A New Duality

BOOK ONE
SONGS OF POWER

ALMA M. VASQUEZ

Exclusive Offer

The last page of this book is not the end. . . if you choose to venture further into the *Songs of Power* world. Your gateway to exclusive content awaits at www.almavasquezbooks.com. Please see the back of this book for more details.

Prologue
A Crux Emerges

L IGHT LEAPED FROM SILVER sconces circling the vast subterranean sanctuary, dancing on the surface of the sacred pool. It frolicked on the polished marble walls and the slim platinum belt worn by the Seer of Kalehala, who awaited him. In a silken aubergine gown, the seer stood still, her silvery hair cascading to her waist. Her aquamarine gaze seized him as he entered the Reflection Chamber.

Lythk bowed, meeting her eyes while taking a knee and pressing both hands to the cool, dark stone tiles. The weight of his gold medallion, marking him as the commander of the vaxili soldiers encamped in Kalehala, strained his white tunic.

"Magisthild Lythk," she said, inclining her head. "Please rise."

Once on his feet, he waited for her words. If he had been before a senator, he would have assumed the delay was tactical. Silence can gather weight and pressure those who are guilty or weak. Lythk was neither.

"I have Seen a Crux," she proclaimed at last.

Lythk unconsciously softened his knees, his muscular frame ready for combat. "How may I serve?" he inquired. His small army in this remote outpost could protect the Drylands, but he questioned their ability to influence pivotal moments in history.

Seer A'zine walked along the edge of the oval pool, peering into its depths. "The vision revealed two futures for the Asthildi Empire. One possibility is renewal and innovation."

She lifted her vibrant gaze to his. "The alternative shows death and darkness for all."

Her words lingered in the cavernous space, the horror in her eyes filling Lythk's mind. He took a step towards the aged mystic, and the movement recalled her from the memory of her vision.

She turned her silvery head away from him. "There are consequences to what I say, and thus, I cannot reveal more."

Lythk stepped back, adopting a vaxili stance he could hold for hours.

When she was ready, Seer A'zine faced him. "Your task is to choose a vaxili to retrieve our jewel from the lands of the People. At all costs, it must be returned to the Empire."

"What is this jewel?" Lythk asked. He did not understand how any valuable Asthildi object could be in the realm across the massive mountain range that formed the western border of the Empire. He was not aware of any contact between the two civilizations.

"If you choose your vaxili wisely, he or she will find it."

In the renewed quiet, Lythk realized he may not receive further instruction. He stared into the seer's bright eyes, urging further disclosure.

Unmoved, she smiled slightly. His gaze, which had unnerved senators, did not have the power to disturb her tranquility.

Lythk studied the Seer of Kalehala, wondering how to achieve this impossibly vague mission. After a long moment, he lowered his head in a nod. Her reticence was perplexing, but he could not question her judgment.

"In three days, bring your chosen vaxili to me, and I shall bless the journey," she instructed.

Lythk bowed deeply, his golden hair, laced with braids, catching the light.

As he left the seer's sanctuary, he donned a peridot cloak that covered everything but his light-green eyes. On glistening pathways, he strode through the sun-baked city of Kalehala, perfunctorily noting the Asthildi bowing to him.

The sight of the Fortress of Knath briefly interrupted his thoughts. Its monolithic walls rose from desolate ground, dark stone against yellow sand. Despite the long years he had served in this desert outpost, the view remained impressive.

In the courtyard, Lythk paused, watching a thousand vaxili moving in unison, performing rapid fist strikes. Then he disappeared into the fortress.

For two days, Lythk stalked the grounds, observing the scores of elite warriors he had trained. Only a few could be considered for the nebulous mission on foreign soil.

On the third day, Lythk presented his chosen warrior to Seer A'zine. Like many vaxili, Mathim matched his commander in height, muscularity, and combat skills. Mathim's unique asset was his intelligence. He excelled at solving puzzles, and Lythk hoped he could interpret the Seer of Kalehala's imprecise directives.

When Seer A'zine saw Mathim, a fragile smile blossomed on her unlined face. "It is a difficult quest we give you, Vaxili. Find the jewel, our Erynannea, and bring it home." She produced an opaque pink shard. "With this transporter, you may travel to the realm of the People and return to Kalehala only once."

She offered the magic object to Mathim, who accepted the gift, his large hands careful and his golden eyes solemn.

After the Seer of Kalehala intoned her blessing, Vaxili Mathim bowed formally to them both. "For the Empire, I will do everything in my power to return with the Erynannea," he swore.

In response, Lythk nodded. He had sent many vaxili into battle, always finding a few words to exhort them into action. Today, he was wordless as he observed his chosen vaxili depart, beginning the mission that would determine the future of all Asthildi.

1

A Departure from Ordinary

I N HER GARDEN, BELRINA de Montañas Alejado planted seeds in the damp soil, which was as rich and dark as her hair. After burying them, she laid a hand over the smooth ground, reciting, "Feel the earth's embrace, drink in rain and sun, then live in light and grace."

It had been two years since she had heard her mother, Erynanne, say that prayer. She missed seeing the tranquility in her mother's golden eyes as she surveyed the burgeoning garden. Attached to every leaf, bud, and weed, there was a memory, for they had spent hours there together, nursing the herbs essential to their craft as healers.

Inhaling the cool air of early spring, Belrina refrained from asking the Gods United why they had only given her seventeen years with her mother, for she had posed the question to them many times, and she was still waiting for an answer.

Standing, Belrina raised her startling blue eyes to the Majesties, the northeasterly mountain range that, by night, touched the stars. She drank in the tranquility of the enduring snowy peaks, now dappled with sunlight.

Moments later, Belrina wiped her hands on her apron before entering her log cabin. Of their own accord, her eyes moved towards the fireplace, coming to rest on Erynanne's chair, which still had her shawl draped over its back. Belrina drifted closer, fingering the gray wool fringe.

Blinking rapidly, Belrina swiveled, retrieving a woven basket and calling to the pale mastiff lounging nearby. "Luna!

Come, Luna."

The mastiff rose, yawning and stretching.

Belrina smiled. "That's a good girl." When Luna reached her side, Belrina petted her soft ears. "Let's see if we can find mushrooms," she said.

Belrina set a brisk pace that Luna matched with a languid amble on the footpath. In a few minutes, the forest surrounded them, its old growth of firs and cedars stretching towards each other and the sky, filling all space.

They had not yet veered from the pathway when Luna sniffed the air and gave a deep bark, promptly sitting.

"Who is it, girl?" Belrina asked. Few people traveled this way, unless they were seeking healing. "Let's go, see." She continued along the path and Luna followed, her eyes trained on a distant point ahead.

Soon, she faintly heard a familiar tune being whistled, and she smiled. "Luna, it is Aurelio!" They rushed to meet her friend.

As usual, Aurelio was grinning beneath his black broad-brimmed hat. Tall and slim, he was a few summers older than Belrina.

"Hello," he called. "I was walking this way to visit you, since I didn't see you at Renewal. Everyone missed seeing you there."

She dropped her eyes. "Oh! So many villages were invited to the festival this year. . ." Every child who had not yet seen her eye color would stare or ask questions. She changed the topic. "Would you like to walk with me as I search for mushrooms?"

"I spotted some on my way here—let me take you to them." He smiled, gazing at her.

"How fortunate I ran into you!" Belrina exclaimed, waiting for him to take the lead, but he remained standing, his warm eyes on her face. She asked, "Shall we go?"

"Ah, yes." Her friend removed his hat to run a hand through

his dark, wavy hair, and then he turned, retracing his steps.

Belrina soon outpaced him, and she glanced backwards, laughing. "What strange day is this? Today, I am faster than our footrace champion."

Aurelio gave a brief smile, twirling his hat by the brim, using both hands. His slow feet stopped walking altogether, and he stared at his hat.

She faced him, drawing near. "Is something wrong, Aurelio?" Her trained eyes examined him, but he appeared to be in good health.

"There is something on my mind," he replied, his voice barely audible above two squirrels chittering as they scampered around a tree trunk.

"Do you wish to tell me?" Belrina touched his arm. "My mother always said 'a shared problem is a smaller problem.'"

He smiled softly, grasping the hand she had laid on his forearm. "My parents, well, really, my mother wishes for me to. . ." Aurelio began. He glanced at her face before looking down at his boots.

"Yes?" she prompted him, hoping she could help him with the situation that was so difficult for him to name.

"Marry."

"Oh." Belrina felt the weight of his hand on hers, and she studied Aurelio's hat, lying on the ground, forgotten by its owner.

He squeezed her hand, asking in a soft voice, "Do you want to know what I wish for?"

When Belrina looked into Aurelio's face again, she saw in those familiar deep brown eyes something new and powerful, and she looked away, focusing on the arcing foliage of a fern.

Aurelio released her hand, permitting Belrina to grip her basket with both hands while she stared into its empty bottom. Strangely, she found she did not wish to learn the contents of his heart, but she would not say so to her friend.

He reached towards her as if approaching a wild bird he did

not want to startle into flight. "Or perhaps you already know?" he asked as his hand grazed her shoulder. The gentleness in his voice was at odds with the intensity of the emotions she had seen in his gaze.

"No, I do not," Belrina responded. "You have never spoken of. . . anything like this." She met his gaze again, looking at her friend.

Aurelio smiled when her eyes met his. "Belrina," he said, stepping closer. "Do you think. . . you could consent to be my wife?"

She gripped her basket tighter, staring at the even stitching on Aurelio's white shirt. In the lingering silence, the sounds of the forest grew in richness and diversity.

"Please say something," he breathed, clasping her shoulder tighter.

"I am very surprised." Belrina raised her eyes. "We have always been friends." She could not remember meeting Aurelio, as he was in her earliest memories of visiting the Nieve Fresca village. It was his cheerful smile that had unfailingly provided the warmest welcome. "Good friends," she added.

Belrina made herself observe Aurelio's face, noticing for the first time how nicely his black brows framed his gentle eyes; how gracefully his plentiful dark hair skimmed his square jawline; how his smooth golden-brown skin seemed to harness the warmth of the sun.

Her friend was now a handsome young man who wanted to marry her. "How do you know this is what you want?" Belrina asked, giving voice to one of her thoughts.

Aurelio smiled, and his dark eyes delighted in the lines giving shape to her face. His touch was light on her cheek. "I have always known. I waited for you."

She stared at her friend. *How do I escape from this moment without hurting you?* she thought.

Aurelio drew closer and then stopped. "Waited to see if you might feel something for me?" His open, expressive eyes searched hers.

"I. . ." Belrina looked down, beginning again. "I care for you, and I want you to be happy." She could not force herself to say more.

"I will be happy if you consent to be my wife." Aurelio smiled, placing both of his warm hands on her shoulders.

Now she wished she had expressed more of her thoughts, and as he bent forward to kiss her, Belrina moved back.

"I'm sorry," she mumbled, unable to meet his dark eyes. "Please allow me time to consider, Aurelio?" She ventured to look at her friend again, burying her thought: *I like our friendship as it is.*

He enjoyed looking at her for another moment before stepping away. "Of course." He retrieved her basket, which had slipped unnoticed from her hands. Then he reclaimed his hat, brushing it off before replacing it on his head. He smiled, asking, "Still interested in those mushrooms?"

Belrina nodded, grateful to see her friend return to normal, and their afternoon proceeded like many others had until he walked her home.

At her door, she was uncertain whether she should invite Aurelio in, and she did not like this uncertainty.

"My mother is waiting for me, and she is not always a patient woman." Aurelio grinned like the boy she knew. Then his grin faded, and he became the man Belrina had met that afternoon.

Aurelio stepped closer, clasping her arm above the elbow. "I love you, Belrina. Please let me take care of you. If you love me even a little, we can have a beautiful life together, a wonderful family."

He looked into her eyes, trying to ascertain their future. "May I come visit you tomorrow afternoon?"

She nodded, and her heart sank when he responded with a luminous smile.

Aurelio bounced down the wooden steps of her front deck,

calling, "Good night, Belrina!" As his long legs strode along the path, he whistled cheerfully into the evening.

Belrina closed the door, finding the interior of her small cabin dim and chilly. As she started a fire and lit the oil lamps, she easily imagined the life Aurelio described. She knew he would fulfill his promises—if she were willing to create a new home with him.

She surveyed her one-room cabin with all her mother's possessions in the same place she had left them. After slipping her feet into the black woolen shoes next to a matching pair Erynanne used to wear, she cleaned and stored the mushrooms they had gathered.

Belrina tried imagining what counsel her mother would have offered. Her feelings for Aurelio did not match those he had for her, and it didn't seem a stable place from which to begin a marriage.

Hours later, after she had eaten dinner and completed her chores, Belrina sat by the fire with Erynanne's journal of herb lore unopened in her lap. She hadn't decided what to say to Aurelio tomorrow—could she reveal her misgivings without causing him pain? Her grip tightened on the notebook she held.

Aurelio had always been her protector, insulating her from incredulous stares and intrusive questions. This was the first opportunity she had been given to protect him.

It was some time before Belrina opened the journal. Perusing the notes and illustrations in her mother's precise hand helped settle her thoughts, and she drifted to sleep where she sat.

S HE WOKE TO A loud, insistent knocking. Belrina blinked in the dark, as the fire had died to embers. As the knocking grew more desperate, she fumbled her way into lighting a lantern.

"Luna?" Belrina whispered. "Where are you?"

She aimed the lantern at the door, finding the mastiff, sniffing at the threshold. Belrina relaxed, concluding it must be someone who needed help. She ran to loose the bolt, opening the door.

It was a tall, middle-aged man dressed in bulky woolens to survive the cold of the high mountains. He struggled to catch his breath.

His dark eyes glanced at Belrina before looking over her shoulder. "I came for help. A-a-a. . . man is injured."

"I am a healer." Belrina left the door open as she grabbed her mother's traveling satchel, checking its contents. The man waited on the front deck as she added a flask of water and a few medicines manufactured in the City.

"Anyone else here who can help?" He looked back into the night. "Might be good to have more people," he muttered.

"The nearest village is four miles away. You were lucky to find me." Belrina wrapped herself in her winter cloak and grabbed the lantern. "Please lead the way."

Belrina, with Luna at her side, followed the man as he strode towards the Majesties. In the frigid air, her breath showed in white puffs within the soft glow of the lantern. With her eyes on the inclining ground, she waited for the mountain man to explain the situation.

After a few minutes, she suspected her companion enjoyed the solitude of the higher peaks of the Majesties for long stretches of time.

"I can carry the lantern," the mountain man finally said, retrieving it from her before resuming his trek.

"Thank you," she replied. "My name is Belrina."

The tall man looked back at her. "I am Adan. Forgive my manners. . . I am not used to company."

"There is nothing to forgive," she replied. As they hiked up stone-studded inclines, Belrina was glad for her stout leather boots. "Please tell me about the injured man?" she asked, prompting Adan as gently as possible.

"He is about two miles up this way. He. . . isn't from here," Adan said, holding himself rigidly. He stared unblinking into the moonlit landscape, keeping his thoughts to himself. He said, "I didn't get close. He has a bad fever."

They continued their trek into the foothills, the air growing frostier, numbing Belrina's fingers and toes. As she buried her hands under her arms, Belrina wondered why Adan seemed afraid of the feverish man. "You said he's injured?" she inquired next.

"I saw blood on his leg," he replied matter-of-factly.

"When a wound is infected, it can cause fever," she explained. Watching Adan's face in the lantern light, Belrina added, "This man's sickness is likely not contagious."

Adan absently nodded, peering ahead.

In the mile they had hiked, the elevation had risen significantly, and snow and ice now dotted the rocky ground. She had to slow her steps to avoid the treacherous patches, and the slower pace allowed the deep cold to infiltrate her woolen skirts and shawl.

To distract herself from the freezing temperature, Belrina considered how she could politely inquire into Adan's anxiety concerning the injured man. She could understand his discomfort around strangers, but did he fear people from other regions? What a strange notion! She shook her head, dislodging the shawl around her face, and the frosty, moisture-rich air attacked her exposed skin. Biting her lip, she repositioned her shawl.

As each moment passed, the silence of the frigid world became more difficult to interrupt. Whatever the cause of the mountain man's fear, Belrina began fretting for her unseen patient, who was suffering alone in these treacherous conditions. Soon she peered ahead more intently than Adan, her eyes searching for the injured man they needed to rescue.

Suddenly, Luna caught a scent and trotted forward to chase it. Adan broke into a jog, but he looked back at Belrina, moderating his pace. In the light of the night sky, she discerned Luna's pale fur. The mastiff was standing with her nose to the ground.

Running, Belrina passed Adan, calling Luna back, and then she saw an enormous man whose skin color matched the snow. His hair appeared to have a bit more color, but none that she had ever seen on a person before. Laying on the snow-dappled ground, his muscled arms and long legs thrashed in the throes of his fever.

Belrina rushed to kneel by his side, mixing manufactured medicine into the flask of water and administering it to the senseless man. The process was slow and messy, as much of the medicine didn't make it into his mouth. While she was busy, Adan started a fire. When her patient had ingested sufficient medicine, Belrina used a cloth to gather snow, placing it on his forehead. That was when she noticed his ears in the firelight. Poking through his flaxen hair, they were long, narrow, and furled to a point.

"He is an elf!" Belrina exclaimed.

Adan's head jerked up. "What is that?" He stared at the pale creature, his forgotten hands extending towards the flames.

Belrina ignored the question for a moment. "Will my treatments work for you?" she muttered, holding the compress against the elf's smooth brow.

The minutes seemed long as she waited for the medicine to take effect, watching the elf's convulsions and praying they would stop. Finally, his thrashing became less severe, and Belrina whispered, "Merciful are the Gods United."

When her patient lay still, she addressed Adan, asking, "Would you please hold this against his forehead? I need to examine him."

The mountain man was slow to comply, eventually clenching the pack of snow with his thick fingers.

Raising the lantern, Belrina examined the elf for injuries, running her hands over his limbs. Discovering no misalignments, she turned to the large patch of blood marring the lower leg of his white, fitted breeches. She carefully lifted the torn cloth, revealing a bone protruding from his shin.

Belrina sat back on her heels, for she had not treated a severe fracture like this before.

"His leg is severely broken," Belrina informed Adan. "We need to get him to my cabin for further treatment." She had spoken of the need easily, but she wondered how they were going to move the massive elf.

Returning to her satchel, Belrina added several powders and herbs to the flask to ease her patient's pain.

"He is awake," Adan announced, retracting his hand and inching away from the pale creature.

Belrina met the elf's alert eyes, kneeling beside him and smiling. She displayed the flask to him. "This is medicine. It will make you feel better." She lifted it to his lips, and the elf drank eagerly. "Good, very good," Belrina murmured. "Oh, that is enough for now!" she exclaimed, withdrawing the flask.

The elf spoke a musical language.

"I'm sorry, but I do not understand." Belrina smoothed her patient's hair away from his eyes. She removed her shawl, and she began creating a pillow to place under his head, but Adan stopped her by offering one of his layers.

"Use this instead," he said, not meeting her gaze. "You need that shawl more than him."

"Thank you, Adan," Belrina replied, holding his hand longer than necessary to show her gratitude. As she ensured her patient was comfortable, she spoke quietly to Adan. "After the medicine takes effect, I'll bind his leg, and you'll need to restrain him."

Adan swallowed, but he nodded firmly.

Belrina smiled at the mountain man. "Thank you again. You were very kind to seek aid for him." She looked down at the elf, who studied her until she lay her hand on his forehead, stroking between his light eyebrows with her thumb. Then he closed his eyes.

"The Goddess of Mercy would have shunned me forever if I had left this poor creature to die," Adan explained. After a pause, he asked, "You said he is an. . . elf?"

"Yes. My mother told me stories about fair creatures called elves. They create beautiful cities, art, and treasures." She did not tell Adan that elves had magic powers in those stories.

"The Gods United love beautiful things," Adan said slowly.

Belrina smiled. "They love all that lives."

"Aye." Adan returned her smile, and then he gestured towards the mountains. "No one uses this path regularly. How long do you think he has been here?"

"Several days," Belrina said. The infection would be difficult to combat. After looking down at her patient, she announced, "It is time."

As soon as she removed her hand from the elf's forehead, he opened his eyes. "I wish I knew your language," she said to him. "I will do my best to explain." She pointed at his injury. "I need to secure your leg."

The elf immediately closed his eyes, breathing deeply.

Belrina hesitated, uncertain if her patient understood. They would soon find out. She stood, and Adan knelt behind the elf, resting his stout hands on his knees, ready to restrain the elf by his muscular shoulders.

Setting the lantern by her side, Belrina started by removing the most finely crafted boot she had ever seen. The elf remained motionless as she began cleansing the intact skin surrounding the wound. As she grabbed her linen strips, she met Adan's eyes, and he nodded in response.

As Adan's hands hovered above the elf's broad shoulders, Belrina entwined a strip around the elf's ankle while he continued his deep, regular breathing. When her frozen fingers cinched the linen around his injury, her eyes leapt to her patient's face, but the elf had no reaction. The crackle of the fire was the only sound as she wrapped his wounded leg, from ankle to knee.

When she finished, Belrina sat on her heels, studying her calm patient, who appeared to be sleeping. The medication would only have dulled sensation. Was the elf using magic to shield himself from the pain?

"What should we do next?" Adan asked.

"Let's let him rest." Belrina moved to the fire, which Luna had long been enjoying. She lifted her hands to the wondrous warmth produced by the flames.

A relieved Adan soon joined her.

"When he wakes, we'll determine if he can bear any of his own weight," Belrina continued. "If he cannot, I'll stay here with him while you get help."

"In this cold? You haven't proper clothing." Adan shook his head emphatically.

Belrina did not argue, hoping further discussion would not be necessary.

The elf raised himself on his elbows.

"Stop! Please be careful!" Belrina exclaimed, raising her hands.

The elf immediately froze, staring at her.

"I didn't mean to startle you," she said, speaking evenly and slowing her movement. When she knelt beside him, she lightly tapped her chest. "I am Belrina," she stated.

The elf sat up slowly, keeping his eyes on her. "Mathim," he said, touching his broad chest.

Belrina gestured towards Adan, introducing her companion of the last few hours, who nodded to acknowledge the elf.

Mathim nodded in return before peering at his injured leg.

"Mathim, can you stand?" Belrina asked, rising to her feet. "Belrina stand. Mathim stand?" She pointed first to Mathim and then up.

In response, the elf brought the knee of his uninjured leg

up, effortlessly pushing himself away from the ground. He left his injured leg stationary while holding out his hand to Adan.

Adan looked at Belrina, who nodded. Grasping Mathim's hand, Adan heaved, and the massive elf soon stood on one foot.

Rushing to his side, Belrina steadied Mathim, wrapping an arm around his waist. With Adan lending his arm and shoulder on the other side, they kept the enormous elf on his feet. Belrina noticed that the top of Adan's head barely reached Mathim's chin.

"Walk, Mathim?" she inquired, pointing ahead. She hoped they could support the elf's substantial weight.

Looking up at the stars, Mathim intoned a single word. Belrina gasped, and Adan's mouth hung open. Mathim's body mass reduced by at least half.

"Go, go, go," Mathim said urgently, using Adan's shoulder to hop forward.

Despite her surprise at Mathim's use of their language, Belrina kept pace with the elf as he propelled himself down the slope. The three of them began an awkward hobble towards Belrina's cabin, Luna leading the way.

With only the light of the moon and stars, Belrina placed her feet carefully, hoping to avoid stones or ice. After a few minutes, they achieved a smoother shuffle, developing a rhythm. She lamented every jolt to Mathim's injured leg, but the placid elf never complained.

The constant exertion lessened the chill of the night air, for which Belrina tried to be appreciative, but it wasn't long before she was praying to the Gods United for strength, as Mathim seemed heavier after the first half-hour. Initially, she thought it was merely a measure of her fatigue, but by the end of the hour, there could be no doubt: Mathim's full body weight was returning.

Belrina's muscles burned with the strain of supporting Mathim, and she heard Adan breathing heavily as well. She focused on taking one more step. Then another. She refused to think about the distance lying ahead. Adan and Mathim kept moving forward, and so did she.

Occasionally, Mathim spoke words in his own language, but he produced no more magic. Every time he spoke, Belrina studied his pale face. His eyes were always fixed ahead, prompting her to take another step forward. Then another.

Finally, Belrina heard a whine from Luna, and she looked up. The cabin was several yards away. With renewed vigor, Belrina aimed for the door, and they deposited Mathim clumsily, but safely, into the single bed designated for patients. The wooden bed frame creaked under the weight of the large elf.

"Can I help with anything else?" Adan asked, still panting. "The fire, it should not be left unattended."

"Will you not rest first? I can prepare some tea for you," Belrina offered.

"Thank you, but you have enough to do." Adan looked at Mathim, whose pale skin was visible in the dim cabin. "Belrina, if you need me, I will stay. What he did. . ." The mountain man froze, his eyes fixed on Mathim's pointed ears.

"He can harm no one in his current state," Belrina said, touching Adan's elbow. "You have saved this poor creature's life, and the Goddess of Mercy will reward you well." She held out her hand, saying, "May your paths always be pleasant."

Adan clasped her hand, meeting her eyes. "May the Gods United always find you," he replied. Then he vanished into the night, returning to his serene life in the Majesties.

2

Introduction to Magic

After barring the door for the night, Belrina turned towards Mathim, who lay still in the undersized bed. There was no guarantee he would live, for under the clean linen bandage, the infection festered, colonizing and invading his body. She had to stop it from killing him.

She arranged a coverlet over her patient, muttering a quick prayer.

After lighting the kitchen lamp, Belrina loaded a bed tray with tea and slices of honey-drizzled raisin bread, setting it before the sleeping elf.

Mathim roused when she called his name. She displayed a manufactured pellet—the only one in her supply—to him. "This medicine will combat the infection. It must be swallowed." She demonstrated, watching to see if he understood.

The elf held out his hand for the medicine, ingesting it before launching into the contents of the tray.

"Good." Belrina nodded. The dose would last twenty-four hours.

In the kitchen, she added a sedative to a second cup of tea. After seeing the rapidity with which Mathim ate the bread, she cut another generous slice.

While he consumed the new fare, Belrina lit a mirrored lamp, arranging all available sources of light near his injured leg. She set her mother's tool kit on the table and began sanitizing the implements.

Mathim studied her every movement.

"I promise, Mathim, I will do everything I can to heal you." Belrina met his eyes, which shone in the increased light, and she inhaled audibly. They were the same color as her mother's. Outside of her family, she had only seen brown eyes. Questions too complicated to ask without a shared language flowed through her mind.

Mathim began blinking drowsily as the sedative took effect. Recalled to her purpose, Belrina finished her preparations and approached Mathim's bedside with her tools. He did not stir.

Cutting his snug breeches above the knee, she carefully removed the bandages. Gaining trust in the sedative, Belrina set a basin below the injured leg, and then she piped distilled water over the ruined flesh in a steady, gentle stream.

As bloody water flowed into the basin, she saw foreign debris and bone shards in the wound that she needed to remove. Using several tools, she tried to eliminate all contaminants. It was essential to saving Mathim's life.

While Belrina worked, the sky lightened, and the first rays of the sun streamed into her cabin through the high, narrow window traversing the length of the east-facing wall. She felt the strain in her eyes and neck, but she ignored these annoyances. Her patient's needs were much more critical.

Belrina studied Mathim's misplaced bone. She had observed her mother treat fractures, but none that had punctured through the skin. It was clear, though, that the bone had to be restored to its original position. Looking at her available tools, she pressed the protruding bone down, looping the suturing thread around it and the bone from which it had separated. After nearly an hour, she could close the wound, replacing damaged tissue with a line of neat stitches. Then Belrina applied an anti-infective herbal treatment before protecting the area with fresh linen strips. She hoped she had done enough. Heavy-lidded, she cleaned and cleared everything away, leaving her bloodied apron outdoors to be washed later. Belrina smiled when she noticed Adan had returned the lantern, placing it on the front deck.

Once in a clean dress, she moved a cushioned chair next to Mathim. Thus far, the only sound from him was steady breathing, and she smoothed his blankets before settling in the chair and succumbing to her fatigue.

A few hours later, she reluctantly roused when Luna placed her head in Belrina's lap. She stroked Luna's forehead as the mastiff patiently waited to be let outside. Belrina glanced at Mathim and started. In a peaceful sleep, his skin glowed. She blinked. As she raised her hand to touch the diffuse silvery light, Luna whined.

Trying to be quiet, Belrina unbarred the door for her, and sunlight streamed in. She turned back to Mathim, discovering the subtle luminosity was gone. Then he opened those eyes so like her mother's.

"I am sorry to wake you." Belrina felt Mathim's forehead, and his skin was cool beneath her fingers. She retrieved the blanket she had used, covering him. At first glance, his face had seemed serene, but she could now see he held himself stiffly. After she gave him her most powerful pain reliever, Mathim peered at his bandaged leg. Belrina considered how to communicate with him, and then she grabbed a notebook and a pencil, sketching his injury.

"You have a severe fracture." She showed him the sketch, and then she retrieved a spool of suturing thread, unwinding a strand. "Until your bone heals, this is keeping it together." Going back to the illustration, Belrina faced it towards Math-im, repeatedly drawing a line around the two pieces of bone. Mathim looked surprised. To ensure he understood, Belrina pantomimed winding the thread around his leg.

She held her hands above his injured leg. "Please do not move." She looked at Mathim. "Do you understand?"

"Mathim understand." The tune his musical voice sounded was mournful. The elf looked down, his shoulder-length golden hair falling against his face, which was nearly as white as a cumulous cloud on a sunny day. Was that his natural color?

Belrina covered one of his pale hands with hers. "The bone can heal, but it will take time. Do not despair." She smiled, trying not to think of the infection that could rob him of the opportunity to heal. "You must be hungry."

She started the stew of oats and dried fruit before retreating to the bathing room to wash her face and quickly braid her hair.

"*Stilth zabina!*" Mathim bellowed.

Belrina ran into the main living area to see Luna frozen in mid-stride at the foot of Mathim's bed.

"Luna!" she cried, sprinting to her pet, who whined and rolled her eyes. "Mathim, did you do this?" Belrina hugged Luna, petting her head. "Luna is my friend."

Mathim uttered another Elvish word and the strange force operating against Luna vanished.

Belrina showered Luna with affection, comforting her. Once she determined Luna had recovered, she said, "Come, Luna, I am going to introduce you to Mathim." She walked towards the elf, Luna obediently following.

"Sit, Luna," Belrina commanded, and the large animal sat.

Mathim stared at Luna, fascinated by her mouth.

"You will be nice to Luna, won't you, Mathim? No more magic?" Belrina implored.

The elf was not listening. Belrina squeezed his hand, and finally, he turned his eyes away from the mastiff. "Luna is my friend. Mathim is my friend."

Mathim's golden eyes reflected confusion.

Belrina petted Luna's soft head, trying again. "Luna is a good dog." She guided his hand towards Luna, but he balked, and she couldn't budge his arm any more than she could an old-growth redwood.

She sighed. "Come, Luna." Belrina led the mastiff to her favorite spot by the fire, where a nest of blankets waited. As she petted her gentle companion again, the image of Luna's immobilized body appeared in Belrina's mind. Luna was unharmed, but she could not dispel her unease. Mathim's injuries did not impede his ability to use magic, and she wondered what else he could do with it.

The smell of breakfast roused her from her thoughts, and after washing her hands in the kitchen spigot, she prepared Mathim's breakfast tray. As she approached him, he sat up without using his arms, keeping both legs motionless. He intoned an Elvish word, transforming a blanket into a pillow. She stared. With another chant, the pillow floated to rest behind Mathim's back, and he settled against it.

"Very helpful," Belrina finally said, setting her legs in motion again. As soon as she placed the bed tray over Mathim's lap, he started eating.

Belrina retreated to the kitchen to eat her own breakfast, but she ate slowly, considering whether to administer Mathim a light sedative.

No, she thought guiltily. *Mathim intends no harm.* She turned her mind towards obtaining more infection-fighting medicine. She could not leave Mathim to visit the neighboring healers, the closest of whom was several hours away. Suddenly, she smiled, remembering Aurelio would come later. She was certain he would help, and with his swift feet, the medicine would arrive as quickly as possible.

Looking towards the elf, Belrina observed his empty bowl. With a smile, she rose from her seat. "Would you like more?" she asked.

With one Elvish word from Mathim, his bowl appeared on the kitchen table near Belrina.

"I think that is a yes," she laughed. After Belrina provided a more generous helping, she took a few steps towards Mathim, but he said another Elvish word and a gentle force tugged at the bowl in her hands. When she released it, the bowl floated to Mathim's tray.

"Yes, magic is helpful. But Mathim, will you not tire yourself?" Belrina asked. She suspected he must have had a reason for not using magic last night, when it had been sorely needed. Perhaps the medication was permitting Mathim to believe he was healthier than he was. She crossed her arms over her chest, looking at Mathim. "You need to rest," she instructed.

Mathim stopped eating to look at her, tilting his head. He asked, "Belrina eat?"

"Mathim rest," Belrina insisted. "It is important you rest. No more magic today, please."

"No? Today?" Mathim repeated, trying to work through the puzzle of her words.

Belrina tried a different approach. She pointed to Luna, who still lounged by the fire. "Luna rests. Mathim rests."

Mathim looked at Luna, nodding. "Belrina eat?" he inquired again, smiling slightly before resuming his breakfast.

Belrina sighed. He was going to be a restless patient—if the infection did not return. Her mother had treated many such.

After breakfast, she adjusted the pillows so Mathim could recline.

"Mathim rest," he said cheerfully.

Belrina suppressed a laugh. "Yes, rest now."

By the time she had finished yesterday's laundry, Mathim appeared to be sleeping, and Belrina needed no other invitation to rest herself. She sat down by the fire, trying to recall every detail of her mother's stories about elves. All too soon, the whistling of a merry tune woke Belrina. Was it afternoon already?

She wearily rose to her feet, and then she froze as the memory of Aurelio's marriage proposal surfaced. She was uncertain she had the courage to be honest with him, but perhaps they would not revisit that conversation now that there were more pressing matters to discuss. After a slow exhale, she slipped out the door to greet her friend outside, seeing as Mathim was still sleeping.

Luna was trotting alongside Aurelio, as if walking him home.

"Happy day to you, Belrina." Aurelio's broad smile faded as he took in her rumpled dress and tired eyes. "Is something amiss?" he asked, striding to her side.

"I am well, but I had an eventful night," Belrina replied, leading Aurelio to the wooden bench on her front deck. Starting with Adan's knock on her door, she provided a full account of what had transpired since they had last seen each other.

"He has magic! How do we know it is safe for you to be alone with him?" Aurelio immediately asked when she finished.

"Aurelio, he understands I am helping him," Belrina countered. "He will not harm me."

"We do not know why he is here or what he wants, Belrina."

"True, but would I question any other traveler before offering healing?" she insisted. Belrina gazed at her friend steadily. "He needs my help."

Aurelio smiled softly, his eyes lingering on her face. "Your kindness is beautiful, Belrina," he breathed, enfolding her hands in his. "Because I love you, my heart warns me to be cautious. If anything were to happen to you. . ."

"Nothing will—" Belrina began.

"You cannot promise that!" Aurelio interjected. "Only the Gods United know what the future holds."

"When did you get to be so serious?" Belrina asked lightly.

He smiled, although not as broadly as before. "I have no idea." He held her hands a moment longer. "Please be careful, Belrina," Aurelio said quietly before standing. "I think it is time I met Mathim."

When they entered the cabin, Mathim seemed to be expecting them, and to Belrina's eye, his peaceful face appeared more tense.

"Mathim, this is Aurelio," Belrina announced, making the hurried introduction before rushing to provide more pain medication.

"Hello, Mathim," Aurelio said, smiling. He stopped short of Mathim's bedside.

"Auralieo," the elf said slowly, trying the name on his tongue.

Aurelio corrected him, stepping closer as Belrina handed Mathim a tumbler of medicated water.

Mathim took a generous drink before trying again. "Aurelio?"

Her friend nodded, flashing his bright smile. Then he noted, "You were right, Belrina. Mistress Erynanne had eyes the exact same color."

"Erynanne?" Mathim sat up.

"Rest, Mathim," Belrina instructed.

The elf complied, easing back on his pillow while staring at Aurelio, who looked around. "This is quite a predicament. Belrina, you need some privacy," he stated, surveying the cabin, pacing through the confined space.

Mathim tracked Aurelio's movement.

"We can erect a screen here," Aurelio suggested, gesturing with his hands. "Master Silvio and I could craft it for you."

"Thank you, but I think medicine for Mathim is more important," Belrina replied, looking at her patient, who continued his close observation of Aurelio.

"I was thinking about that," he replied. "I could run through our circle of villages. Perhaps our neighbors have some."

Belrina considered. "Mathim needs at least six more doses. It would be better to go directly to a healer."

"Master Valerio is the closest. I can be there and back in a day," Aurelio said, smiling proudly.

Belrina crossed her arms over her chest, gripping her elbows. "What if Master Valerio doesn't have enough? I only had one dose."

Aurelio crossed the room and clasped her arm. "We'll send messenger pigeons to all neighboring healers. I'll find the medicine for you, Belrina," he affirmed. "Please, don't worry." He stepped closer, his dark eyes fixed on her face.

Belrina dropped her own eyes. "It is a blessing to have a friend like you." She met his gaze, adding, "With your help, I believe we can save him."

Aurelio smiled, murmuring, "I hope so." It was a long moment before he stepped away. "I'll send word so you know when to expect me."

Hurriedly, Belrina retrieved a string of bartering beads, handing them to Aurelio as she walked him to the door.

"I shall return as soon as I can," he declared, turning to face her on the front deck.

If he had not proposed to her yesterday, Belrina would have thrown her arms around him. Instead, she gripped his hand and said, "Thank you, Aurelio. I will pray for your safe journey."

He clasped her hand, gazing into her eyes. "And I shall pray for you, Belrina," he said, his voice low. "Stay safe." His eyes darted to where Mathim lay beyond the cabin's wall. Turning abruptly, he jogged back to Nieve Fresca, Luna trotting at his side for a bit.

When Luna returned to the front door, Belrina ruffled her soft ears. "Why can't I say yes, girl?" she asked softly.

When Belrina entered the cabin, Mathim greeted her with a hopeful question. "Eat?"

She smiled, preparing a plate of dried fruits and nuts for him.

Mathim gratefully accepted the fare, and as Belrina turned away, he reached for her elbow, stopping her.

"Erynanne?" he asked.

"She was my mother," Belrina replied.

"Mother?" Mathim questioned, stumbling over the foreign word. He shook his head.

Belrina considered how to explain. She went back to her notebook, sketching a woman with a baby in her arms. Showing the sketch to Mathim, she pointed to the woman, saying, "Erynanne." Then she pointed to the baby, stating, "Belrina."

Mathim stared. "Erynannea *etz* Belrina," he breathed.

"I do not understand," she said, shaking her head. Belrina returned to her drawing, trying to make the eyes on the woman more realistic. Belrina pointed to them, showing Mathim. "Erynanne has gold eyes," she said. Then she pointed to Mathim's eyes, saying, "Mathim has gold eyes. Do you know how that can be?"

He provided an explanation in Elvish.

Belrina shook her head, offering Mathim the notebook, but he set it aside, preferring to eat.

She sighed, deciding it was time for a proper bath. Retreating to the bathing chamber, Belrina opened the spigot to fill the ceramic tub with spring water, and then she started the fire to warm the water.

For the first few minutes of her bath, Belrina's fatigue allowed her to lounge without thought. All too soon, one question kept reverberating through her mind: *how long? How long can I keep him alive?* She devised a treatment plan using her current supply of medicine.

Once she emerged from the bathing chamber, Belrina applied another herbal salve on Mathim's wound, which she would do every four to six hours. She studied her patient. Judging from his build, he was accustomed to physical activity.

"Luna, do you want to play fetch?" Belrina called.

The white mastiff scrambled for her well-used ball, grasping it in her powerful jaws and dropping it at Belrina's feet.

Mathim studied the mastiff's movements.

"Good girl!" Belrina tossed the soft ball again, which bounced off the wood floor boards into Luna's waiting mouth.

When Luna happily returned the ball to Belrina, she handed it to Mathim, who sent it arcing towards Luna. The mastiff hopped and caught the ball in midair, causing Mathim to exclaim in his language.

Smiling, Belrina patted the bed. "Bring it right here, Luna. That's a good girl—you are so smart!" She fondled Luna's ears. "Go ahead, Mathim," she said, nodding to the ball.

Mathim picked it up, and Luna immediately fixed her eyes on her toy. He tossed the ball between his hands, watching Luna's head swivel. Then he looped it over the mastiff.

Belrina ensured Luna returned the ball to Mathim's bed before looking out her kitchen window. Soon, they would send the pigeons, and she wondered if Aurelio would set off tonight.

The next morning, Mathim was rosy-cheeked, and after feeling his forehead, Belrina rushed to give him medicine to reduce the fever. She had continued the herbal treatments throughout the night, but they were already failing to prevent the infection's resurgence.

Belrina scoured her mother's journal, discovering she could double the strength of a few key ingredients. After she applied the stronger salve, there was a gentle knock on her door.

Victoriano, whose curly dark hair matched his thick curly eyelashes, stood on the front deck, holding his hat in his hands.

"Morning, Belrina," he said, nodding. "Aurelio sent me. He wanted you to know he left for Mistress Petra's village last night. He'll be back in four days. Maybe quicker the way he runs." Victoriano finally drew a breath.

"Ah, thank you. Would you like to come in, Victoriano?"

"No—you must be busy." He started edging away, replacing his hat. Then he planted his feet, staring down at them. "Is there anything you need?" He briefly met Belrina's eyes. "All is well?"

"I am well," Belrina assured him. "I am only concerned about Mathim." *Could he hold out for four days?*

"Aurelio will be here soon," Victoriano affirmed. "He'll get that medicine." His feet began moving again. "Uh, good day to you."

"Good day," Belrina said, distantly noticing her powder-stained hands. She looked towards the towering Majesties, luminous where sunlight blossomed on the snow, and she filled her lungs with the fresh spring air.

As she entered the cabin, Mathim was playing fetch with Luna, and when the mastiff placed the ball on his bed, he hesitantly touched her forehead. Luna licked him encouragingly, but Mathim retracted his hand, studying it. With one magical word, his hand was clean once again.

That morning was the last time Mathim was healthy enough to play with Luna. Over the next two days, Belrina administered herbal or manufactured medicines each hour, and she used every bit of knowledge she had gained from her mother, but the fever kept worsening. Almost constantly, Mathim closed his eyes to bear the pain untouched by her medicine, breathing as he had when she first touched his injured leg. He clung to his stoicism as fervently as she clung to her fading hope, but they both knew they were losing the battle against the infection.

I do not know if my words have any power at all, Belrina prayed to the Gods United at one point. *But I cannot help asking you to spare Mathim's life. Please.*

With no other remedy, Belrina continued her prayers, offering gratitude every time Mathim opened his eyes, not knowing he would do so again the next time he closed them.

On the dawning of the third day, Belrina woke when light streamed across her face. She had fallen asleep in her chair next to Mathim, and she immediately cast her eyes on him.

His skin glistened with sweat, but he was not yet thrashing. He gripped a pink shard in his hands.

Belrina moved closer, staring at the opaque crystal, wondering if it held magic. She jerked when Mathim clasped the side of her head, intoning an Elvish word.

Then she could see only his golden eyes while his voice filled her mind.

'Belrina, I am dying here. I need to return home. Please come with me. You are Erynannea. It is important we return together.' He wrapped her hands around the crystal, and then he covered her hands with his.

Belrina's thoughts oozed through her sleep-deprived mind. Mathim would live if she returned with him? Her hands were sweating from the heat of his feverish flesh. If Mathim stayed, could she heal him? Only the Gods United knew if the medicine would work at this advanced stage of the infection. And it would not arrive until tomorrow. Mathim might not have a tomorrow. As Belrina's eyes filled with tears, she gripped the crystal, its hard-edged facets digging into her palms.

'Will you come with me to the land of your mother's ancestors?' His golden gaze was steady and tranquil.

Belrina blinked in confusion. Her mother had elven ancestry? How could that be possible?

He waited for her answer patiently, ignoring the infection boiling his blood. His smooth, pale face was a mask of serenity as he also disregarded the pain. A tear ran down Belrina's cheek, and she knew she couldn't continue watching Mathim die.

"Yes," she replied, uncertain if she had voiced the thought aloud.

'Focus on your desire to be in my homeland,' Mathim instructed.

Belrina filled herself with prayer, yearning to be in a place of magic where Mathim could be healed.

When Mathim intoned an Elvish word, an invisible power swirled around them.

Belrina closed her eyes against the whipping force, and then the world dissolved into pain and searing heat.

3

ANOTHER DEPARTURE

LATER THAT AFTERNOON, AURELIO returned to Belrina's cabin with the medicine. When she did not answer his knock, he entered, finding Luna alone. The mastiff was sniffing, crossing the room in a bewildered manner. Aurelio's eyes absorbed the confusing details: Mathim's empty bed, Belrina's boots left by the front door, and the open door to the bathing chamber.

"Belrina?" Aurelio called. He hoped for—but did not expect—a response.

He watched Luna's frenzied pursuit, realizing that she was following Belrina's scent trails. They did not lead outside. Aurelio joined Luna in searching the cabin's interior, looking for clues to explain Belrina's disappearance. Everything was in its usual place.

When Luna howled in frustration, he felt like doing the same. Belrina had been taken by no ordinary means.

"Magic!" Aurelio growled. He tossed his hat off, running his hands through his wavy hair. "Mathim, where did you take her?" His face crumpled. "Why?"

The young man sat down in Belrina's chair by the fire. Luna whined and placed her head on his lap. He petted the mastiff for several minutes.

"How do we find Belrina, girl? Gods United, please help me." An idea struck him, as if in answer to his prayer. "The Old Ones! In the stories, they grant wishes, so they must understand magic. They can help me find Belrina."

Aurelio rose, extinguishing the fire. He closed all the curtains before slowly shutting the door.

"Come, Luna, we have a long journey ahead of us. We must go to the City to speak with the Old Ones."

On his way home, Aurelio mentally composed a list of the items he would need for his journey. As he strode through the door, he saw his mother cooking supper. He would miss the comfort of this normalcy, which his departure would disrupt for the entire family.

As his hands fumbled with his hat, his mother turned. Sophia immediately abandoned her spoon, sitting him down at their kitchen table.

"What's wrong, mijo?" she asked.

"Mama, the elf-man took Belrina. I need to find her!"

Aurelio's eldest niece, who had seen but seven summers, stopped playing with her cloth doll and looked at him with large, dark eyes.

"It's alright, Maribel," Sophia said soothingly. Lowering her voice, she whispered to Aurelio. "Mijo, let's not frighten the children. Now, the elf-man was sick and injured. How could he take Belrina anywhere?"

"Magic," Aurelio hissed. Hearing this word, Sophia placed her hand over his. "There is no other explanation. Luna tried to find Belrina, but not one scent trail left the cabin." Aurelio patted Luna's head with his free hand. The mastiff had not strayed far from his side. "Mama, I can't rest until I know Belrina is safe."

"I know what she means to you, my boy. I'll pray to the Gods United to keep Belrina safe. What are you planning to do?" Sophia asked cautiously.

Aurelio's second eldest brother walked in, exclaiming as he did, "Mama, the stew smells delicious. I hope it's ready to eat!" Then Nazario noticed the serious faces. "What happened?" he asked.

"Belrina and the elf-man have vanished. I am going to look

for them," Aurelio explained again, more quietly. "Mama, I intend to ask the Old Ones for help. They grant wishes, so they must have magic. They are the only ones who can help."

"The Old Ones." Sophia crossed her arms over her chest, leaning back in her chair. "There must be another way."

Aurelio placed his hands on his knees, meeting his mother's eye. "I cannot think of one."

Sophia arched a black eyebrow. "Are you thinking at all? You clearly want to run off right this minute." She drummed her fingers on her forearm. "Tell me. What is the rest of your plan? How are you planning to get through the unprotected woods alive?" Both eyebrows had climbed upwards, furrowing his mother's brow, and she leaned towards him expectantly.

Swallowing, Aurelio sat straight in his chair. "The Gods United will provide a way," he said stiffly.

Nazario cleared his throat. "Uh, Aurelio, let's think it through together. We don't know where they went. What if they are somewhere in the Mountain Region? Shouldn't we search here first?"

Aurelio slowly shook his head. "It is possible, I suppose." He raked a hand through his hair. "But my heart tells me Belrina is far away." He took to his feet. "I need to leave now—she could be hurt!"

Sophia stood, fastening her fists to her hipbones. "What you need to do is rest! How many miles did you run in the last few days to get medicine for Belrina?" Aurelio opened his mouth to speak, but Sophia continued, "You need to calm down, eat, sleep. If you do not, how can you help Belrina?" She fixed him with a stare. "After you eat, you can prepare for the journey. I will visit the village council, and we will have pigeons sent throughout the region." She nodded. "Tomorrow, after a good night's sleep, and if the pigeons bring no news of Belrina, you can leave for the City."

She turned to her other son. "Nazario, please watch the stew and feed all little ones."

"Yes, Mama," Nazario replied.

Aurelio remained standing, earning his mother's attention again.

"You are staying here to eat that stew as soon as it is done, right?" Sophia tilted her head, staring at Aurelio.

"Yes, Mama," Aurelio echoed his older brother, sitting down. He would have more endurance for the journey if he ate well now. With luck, fast feet would get him through the deep forest undetected by the predatory beasts who lived there.

Sophia nodded her head in satisfaction and then swept from the room.

Nazario picked up the wooden spoon abandoned by their mother. As he stirred the stew, he said mildly, "The Old Ones grant wishes, but there are no happy endings."

"I need their magic to find Belrina."

Nazario turned his dark eyes on Aurelio. "What will it cost?" he asked. "To ensure Belrina's safety, you risk your own. Please be careful, brother."

"I will be as careful as I can be," Aurelio replied, lowering his eyes. He could not promise his family more. To protect Belrina, he was prepared to make any sacrifice.

"As careful as you were when you chased that bag of seeds that bounced off our cart? You tumbled along with it down a ravine."

"Thanks for not telling our parents about that." Aurelio stood, reaching to clasp his brother's shoulders. He met Nazario's eyes. "I will do my best. That is all I can promise." He looked into the cook pot. "Is it about ready? It's been a long time since I've had a warm meal!"

Nazario began ladling out the stew, and Aurelio helped by setting the bowls on the table. Soon, the children of the family surrounded them with their cheerful chatter. However, as soon as he could, Aurelio retreated to the room he shared with his unmarried brothers, and Luna followed him. The mastiff's silence suited him as he packed a satchel for his journey.

"Do you want to come with me, girl?" he asked, ruffling the dog's soft ears. She would warn him if any predatory beasts were near, but he also needed a weapon.

He crept to the toolshed, examining the hunting supplies. Aurelio fingered the tight hemp weave of a sling. His aim was more accurate with a sling than a bow, and projectiles for arming it were easy to find, unlike arrows. He placed it in a side pocket of his satchel, hoping he would not have to use it.

The next day, messenger pigeons confirmed no one had seen either Belrina or a large, pale man in the area, and then Aurelio had another conversation with his mother, which ended in him conceding that anyone who wished to help find Belrina could join him.

When Sophia raised the call, volunteers and well-wishers filled their home, donating provisions or opinions (and often both). None approved of Aurelio's plan to visit the Old Ones, but everyone agreed someone should search for their missing healer.

When Master Silvio had appeared at their door, offering his mule to Aurelio, the young man had tried to refuse his mentor's gift.

"Master, this is too much!" he had said.

"Nonsense," Master Silvio had replied, waving away his objection. "You will need her more than me." He had patted the mule's back and rubbed her between the eyes. "Be as faithful to Aurelio as you were to me, Sadie." Then Master Silvio had turned to Aurelio, saying, "Be on your guard—not only for wild cats and ositos. Be careful with those Old Ones, my boy. I'd like my apprentice to return to my woodshop soon."

"I'll be careful, Master Silvio," Aurelio had vowed. "Thank you for understanding that I need to do this."

When the bustle finally died down, three long days had passed. Now, Aurelio and twenty companions were ready for their journey to the City, and although the sun had scarcely crested the horizon, his feet were eager to move.

The inhabitants of Nieve Fresca lined the route, waving and calling out final farewells and last-minute advice.

Lifting his hat in reply, Aurelio led the group, holding the halter for a provision-laden Sadie. As Luna trotted at his side, he used a barely perceptible path slanting westwards through woodlands.

As the voices of their family and friends faded, silence prevailed among the company while they marched away from the village in a long line. Most in the group were of an age with Aurelio, and there were several with whom he had shared boyhood adventures. He prayed they would all get to the City safely.

A petite boy called Cesario, known to be short-sighted and a lover of old books, was the first to break the silence by telling a story.

"My nanita told me about a girl who visited the Old Ones. She asked them to cure her father's rare illness. The girl returned home fifty years later, looking the same as when she had left. She had a healing potion, but of course, her father was long dead. She believed she had only been gone six weeks."

Exclamations and uneasy murmuring erupted.

"Why didn't she come home right away?" Aurelio's friend, Epifanio, asked.

"She had to do something for the Old Ones before they gave her the potion," Cesario explained. "Aurelio," he called, "in the stories, the Old Ones give nothing without asking for something in return."

Without turning around, Aurelio said, "I'll give them whatever they want." The silence that followed seemed disapproving. He knew his mother would certainly object.

It was Epifanio who disrupted the silence. "Do you know something? I can't remember any story that says what the Old Ones look like."

"Well, they must look old! That's why they are called the Old Ones," chuckled Noelio. A lean man with a prominent mustache, he was a few years older than Nazario.

"But how many of them are there? Are they male or female? Don't you think it's strange that anyone who has seen an Old One doesn't say what they have seen?" Epifanio insisted.

"Of course it is. Everything about the Old Ones is strange," Noelio quickly retorted.

"I think it would be helpful to consider what we know about the Old Ones," Cesario said. After a pause, he added, "If an animal was attacking a henhouse, wouldn't you want to know what kind of animal it was? Knowing if it were a raccoon, weasel, or dog, you could better plan how to protect the chickens."

"Or perhaps it is more like courting a girl? I heard you should get to know her preferences and bring her gifts that will please her." Aurelio turned to see Victoriano finish his statement with a blush, ducking his head, which set a bouquet of spiral curls into motion.

The boys laughed.

"And what do you know about courting, Victoriano? All the girls come to you," Noelio said testily.

"No, not all the girls—just your sisters!" Epifanio laughed, clapping Noelio's back. "Come, man, you know Victoriano does nothing to encourage them. I have never seen him voluntarily speak to a girl first."

"No, I suppose he does not encourage them," Noelio admitted.

"I try to avoid your sisters, Noelio. Once, I fell as I ran away from Sola, twisting my ankle," Victoriano recounted. "I hid in a hollow tree for an hour, listening to Sola call my name. Luckily, she never found me."

This eruption of laughter was louder than the first.

"Victoriano can't help having a pretty face, Noelio," Aurelio chuckled. After a pause, he considered, "Maybe I should give the Old Ones a gift? What did they ask for in the stories?"

There was a long pause as the young men tried to remember. They were walking through a dense canopy of trees that only occasionally allowed pockets of sunlight to warm them.

"Remember the story about Paulino?" Cesario asked. "He began losing his hair when he was seventeen. He stole a stallion to travel to the City, and he asked the Old Ones to cure his baldness. In exchange for the stallion, the Old Ones granted his wish. They told him that every oat plant he grew on his farm would be matched by a hair on his head. It worked! But what the Old Ones didn't say was that if he sold his oats for profit, his hair would fall out. To support his family, Paulino couldn't grow all the oat plants he needed to maintain a full head of hair, but everyone in his village received a lot of free oats."

"If they accepted a stolen stallion as a gift, maybe they will accept Sadie?" Cleofas, the tallest in the group, suggested in his deep voice.

Aurelio patted Sadie's nose. "A stallion is far more impressive than Sadie, though she is a good little beast."

"Paulino was a thief with a stupid request. I don't know why the Old Ones helped him at all!" Gavino, the youngest of the group, exclaimed.

"But it was the village that benefited most, right?" Victoriano pointed out.

"Well, what about that poor girl with the sick father? She deserved their help," Gavino continued.

"There will always be illness, Gavino. The Old Ones cannot use their magic to save every person from death."

"Noelio, she deserved help more than Paulino. And it sounds like she did what they asked her to do. They did not deliver on their side of the bargain," Gavino insisted.

"Bargain?" Aurelio adjusted his hat on his forehead. "Yes, that might be a good way to think about dealing with the Old Ones."

"But they are not honest bargainers. They always leave something important unsaid," Cesario declared.

"Well, I'll ask how they will fulfill their promise," Aurelio concluded.

"And you'll need to ask them *when* it will be done," Cesario added.

Gavino spoke up again. "But what does Aurelio have to bargain with? I don't think they'll want bartering beads."

Several of the boys tried to shush him.

"I haven't figured it out yet, Gavino," Aurelio responded. "But I have time to think about it, don't I?"

"Well, I'm hoping we can find Belrina without the Old Ones," someone muttered. Aurelio looked back, but he couldn't tell who had said it.

He patted Luna's head. "If the elf-man hadn't used magic to take Belrina away, Luna would have followed their trail." He stared into the dim forest ahead. "We would have found her by now."

They all walked on in the silence, listening to the birds chittering.

"Well, maybe you can ask the Old Ones what they want?" Victoriano suggested.

"Isn't that risky?" Cesario was quick to reply. "What if they ask for something Aurelio cannot give them? If he can't honor their request, they might get angry."

Aurelio grimaced at Cesario's words. Through a break in the evergreen canopy, he saw the sun directly overhead.

"Let's stop for our noon meal." Aurelio looked for a comfortable place to sit. "Be mindful of the water supplies, though. My father said the next water source won't be for days yet."

Gavino promptly sat on the damp forest floor, unwrapping flatbread from his satchel. Most of the group chuckled.

"What?" Gavino asked. "It has been a long time since breakfast," he said, between bites.

"Aye, little brother. I had an apple a few miles ago. It is

possible to eat and walk, you know," said Epifanio.

"I know, but I just didn't think about it!" Gavino retorted. "It was all that talk about the Old Ones."

"Are you scared, Gavino?" His older brother loomed over him.

Gavino shooed him away. "Of course, I'm scared. Anyone who says they aren't is lying!" He glared with defiance at anyone looking at him.

Epifanio raised his hands in defeat. "Hey, don't be so serious. Let's eat in peace."

As everyone began eating, most young men indulged in light-hearted banter, but Aurelio did not join in or eat. Fear gnawed at his belly, making it an inhospitable place for food. Instead, he prayed for Belrina's safety as he massaged Luna's head.

Cesario approached Aurelio. "May I sit?" he asked quietly.

After Aurelio nodded, the round-faced young man sat on his sleeping roll and used the open flap of his satchel to spread out his meal of jam-filled flatbread and a lemon puff.

Cesario eyed Aurelio. "Does Belrina approve of skipping meals?"

Aurelio shook his head and dutifully opened his satchel, unpacking some nuts and raisins. "Does your mother approve of all that sweet stuff?" he asked. The nuts in his mouth crumbled into dry pieces.

"She packed this lunch herself." Cesario grinned, taking an enthusiastic bite.

At first, Aurelio took one mouthful for every three taken by his plump-cheeked companion, but as the silence between them stretched, Cesario began taking side-long glances at Aurelio, which made him neglect the flatbread in his hands.

Surveying the other young men, Aurelio was pleased to see they weren't neglecting their lunches. They would soon be ready to depart. He turned his attention back to Cesario, meeting his gaze.

"You probably know little about me," Cesario said. He looked at the uneaten puff in his hand. "I read a lot—I might have information that would be useful when dealing with the Old Ones." He briefly met Aurelio's eyes. "I can speak to them on your behalf."

"No, it's too dangerous." Aurelio paused for a deep breath, moderating his tone. "Cesario, I appreciate your offer, but I would never forgive myself if. . ." He didn't want to finish that sentence. "Any sacrifice should be mine alone."

"I—we—came, so you wouldn't have to do everything alone," Cesario replied. He fixed an intent gaze on Aurelio. "You are prepared to risk everything for her, but if you let us help, you'll face fewer risks and have a greater chance of success." His dark eyes shone. "You have more courage than all of us here combined, but it takes more than courage to succeed." Cesario stopped to draw breath. "Sometimes you need friends."

Aurelio stared into his new friend's determined face. He had rarely seen this diminutive young man outdoors, and he had never seen him pick up a bow or finish a foot race. Yet, he exhibited no fear as he advocated for the opportunity to meet the Old Ones.

"You are not without courage, my friend." Aurelio smiled. "As for your offer, I will think about it." When Cesario opened his mouth again, he added, "I will consider anything to keep Belrina safe."

Cesario nodded, compassion flashing over his face. "We'll come up with a plan, Aurelio. We will."

Aurelio clasped Cesario's shoulder, and then he stood. "Enough lounging, boys! Let's see if we can reach the meadow before nightfall."

"I haven't seen the meadow before!" Gavino exclaimed. He surveyed his surroundings. "You know, we have walked so many miles already, but everything still looks the same."

"You are not truly looking," Epifanio retorted. "The canopy

overhead is not as thick, and look at those ferns—they are much smaller than the ones at home. The forest is thinning as we go lower."

Gavino looked around again, coloring with embarrassment.

"Don't worry, I didn't notice either," Cesario whispered to Gavino. He squinted up at the trees.

As the flush on Gavino's face deepened, Aurelio suppressed a chuckle, grabbing Sadie's halter.

Epifanio called, "Hey, Aurelio. These are fertile hunting grounds. How about Cleofas and I rustle up a few things to put in a pot?" he asked.

"It would be good to eat well while we can," Noelio opined.

Aurelio shrugged, replying, "As long as we don't stop walking until nightfall. . ." He started his feet moving again.

With that encouragement, the two young men grabbed their bows and arrows, setting off.

"And be careful," Noelio called after them. "We'll soon be outside the protected zone."

Several minutes later, Aurelio spoke his thoughts aloud. "I wish this were summer. With more daylight, we could walk to the City in a week."

"Maybe if we had wings on our feet!" Noelio snorted.

"We will make better time in the lower lands," said Emiliano, a thin boy whose thick curly hair rivaled the width of his shoulders.

"Yes, yes, of course," Aurelio replied, whistling and picking up the tempo.

Without further discussion of the Old Ones, the afternoon proceeded more cheerfully for everyone. When none complained about the pace Aurelio set, his spirits heightened further, but all too soon, they began losing daylight and the warmth of the sun.

Noelio called, "Lads, this is about the time wildcats prowl. Bring out whatever weapons you brought. I'll keep an eye at the rear."

"I didn't bring a weapon," Gavino blurted.

Aurelio looked over at Cesario, who shook his head no. He considered, but before he could say anything, Noelio had a solution.

"Anyone who didn't bring a weapon, keep to the center," he instructed. "Those who have bows, let's have you spread out."

A young man named Eustacio added, "Anyone with a sling, make sure you have some projectiles ready. Remember, Luna should warn us if any wildcats approach."

Aurelio and the rest of the crew followed those instructions with a bit of jostling.

"And Gavino," Noelio called. "I saw you had a knife. If need be, it can do more than cut apples."

After he had his sling and a few stones in his hand, Aurelio weaved through his friends, stopping when he was at Noelio's elbow. "Thanks for speaking up. My mind is so set on getting to the City. . . well, I will try to be better at looking out for everyone."

"No problem. I have an interest in saving my own skin," Noelio replied with a smile. The mirth vanished from his face as he added, "But, um, don't feel responsible for everything. You already have too much on your mind. We can look out for ourselves." He glanced at Gavino. "Well, most of us can. Just remember, we all came because we want to help."

Aurelio nodded. "Thank you."

"Eustacio and I can scout up ahead to find a suitable place to stop for the night," Noelio suggested.

"Ah, yes. Thank you again," Aurelio said. There was a lot he needed to learn about leading this group and keeping them safe, but he would do it.

"I'll keep an eye out at the rear then," Rogelio volunteered. His deep voice complemented his thick muscles. He bounced a large stone in his hand, ready to use his sling.

"Much appreciated, my friends." Aurelio strode to the front, and the young men marched forward, their eyes roving the surrounding forest for signs of the unfriendly beasts who could be hiding among the dense foliage and thickly growing trees.

Luna barked once, and the group halted. In silence, they studied the spot of woods at which Luna appeared to be staring.

"It is Epifanio and Cleofas," Emiliano announced.

"Sharp eyes, Emiliano! I can't see. . . oh, yes, I see them now. Let's continue walking," Aurelio said. "They'll catch up soon." He nodded appreciatively as his friends resumed their vigilant trek.

He estimated they would cover twenty miles on their first day. Tomorrow, they might travel thirty due to the expansive flower-rich meadow on level ground.

Finally, Aurelio could allow himself to believe his actions were taking him closer to Belrina.

Hold on! I'm coming, Belrina. Aurelio's thoughts became a prayer. *Please, merciful Gods United, protect her because I cannot.*

4

THE SILVERY DOME

BELRINA OPENED HER EYES in panic, expecting scorching, blinding light. It was gone, but waves of agony rolled through her head. She closed her eyes, retreating from the dim light in the unfamiliar space. As she strained to hear any sound, she realized her leaden limbs were nestled in soft, clean bedding.

She breathed shallowly, afraid movement would antagonize her headache. Each brief inhale captured a strange scent, strong and calming. She struggled to remember anything before the pain. Darkness overtook her again.

Soft voices woke Belrina, and she instinctively moved her head towards the sound, not in full control of the movement. A line of light pierced the gloom, lashing her head with pain. She closed her eyes, moaning, unable to watch who walked into the room.

The door quickly shut, concealing the brighter exterior world again. As soft footsteps approached, Belrina could only hope that these intruders intended no harm.

Soon, a cool, gentle hand touched her forehead, and a feminine voice spoke a strange word. The pain vanished.

Belrina gasped. "How did you do that?" she asked, cautiously opening her eyes.

Two slender golden-haired women in topaz robes flanked her bed. Their kind, beautiful faces were so similar she thought they must be sisters. Then Belrina noticed their delicate, furled ears, and she remembered.

Mathim had brought her to his homeland.

"Where is Mathim? Is he. . . well?" Belrina asked. As her mind awakened, it generated more complicated questions, and she remembered Aurelio's sage warning about Mathim's magic.

Oh, Aurelio, she thought, gripping her bedsheets as she envisioned his reaction when he discovered she was gone. She had left no word, abandoning poor Luna. *Please forgive me.*

The taller elf spoke another word, erasing Belrina's emotions. She blinked, confused by the sudden emptiness. Did elves think human emotion was an affliction to be healed?

The two elves took turns speaking to Belrina. Although she did not understand their musical language, she recognized they were trying to keep her calm. Agitation worked against recovery.

The sister, who appeared to be younger, with a plumper face, administered a cool, bitter drink. Belrina could have suggested a few herbs to make the drink more palatable, but in a few moments, she was asleep again.

When Belrina next awoke, a delightful dream lingered in her mind. Her mother had been mixing remedies while she played with Luna by the fire. She reluctantly opened her eyes to her new reality, staring at a white ceiling. Judging by the light in the room, it was early morning.

Belrina inhaled deeply and then closed her eyes in relief. Her headache was gone. A residue of trauma lingered, as if her skull was bruised on the inside, but it would fade.

She would recover from the torturous journey, but would Mathim, who had been barely clinging to life?

Slowly, Belrina turned on her side, tucking her hand beneath a silken pillow. Had Mathim, unlike her, known how painful traveling by magic would be? He should have warned her. But then, it may not have dissuaded her. As long as Mathim survived, she would not regret her decision.

"Gods United, can you hear me here?" Belrina whispered. "Please spare Mathim's life." After a moment, she sighed. If her prayers had any power, she wouldn't have had to seek out the magic of this foreign place.

She looked towards where the elf healers had entered, finding only a faint outline marking a door. If she discovered how to open it without a knob, she could search for Mathim—assuming she was able to rise from the bed.

Belrina turned on her back, testing her motor skills. All her fingers, toes, and joints were responsive. She drew up her knees and gingerly raised herself up onto her elbows. The movement cast a shimmering veil before her eyes. Rapidly blinking, she waited for her vision to clear, and then she clasped her knees, slowly rolling up to a sitting position. She was careful to keep her head stationary, but the shower of motes returned, obscuring her vision.

It was a few minutes before she perceived there were three square pedestals of equal height in her line of sight. A frosted glass bowl resembling an open blossom was on the middle pedestal. It emitted vapor, but she could not imagine its purpose.

Cautiously, Belrina surveyed the small room. There were no windows, lanterns, or fires, but somehow there was light. In the perfect silence, she heard rustling at the door before it opened.

A line of light appeared, preceding the entrance of a silver-haired lady who seemed the Goddess of Light personified. Belrina stared into her incredible eyes, which were the same hue as an alpine lake. She noticed the presence of the younger sister-healer when she intoned an Elvish word, erasing the lingering effects of the headache.

"Thank you," Belrina breathed.

Then the silvery lady spoke in a melodious voice, her words repeated in the language of the People by a reedy voice: "I am A'zine, the Seer of Kalehala. On behalf of the Asthildi Empire,

I welcome you home."

As Mistress A'zine spoke, an emerald jewel on her cloak flashed with each word. "You have journeyed far in an unfortunate manner. Now that you are in Kalehala, I will protect and care for you."

Belrina smiled, sensing the enormity of the protection this luminous person offered.

With an Elvish chant, a blue jewel appeared on Belrina's white linen robe. "This device is imbued with magic. It will translate everything you say. Try it, dear one."

"It is lovely to meet you, Mistress A'zine. My name is Belrina." The stone fluoresced as it translated Belrina's words into Elvish. "Please, will you tell me if Mathim is well?"

"Call me Seer A'zine," she replied with a soft smile. "I am pleased to say Vaxili Mathim is recovering well. You seem very concerned about him."

Belrina released the breath she had been holding. "I am glad to hear that. I am a healer, and I was trying to save his life." Belrina looked down at her hands, which contrasted with the white bedding. "But I almost failed. I hoped the magic of the elves would save his life."

"You came to the Empire for Vaxili Mathim's benefit? Without training, you used magic to transport yourself to a foreign place to save the life of a stranger?" The question did not affect Seer A'zine's tranquil expression, but Belrina shook her head vigorously in response.

"I did not use magic," Belrina replied. "I have no such abilities. Otherwise, what you said is true. I couldn't bear to watch him die."

"Do you always value the needs of others above your own?" Seer A'zine asked. Stepping forward, her aquamarine eyes grew more vibrant. "Be careful, dear one. Are there not perils in doing so? Using magic inappropriately can lead to death."

Belrina lowered her eyes instead of correcting the ancient elf again. It had been Mathim's magic that had transported her here—she had only prayed.

"We need not dwell on it now," Seer A'zine said softly. "May I address you as Belrina?"

"Yes, of course," Belrina responded automatically.

"Thank you." Seer A'zine inclined her silvery head. "Belrina, any person with elven blood can wield magic, and I sense you have Asthildi bloodlines. Please tell me about your parents."

Belrina stared into Seer A'zine's serene face. "My father, I did not know," she began slowly. "He died when I was a baby. My mother's name was Erynanne. She was a talented healer." Her voice grew quieter. "She had golden eyes and chestnut hair."

"Traits she received from her elven ancestors." The silvery elf drew nearer to Belrina. "You are speaking of your mother in the past tense. Am I to understand she is no longer alive?"

Belrina lowered her gaze. "She died two years ago. She had a sudden headache, which was not uncommon. But this time, she fell asleep and never woke again."

"My deepest condolences, Belrina," the Seer of Kalehala said softly. "As you recently experienced, using magic without training can lead to bodily pain. Do you often have strong headaches?"

Belrina nodded, her throat growing dry.

"Do not worry, dear one. You are safe now from that danger. You will heal, and I will teach you how to handle magic properly." Seer A'zine gestured to the healer standing at the foot of Belrina's bed. "This is Lakri Njal."

The apple-cheeked elf inclined her head gracefully.

"She predicts you will fully recover in three days, and then we can start your lessons."

"Must I learn how to use magic, Seer A'zine?" The question leapt from Belrina's mouth.

"Yes, Belrina. Magic energy flows through your body, and you must learn to control it. If you do not, your life will always be in jeopardy." The seer's voice was gentle. "While you are recovering, a tutor will teach you Asthildi culture."

"May I learn more about Asthildi healing?"

"Yes, Belrina, but first, you must learn to use magic."

Belrina looked down and her loose hair fell forward.

"You are beautiful, Belrina," Seer A'zine remarked. It did not seem an idle compliment.

Belrina looked up, observing the seer's solemn expression as she looked at Lakri Njal.

"We shall conceal your presence here," Seer A'zine intoned in her musical voice.

The younger Asthildi bowed, acknowledging the subtle command.

Belrina watched the two, uncertain whether to voice her questions.

The silver-haired elf returned her attention to Belrina. "Much must be confusing. Trust that you are shielded and safe." She raised her hand, intoning a word, and a silvery light briefly traced the outline of an invisible dome encompassing the entire room.

Seer A'zine's face softened as she looked at Belrina. "I hope to see you happy here."

"Thank you," Belrina replied, her voice breathy. Under the beautiful arc of light, Belrina had felt the immensity of the Seer of Kalehala's power.

"Tomorrow, you'll begin your lessons on Asthildi culture. Before me, the tutor will swear an oath to protect you," Seer A'zine said. "It is an oath sealed with magic."

"Will you come see me, too?" Belrina asked.

Lakri Njal seemed startled by the question, but Seer A'zine simply smiled. "When you are well, you will come to see me."

Belrina nodded. "I would be happy to do so." She fingered the jewel that had been transformed into a useful device by magic. "Thank you for everything, Seer A'zine. I am very grateful."

"Do not overly rely upon the translation device. You should

learn our language as soon as you can," Seer A'zine instructed. "Until we meet again, Belrina." She inclined her silvery head.

"May your path be pleasant," Belrina replied.

Lakri Njal took a knee and pressed both hands to the floor as the Seer of Kalehala glided from the room, which now seemed dimmer for her absence.

Belrina rested back on her pillow. Her mother had died because she couldn't control her magic? When had her mother used magic? Belrina shook her head. How did they have elven blood?

It was too difficult to believe. If Seer A'zine was mistaken, Belrina wouldn't need magic lessons and perhaps she could return home soon. . . she slowly shook her head again, remembering the mystical elf's presence. The Seer of Kalehala seemed the very manifestation of truth.

"I've never met anyone like Seer A'zine before," Belrina said aloud, her words translated by the blue gem.

Lakri Njal responded, her Elvish words flowing quickly.

"Would you please say that slower?" Belrina asked.

"*Frinth tal viw de apsom palinth*," the topaz-robed healer said, drawing out her words.

Belrina repeated it as best she could for the device, but it didn't offer any translation. "Pardon, do you know why it isn't working?"

Lakri Njal provided another untranslated Elvish statement.

Belrina considered, and then exclaimed, "Oh! The device only translates my language to Elvish, but not the reverse."

"*Jas*," Lakri Njal said.

"Yes," Belrina repeated, and the device said, '*Jas*.' She smiled, saying, "I have learned my first Elvish word."

Smiling, Lakri Njal brought a fresh white linen robe, helping Belrina stand and disrobe. Belrina's muscles felt the weight of gravity. When loosely wrapped in the fresh robe, Belrina promptly sat on the edge of the bed.

Njal rubbed a soft cloth on her arm.

Belrina gasped at the tingle it created on her skin. She fingered her cleansed arm, encountering smooth, perfectly moisturized flesh.

"What is this?" Belrina inquired.

Njal pointed to the cloth. "Utilth."

"*Utilth*. That is the substance on the cloth?" Belrina clarified.

The elf nodded, stroking Belrina's back with the cloth.

"It is wonderful."

Njal smiled, continuing her soothing strokes.

When the bathing was done, Belrina observed to Njal, "No wonder elves are so beautiful. I feel radiant." A soak in a hot bath was more satisfying, but she could not deny the results of the utilth.

Lakri Njal laughed, replying in the musical language of the elves, and then she went to the center pillar. Belrina could not see what she did, but she returned with a vial, offering it to Belrina.

Belrina sniffed it, but she wished she had not. She downed the drink, for it would have been impolite to do otherwise. It must be laced with nutrition, for the one she had consumed hours earlier had staved off hunger. What strange things magic could do! However, she looked forward to eating solid food again.

The tonic must also have contained a sleeping draught, for Belrina soon felt the allure of the pillow and soft blankets again.

"Surely I do not need to sleep so much?" Belrina murmured drowsily, settling into the comfortable bed. If Lakri Njal answered, Belrina did not hear it.

T HE NEXT MORNING, BELRINA woke, feeling normal. Cautiously, she rose from the low bed. Feeling fully recovered, Belrina explored the room, which was brighter this morning.

A small table and two chairs had been placed in the corner, reminding her she would meet her tutor today.

Belrina studied the objects on the pillars. Thinking it wise not to touch them, she waved her hand above the wavy vessel emitting vapor, discovering the air was cooler there.

Turning to the adjacent pillar, she explored the air above a softly glowing sphere, but she could feel nothing and nor could she see anything on its smooth surface.

Lakri Njal entered, calling an Elvish greeting.

"Good morning," Belrina replied. "What is this?"

Njal said a word, briefly touching the orb. The room grew brighter and the orb's brightness similarly increased.

"Amazing!" Belrina exclaimed.

Lakri Njal nodded, a subtle smile on her face. She led Belrina away from the pillars, placing a hand on Belrina's forehead. The healer chanted a few words with closed eyes.

A tingle of energy swept through Belrina's body. When she opened her eyes, Njal nodded, apparently satisfied with Belrina's recovery.

Njal opened a compartment in the third pillar, retrieving an utilth cloth for Belrina. With a brief explanation, Lakri Njal left. Belrina had the impression that she would return soon.

Enjoying her privacy, Belrina bathed, loving the feel of the utilth on her skin. As she finished braiding her hair into a thick plait, Lakri Njal returned with a dark green tunic, which she donned over Belrina's shoulders. It was much too long; the sleeves trailed over her hands and the hem pooled on the floor. Njal chanted, folding and molding the tunic until a simple dress took shape.

"Thank you, Lakri Njal," Belrina said. "It's beautiful." The fine fabric caressed her skin when she moved.

Smiling, Njal fingered an escaped curl along Belrina's face, repeating the Elvish word most recently translated.

"Thank you," Belrina attempted in Elvish, realizing that all the elves she had met had silky, straight hair. Then Lakri Njal guided Belrina to the table, patting a chair. Belrina sat as directed, eager to pose questions to her tutor.

A moment later, Lakri Njal escorted in a young elf with light chestnut hair, loose to his waist. He wore a black tunic with voluminous sleeves adorned by sinuous designs, which were repeated on his knee-high boots. His blue eyes widened when he saw Belrina, but he smoothly bowed, bending forward at the waist.

"I will be your tutor. You can call me Rakti Za," the newcomer said.

Njal sighed as she gazed at Za, drawing his attention. He spoke to her briefly in Elvish, and she inclined her head gracefully before departing.

"Rakti Za, I am pleased to meet you. I am Belrina." She rose from her chair. "I am surprised you speak my language."

"I do not speak your language often. Please correct any mistakes I make." Za smiled, revealing symmetrical white teeth. "I would love to learn more about the People. Perhaps you can teach me about them while I give you lessons on the Asthildi Empire?"

"Agreed." Belrina smiled in return. "You did this"—she bowed—"when you saw me. Should I do that as well?"

"Yes, but how you bow depends on who you are greeting. This is how I would greet a seer." He knelt on one knee, lunging deeply to place both hands on the floor. "This is how I would greet a senator." He remained on one knee with his head bowed, but he raised his arms, holding them outstretched to either side.

"What is a senator?" Belrina asked.

Rakti Za stood up, gesturing for Belrina to sit at the table. He took his seat. "Asthildi elect senators to speak for us and represent our interests in the. . . I am not sure I know the correct word—council is the closest word I know."

"We have village, regional, and national councils. Is a senator a national council member?"

Rakti Za hesitated. "Approximately." He continued, "I am curious. What is the size of the village you come from? How many people live there?"

"I live outside a village. All villages have only twenty-five families, as this ensures village councils will make timely decisions." Belrina realized she needed to explain further. "Each family selects a member of their household to serve on the village council."

"About fifty individuals in the village, then?"

"A family can include adult children and their children. A village may have three hundred residents."

Rakti Za sat back in his chair. "There is no attempt to limit the number of children?" he asked, his azure eyes wide.

"No." Belrina looked at Rakti Za in confusion. "Why would that be necessary?"

Za considered. "Asthildi have the ability to live forever. We need to limit births to prevent overcrowding in the Empire. In Kalehala, there are over ten thousand Asthildi, and this is a small town."

"Ten thousand? Ten sets of one hundred is one thousand, correct?" Belrina sought to confirm.

"Yes. And that number excludes vaxili, who can be ordered to another outpost."

"Are there many cities?" Belrina inquired.

"A great many. The Asthildi nation has seven prefectures, and each prefecture has at least one senatorial city, where senators conduct their business. The greatest city is our Capitol, and it has over fifty million residents."

Belrina stared, uncertain she had seen even one million objects of any kind. "It seems Asthildi are as numerous as the stars."

Rakti Za looked amused.

"Do you think I can find my mother's family?"

He sobered. "I do not know," he said. "Please inquire with Seer A'zine, for she has the resources to initiate such a search."

Belrina nodded, looking away. Her mind reviewed all the information her tutor had provided. "What are *vaxili*?" she asked, her mouth finding the Elvish word strange.

"Warriors who are necessary to keep the peace."

Belrina shook her head. "I do not understand. How can violence keep the peace?"

"When every prefecture has its own army, senators know it is unwise to attack another prefecture."

"Why would senators wish to attack?" Belrina felt her brow furrow.

"The wars first started over access to natural resources. Senators tried to redraw the boundaries of their prefectures to include rivers and other water sources." Rakti Za shifted in his seat. "That was many, many centuries ago. We have had peace for nearly a millennium. Senators devised a system of rights; each prefecture has an allotment of water and magical energy."

"Why does water need to be allotted?" Belrina asked, struggling to understand Rakti Za's history lesson.

"There is not enough for us all to consume as much as we wish," Rakti Za said quietly. "Do the People have no limits on water consumption?"

"No, I have never heard of such a thing!"

"Water is so limited in the Empire that we regulate all agriculture. For the last eight hundred years, only those with a special license can grow fruit and grains."

"Most elves do not eat solid food?" Belrina sat back in her chair. "There is only magic liquid for meals?"

Za's eyes were solemn. "Nutritive vials provide our bodies with all the fuel we need." He forced a smile. "Let us return to the subject of bowing, which nicely illustrates the hierarchy of Asthildi society."

"I apologize, Rakti Za, but I do not understand." Belrina

shook her head. "Can't magic be used to create more natural resources? More water?"

"No, it cannot." He paused. "I am not a magician, so my explanation will be rudimentary." He smiled apologetically without rumpling his smooth skin. "Magic cannot create a tangible object from nothing. It can only transform preexisting material into different material. Now, I can take sand"—Za intoned an Elvish word and a pile of tawny granules appeared on the table—"and transmute it into water." With a series of Elvish words, the sand gathered into a small globe in the air, swirling into a suspended circle of water. "This looks like water. Feels like water." He nodded at Belrina, signaling for her to touch it.

She cautiously touched the bubble, her finger penetrating through the surface. The water droplets continued to circulate around her finger.

"And tastes like water."

Belrina removed her finger and tasted a lingering water droplet. She nodded.

"But it will not give you the sustenance you need."

"Magic is a sophisticated illusion?" Belrina said.

Rakti Za shrugged. "I, like most Asthildi, know little more than how to activate devices created by magicians." At his word, the swirling circle of water vanished. "Now, I should finish the lesson on proper greetings in Asthildi culture. Some can be. . . sensitive about etiquette."

Belrina's session with Rakti Za continued for several hours. Each answer generated more questions, and she became less and less certain she would ever understand Asthildi society.

5

A New Mission

MAGISTHILD LYTHK ENJOYED THE chill and quiet of the desert night on the ancient ramparts of the Fortress of Knath. By the celestial light of the cloudless sky, he could barely discern the orderly line of vaxili tents spreading for acres across the leveled sand. Beyond the slumbering vaxili under his command, the small community of Kalehala lay. At this distance, the lights within the town mimicked the constellations in the midnight firmament. It was the only aspect of architecture in Kalehala that could be mistaken for any part of nature.

The two primary thoroughfares ran perpendicular to each other, prevented from intersecting by the main plaza. On this plaza, the swirling porcelain tower belonging to the kaolin-masters fluoresced, and the metallic headquarters of the silvermasters, shaped like a string of bells, shimmered in the open night sky.

After growing accustomed to wearing sun-shielding cloaks to combat the searing heat, Lythk had discovered Kalehala, on the southeastern tip of the Prefecture of Knath, to be a pleasant post. As a vaxili, he had served in most prefectures, earning a braid in his shoulder-length hair for each location. Kalehala was his first assignment as magisthild, where he had served for forty-three years, not yet earning a horizontal braid to mark a half-century of service.

Lythk looked at Seer Azine's sanctuary, concealed within a craggy ridge that rose from the sand like the plates of an armored lizard. In these arid lands, it was difficult to believe a natural water reservoir lay beneath the stone.

It had been seven days since Mathim arrived in Kalehala with the girl, both unconscious. Seer A'zine had not yet summoned him, but tomorrow, he would question Mathim directly, as the lakri were finally permitting him visitors. Soon, Lythk would learn why the vaxili had brought the human instead of a jewel. Only the Seer of Kalehala knew whether Mathim had averted disaster for the Asthildi Empire. Her silence on the subject did not seem promising.

Lythk began pacing the length of the rooftop, and after a few circuits, he planted himself in the middle of the space. He moved into a slow and methodical sequence of hand and foot strikes, the first of the ten forms of physical combat, which taught control. After completing the first form twice, Lythk moved on to the second form, which generated some energy, hinting at the power a skilled vaxili could produce. He ended the form with a double-fisted pulse, a strike fueled by magic energy. The exercise was so invigorating that he went on to complete all ten of the forms, each increasing in intensity and speed. The pulses he generated in the later forms were manifested visually, magic energy sparking in purple arcs, green jagged bolts, and showers of light.

Every year, vaxili competed to create the most vibrant displays of power, but Lythk had never entered. In the freedom permitted by solitude, Lythk's pulses lit up the night, a display intended only for his eyes. After he completed the ultimate form, he glided into the first form, finishing his exercise with the meditative movement.

Lythk returned to his sleeping quarters using narrow causeways. It was several minutes before he reached the hallways lit by the keepers, the personal attendants for all vaxili. When he reached his chamber, he did not activate the device to regulate temperature. Lythk hastily unlaced his white boots and stripped off his clothes, laying them neatly on a bench, where a keeper would retrieve them for cleaning. The nightshirt he donned did not protect against the chill in the room, and nor did his bedsheets initially, but after the exertion of performing forms, Lythk slept well.

A S THE FIRST RAYS of the sun entered his window, Lythk cleansed with utilth and hastily dressed. He used a transporter to travel to the roof of the medical facility, and then he stepped into an ardhendir, which lowered him to the reception area where a lakri swiftly bowed and offered to escort him to Mathim's recovery room.

As Lythk entered the sparse, windowless chamber, the vaxili attempted a bow from his bed.

"Rest, Vaxili Mathim," Lythk instructed, assessing Mathim's condition. "I am glad to see you safely returned. You appear to be well."

"Good morning, Magisthild. My injuries are healed, and I feel fit for service."

"When do the lakri estimate you can return to duty?"

"In three days." Mathim looked at the door, lowering his voice. "It seems a conservative approach."

Lythk suppressed a smile. "If we need your unique skills before then, I will speak with the lakri. It is possible they can be persuaded to adopt a different approach." He moved closer to the bed, adopting a comfortable stance. "I have not yet conferred with Seer A'zine regarding your mission. Please brief me."

"Yes, Magisthild. I started my mission in the People's City, where a few Banished Ones reside. After questioning them, I learned that humans do not mine for jewels or precious ores, believing it destroys the environment. I turned to the countryside, searching for mystic practitioners. For two months, I explored three regions, finding none who knew of Asthildi, let alone any jewel originating from the Empire. I began traveling at night because my appearance was disturbing to most humans."

Mathim shook his head. "Traveling at night in icy mountainous terrain was how I slipped, injuring my leg. I don't recall how many days I was stranded before a man and a girl rescued me. Her name is Belrina, Magisthild." His tone became less brisk. "She attempted to heal me, and I was better briefly. I sensed Belrina is of Asthildi blood, and Magisthild"—Mathim's golden gaze grew intense—"she is the daughter of Erynanne."

Lythk blinked.

"I thought it too great a coincidence. I do not know if she is the Erynannea, but I was dying. My choice was to die there and fail, or return with Belrina so Seer A'zine could judge if she was the Erynannea. I had to gamble that the transporter would work for us both." He looked down.

"Ah. It was an enormous risk, but I have been informed the girl will recover," Magisthild Lythk replied. "You did well, Vaxili Mathim." He briefly clasped Mathim's shoulder. "I shall leave you to rest. Good morning."

"Good day to you, Magisthild." Mathim inclined his honey-gold head.

As Lythk turned to leave, the door opened, admitting a lakri and a child-sized figure wearing a cloak hiding their eyes. An Asthildi child would be slimmer and not need a disguise in Kalehala. The two dropped quickly into respectful bows.

"Forgive our intrusion, Magisthild Lythk. Please allow me to introduce myself. I am Lakri Njal, and I am escorting a visitor to Vaxili Mathim. We did not expect another visitor at this early hour. We shall return at a different time, so as not to invade your privacy."

"No forgiveness is necessary, Lakri Njal. Please rise," Lythk commanded.

Njal promptly did so, but her companion was slower.

"Your presence is not an inconvenience. Please stay. I should like an introduction to Vaxili Mathim's guest." Magisthild Lythk swept back his peridot cape as a subtle reminder of his position.

"Magisthild Lythk," Njal began, inclining her head, "I wish I could grant your request. Please accept my sincere apologies—"

Her companion suddenly gripped her arm. "I invoke medical license," Njal exclaimed, intoning a spell to bind all those present to secrecy.

"Are you ill?" Lakri Njal asked as she quickly removed the cloak, revealing a large-eyed girl with warm-colored skin and dark hair undulating to her waist.

"*Estoy bien*," came the reply, quickly interpreted by a translation device as "I am well." Her dark blue eyes darted to Mathim before she continued in her native language, speaking in a hushed tone. A moment later, Lythk heard the interpretation: "I am now hearing every Elvish word translated in my head. It startled me."

"You can understand every word I am saying?" Njal queried.

The girl said, "*Sí*, Lakri Njal," which the device translated as "Yes, Lakri Njal." The delay in translation was a temporary nuisance.

"Belrina, you must have used magic," the lakri declared. "I need to examine you, and I must summon Seer A'zine."

"I will summon her," Lythk offered, activating a communication device.

"Thank you, Magisthild." Njal conjured a second bed, and Belrina sat on its edge while the lakri examined her.

The girl gripped her knees, speaking haltingly, "*No quise hacerlo. . .*" Lythk focused on the translation. "I didn't mean to. . . I didn't want to use magic." Agitation enhanced the color in her face. "Am I. . .?" She glanced at Lythk, falling silent.

"You are fine, Belrina." Njal held the human's shoulder. "You are in perfect physical health."

Belrina relaxed, smiling at the lakri with gratitude.

Lythk wondered how this guileless child could hold the key to the Empire's survival. In her current state, she would be defenseless against all Asthildi, not only the elite who sought unlimited pleasure or power.

"Lie down now and rest until Seer A'zine arrives," Njal instructed gently.

The girl promptly complied, looking towards Mathim in the adjacent bed. "Greetings, Vaxili Mathim," she said in Elvish. Then, the exclamation in her language was translated as, "I am happy to see you recovered!" Her emotions lit her face, a luminous display as interesting as magic power pulses.

Mathim said a few words in the human language, smiling broadly by Asthildi standards. Then he said, "Your happiness cannot exceed mine, Belrina. I am relieved to see you in good health, as it was I who placed you in danger. Please forgive me."

The child shook her head, replying through the translation device. "What little I suffered is long forgotten now, Mathim. What matters most is that we are both alive."

Lythk stepped forward, studying the girl. No human child would express such a sentiment, nor any Asthildi of any age. "The seer will be here shortly," he announced. "Lakri Njal, will you please introduce me to Vaxili Mathim's guest?" Lythk asked, approaching the girl's bed.

"Magisthild Lythk, this is Belrina of the Forest People," Njal said. "Seer A'zine commands all to conceal her presence."

Lythk nodded, saying, "I am pleased to make your acquaintance, Belrina of the Forest People. Please allow me to observe that your current disguise needs to be improved. It will attract the attention of any Asthildi hunting for information."

Belrina appeared confused, but she said, "Thank you, Magisthild Lythk, for your help." She only occasionally met his eye.

"Seer A'zine should provide you with a device to transform your appearance." As Lythk spoke, it occurred to him that the seer had not done so because the girl would need to use magic to invoke it. "If I may inquire, Belrina of the Forest People, prior to your arrival here, did you understand the Elvish language?"

"No, Magisthild," Belrina replied.

Lythk looked briefly at Mathim, who confirmed with a surreptitious nod. "And how do you understand what I am saying now?"

Belrina looked down. "It is as if there is a translation device in my mind, repeating every Elvish word into the language of the People."

"May I test this translation device you hear in your mind? If you would please repeat after me: 'the first principle of magic is that it cannot exist without light.'" Lythk quoted the catechism every Asthildi child learned.

Belrina repeated every word faithfully in the human language, which was translated back into Elvish by the device she wore.

"Very good," Lythk said. The girl smiled at his praise. "Please tell me, have you ever used magic before?" He could not create a telepathic translation device, and yet, the girl had done so without any training.

"No, Magisthild," Belrina said quickly, and then she continued more slowly, "I suppose I cannot be certain. I wasn't aware of using magic just now." The girl looked frightened again.

"There is no need to be frightened of magic," Lythk said, causing the girl to stare at him. He now seemed to be the object of her fear, although he couldn't guess why.

The Seer of Kalehala swept in the room, and Lythk promptly bowed, along with Lakri Njal.

"Rise, please. Belrina, I shall ascertain your magical state," the seer announced. As she chanted, her hands hovered over the girl, and after a few minutes, she concluded, "A few adjustments are necessary."

"I shall leave you to your ministrations, Seer," Lythk stated.

"Stay, please," A'zine commanded, before beginning her magical manipulations.

Lythk assumed a comfortable position next to the door, observing the cleansing. One of his devices registered the tremendous flow of power used by the Seer of Kalehala. Belrina lay calmly, breathing easily when most Asthildi would be convulsing. For criminals, a cleansing by a seer was a form of punishment.

Several minutes later, the seer concluded her chanting. "You are cleansed and your balance has been restored," she intoned the ritualistic words terminating the cleansing. "How do you feel, Belrina?" A translation device performed the interpretation.

Belrina smiled brilliantly, exclaiming, *"Espléndida! Gracias!"* The emotionless voice of the device said, "Splendid. Thank you." The girl sat up, still beaming.

"You must train with me beginning tomorrow morning. Until then, be careful with your thoughts. Do not wish for anything too intently," Seer A'zine warned.

Belrina nodded solemnly, but Lythk did not understand the warning. What did wishes have to do with using magic? He had learned how to channel magic energy by precisely following the formulas identified by the rakti.

"To ease your consternation with understanding our language, I will give you this—" A'zine opened her hand to display a translation device—"so that you can converse with Asthildi."

Belrina took the proffered stone with reverence. "Thank you. You are very kind to me, Seer A'zine."

The ancient mystic smiled, and to Lythk's surprise, she smoothed the girl's impossibly dark hair, which reflected the light in the room.

"Lakri Njal." The seer turned to the young healer. "This is for you. I crafted a magical device you can invoke for Belrina. It will disguise her as an Asthildi. Please try it."

Belrina stood while Njal accepted the dark cube sized to fit into a pocket. When Njal invoked the device, Belrina appeared to be a nondescript blonde wearing the navy tunic of a personal attendant.

"Did it work?" Belrina looked at her hands and down at her dress, unable to see the illusion.

To answer the girl, Seer A'zine conjured a large mirror.

Belrina gasped at her reflection, and she stepped closer, the elf-image mimicking her actions perfectly. "Extraordinary," the girl said, trying a few gestures. The synchronicity with the elf-image, including facial expressions, was perfect. When the girl turned away from the mirror, it vanished.

"Lakri Njal, I will send for Belrina tomorrow. Good morning to you all." Turning to him, A'zine said, "Magisthild, I apologize, but I must detain you a moment longer."

"I am at your service, Seer." Lythk bowed. His eyes swept the room, lingering on Belrina. In her Asthildi disguise, she appeared unremarkable, but even if she was not the Erynannea, her heritage was anything but ordinary. "A good day to you all." Then he held the door open for the seer.

Once in the bright hallway of the medical facility, A'zine held out her hand to him. "Magisthild, if you would please accompany me to my sanctuary?"

In reply, Lythk joined hands with her, wondering why she felt the need to expedite their travel.

The silver-haired mystic chanted furiously, generating a swirl of magic around them. Lythk closed his eyes, and in the next moment, they were standing in darkness.

With a one-word chant, a soft globe of light appeared in the seer's hands, revealing the outlines of a dark lake within the basalt cavern. Lythk peered into the gloom, sensing, rather than seeing, the greatest body of water in the Empire.

"I have spent many hours here since Belrina arrived, Magisthild, seeking insight."

Lythk turned his attention to A'zine.

"Now, I must turn to action, and therefore, I need your help." She held his gaze. "Belrina must be protected."

"I am honored to serve, Seer." Lythk inclined his head. His words extended into the sacred space, gaining significance. "To protect her, we must prevent anyone with a modicum of influence from learning of her existence."

"We have a complication on that front," A'zine replied. "A seer. . . associated with Senator Primth has contacted me 'in the spirit of sisterhood' to inquire about the magical anomaly caused by Belrina's arrival." After observing Lythk's face, she offered further explanation. "Mathim's unorthodox use of the transporter to bring her here created a surge of energy that disrupted the magic energy grid."

"Senator Primth." Lythk was uncertain he prevented a grimace. He began pacing. "How much must be revealed to Primth's seer?"

A'zine replied, "I need to provide a complete explanation composed from veritable facts."

Lythk paused mid-stride. "Would it be possible for someone who has not taken the Oath of Veracity to answer this seer's inquiry?" he inquired.

She shook her silver head. "I think that would be too transparent. There is no reason for someone else to respond except to circumnavigate the Oath." She breathed deeply. "Until this moment, I have always found the Oath to be liberating."

"Let us list the facts we can safely disclose," Lythk continued, pacing once again. "First, a transporter was used incorrectly."

"Second, an Asthildi used it to transport to Kalehala," A'zine joined in.

"Let's pause there. How does an Asthildi use the device incorrectly?" Lythk inquired.

"If the Asthildi was young and untrained, it would be possible," she responded. "It is the truth in Belrina's case. Due to lack of training, her magic energy flowed not only into the device but also into surrounding matter."

Lythk nodded. "A child misused a transporter. Will that story work?"

"That may do, but I do not believe I can call Belrina a child," Seer A'zine concluded. "Although a young one, Belrina is an adult."

"In stature and experience, she seems a child." Lythk permitted himself to share his opinion. "How can she be the jewel, Seer?" he asked quietly.

A'zine fixed her vibrant gaze on him. "I see tremendous potential in Belrina," she affirmed. "Until she fully develops her abilities, though, I must ask you to provide security for her."

"I must review the matter with the vaxithild before employing all vaxili resources." Lythk added, "It is likely Primth will dispatch an intelligence officer to investigate your story. We should protect anyone with information about the girl as well."

The seer nodded. "I will do so, and I will speak with the vaxithild." She held herself erect. "I cannot overstate the importance of protecting Belrina. A threat to her security could be a threat to us all."

As Lythk bowed, he confirmed, "I will employ a full security team, Seer." He gazed at the deep, dark waters for a moment. "A human with Asthildi bloodlines, hitherto only existing in legend. . . it will be an enormous enterprise to protect Belrina of the Forest People." Lythk met the seer's vibrant eyes. "Any information you have about this young one could help me keep her safe."

A'zine smiled. "Magisthild, I may not always answer your questions, but please know I will support you in every way I can and often in ways you will not see."

Lythk's lips quirked into a smile. "I appreciate the Oath of Veracity, Seer. I will keep you apprised of the security plans, which I shall begin enacting now." He bowed formally in farewell.

"Thank you, Magisthild. I wish to remain here, but I will show you the way to the antechamber." The seer intoned a word and small orbs of light lit the winding steps of a stairway hewn from the rock.

Lythk bowed again and as he followed the ascending lights, he considered how to protect the Erynannea from Senator Primth. In past missions, Lythk had undermined members of the elite, but none had been as powerful as Primth, who governed the Empire in all but name. Primth's tastes were infamous, and the novelty of a young elf-human hybrid would excite him.

Lythk's stomach soured at the thought of that innocent child in Primth's hands. Protecting the all-too-human girl was going to be the most complicated sociopolitical campaign of his career.

6

Traveling the Road

LUNA'S LOW GROWLS WOKE Aurelio. He blinked in the darkness, realizing the fire had died down. He strained to hear the cause of Luna's anxiety, but the forest seemed still and quiet.

"Eustacio!" Aurelio called to his friend on watch, slowly rising to a crouch. He could barely make out his sleeping companions as the forest canopy blocked the light offered by the night sky.

Luna continued growling, her pale head swiveling as she peered into the surrounding forest.

"Eustacio!" Aurelio called louder.

"Eustacio!" his voice seemed to call back to him.

"Ositos!" Aurelio roared. "Grab your weapons! Get the fire going. Eustacio!"

Without time to find stones for his sling, Aurelio picked up a bow. He was not the best archer, but he could hit his targets most of the time. The experienced hunters of the group were the first on their feet and they began directing the others.

"Light some torches!" Noelio yelled, while nocking an arrow to his bow. "Eustacio, where are you?"

"Circle up! Everyone spread out in a circle," commanded Epifanio. "You'll see their eyes first."

Cesario had stoked up the fire, bringing Sadie near it within the circle. He hurriedly handed Aurelio a torch, who staked it in the ground.

"There!" Emiliano called, letting loose an arrow. When it

found its mark, the struck beast let out a high-pitched screech, echoed by the rest of the pack.

The screeching beasts had them surrounded.

"Wave those torches!" Noelio shouted. "They hate fire."

His friends complied, aiming their torches towards the trees and streaking the darkness with flame. A dark dog-sized shape raced through the shadows, its yellow eyes gleaming in the torchlight for an instant. Too late, Aurelio launched an arrow.

To his left, Noelio quietly released an arrow, and they heard a scream. Again, the pack repeated the full-throated shriek until Cesario's torch exploded in blinding white sparks.

"What was that?" Aurelio shouted above the surprised din made by his friends.

"Sugar. It's highly combustible," Cesario bellowed. "Did it scare them off?"

The group collectively quieted as they strained to perceive the presence of the ositos.

Gavino yelled, "I hear something." He pointed his torch towards the sound.

The crunch and crackle of branches grew louder, closing in quickly.

"Don't shoot!" Noelio ordered. "Ositos aren't that loud."

Eustacio ran into the camp, stumbling and struggling for breath. Gavino helped him regain his feet, pulling him into the circle.

"What happened?" Gavino cried.

"Keep looking for ositos," Aurelio directed his friends. He spared a glance at Eustacio, noting his scratched face and bloodied arm.

Then the growling started, fierce and sustained, from every direction.

"They're preparing for a charge," Noelio said calmly.

"They're challenging us," Cesario cried. "Make a lot of noise!" He warbled as loud as humanly possible, "Ah-yah,

Ah-yah, Ah-yah." He aimed his torch at the ositos, waving it back and forth in a blur.

Gavino spun his torch before him, shouting, "Leave us alone!"

Aurelio added his own shouts, and the others followed. Those who had torches waved them frenetically, and Cesario generated more pyrotechnics. Luna's barking added to the cacophony. For a few long moments, Aurelio waited for the attack, continuing his wordless screaming. The attack did not come.

He yelled louder, shaking his bow above his head. They would fight if needed, and they would be the ones to survive. Aurelio felt the certainty of it, and he communicated his confidence to the ositos with all the air in his lungs.

For several more minutes, the young men maintained the pandemonium, ready to face a charge of ositos. Eventually, they quieted down, and although all seemed still in the surrounding forest, Aurelio knew the ositos could be watching, concealed within its dark depths.

"Do you think they're gone?" whispered Gavino.

"Ositos are crafty. They could wait until we sleep to attack," Noelio replied.

"Let's stand ready," Aurelio decided, maintaining his stance. His eyes roved the dark forest. "Eustacio, are you okay?"

The rest of the group maintained their positions as well, waiting for Eustacio to speak.

"I-I'm fine." Eustacio's voice was hoarse. "I'm sorry I failed to give warning. I fell into their trap."

"Tell us what happened," Cesario said gently.

"About an hour ago, I thought I heard women's voices. I was going to invite them to join our camp." Eustacio cleared his throat. "I thought the tales of ositos mimicking human voices were just stories. But it sounded exactly like two women whispering a few feet away. Stupidly, I left the camp, and immediately, I saw an osito. I backed away, but there was another one ready to block me. I tried to circle around to one side, but there was another one. They herded me away from the camp. When I realized what they were doing, I figured they were planning an attack. So, I made a run for it." Eustacio fingered his tattered shirt. "But I was too late to warn you all. I wasn't a good watch. I-I'm sorry."

"No harm has come to anyone but you," Cesario replied. "I forgive you for my part."

The others murmured their agreement.

"How many do you think were herding you?" asked Noelio.

"At least five. It seemed like more, but I don't think I would have survived had there been more."

"This is a large pack," Noelio stated matter-of-factly.

Aurelio looked at Luna, who sat at his side, alert but no longer peering into the forest. "We have maybe five hours until dawn. At least half of us should remain on guard."

"Can anyone sleep, knowing the ositos are out there?" Gavino shook his head. "I know I can't."

"But we must move on at first light. Those of us who can sleep should," Epifanio noted.

While the rest of the boys decided whether to stay on watch or attempt to sleep, Aurelio watched Cesario examine Eustacio's arm. The six claws of the osito had left bloody rows starting at the shoulder and running down to the elbow. He stepped closer, wincing when he saw the depth of the grooves. He hoped Cesario had read some books on healing.

"We should wash and wrap this. Take off your shirt, please." Cesario retrieved provisions from his satchel by the fire.

Aurelio searched his own bag for the medicinal pack provided by his mother, and then he stood by Cesario, who was kneeling by Eustacio.

"Can you move all your fingers?" Cesario was asking. In response, Eustacio slowly wiggled his fingers. "Hmmm, that's good," he muttered, as he cleansed the wound.

Aurelio searched through the medicine in his pack, which

his mother had labeled in her slanting script.

"I can brew tea to help with the pain." Aurelio lifted his eyes from his friend's ruined arm to look into Eustacio's face. "I'll wager Cesario will have you feeling better in a week."

"The manufactured medicines I brought will do much of the work," Cesario said, offering Eustacio a pellet.

"You see? Cesario has everything under control." Aurelio closed up his pack, putting it under his arm. He briefly surveyed the camp, hoping the activity and torches would keep the ositos at bay. Then he knelt beside Eustacio, meeting his dazed eyes. "I didn't want anyone to get hurt." Aurelio swallowed. "I'm sorry this happened to you."

"It was my own fault," Eustacio muttered. "My mistake."

Aurelio felt Cesario's eyes on him as he gripped Eustacio's hand. "I'll pray for your swift recovery." Standing, he finally asked Cesario, "How did you know the ositos wouldn't attack if we put on that noisy show?"

"I didn't *know*, but it made sense to me. We acted like we were bigger and stronger, making them rethink their plan to attack."

"Lucky for us, your instincts were right," Aurelio replied. "Thank you, Cesario."

Cesario glanced up at Aurelio, smiling. "You're welcome."

Aurelio left him to treat Eustacio, while he stood on watch. No one on patrol with him spotted another osito, but he knew they were out there.

As soon as there was light to see the path, the young men loaded Sadie with their provisions and left camp, eating breakfast while they walked. Aurelio would have preferred Eustacio to ride Sadie, but he had declared that his legs weren't injured and vowed to keep up with them. Thus far, he was keeping his promise.

"We won't be safe until we are out of the forest," explained Cesario to Gavino, when he asked why they were not having breakfast in the camp. "The ositos may be asleep now, but they can quickly catch up to us."

"How long until we are out of the forest?" Gavino asked.

Cesario shrugged. "I looked at Master Orphelio's map before we left. He said the forest extends for about a week's walk." He shook his dark head vigorously. "So imprecise."

"We may have another three days before we are out of the forest?" Gavino bemoaned, quickening his step.

They all pushed themselves hard, traveling during every moment of daylight. Hunters ran ahead to shoot small game before the sound of the group's marching frightened them. They chose campsites on high ground, and they kept a routine of sleeping in four-hour shifts alternating with four hours of watch. There were signs the ositos were stalking them, but they did not threaten them again.

By mid-morning of the third day after their encounter with the ositos, the young men emerged from the forest onto the grassy rolling hills of the Lowlands Region, known for its rich farmlands. That night, they camped early, as all were exhausted. Yet, at least two kept watch at all times. Although ositos would not leave the forest, wildcats would, especially if they were hunting livestock. . . or Sadie.

T HE NEXT MORNING, AURELIO and his companions permitted themselves a leisurely breakfast for the first time in days. Their camp was a slight hollow in the land, partially shielded by a velvet mesquite whose branches spanned a greater width than its height. As he looked in the City's direction, Aurelio could see few trees. Soon, they would discover what it felt like to sleep under the open night sky.

Gavino slowly chewed flatbread they had procured from a farmer, exchanging some game for the bread and fresh fruit.

"I never realized how wonderful bread tastes. When I get home, I will eat fresh bread every day." Gavino chewed some more. "Twice a day!"

"Mama has better things to do than make bread for you twice a day," Epifanio retorted.

Cesario stopped looking up at the empty, unobstructed sky. "I know how to make bread. I could teach you."

"Or better yet, you could get married!" Epifanio teased.

"Married!" Gavino jumped up as if to run, but seeing the unfamiliar terrain, he promptly sat back down.

The young men laughed.

"When you find the right person, Gavino, the idea will not seem so strange," Aurelio said quietly. He had finished his breakfast, and he was already on his feet, staring again in the City's direction.

"Come on, boys," said Cesario, "let's get moving." He rolled up his blankets, securing them to his back.

Aurelio looked at his friend gratefully, and he began packing up camp, too.

"Here comes Noelio," observed Eustacio, unconsciously itching his bandaged arm. "It looks like he has a rabbit. And"—he squinted—"something else."

Noelio quickly put the rabbit and a squirrel in a bag, tying it to Sadie. "I set four traps," he informed Aurelio. "I can set more, but it will take more time to retrieve them."

It appeared woodland creatures were vanishing with the trees.

Noelio raised his voice. "The squirrel is for Luna." He patted the mastiff's head. "She deserves a treat."

"What happens if there is only squirrel?" Gavino asked as Cesario attached a blanket roll to his back.

"Well, maybe we can barter with them. A farmer might need them for feed. Or maybe we find out what they taste like." Cesario shrugged.

"Yuck! You would really eat one?" Gavino grimaced.

"Honestly, I wouldn't eat the meat of any animal if I had a choice. Squirrels, rabbits or hens, I would prefer they live than end up in my belly. But," he concluded, "I need to live, so I will eat any of them if I must."

Aurelio studied Cesario's profile, wondering what other original thoughts his mind could generate.

Gavino frowned. "Well, I don't have to like it."

Cesario smiled. "No, you do not."

As they began walking, Gavino and Cesario assumed their positions in the middle of the group. Aurelio thought it best to be prepared for anything unexpected. They could not afford any delays in reaching the City.

"You know," said Cesario, "I think I could grow used to living in the Lowlands. The weather is warmer, and you can see so much of the sky. Look at that sunrise."

A soft pink spread across the horizon as the sun crested a hill.

"Uh, I don't know about all this openness. I miss the trees," said Hector.

Victoriano stopped scanning the countryside to glance at Hector. "I think we should enjoy the beautiful things we see here. When we return home, we will see trees for the rest of our lives."

The effect of Victoriano's words on the group was immediate. Gavino looked up more, trusting his feet to keep to the path. All with weary feet stepped lighter as eyes searched for the next moment of beauty.

There were many, as the Lowlands contained fields of wildflowers and orchards of budding fruit trees. Cultivated fields harmoniously blended with nature, creating a vibrant continuity of flora and farmland. Without thick groves of towering trees, the green landscape unfolded for miles, complementing the expansive cerulean sky dotted with cumulous clouds.

The morning quickly passed, conversation sparked by visual points of interest, such as a new species of bird someone spotted. Shortly before their noon meal, the pathway brought them to a wide, dirt-packed lane. Leading straight to the City, it cut through the land for as far as Aurelio could see. Putting his boots on the road, he started whistling.

"The road to the City!" Gavino exclaimed. "Oh! It's dusty." He waved his hand in front of his face as the boots of his companions churned up the roadway's surface.

Cesario tied a handkerchief over his face, and most boys did the same.

Several minutes later, Luna barked once, staring at the path straight ahead. The mastiff continued to walk, so Aurelio did, too.

"I think we are about to meet a traveler. Maybe someone returning from the City." Aurelio quickened his pace.

"Aurelio, it is most likely a local farmer," Cesario replied.

"It looks like a horse and a rider," Noelio said.

Aurelio was not accustomed to seeing horses used for anything other than pulling plows or wagons. But Red Cliff People held horse-riding contests rather than tree-climbing contests for the Flourishing Festival.

"Maybe there is a horse breeder nearby?" Victoriano suggested hopefully. "Can you imagine a ranch of *horses*?"

Several minutes later, the single rider paused on top of a hill.

"Do you suppose the rider is afraid? We outnumber him and many of us have bows," Cesario mused.

Noelio shrugged. "Only rabbits and pheasants should fear our hunting bows."

"Let's move over to one side of the path and allow the rider enough room to pass," Aurelio suggested.

He moved Sadie to the opposite side of the path. "Cesario, please mind Luna."

Cesario promptly moved forward, keeping a hand on the large dog's neck. When they had done so, the rider walked the horse towards them, and the boys unconsciously slowed their pace, leaving Aurelio walking alone ahead of them.

Aurelio couldn't clearly see the rider's face, but he seemed within earshot, so he called out, "A good morning to you, sir."

A girlish voice laughed, calling back, "You boys are a long way from home, I think."

"Uh, excuse me, miss," Aurelio responded. "Yes, we are from the upper Mountain Region."

"Have you come from the City?" Gavino blurted.

The rider paused her mount several yards in front of them, and the group paused as well. "No." She looked them over. "I can see you do not know the etiquette of traveling the road. Keep to the right to allow someone to pass you going the opposite direction. Also, most travelers do not exchange more than polite greetings." She smiled sweetly. "You do not need to know my business, and I do not need to know yours. We are not neighbors. We are travelers." She nudged her horse into a walk. "A good day to you, gentlemen."

A good many of the young men stared at her while she passed, her long braid swaying with the movement of the animal. The others stared at the horse, a long-legged chestnut with white markings on its nose.

"What a beautiful creature!" Victoriano commented.

"The girl or the horse?" Cleofas grinned. "She was pretty."

Aurelio did not hear the reply as he had begun marching again.

"We met our first traveler, and we are going to meet more. Keep to the right, everyone," Aurelio directed. "We will not stop until the next village." Hopefully, they could purchase some medicine for Eustacio, whose steps were as steadfast as his companions, but by the end of the day, his grim face would reveal he needed more than herbal remedies.

As the day wore on, they saw many young women riding horses, and Aurelio kept his feet moving while tipping his hat to say hello.

"I think that is their job—delivering horses to their new owners," Cesario postulated.

"But how do they get back to their homes? After they deliver the horses?" Victoriano asked.

Cesario shrugged. "Walk, I suppose." He muttered under his breath, "This could get interesting."

Aurelio refrained from asking what his bookish friend meant. The road was now open with a blue sky above, and he could celebrate both with a tune. He whistled, giving their feet a rhythm to follow.

As they traveled deeper into the Lowlands, farms and homesteads dotted the landscape in increasingly dense clusters. They repeatedly abandoned the road to allow the oversized farmers' and merchants' carts to pass. Aurelio tried walking alongside the roadway, but sometimes the uneven terrain was too difficult for Sadie. Aurelio began gritting his teeth every time he saw another cart.

In the late afternoon, the female riders began walking home, often in pairs or larger groups, cheerfully chatting with each other.

To avoid conversation with the horseriders, Aurelio tried to keep his friends moving. More than once, the girls' whispers and sudden laughter startled them, spurring most of them on. A few young men loitered, though, hoping to discover what the horse riders found so entertaining, and those young men had to be rounded up by Aurelio or Epifanio, which often engendered more merriment rather than the desired forward movement.

Until the last horse rider was off the road, Aurelio didn't have a moment of peace. Then it was time to scout for a place to camp for the night.

Once Victoriano had set off on that task, Aurelio fell back to speak with Cesario, who had anticipated the afternoon's events. It was the latest example of his friend's keen intellect, and Aurelio wanted to know if he had any new theories about the Old Ones. There were far too many days remaining until they arrived in the City, but he wanted to arrive with a plan.

7

A CHOICE

I T WAS THE MORNING of her first lesson with Seer A'zine, and Belrina waited in her room alone, wrapped in the magic disguise and a sun-shielding cloak. She ambled around the small chamber, her mind replaying the conversation she had had with Mathim, which had led to him swearing to protect her. Magic had spontaneously sealed the oath.

Everywhere, magic was waiting, unable to be controlled. Leading to death. She shook the thought from her mind. Seer A'zine had said it was only dangerous if she was untrained.

Belrina turned towards the door. Any moment, her escort would arrive, and she would soon thereafter be opening herself to magic and its immense power. She would try to touch as little of it as possible.

Pivoting, she strode to the table where she received her lessons with Rakti Za, her mind also turning with the change in direction. As she perched on a chair, Belrina reflected again on what she had learned from her conversation with Mathim. He had explained his mission had been to find the Erynannea and return it to the Empire.

According to Asthildi custom, the daughter of Erynanne would be called Erynannea by her parents. She understood the logic of Mathim's theory, but she didn't believe she was the Erynannea sought by the Seer of Kalehala—what could one human do to affect the future of the Asthildi Empire?

However, if Seer A'zine believed otherwise, would Belrina be allowed to return home?

She stood up. She was learning that some Asthildi rules of etiquette were inviolable, and the greater the difference in rank, the more deferential the individual with the lower status had to be. Thus, the wishes of a person of eminent importance, like the Seer of Kalehala, acquired the force of law. Belrina shook her head. It was a complicated, confusing system.

The door to her room opened, and a male attendant entered, closing the door behind him. Belrina rose and bowed.

With a one-word chant, the attendant transformed into Magisthild Lythk. Belrina blinked in surprise, taking a knee, and then she met his green eyes, which were as bright as the first buds of spring.

"Please rise," he commanded through a translation device. "I shall escort you to the seer's sanctuary." He intoned another word. "I have created a privacy screen. Our conversation will be confidential, but it is best if we speak sparingly."

"Yes, Magisthild," Belrina acknowledged in Elvish, wondering why a military leader was escorting her. Perhaps he had business with Seer A'zine.

He reactivated his disguise before opening the door, permitting Belrina to exit first. Then he escorted her through a maze of identical white corridors, and she soon lost track of the turns leading to a large, gray metal door.

When Magisthild Lythk lifted his sunshield over his face, Belrina did the same. The moment he intoned a word, the door smoothly opened, admitting the shimmering rays of the dawning sun. It had been this Kalehala sun that had seared and blinded her when she first arrived.

Belrina surveyed the parched landscape in the soft, early morning light, hesitating to step into this sun-blasted world, although Njal had assured her the sunshield would prevent even the most intense heat of the desert from reaching her skin.

Instead of rich soil, deep yellow granules—sand—extended

as far as she could see. If she dipped her hands into this form of earth, which did not sustain plant life, what would it feel like? A glint from the sun revealed the pathway, which was the same color as the sand and visible only by its subtle sheen.

When Magisthild Lythk offered his arm, Belrina could not recall where to place her hand. After she lightly held on to his forearm, they set off at a quick pace. Once beyond the large medical facility, Belrina stopped.

The city stretched for miles, but her eyes traveled beyond the gleaming elven constructions to the dark, craggy mountains rising into an impossibly open, cloudless sky. A rosy-orange glow stretched across the length of the rugged peaks, announcing the desert sun's arrival.

After a moment, Belrina recalled Seer A'zine was waiting, and she looked for the commander, finding him one pace ahead. In the disguise, his eyes were blue but no less penetrating. "Please forgive me, Magisthild." She listened to the translation provided by the device she wore.

"No need to apologize. One's first sight of Kalehala is arresting." Magisthild Lythk offered his arm again. "If you would place your hand here." He tapped the top of his hand. When she did so, leaving her arm extended, he moved closer, adjusting his forearm to be beneath hers. At home, only a friend would stand this close.

"Let us proceed," he directed, setting a quick pace again. With his arm beneath hers, she was whisked away, her feet churning as quickly as a quail fleeing from Luna.

Not wishing to invoke his ire, Belrina keep her eyes forward as they marched towards the seer's sanctuary. As they entered Kalehala, elves, garbed mostly in dark blue cloaks, began sharing the path, stepping just as briskly. In their magical disguises, she and her vaxili escort were indistinguishable from them.

Their trek ended at a cave-like entrance, invisible until almost upon it. The magisthild gestured for Belrina to enter, and she found a lavender-clad apprentice waiting to receive them. After a brief exchange with Magisthild Lythk, the seeker escorted them further into the seer's sanctuary. Beyond the antechamber, broad columns lined the smooth stone walls, which were united by softly glowing archways.

After descending a spiral flight of stone steps, Belrina spied a glistening vast chamber beyond an expansive archway. The apprentice led them inside, immediately dropping into the deepest Asthildi bow. Belrina and Magisthild Lythk swiftly did the same.

The Seer of Kalehala dismissed the seeker before speaking through her emerald translation device. "Rise, rise, please. Good morning to you both."

Once on her feet, Belrina delighted in her surroundings. Delicate silver-encased lights rested on a mahogany cornice originating from wooden pillars, as if growing in the manner of a tree. White marble walls balanced the natural basalt ceiling distantly overhead, and at the center of the chamber, concentric stone rings levitated above a calm oval pool.

The seer's voice drew Belrina's attention. Then the translation followed: "Magisthild Lythk, please help Belrina with her cloak."

Belrina immediately felt the back of her cloak lift, and she slid her arms out, stepping away from the magisthild. "Thank you," she said quietly in Elvish, hoping she had managed that properly. Rakti Za had not explained this protocol. Why would she need help removing her cloak?

"I have sealed the Reflection Chamber," Seer A'zine was saying. "We have absolute privacy. Let me remove your disguise, Belrina." She intoned, "*Ophedyn,*" which her device translated as "cease."

Although Belrina could detect no change in her appearance, the seer said, "I see Lakri Njal made good use of the textiles I sent. She has some skill with fashion."

"Thank you, Seer A'zine. I've never worn anything so lovely." Belrina smiled, looking down at the crisscrossing bodice of the emerald-hued silken gown.

"I am the one who should thank you, Belrina. Your presence here is a gift to us all." Seer A'zine stretched out her hand. "Come."

Belrina swiftly moved to grasp the ancient elf's delicate hand, wondering if the seer actually believed she was the Erynannea.

"Have you used any magic since yesterday?" Seer A'zine inquired.

"No, Seer," Belrina responded quickly.

"Will you permit me, Belrina, to ascertain your health?"

"Yes, of course."

Seer A'zine placed her hand on the crown of Belrina's head, and Belrina shivered, feeling the chill of magic energy enter her body.

"We can begin your lessons," Seer A'zine said, smiling and removing her hand. "Look at me, Belrina."

Belrina raised her eyes to those aquamarine pools, feeling an instant psychic connection. The seer spoke directly into her mind, as Mathim had.

'Magic is energy. It exists without form. It is a natural element of our world, much like water or fire. As magical beings, elves can use currents of magic energy for our own purposes. We give magic form, shaping it into patterns for a specific purpose.'

"Magisthild Lythk, we shall spend most of the day training," Seer A'zine said aloud. "You have my permission to secure the area and depart."

The magisthild was standing by the door, his feet planted shoulder-width apart and his arms crossed in front of his broad chest. He had folded their cloaks neatly, placing them on a wooden bench near the entrance.

"Thank you, Seer A'zine," he responded, uttering a string of magical chants. "I have secured the area. It is less suspicious if I remain here."

"As you wish, Magisthild." The seer fixed her aquamarine eyes on Belrina again. *'Magic requires a focused mind. Directing magic energy is done with your will, which is the combination of your mind and spirit to achieve a certain purpose. That is why wishing for something strongly opened the path to magic for you.'*

Seer A'zine moved to sit on a birch bench whose curve mirrored the adjacent sacred pool. *'Come sit beside me, Belrina.'*

Belrina's steps were slow as she complied.

'There is no need to be frightened. I will guide you through every step.' A feeling of calm accompanied the thought.

Gazing into Seer A'zine's tranquil eyes, Belrina nodded.

'Now, let us start with some breathing exercises. Close your eyes and breathe deeply, drawing out your breath slower and slower. Let me know when you feel magic gathering in your body.'

Belrina did as she was told, breathing slowly. She did not know what magic energy would feel like. She controlled her breathing, releasing tension with each breath. More than a full minute later, she felt a tingling below her chest.

With a few more breaths, the tingling became a soft orb of energy, as if invisible particles were circling around each other. "I feel it, Seer."

'Good. Open your eyes, but do not lose connection with your point of power.' Seer A'zine intoned a word, and a triangular colorless gem floated in the air before them. *'This is a claryth, a device that measures your abilities. To invoke it, touch your magic energy to the jewel.'*

"What will happen, Seer?" Belrina asked.

'The device will glow. Its color and brightness will reflect your magical aptitude. Send the energy you feel into the gem.'

"How do I move it?" Belrina felt the percolating magic expanding.

'The energy will respond to your desire.'

Eager to release it, Belrina imagined pushing the energy towards the gem. Vivid magenta light burst from the gem, flooding the chamber. As intense as the sunrise, the air itself glowed. Shielding her eyes, Belrina tried to suppress the magic, losing connection with the energy, but the explosive light continued.

'*You did well, Belrina,*' Seer A'zine conveyed. '*The light is a manifestation of your ability. You have great capacity, dear one.*'

Belrina could sense the seer's satisfaction, but to her eye, the world appeared unnatural and unsafe in the red-hued light. '*Can you please make it stop?*'

'*It will fade on its own.*' After a pause, Seer A'zine noted, '*You have discovered how to communicate telepathically, Belrina! Telepathy is an exercise of the mind. Magic is not involved.*' The seer touched Belrina's hand. '*Why are you so frightened of magic, dear one?*'

'*It took my mother from me.*'

'*I could have saved her.*' Seer A'zine's expression did not change, but her communication was laced with sorrow. '*Although I could not protect her, I will protect you. You know that every word I say is true?*'

Belrina nodded. Rakti Za had informed her about the Oath of Veracity. The brilliance of the gem was receding, as the seer had predicted.

'*I will always protect you, Belrina.*'

'*Thank you, Seer.*' Belrina squeezed her soft hand. '*Am I the Erynannea?*'

'*It is unwise for me to answer,*' she replied. After a moment, the seer sent another thought. '*I will do my best to set your mind at ease. I shall invite Magisthild Lythk to this conversation.*'

Belrina looked at the vaxili, who had removed his disguise and was standing with his eyes closed, facing the glowing gem as if it was the sun on the first warm day in spring, erasing the memory of winter snow.

With the seer's chant, a bench appeared opposite them, and she addressed the magisthild. Before the translation device finished, the commander had taken a seat, dividing his green gaze between Belrina and Seer A'zine.

"Magisthild Lythk, please join us," the reedy voice of the translation device concluded. The delay in communication underscored the convenience of telepathy.

"Belrina has inquired whether she is the Erynannea," Seer A'zine announced.

The magisthild's expression did not change, but his gaze on the seer's face intensified.

"What I say will not change fate, but it may alter the future." The seer turned her tranquil eyes on Belrina. "I must protect the future, dear one. My silence guarantees that all choices will be your own."

"If I choose to return home, you will help me do so?"

"Yes, Belrina." The seer inclined her silvery head. "Although I will remind you of the dangers of using magic without training."

"Seer, can you teach me how to never touch magic again?"

"The choice to use magic will always be yours, even if you were to master the ability to block yourself." Seer A'zine folded her hands in her lap. "For most Asthildi, it would be akin to learning how to live without the ability to breathe."

Belrina looked at Magisthild Lythk's smooth face, unable to discern his opinion. She remembered Mathim's urgent voice, saying it was important she accompany him. He had been fighting for more than just his own life. "Do you want me to stay in the Empire, Seer?"

"Yes, very much so, Belrina," she replied, smiling softly. "I know you wish to know why, and thus, I will tell you this: I fear if you return to the Forest People now, there will be widespread suffering in our Empire."

Belrina gazed into the still water of the oval pool, considering. The view of the Majesties from her garden was more beautiful than the entire Reflection Chamber. There was no superior comfort than the warmth of her fireplace and Luna's soft fur under her fingertips. But if she returned now, she would never be at peace. "I cannot be responsible for any suffering." Belrina shook her head. "I will stay as long as you believe it necessary, Seer." *Though, may the Gods United allow me to return home soon.*

"Bless you, Belrina." A loving energy emanated from Seer A'zine. "You must not seek your fate. You will discover the future in each choice you make." She turned her aquamarine eyes on the impassive vaxili. "I have asked Magisthild Lythk to keep you safe."

"Why am I not safe?" Belrina swiftly inquired.

After a few moments of silence, the green-eyed vaxili answered, "Not all Asthildi may treat you respectfully." His eyes flickered over her face. "Until you are ready to protect yourself, vaxili will guard you at all times. We will ensure no one knows you are in the Empire."

"Ready to protect myself from who? Elite Asthildi?" Belrina gripped the edge of the bench. "But how can I do that?"

"I will teach you self-defense," Magisthild Lythk responded, glancing at the hovering triangular device, which was now colorless again. "I would also advise you to develop your magic power."

"As would I," Seer A'zine chimed in. "Will you trust me, dear one, to teach you safely?"

"I trust you." Belrina reached for the seer's hand again. When she breathed deeply, magic energy swirled within her chest, threatening to burgeon into inexplicable creations. "But I am still afraid." She looked down at Seer A'zine's longer, elegant hand, clasping her own. "It feels uncontrollable."

"You will learn to control it, Belrina," she said, sounding certain. "When you embrace your own power, you will be better able to serve others."

Belrina looked up, staring into the seer's vibrant eyes. *She believes I can learn how to use magic to heal and protect.* The magic energy swirled gently now.

'Are you ready now, dear one?'

'Yes, Seer,' Belrina responded, growing accustomed to telepathy.

"Magisthild, we will resume training now."

The muscular vaxili smoothly rose, bowing slightly before resuming his post by the entrance to the Reflection Chamber.

'Focus on the currents and patterns created when I use magic.' Seer A'zine intoned a one-word chant and the triangular gem disappeared. Belrina sensed a small ripple of magic energy.

'I will invoke a conveyance spell again.' When she chanted, the same small ripple occurred, a vibration with the frequency of a woodpecker's hammering. Seer A'zine opened her hand, showing Belrina a small onyx bead.

'Now, I will use a transporting spell.' With another chant, the bead appeared in the seer's other hand. Faster than a heartbeat, magic energy leapt and then dissipated.

'Breathe deeply, Belrina. Gather magic energy, and then send it into the stone. Command it to your hand.'

Before Belrina completed her first breath, energy tingled within her chest. She directed it towards the bead, but the stone did not move.

'You are sending energy, but you are not giving it purpose.'

Belrina sent more energy, wishing the stone would move. Magic surged, and the bead launched upwards, as if flung by a sling. "Oh! I'm sorry," Belrina yelped.

Seer A'zine raised her hand towards the disappearing onyx, performing the transporting spell again, and with a larger spike in energy, the bead reappeared in her hand. *'No need to apologize, dear one. The spell works on objects in motion as well,'* she sent. *'Your directive was imprecise, Belrina. Please try again.'*

Eyeing the bead in the seer's raised hand and then her own open palm, Belrina tried to replicate the pattern of the transporting spell by pushing her magic energy down so that it could recoil upwards. An invisible wave lifted her from the bench, setting her on her feet.

"Wh-what happened?" Belrina breathed, turning one way and then another while staring down at the floor upon which she was suddenly standing. With her heartbeat thundering in her ears, Belrina looked down at the calm, seated Seer A'zine. "I-I don't think. . ."

The seer stood, placing a hand on Belrina's shoulder. *'I think you are learning valuable lessons. Magic cannot be manipulated as if it were a material substance, like water. It will naturally create the pattern to accomplish your objective. Impress your desire onto the magic.'* She returned to her seat, exposing the bead on her palm.

'Am I safe, Seer?' Belrina sent. Her pulse had not yet returned to normal.

'Yes, Belrina,' the seer conveyed, with a touch of loving confidence.

After a few more deep breaths, Belrina inhaled slowly, commanding the rising magic energy as if she were issuing a command to Luna. The onyx bead appeared in her hand. She jumped back. *'Did I truly do it on my own, Seer? It felt. . .'*

'Natural?' Seer A'zine suggested when Belrina could not finish the thought.

'I suppose so,' Belrina admitted.

'That is how magic should feel, as it is a natural part of you.'

Training continued for the rest of the day. Each magic act revealed another aspect of a complicated system of energy. As Belrina experienced magic currents, she began understanding their purpose. In the same way as she would discern whether a melody was sad or joyful, Belrina perceived the logic of the magical patterns, and Seer A'zine pointed out the subtleties of the currents, aiding Belrina's intuition.

The most useful lesson was learning how to implement a magic block, which the seer advised her to maintain until she was in full control of her abilities.

I N THE SHIMMERING LIGHT of dusk, Magisthild Lythk escorted Belrina to the medical facility. Now, the air was alive with magic. For long stretches of time, Belrina closed her eyes to sense the currents, for understanding magic was essential to controlling it.

Small bursts of energy were used to accomplish prosaic tasks, such as transporting newly purchased goods home. Continuous bands of energy flowed around buildings, performing unknown feats. Within the medical quarters, the halls vibrated with magic energy to aid healing. Belrina smiled, imbibing the subtle therapeutic energy.

Without knocking, the magisthild entered Belrina's room, startling Lakri Njal. Njal began saying something in Elvish, breaking off when she recognized Belrina's disguise. After Magisthild Lythk closed the door, they removed their magical disguises, and Njal gave the decorated vaxili the bow befitting his station.

"It is late for a medical treatment, Lakri Njal," he mildly observed through his translation device.

Njal provided an untranslated Elvish explanation, but Belrina had already surmised she was there to help remove her gown.

"It is fortunate you are here. Belrina shall move to the seer's sanctuary early tomorrow morning. Will you please make the preparations?" the magisthild instructed.

"Yes, Magisthild Lythk." Njal finally said Elvish words Belrina understood. The lakri hastily left to execute his command.

As soon as the door closed, Lythk inquired unceremoniously, "Do you trust her?"

"Yes, Njal is my friend." That morning, Njal had invited Belrina to drop the honorific. The young lakri's kindness truly extended well beyond medical necessity.

"Who else do you trust?" His light-green eyes studied her.

"Seer A'zine." Belrina stopped answering his question, realizing she had to trust him to answer fully. "My apologies, Magisthild, everything is so new that I cannot be certain. . . of my opinions."

Before arriving in Kalehala, Belrina had not realized trust could operate in degrees. She wanted to trust Mathim, but he had sworn the Oath of Obedience to his commanders, including the magisthild who was observing her now.

Unreadable, his penetrating eyes remained on her face for a moment longer before he removed his cloak. "I am going to secure the room," he said.

He performed an incantation, and Belrina stepped closer to sense the magic currents. It was a sophisticated pattern, setting alarms to monitor physical and magical intrusions into her room.

When she opened her eyes, Belrina realized she was standing near the enormous vaxili, and she hastily stepped away.

The magisthild gestured to the table. "Let us sit. I shall stay with you this evening."

Belrina inelegantly sat. "Throughout the night?"

"Yes, you will have a vaxili guard at all times." He continued, "All will adopt disguises, for no one should know they are guards. I will select a team tomorrow." Magisthild Lythk paused. "Do you have any requests for the team?"

She shook her head.

"Please speak freely," he instructed. "What is your concern?"

Belrina opened her mouth, then closed it. She looked away. "Among Forest People, it isn't proper to share a bedchamber with a man who isn't your husband," she whispered.

"What is a husband? I am not familiar with that custom."

Belrina stared at the magisthild's smooth, expressionless face. "A husband and wife are married. They promise to live together for their entire lives."

After a brief nod, he said, "Then I shall select female vaxili to guard you at night."

"Thank you, Magisthild." After a pause, Belrina asked, "Would you please help me understand why I am in danger?"

"There are few elite who can override a seer's wishes. One of them is Senator Primth, who commits egregious crimes without punishment. He is the most dangerous person in the Empire, and we have reason to believe he will be. . . interested in you."

Belrina pondered the magisthild's statements. Rakti Za had described crimes and other incomprehensible historical occurrences, like war.

"Why would he commit a crime against me?" she asked. "I have learned that Asthildi commit crimes for personal gain. This senator already has wealth and power. What could I give him?"

Magisthild Lythk fixed his green gaze on her for a long moment. He was the first to look away. "Asthildi value novelty, and as you are the only human-elf female known to exist, you will be highly prized."

Belrina sat back in her chair, barely hearing the knock on the door preceding Njal's entrance.

"Lakri Njal, I will allow you to attend Belrina." The magisthild rose, stepping outside.

"Belrina," Njal began, peppering her with questions in Elvish that Belrina didn't yet understand. Then she rattled off something that included the words for "tired" and "sleep."

Belrina gratefully agreed, and Njal hurriedly unwrapped the long ties crisscrossing to form an intricate pattern on the bodice of Belrina's dress.

Soon, Belrina was in bed, covered to her neck with soft linens, and although she tried not to notice when Magisthild

Lythk returned, his quiet, solid presence was difficult to ignore. She turned on her side, facing her back to him, but sleep did not come.

Her mind could not rest. Why would an elite commit a crime against someone highly prized? What would Senator Primth want from her? She turned again, forcing her mind to turn as well.

She imagined sitting in a hot bath, but rather than bringing comfort, the image conjured an intense longing for home and those she had left behind. She had abandoned poor Luna so suddenly, but Aurelio must be taking care of her now. Belrina could take some comfort in believing they were together.

Magisthild Lythk moved, and Belrina bolted upright.

He stopped in his tracks, offering an Elvish explanation. The translation promptly followed, loud in the dark chamber: "I thought you might like a sleeping draught? Seer A'zine said you need rest."

Belrina did not trust herself to speak, so she nodded.

He handed her a vial, saying something in a low voice, which was translated as: "Drink and all will soon be forgotten."

Until tomorrow morning, Belrina thought. Lakri remedies could suppress human emotions, but they could not solve the issues which caused them.

She contemplated querying Magisthild Lythk further. However, there was something in his manner that suggested he was uncomfortable discussing this Senator Primth's crimes. What ungodly acts was this elite capable of?

She lay back on her pillow, breathing deeply to suppress her tears. Asthildi seemed discomfited by any emotional display; if she cried, she would likely distress the emotionless magisthild.

Belrina fingered the vial, reciting a proverb to herself. *Do not worry about the path ahead or dwell on the path you left behind. Make the choices in front of you today.*

She consumed the sleeping draught, vowing to make her choices, one by one.

8

A Warrior's Training

BELRINA WOKE TO A soft touch on her arm, and she sprang erect, startling Njal.

"Are you well, Belrina?" the lakri asked, followed by additional inquiries in Elvish that Belrina could not yet understand.

Without uttering a word, Belrina summoned the translation device to her hand. Staring at the gem, she whispered, "I didn't mean to do that." She had fallen asleep with the magic block in place but had forgotten she couldn't maintain it through unconsciousness.

"Belrina?" Njal was studying her.

"I am well, Njal. Thank you," she replied in Elvish, giving Njal the translation device. In truth, Belrina was well-rested, benefiting from her dreamless sleep. The contrast with her emotional state was disconcerting. She scanned the room, relieved to find Magisthild Lythk gone.

Without a word, Njal strode to the pedestal where her chest of remedies was concealed.

Belrina restored the block, imagining a black box to seal her body from the magic energy, which seemed as plentiful as air. Breathing easier, she sat on the edge of the bed, using her fingers to untangle her hair.

Njal approached with a few vials on a tray. The first draught spread a subtle warmth through Belina's body, releasing tension. The second vial was breakfast, which Belrina downed quickly, attempting to keep a grimace from her face.

Sprinkling a few drops from another vial on her fingertips, Njal applied the cool substance to Belrina's temples, massaging her head and working the substance through her hair. A light tingling lingered where Njal's fingers had been.

Belrina closed her eyes to enjoy the massage, unfazed when the lakri's chanting instantly plaited her hair into a crown. With another incantation, Njal summoned glittering glass pins, fixing them manually, careful with their placement.

When she was done, Njal stepped back to admire her work. Smiling, she held out her hands to Belrina, who rose from the bed to grasp them. With another chant, her friend attired her in a vibrant blue gown.

"Thank you, Njal," Belrina said in Elvish, squeezing the young Asthildi's hands.

"It is my pleasure, Belrina," Njal replied, and then her smile faded. "I do not know why the magisthild was here, nor why there is a vaxili waiting outside. Our medical facility is secure. I-I will be wishing you well." Her blue eyes conveyed her concern. "Belrina, please take care."

"I am not in any immediate danger," Belrina said to assuage her friend's anxiety. "Please do not worry, sweet Njal."

"You seek to comfort me." Njal stared at her a moment before retrieving Belrina's sun-shielding cloak. As she wrapped Belrina in the cloak, Njal lightly squeezed Belrina's shoulder. "Stay safe, my friend."

Then Njal opened the door with a chant, and Belrina felt an unfamiliar swirl of magic enter the room. Closing the door behind the magical occurrence, Njal returned to stand next to Belrina, who refrained from grabbing Njal's hand. Instead, Belrina stood as tall as her frame would allow.

A male voice said, "*Ophedyn*," and amid a torrent of magic energy, Mathim emerged.

"Good morning, Vaxili Mathim," Belrina said, as she bowed.

"Good morning, Belrina," Mathim said in the People's language, bowing in turn. Belrina gave him the translation stone

Njal had returned to her.

Njal quickly bowed to them both, departing to attend to other patients.

"Good day, Lakri Njal!" Belrina called to her friend, then she turned to Mathim. "I am glad to see you back on duty, vaxili."

"Please call me Mathim," he said promptly. "I am grateful Magisthild Lythk persuaded the lakri to release me for service." His golden eyes sparkled with triumph.

"Then you will be on my security team?" Belrina said the last two words slowly in Elvish.

He nodded.

Belrina searched Mathim's face. "Please tell me, what danger do I face from Senator Primth?"

Mathim conjured a magic device to his hand, looking down at it. "It must be difficult for you to understand crime. It is a shameful part of Asthildi society." He frowned, still not meeting her eye. "Primth does not obtain consent before taking what he wants, which includes interacting with a young woman like a. . . what is the word for lifelong partner?"

"Husband?" Belrina clutched her chest. When Mathim nodded, she stepped back, her belly twisting. "Without consent?" *Gods United!* Belrina thought. *How can creatures of your creation be so vile?*

"We will protect you, Belrina. He does not know you exist." Mathim eyed her worriedly. "Are you well? Should I call the lakri?"

"No." Belrina removed her hand from her chest. "Thank you. I merely need a moment. . . to compose myself." She looked at her elven slippers as she attempted to erase any emotion from her face. As she breathed deeply, she felt the magic block disintegrating. "We should hurry to the seer's sanctuary."

She reached out to magic to assume her Asthildi disguise, and energy flooded into her body, currents of power racing through her veins. *No!* Belrina thought. *It is too much.*

She held her breath, releasing the energy, careful to keep her mind blank. When the smallest trickle of energy remained, she activated the disguise-generating device as the seer had instructed her. Then she hastily recreated the magic block.

"As you wish," Mathim said, invoking his own magic disguise, becoming an unremarkable personal attendant. "The translation devices will attract attention, so we mustn't speak."

Mathim offered his arm, which Belrina accepted, and as they strode through the bright corridors of the medical facility, she focused on remaining calm, because magic seemed to respond to her emotions. Unfortunately, she did not have the innate serenity of the elves. Belrina pictured the soaring, snow-peaked Majesties, remembering how it felt to be near their enduring beauty. When it was time to fix a sunshield across her face , she had regained her emotional equilibrium, inching closer to achieving control.

Once on the glistening path to the seer's sanctuary, she allowed herself to be distracted by the sights of Kalehala. She gaped at a spiraling pearlescent tower with empty air supporting several upper stories. Impossibly, an Asthildi on a platform resembling the white petals of a flower moved through the empty space, ascending to the apex.

All too soon, Belrina and Mathim were exchanging bows with a seeker, who permitted them to proceed to the Reflection Chamber on their own.

In her deep purple robes, Seer A'zine sat next to the sacred pool, looking into its depths. Mathim and Belrina bowed deeply in unison.

"Good morning to you both. Please rise. We are sealed in privacy, so you may reveal yourselves," the seer said through her translation device.

Mathim immediately deactivated his disguise. Belrina was slower, removing her self-imposed magic block first.

"Vaxili Mathim, it is nice to see you." Seer A'zine smiled.

"Thank you, Seer. Do I have your permission to secure the chamber?"

"Yes, of course, Vaxili." She turned to Belrina. "You look lovely today, dear one. Please make yourself comfortable, and then come join me." The seer gestured to the space beside her.

Seer A'zine seemed to be inviting Belrina to remove her sunshield without Mathim's assistance. Did she wish for her to do so with magic? Closing her eyes, Belrina breathed deeply, performing conveyance and alteration spells so that the robe would appear on the bench neatly folded, duplicating what the magisthild had done the previous day.

When the currents of magic swirled around her, Belrina knew her incantation had been successful, but she still glanced backwards. Mathim had adopted the same stance the magisthild had the day before, and he nodded encouragingly. She smiled at her friend before joining the seer.

After Belrina took her seat, Seer A'zine lightly touched one of the sparkling pins in her dark hair. "Like stars in the night sky. Njal excels at enhancing your unique beauty. I obtained permission for her to join you here."

"Thank you, Seer!"

'Today, we shall focus on regulating magic energy,' the seer conveyed, placing her hands on her knees and closing her eyes. *'Breathing deeply, I feel my magic energy coalescing, and when I direct all my energy into that one point of power'*—she paused, as a silver orb of light appeared at her forehead—*'there is a visual manifestation. Now, I release the energy, allowing it to flow throughout my body.'* The light vanished. *'Each Asthildi has a unique point of power. Find yours, Belrina.'*

Belrina permitted a rivulet of energy to enter her body, allowing it to circulate freely. After a few minutes, the magic still had not settled in one area.

'Draw more energy, dear one.'

She did as instructed, opening herself to more magic. As energy streamed through her, it swirled into a circle slightly below her chest, as it had the previous day.

'Open yourself further, Belrina.'

Belrina met the seer's vivid eyes, asking, *'What if it is too much for me to control, Seer?'*

'As long as your mind is focused, there will be no harm, even if you harness all the magic in the Empire within your body.'

'But the power feels. . . like lightning. How can I control such immense power?'

'Great or small, we control magic with our will. If you desire control, it shall be yours.' The seer smiled. *'Are you not controlling the flow of magic as we speak? You have a focused mind, Belrina. You are in control.'*

Belrina stared at Seer A'zine, realizing she was indeed fending off the greater flow of magic. "I am in control," she whispered. Then she opened herself fully, allowing the magic to course through her. It converged on her point of power, flaring into a sphere near her chest before settling into a soft glow. Belrina marveled at how the storm of energy transformed into a delicate, tranquil orb.

'Do not hold it too long. Release it slowly when you exhale,' Seer A'zine coached.

Belrina pressed a hand to her chest. *'What was that flash of light, Seer?'*

'Your body is not efficient at circulating magic, as you have suppressed the use of magic all your life. Only by using magic can you achieve greater balance. Therefore, using magic blocks will prevent you from gaining greater control of your abilities.' The seer rose from the bench and Belrina followed.

'Send a stream of magic energy into the bench.'

Belrina complied, energy flowing out of her body. The bench remained unchanged.

'You can stop, Belrina. Why did nothing happen?'

After a moment of reflection, Belrina answered, *'I did not give the energy any purpose. You explained yesterday that magic has no purpose on its own.'*

Seer A'zine smiled. *'Correct. The energy we call magic needs no purpose. It simply is. Yesterday, you learned incantations to use magic energy. I believe you can execute spells without chanting. This will be a significant advantage.'*

The seer pointed at the wooden bench. "*Nilkath*," she intoned. It smoothly rose into the air a few feet. Belrina recognized the spell, having used it to levitate the onyx bead yesterday. The pattern of energy was the same, but the waves had higher crests to support the larger object.

"*Nilkath*," Seer A'zine repeated. The long solid bench continued upwards as if it had no weight at all. *'To return an object to its original position,'* the seer explained telepathically and then intoned aloud, "*Celiteth*." She let her hand fall to her side and the bench swiftly returned to the stone floor. The current of energy undulated in the opposite direction, dissipating when the bench was motionless. *'Now try the spell as I showed you.'*

'Perhaps I could try a smaller object?'

Seer A'zine smiled. *'This requires a minute amount of energy.'* She measured with her fingertips, leaving an inch of space between them.

'That small? To accomplish this?' Belrina judged the weight of the bench to be eighty pounds or more.

'It is a minor task. It is nothing compared to traveling from your home to Kalehala.'

'I don't know how I did that.' Belrina looked down.

'You believed you could go to the land of your mother's ancestors. Belief gives magic strength and doubt achieves the opposite. Do you believe in me, Belrina?'

'Yes, of course, Seer A'zine.'

'Then, believe me when I say you can do this.' She waited, as still and graceful as the Majesties.

Belrina closed her eyes, drawing a deep breath, and energy gathered in her body. "*Nilkath*," she intoned. Energy leaped from her hand, but the bench remained rooted to the dark polished floor. She maintained the flow of energy, closing her eyes to sense the magic currents. The waves were too short, so she released more energy and the birch bench responded, lifting into the air.

As the seer predicted, Belrina perceived no expulsion of effort as the bench glided upwards. Then, with the directive "*celiteth*," the object returned to its original position, the energy currents reversing and then vanishing. The logic of it was satisfying.

'*Now, use only your mind,*' Seer A'zine instructed.

Without the incantations, Belrina lifted the bench several more times, carefully replicating the pattern of magic currents.

'*Seer? Why do Asthildi need to use incantations?*' Belrina inquired.

'*I had not considered this question before.*' Seer A'zine paused. '*We start using magic when we are children, and we need incantations to focus our minds. For your disciplined mind, they are unnecessary.*' The communication was laced with pride. '*Let us try a few more things, shall we?*'

For the rest of the morning, the seer demonstrated spells, and Belrina repeated them, learning how to transmute material and create illusions. Seer A'zine welcomed her questions, and she always provided satisfying answers, revealing an intriguing system of magic, complicated but rational, unlike the rules of Asthildi society.

After a lunch break, the seer summoned a glass jar filled with black powder.

'*This is more advanced. It will aid you in gaining balance.*' Seer A'zine summoned and suspended a colorless gem in the air. '*Examine this diamond, Belrina.*'

Belrina summoned the diamond to her hand, admiring its

brilliance. "It is exquisite."

'We will heat and compress the carbon in this jar to create a diamond.' The seer opened the jar, setting it on the floor. With a string of chanting, she gathered the carbon into a sphere, lifting it into the air. A torrent of magic energy rotated around the shrinking carbon sphere.

'Join me, Belrina.'

Belrina opened herself to magic, allowing it to flow into her body. At first, she sent a small amount of energy into the seer's spell, which was swept into the magical vortex. Belrina drew in more and more magic energy to contribute to Seer A'zine's work. With the rhythm supplied by the seer's chanting, Belrina focused on compressing the carbon. Magic energy flowed freely through her body.

After several minutes, the black sphere became white flame, pulsating with light. Belrina imagined the diamond that would emerge from the incandescent blaze, pouring herself into bringing it into existence.

Power swept through her, a cleansing, vibrant energy, connecting her to the seer's torrent of magic, manifesting as a wind rippling her gown. Light exploded, flooding the chamber as the magic climaxed.

When Belrina opened her eyes, an enormous diamond twirled midair, fluorescing as magic continued to swirl in diminishing eddies.

'You may take it, Belrina,' the seer conveyed.

Belrina reached for it with an unsteady hand, encountering a warm gem.

'This is for ornamentation. You have earned the right to wear it.'

'Oh, Seer! It is enough to see it. I cannot imagine wearing something so precious.' Belrina offered the diamond to Seer A'zine.

"I will keep the diamond for you. Whenever you should need it, it will be yours," the seer said aloud, using the translation device.

"Seer, why would I need to wear a diamond?" Belrina inquired.

There was a pause as Seer A'zine waited for the translation device to finish. "Wearing gems is a sign of wealth and power. It earns you respect among the Asthildi elite."

Belrina gazed at the diamond. "Will it earn the respect of Senator Primth?"

"He respects nothing other than his own power." She looked at Belrina steadily. "If you do not either advance his power or provide him pleasure, he will consider you an enemy."

"There was no translation for that last word, Seer."

"Seer, if you will permit me?" Mathim spoke for the first time in several hours, using the translation device Belrina had provided that morning. At Seer A'zine's nod, he explained, "The individuals you fight in a war are your enemies."

Belrina's eyes widened.

"Do not be frightened, dear one. You and I are on the same side in this war," Seer A'zine replied serenely, raising her hand. *'Be at peace.'*

Belrina felt the effects of the blessing, her anxiety washed away by the seer's love.

"I wish you could rest after today's work, Belrina, but there is much you must learn." Seer A'zine smiled. "It is fortunate you learn quickly." She added telepathically, *'If possible, do not use a magic block until our next lesson.'*

Belrina nodded.

Seer A'zine looked to Mathim. "Now, you must go to your lesson with Magisthild Lythk."

Belrina tried to keep her face blank. "Yes, Seer. Thank you for the lesson today." She and Mathim bowed in farewell.

Outside the sanctuary, Mathim took a narrow path leading away from the town. Into the quiet, lifeless desert, they walked past sand dunes cresting against the sky. Remembering the searing heat of the fiery sun overhead, Belrina gripped her sun-shielding cloak.

Soon she saw the Fortress of Knath, the vaxili stronghold, rising from the sand like a lone mountain on a plain. If humans had built those smooth stone walls and sky-riding towers, it would have taken many lifetimes.

In front of the fortress, thousands of neat rows of vaxili tents, tinted the same color as the sand, created a secondary town, empty at this hour. The fortress entrance, which was an arched, metal double door, stood as tall as the birches in the grove near her cabin.

Mathim intoned a spell, and the doors smoothly swung open, revealing a courtyard alive with training vaxili. On the left side, hundreds of warriors moved in unison through a sequence of stances, kicks, and punches. On the right, lines of vaxili sparred manually, their leaps and flips startling Belrina. Was she expected to learn this?

Mathim led Belrina into the dark fortress, veering quickly to a side stairway. Soon, she gripped his arm, relying upon him to guide her, for she could see nothing in the pitch-black halls. In silence, they climbed countless ramps and stairs, meeting no one.

Then Mathim withdrew his arm, and Belrina heard, but did not see, movement.

"Good afternoon, Magisthild Lythk," Mathim said, dropping into his bow.

Belrina bowed quickly as well.

"Please rise," the magisthild said without a translation device. He said something to Mathim that sounded like a dismissal.

"Good afternoon to you both," Mathim said, placing the Asthildi translation device in Belrina's hand before departing. She wondered if she should offer it to Magisthild Lythk. No one had instructed her on whether it was safe to speak with the translation devices here. She detected several magic security measures, but there were too many for her to determine if a privacy shield was one of them.

"Please follow me," the magisthild instructed.

Belrina could not hear his footfalls, so she could not comply.

His voice was suddenly near, asking a question.

Belrina stepped back. "I cannot see you," she whispered. The translation device did not whisper its Elvish interpretation, and its reedy voice echoed in the vast space. She winced, disabling the device. "Pardon, but would you like to use this?" Belrina offered the translation device to the magisthild, hoping he would understand her gesture even if he couldn't understand her language.

His fingers brushed her palm as he extracted the device. In the next moment, he used it, saying, "We have privacy. My apologies for assuming you have elven eyesight." At his word, a dim globe appeared above him.

Belrina memorized the magic currents giving the light existence. Magisthild Lythk, who was not wearing a disguise, began ascending a spiral stone staircase, taking the light with him. She glanced backwards, seeing only an empty stone-walled corridor.

She hastily followed the magisthild, and when they finally emerged into the open air, she was glad to see the sun again. Belrina studied the training area; a chest-high stone wall surrounded a mostly empty, dark, smooth floor.

Magisthild Lythk gestured to pegs set into the stone wall encasing the stairs. "You may place your cloak here."

Belrina removed her magic disguise as well, alert to a strong magic resonance overhead. She briefly closed her eyes to sense the currents, discerning a magic canopy serving as a sunshield for the entire area.

As Magisthild Lythk walked to the center of the space, Belrina observed the intricate patterns in his braid-laced golden hair. Rakti Za had said each braid had a significance known only among vaxili.

"We will begin with the first form of physical combat. Forms must be executed with discipline. I will command, and you will obey without question." The magisthild's eyes held hers.

After a pause to allow the translation device to finish its work, Belrina affirmed in Elvish, "Yes, Magisthild."

He nodded. "Now, I will demonstrate the first form." Standing straight with his palms together, he swept a foot to the side. He then flowed into a lateral lunge, pointing the palm of his hand in the same direction as his thigh, and then he glided into the same position on the other side. Moving to the center, he clenched an upturned hand at his waist while pointing his other palm straight ahead, slowly exchanging the position of his hands.

In a blur, the magisthild's hands struck the air in a myriad of positions, palms always exposed. The form continued for several minutes, a mixture of lunges, turns, and palm strikes. He concluded the form in the same position from which he had started.

"Come," he instructed, observing Belrina's full-skirted gown as she joined him. "You need proper attire." He produced a magic device. "If you will permit me, I can use this to fit you in vaxili training garb."

With wide eyes, Belrina stood upright. "Yes, Magisthild."

He activated the device, and when the magic receded, Belrina was clad in a white tunic over leggings. She marveled at the lightness of the garb until she noticed the tunic ended above her knees. Then her face grew warm, as she realized how much of her thighs would be revealed when she moved.

"Stand in the starting position," Magisthild Lythk ordered, moving aside.

Belrina responded to the command, her concern about her indecent attire replaced by her apprehension of angering the magisthild. She stepped quickly to compensate for the delay caused by the translation devices, planting herself in the place he had left vacant and pressing her palms together.

"Every position should coincide with the inhale or exhale of your breath." Magisthild Lythk conjured a slim wooden pole, tapping a slow cadence. "Breathe with the rhythm I am tapping. Close your eyes if you need to concentrate." When he was satisfied with her breathing, he said, "Now, with your next inhale, move to the first lunge, and with the exhale, your palm extends."

Belrina attempted the lunge, finding it awkward.

The magisthild approached, tapping a spot a few inches to her left with the pole. "Here is where your foot should be. And your knee should be lower."

Belrina sank down lower.

"Good. Now square your shoulders."

She looked up questioningly.

In answer, the magisthild pressed her shoulders back. "Center your weight in your hips."

Belrina quickly tried to do so. He wouldn't touch her hips, would he?

"Now this hand"—Magisthild Lythk lightly tapped her hand—"moves forward into a strike. Imagine you are going to strike with force."

She exaggerated the thrust of her palm.

"That would break your wrist." He fixed her hand position, and then his head tilted as if listening. "Is your magic evenly distributed throughout your body?"

"I think so, Magisthild." Her work with Seer A'zine had purged and depleted her magic reserves, and now the minuscule amount of energy in her body was hard to detect.

"Balance within is the foundation upon which vaxili build. Breathe evenly and balance will naturally follow."

Belrina realized she had not breathed normally since the magisthild had drawn near. She closed her eyes, ignoring his presence to breathe easily again.

"Now, with your next inhale, move into the second position," he instructed.

With the magisthild's corrections and her failure to remember most of the positions, the form he had executed in minutes took Belrina more than an hour to complete. The relief she felt when she finished was short-lived.

"Start again," the magisthild said calmly, holding the fighting pole perfectly vertical.

Belrina's legs and arms had long since fatigued, but she did as commanded, reminding herself that the seer believed this training was necessary.

The second time, she completed the form somewhat quicker, and the third time, Belrina remembered all the positions, but she still needed to be corrected, mostly because her legs struggled to hold the poses.

In the next execution of the form, Belrina struggled both mentally and physically, making mistake after mistake. Her mind wandered, finding Senator Primth to blame for having to learn the unnatural vaxili form. Thinking of the threat he posed, fear threatened to overpower her, but then she grew angry at the fear.

When it came to the sequence of fast palm strikes, she did them double-time, and with the final strike, a silver light leapt from her hand, narrowly missing Magisthild Lythk, who smoothly ducked. "I'm sorry!" Belrina exclaimed, horrified by the delicate tendrils of smoke rising from the scorched stone wall where the bolt of light had struck.

"Center yourself," he intoned, as if uttering a spell. "Hold there until you achieve balance." The magisthild's eyes bore into hers. "You will finish the form."

Belrina closed her eyes to his scrutiny, gathering herself. Then she gave every part of herself to executing the form. The commander did not make further corrections, although she knew she blundered. She corrected her mistakes as well as she could.

When finished, Belrina was breathless and sweating. She faced the unchanging Magisthild Lythk, as fresh as his pristine tunic.

"You were not balanced," he remarked. He eyed the smoking wall, muttering an incantation, erasing all evidence of her eruption as easily as a lakri easing pain.

She looked down at the smooth floor. "Just as I do not have elven eyesight, I do not have elven serenity," Belrina said quietly, resurrecting the magic block.

"Asthildi do not display emotion, as it may be used against us, but we experience all the emotions humans do," Magisthild Lythk replied.

Belrina's head jerked up.

"We all must learn control," he continued. "It comes with practice, and Asthildi have the advantage of long years to cultivate restraint." With a few chants, he exchanged the wooden pole in his hands for a sun-shielding cloak. "We are finished for today. I shall escort you back to the seer's sanctuary."

He activated his magic disguise and donned his sun cloak, and then he assisted Belrina with hers. As they descended the stairs, Belrina's thighs trembled and protested. Without a word, the magisthild offered his arm. Abandoning protocol, Belrina wrapped both hands around it.

"You will adapt to the physical exertion," the vaxili commander said. "You will get stronger."

As she leaned heavily on his solid arm, Belrina thought, *Yes, I will get stronger, and I will gain control. I must.*

9

OVER THE SHINING BRIDGE

A URELIO STROKED LUNA'S HEAD while he gazed into the night sky, comforted by its familiar constellations. Tomorrow, they would be in the City. Since leaving Nieve Fresca, his mind had worked as tirelessly as his feet, and tonight, though they had stopped to rest hours ago, he could not stop his recurring thoughts: would he find the Old Ones, would he learn if Belrina were safe, could they help her, should he allow Cesario to accompany him?

Cesario had engineered a plan, but Aurelio was uncomfortable with involving his intellectual friend. Every day, Eustacio's injuries reminded him he did not want his friends to pay the price for helping him. He desperately wanted to save Belrina, but he also didn't want any friend of his to be harmed.

"What should I do, Luna?" Aurelio asked the sleepy mastiff. Luna shifted her head on his lap, offering no other response. He sighed.

At least Eustacio was comfortable now in the home of Master Jasefo, the rancher whose stalls they had mucked out to earn tonight's dinner and beds in a bunkhouse. Over two weeks of travel had left them with few provisions and no bartering beads, as they had used them to purchase medicine for Eustacio. Yet, even with the medicine, his arm had not healed well, and the kind mistress had insisted on tending to his wounds. Aurelio said another prayer for Eustacio's recovery.

He sat in the open night air for some time before crawling into his bunk in the narrow wooden building. All his companions were already asleep, their soft snores displaying their appreciation of the lodging.

"We'll see Belrina again, girl," Aurelio whispered, petting the mastiff's supple ears as he drifted to sleep.

H E SLEPT SOUNDLY PAST sunrise, waking to the smell of breakfast cooking. The delightful scents had already lured Luna outdoors. Aurelio had not eaten a warm breakfast since leaving his village. His companions, who were talking and enjoying themselves around the fire, quieted when he joined them.

"Good morning, my friends. Please enjoy your warm breakfast—you all deserve it." A thought occurred to him. "Master Jasefo is looking for ranch hands. If anyone wants to stay and work, Eustacio could recover fully here before going home."

Several young men began talking at once. Aurelio let them sort it out while he chewed on some dried fruit.

"If you are certain, Aurelio, I will stay." Gavino was the first to volunteer.

Aurelio nodded. "I am. I'm grateful for your help, as I wouldn't have made it through the forest alone." He looked into his friends' faces. "But now Eustacio needs help getting home."

"I intend to see you safely to the City, Aurelio," Emiliano said quietly.

"Aye, I mean to take you all the way to the Old Ones' door," Noelio quickly chimed in. "Wouldn't mind catching a glimpse of one, either," he chuckled.

Several of the young men laughed, but Aurelio nodded somberly. "Thank you, both. I will be glad to have your company."

"What is the smallest group that can travel safely through the unprotected zone?" Cesario asked. "Gavino and Eustacio will need help, I think?" He did not volunteer himself.

When all the young men had made their decisions, a dozen would be continuing on with Aurelio, among them Victoriano and Epifanio.

"Something is telling me I must go with Aurelio, Gavino," Epifanio said, trying to explain his decision to his younger brother. "I promised Mama to look after you, but you will be safe here. Safer than. . . well, you will be safe. Our friends will make sure you get home."

Gavino opened his mouth and then shut it. Finally, he said, "I don't understand this 'feeling' of yours, but I guess you must listen to it."

Epifanio smiled. "I don't understand it myself, but I am glad to see you are learning to think before you speak." He ruffled his brother's midnight-colored hair.

Gavino half-heartedly tried to dodge his brother's hand. "Hurry in the City, 'Fanio, and then we can go home together."

"That's a good plan, Gavino." Epifanio's broad smile faded, and he clenched his younger brother's shoulder. "Promise me, no matter what happens, you will go home."

Swallowing hard, Gavino nodded. "But I want you to come with me," he said softly.

"I hope I can," Epifanio replied, releasing his brother, who barreled into Epifanio's chest to give him a fierce hug.

"That's not a promise," Gavino complained as Epifanio patted his back.

For a few moments, Aurelio looked down at his hat twirling in his hands, and then he set it on his head.

Those who were leaving the ranch quickly finished their breakfast and packed up their gear.

"We'll leave Sadie here," Aurelio decided, shouldering his baggage. He looked in the City's direction and then turned to face the two groups. Everyone was expecting him to say something.

Aurelio addressed his friends remaining at Master Jasefo's

ranch. "Thank you for helping Eustacio." He looked towards the house. "Please tell him I said goodbye." He turned back to Gavino's group. "May the Gods United grant we see each other soon, but if we don't return within a month, please go home." His face softened at the thought of Nieve Fresca. "Be well!"

Turning on his heel, Aurelio set off for the road, which was now wide enough to accommodate two carts passing in opposite directions. Before his next foot hit the ground, Luna was by his side.

His friends, those standing by the breakfast fire and those joining him, shouted their farewells, noisy in the early morning light.

The cerulean sky promised a warm day for those accustomed to alpine temperatures, and feet stepped quickly towards the City. For Aurelio's friends, the promise of novel sights kept their strides as lively as his.

In the last few days, their curious eyes had had plenty to see. Towns now dominated the area, and their multistoried buildings housed artisans and merchants. Anything Aurelio could ever wish to own, he saw for sale—and many other items besides. One vendor of cooking gadgets was selling a bowl scraper. Noelio had had a good chuckle over that one, observing that spoons already did that job.

Aurelio had noticed himself eagerly looking for the next community garden or cultivated grove to offer respite from the bustling towns. He had been grateful for the spontaneous fields of wildflowers and tall native grasses, sheepishly observing to Cesario, "The closer we travel to the City, the deeper grows my appreciation for the beauty and serenity of our village."

Cesario had smiled and replied, "I think Gavino feels the same way."

Today, the young men scarcely looked at the noisy workshops and flourishing businesses they passed, often using wooden bridges to traverse the waterways for which the Riverland Region was named.

All looked ahead, anticipating their first glimpse of the City.

A few hours after breakfast, Aurelio and his friends crested a slight rise, and they saw the City, a few leagues away. Nestled against purple hills, buildings of varying heights and shapes sprawled around a dense copse of evergreens at the city center. A wide river wound around a portion of the City, its deep blue water shimmering in the morning sun.

The road led to a glistening bridge that arched across the river, supported by a graceful lattice of trusses.

"The Bridge of Josias," someone whispered behind him. After a brief pause, Aurelio kept on walking, and the group followed.

"How steel shines!"

"How long do you think it is?"

"It's over a thousand feet," Cesario answered. "And a single meteorite provided all the metal. Can you imagine?"

"I'm trying to imagine how many people live in the City," Victoriano commented.

"Thousands!" Cleofas proclaimed.

"Over ten thousand," Noelio opined.

"Which building is the tallest?" Epifanio's voice was hushed. "What do you think it's like to live at the same height as trees?"

"Look at that house there!" Rogelio exclaimed. "The children in that family don't have to share a room."

"That would be nice. When we were children, Gavino gave me a black eye when he had a nightmare. Punched me and he kept on sleeping!" Epifanio laughed.

As they grew nearer, they could distinguish the quadrants representing each region of the People. The cluster of red tile roofs adopted the architecture of the Ocean People, and a sector of flat-topped adobe squares represented the Red Cliffs People. In a neighboring section, the brightly colored adobe structures reflected the style of the Palms People.

"I wonder where the Old Ones live?" Epifanio asked. "I don't see anything that looks. . . well, magical."

"I didn't see anything magical about Mathim," Aurelio said softly.

They proceeded in silence for some time. Soon, a steady stream of travelers filled the road, eliminating the possibility of private conversation.

Once at the foot of the bridge, Aurelio paused, looking through the mesh deck to the swift river far below. He ran his fingers over the railing, feeling its cool, smooth surface. After gripping it, he took a step, his boots sounding strange on the metal. The deck was stable despite its porous appearance. He strode forward, Luna keeping pace with him.

After several feet, he checked on his friends and realized that most did not share his confidence in the deck's stability.

"Focus on the City ahead and don't look down," Aurelio called back, feeling a strong breeze. "And hold on to your hats!" He proceeded, glancing behind him often.

Cesario was crossing confidently, but most of his other friends had white-knuckled grips on the railing.

Emiliano had his eyes closed, allowing Noelio to lead him.

Nearly halfway across, Aurelio noticed Rogelio was still standing at the foot of the bridge. Epifanio was at his side, talking, but Rogelio was shaking his head.

Aurelio turned back, encouraging the friends he passed until he stood by Rogelio. He called his friend's name, looking into the larger boy's unfocused eyes. He removed Rogelio's hat for him, giving Epifanio both of their hats. "We are going to the City." He held both of Rogelio's muscled forearms. "Walk with me."

When Rogelio held his gaze, Aurelio stepped backwards, and his friend followed. "We'll find a place to have tea." They stepped together. "Maybe they will have sweet breads." More steps. "I love the cinnamon ones." More steps. "With raisins."

After another step, the wind started tugging at their shirts. "And walnuts."

"I don't like walnuts," Rogelio muttered. He kept his feet moving, but his eyes strayed from Aurelio's face.

With a quick hand, Aurelio gripped his friend's chin. "Hey, look at me, okay? I'll be sure to find you sweet bread without walnuts."

Rogelio nodded slightly.

"Okay, we're moving again." Aurelio continued walking backwards, using his peripheral vision to spot the metal railing. "We'll get to the City together." Until they reached the other side of the Bridge of Josias, Aurelio was going to maintain constant eye contact with his friend. "All of us will be safe." *Gods United, please let it be so!*

With Epifanio quietly trailing them, they slowly traversed the longest bridge in the world, every strong gust of wind stoking Aurelio's concern for his pale-faced friend. When they finally joined their friends on solid ground, he clapped Rogelio on the shoulder. "We did it!"

Rogelio smiled weakly. "Thank you, Aurelio." He edged away from the bridge, putting on the hat handed to him by Epifanio. He had not yet regained his color, but he said, "Let's get to the City. I want that sweet bread you promised."

Epifanio laughed while Aurelio looked towards the wood-sided buildings that started the City's sprawl. The Old Ones were less than a mile away, and Aurelio could not stop his feet now. A few moments later, he heard someone breathing heavily at his side. It was Cesario, who was nearly jogging to keep pace with him.

"Have you decided on the plan?" Cesario ventured.

"As you suggested, we will find a good meal and comfortable accommodation for everyone. Then you can help me find where the Old Ones live," Aurelio announced.

"Perhaps we can sleep in that woodsy area at the city center?" Cesario asked, running every few steps to keep up with

Aurelio.

Aurelio slowed his pace to accommodate Cesario. "Maybe, but let's try bartering for lodging." He looked down at his petite friend. "Let's ask the people in that first row of houses for help. We might find out if your theory that all city dwellers know where to find the Old Ones is true."

"So near the road, the people living there should be used to answering questions," Cesario replied.

Several minutes later, Aurelio and his companions officially stepped into the City, promptly stopping as there was no longer a forward route. The road curved around shops and residences in both directions as far as they could see.

"How can you see where you need to go? You can't see anything with all these buildings," Noelio observed.

"Where do you want to go, lads?" An older woman with ruffled black skirts and a bright blue blouse leaned against a post in front of a small log cabin. A basket with fruit, balls of yarn, and other assorted goods was at her feet.

Most boys looked to Aurelio, but it was Cesario who stepped forward. "Good morning, Mistress. How do we get to the patch of forest at the center of the City?"

The woman frowned. "Are you lads, searchers? A silly business. I'll have no part of it. Stay away from the woods!"

The boys exchanged confused glances.

"My name is Cesario de Nieve Fresca. We come from the Mountain Region, and it would be comforting to see real trees again. If you please, Mistress, what are searchers?"

"Hmph! Searchers are those fools who want to deal with the Old Ones."

"We have come to the City to find a friend, Mistress. It has been a long journey, and we will need to barter for any lodging. If you would be so kind as to suggest where we may go, if not the woods?"

"Stay away from the woods," the woman warned again. Then she added, "I could offer suggestions." She pointedly looked at her basket.

"Forgive us, Mistress. It is our first time in the City. We are not familiar with your customs." Cesario looked through his satchel, removing something and holding it in his fist.

The woman, who had not yet named herself, drew closer in curiosity.

"Would you care for this bracelet my sister weaved? It was woven with great care and given to me with love."

"You are a well-spoken young man, Cesario." The woman considered. "I'll have a closer look."

As he walked towards the city dweller, Cesario displayed the threaded bracelet, its cream patterns swirling in a rusty red base.

She reached out to rub her thumb over the weave, examining the work and saying, "Your sister did a fine job."

Cesario smiled broadly. "She will be pleased to hear of your praise, Mistress."

The woman finally smiled. "My name is Maurina." She cast her eye over the young men. "For a group of your size and a dog, I think Mistress Helena of the Yellow Lodge might take you all in. She is the yellow house on the fourth row in the Riverlands sector." Mistress Maurina noticed their blank stares. "It is to the left."

"Thank you kindly, Mistress Maurina!" Cesario exclaimed, and his friends joined him in expressing their gratitude.

Mistress Maurina beamed, laughing and gesturing which way they should go.

"Good work, Cesario." Aurelio patted his friend on the back when they were out of earshot.

Stepping lighter, Aurelio and his friends made their way down the long curving path, passing city dwellers intent upon their destinations. A path crossed in front of each organic line of houses, but most ended after a short distance. Roads intersected at various points, angling in different directions.

"I didn't consider the possibility of needing a map to navigate the City." Cesario shook his head.

When the young men reached the fourth row, they eagerly looked down the lines of houses.

"Is that a yellow roof there?"

"I think it is more like orange."

"There is a yellow door over there."

"No, look further down. There is a yellow post like the one in front of Mistress Maurina's cabin." Noelio pointed to a taller building with faded yellow siding.

"That must be it," Cesario agreed.

Aurelio studied the lodge as they approached, noticing a window was secured with boards, and in the yard, he noted the weeds, untrimmed hedges, and a railing missing some spindles. There were ample projects they could undertake.

As they walked up the creaking front porch, Aurelio dusted and straightened his clothes as best he could. He heard the others doing the same.

He knocked softly, and then louder when there was no answer.

A short, round woman in her middle years, wearing an apron dusted with flour, opened the door. "I am Mistress Helena. Welcome to the First Yellow Lodge," she said, smiling.

"Good day to you, Mistress Helena. My friends and I are looking for a meal and lodging for the night," Aurelio began. "In return, we can tend your yard and do some carpentry work."

She peered behind Aurelio. "Come in, come in. Let me see all of you."

He made space for his friends to enter, and Luna was the first to cross the threshold, followed by the rest of the group.

The mistress stared at the mastiff.

"Sit, Luna," Aurelio directed, and she promptly complied. "She's very obedient and friendly."

Small tables crowded the front room, surrounded by chairs and stools, none of which appeared to have been made by the same hand. A young couple in a corner were the only patrons, their quiet conversation rendering them oblivious to the new arrivals.

Mistress Helena beckoned for Aurelio to come closer. When he bent towards her, she whispered, "Will the dog chase away rats?"

Aurelio blinked. "If she does not, we can."

The mistress nodded. "Then I can make room, as long as you do not mind at least two to a bed." She looked at Luna again. "Keep that dog away from my other guests, okay?"

"Of course, Mistress," Aurelio promptly replied, and his friends added their assurances.

She nodded, looking them over more closely. "Looks like you'll want to wash up before a meal. Please follow me." She led them up the stairs, which creaked under the weight of so many.

Mistress Helena looked back at Aurelio. "It appears you have traveled a great distance. You are welcome to stay for as long as the. . . problem is getting solved."

"I appreciate that, Mistress, but we are hoping it won't be long," Aurelio replied. No one would want to wrangle rats for an extended period of time.

Mistress Helena stepped into a wide hallway with several doors and opened two of them, revealing large rooms with oversized beds.

"You can also have a room on the third floor." Mistress Helena ascended the next stairway, which angled in the opposite direction from the first.

Aurelio and Cesario followed her to the upper story, which had low, slanting ceilings. Aurelio removed his hat and ducked his head, following Mistress Helena to a cramped room with three narrow cots.

"Thank you, Mistress. We'll take care of the problem," he called as their patron left the room, and then he claimed the bed nearest the door, removing his pack. He noted the lumpy pillow and moth-eaten wool blankets.

The beds may not be all that comfortable, but his friends had an adequate roof over their heads for the night, even if there were a few leaks—he had spotted several sizable watermarks on the ceiling.

Cesario stared out the window. "This might be better than climbing a tree. I can see the woods from here. Can you make out a path, Aurelio?"

Aurelio stepped to the window, studying the maze of pathways. "Thanks to Mistress Maurina, I know where to find the Old Ones. You can stay here."

"If you wish," Cesario said quietly. Then, more boldly, he added, "Do you know what I wish?"

Aurelio swiveled to look at his friend's round-cheeked face.

"I want to unravel this puzzle. I have spent my life reading about the world, but not living in it. For the first time, I feel like I can do something important. I believe I can help you and Belrina."

"But the risks—"

"All who climb mountains face risks." Cesario's voice was calm, and his eyes confident. "This is my mountain. Let me climb it, Aurelio."

Aurelio nodded slowly. "I will protect you if I can."

Cesario chuckled. "And I will do the same." He nodded towards the window. "Any luck?"

"It may take some time. . . these paths are one big tangle."

Cesario sat on a bed. "I wish I could see for myself."

Aurelio stole a look at his short-sighted friend, marveling at the depth of his insights into a world he barely saw. "I can meet you downstairs after I find a route."

Cesario withdrew a small notebook and nib from his satchel. "I'll take notes once you find it. I'll wager there will be too many turns to remember."

He was right. Once Aurelio found their path to the Old Ones, it took several minutes to jot down the route.

When they joined their friends in the front room, all were busy filling their bellies with warm food, although a few paused occasionally to scrutinize shadowy recesses, watching for signs of the problem they needed to solve for Mistress Helena.

"I love the smell of baking bread," Cesario said, reaching for a piece of flatbread as he sat down on a stool. "Is the stew good?" he asked his friends at the adjacent table.

Epifanio merrily volunteered, "It is a fine stew. Although I can't identify the meat." He chewed more thoughtfully. "It is a little like chicken."

"Well, it is much better than cold, dry biscuits," Noelio commented, helping himself to more stew. "So, are you two leaving now?" he kept his voice low.

"Well, no, I was planning to help with Mistress Helena's problem first," Aurelio replied. He offered to ladle stew for Cesario, but his friend protected his bowl with his hand, shaking his head vigorously. Aurelio examined the contents in the ladle more closely, opting to return it to the pot.

"We'll handle that, Aurelio." Epifanio leaned forward. "You go do what you need to do."

Noelio added, "It is our lodging that we need to earn. There is plenty of daylight left, Aurelio, and I think you should use it."

"Thank you." Aurelio swallowed. "The Gods United have blessed me with wonderful friends." He leaned towards Noelio and Epifanio, saying quietly, "I trust both of you will lead the others if we don't return."

Noelio nodded soberly.

Epifanio managed a smile. "I'm sure we'll see you both soon."

Turning to Cesario, Aurelio said, "If we can slip out quietly, we should."

He tried to enjoy the rest of the meal, but the sounds of his friends' merrymaking brought him more comfort than the food he consumed.

Leaving the table to pack their satchels did not interrupt their friends' chatter, but all grew quiet when Aurelio and Cesario returned to the front room wearing their satchels on their shoulders.

"Gods United be with you." Hector was the first to break the silence, but all their friends added their own words of encouragement.

"We'll be back as soon as we can," Cesario said in farewell.

"Thank you for everything, my friends." Unable to say more, Aurelio petted Luna, commanding her to stay, and then he left the Yellow Lodge to face the Old Ones with Cesario.

While his friend consulted the notebook, Aurelio surveyed the neighborhood, finding tokens of nature in the presence of small gardens and dwarf trees. Searching for a greater piece of nature, he looked to the sky.

The crescent of the moon was faintly visible above the hills outside the City. He smiled softly. His mother had always said whenever the moon and sun shared the sky, good fortune would follow. He hoped that was true, but he would need more than luck.

Closing his eyes, Aurelio prayed, *Please, merciful Gods United, grant me serenity in my heart and clarity of mind.*

"It's this way." Cesario pointed.

As they walked towards the Old Ones, Aurelio fingered the soft leather prayer satchel given to him by his mother, not yet experiencing the peace he sought.

10

UNUSED SPACES

KNEELING, THE SEER OF Kalehala inclined towards the deep, subterranean waters in her sanctuary, staring into their depths. With a sharp gasp, she recoiled from her visions, her first movement in hours.

As she breathed deeply to center herself, she processed the images. Innumerable possibilities for the future culminated in darkness, guided by the corruption of Primth.

Bolts of power had extended from his hands, racing towards Belrina. When Mathim and Lythk had tried to repel the attack, they were obliterated and Belrina became Primth's creature, deprived of independent will. With clarity, she could see Primth with ochre skin, inciting the Asthildi elite with wild speeches. She heard his laughter as dead bodies in the People's City were set aflame by Asthildi wearing ochre-sashed robes. The face of one murderer, a golden-haired elf with cerulean eyes, aged and crumbled into dust in a matter of seconds, portraying the pestilence that would destroy the Empire.

A tear slid down her cheek, recalling A'zine back to her body. She felt the ache in her knees, despite the magical cushioning fashioned by her apprentices, and she carefully unfolded herself, sitting back on her heels.

Life and magic needed light, and she had to preserve the light! If Belrina succumbed to Primth, he would eradicate the People, and the Empire would then face its own end. It was still possible to avert this future, but how to do that remained frustratingly unknown. She would try again tomorrow.

A seeker was at her side, assisting her to her feet.

"Thank you, Saolmyn." A'zine stood for a moment before attempting to walk. She fingered an amulet on her necklace, releasing its store of healing energy. As the magic eased her fatigue, she surreptitiously wiped her cheek.

"Let us leave now," she commanded.

A'zine accepted help from her apprentices as they climbed the stairs hewn from the basalt, and when they passed rarely used chambers, she felt a tug on her point of power, a gentle pull on her magic energy. She broke away from the seekers, following the sensation into the darkness to her right.

Suddenly, she saw Belrina in a sakitha tent, a shimmering energy reaching towards her. When it bonded to her, the Sight showed a beautiful sunrise at the People's City, its dawning rays extending across peaceful dwellings.

A'zine probed the vision, trying to see more. After a moment, she returned to her apprentices on lighter feet, issuing orders.

"Menilth, summon Vaxili Mathim immediately. I will receive him in my private garden, and Saolmyn, please arrange refreshments."

"Yes, Seer," the apprentices chorused together.

Reaching the surface, A'zine found a lavender-clad seeker waiting with a message. After a bow, she conveyed, "Magisthild Lythk is requesting an audience."

"Ah." A'zine considered. "Please have him wait in the Reflection Chamber. There is another matter to which I must attend first."

As she entered her private garden, A'zine took a moment to appreciate the chamber. Leafy vines, crafted from silver, adorned an entire wall, sprouting pearl, ruby, and sapphire flowers. Gray and white marble tile created a trellis pattern on the floor.

Lighting the room, a silver grid traveled the ceiling, alternating white orbs of light with circulating orbs of water. In the corner, a fountain topped with a self-contained orb of water provided a soothing melody.

A'zine gazed at the steady flow of water, recalling every detail of her vision.

It seemed but a moment before Vaxili Mathim arrived. As A'zine gave him permission to rise from his bow, she studied him. He was impressively muscular, and the honey color in his hair was echoed in his eyes.

"Good afternoon, Vaxili Mathim. Please"—she gestured to a small table with two chairs—"let us sit and enjoy a cool cup of water together."

"Thank you, Seer. I am honored," he said, bowing again before perching on the seat across from her.

With an incantation, water poured from a silver pitcher into two goblets. The vaxili waited for her to grasp her chalice before drinking. The water was especially sweet, cooled to the perfect temperature.

"I wish to speak of Belrina," A'zine began, her eyes on his face. "Our current plan to protect her will fail."

Mathim deliberately set down his chalice before laying his hands on his knees, regulating his breathing.

"I see this disturbs you," A'zine probed.

"Yes. Belrina worked tirelessly to heal me," Mathim responded, meeting her gaze. "I repaid her kindness by exposing her to danger. I performed my duty, but I loathe being responsible for ruining her happiness, her innocence. I would protect her from all harm if I could."

"You are not responsible, I am." A'zine held Mathim's gaze. "And we have not failed yet! I have Seen a way to protect Belrina—one that none of us considered."

The tranquil sounds of the trickling fountain prevented the ensuing silence from being absolute.

"Seer, you have summoned me, not the magisthild," Mathim began slowly. "I will certainly do anything in my power as a vaxili to keep Belrina safe. Please tell me, is there some action I can take?"

"I am trying to assess whether you are the one who needs to take action." Seer A'zine laid her hand on the table, palm up towards Mathim. "Given the circumstances, please provide an Oath of Silence."

Mathim firmly clasped her hand without hesitation. "I shall be silent regarding all words you now speak in my presence."

After the eddy of magic swirled around the vaxili, sealing the vow, A'zine announced, "The solution I have Seen is the sakitha."

Mathim stared, his golden eyes wide. "Seer, I have not been unaffected—that is, Belrina is very—"

"Mathim," A'zine interrupted, her voice quiet. "Please consider it fully. Look deep within and answer, not as a vaxili, but as a person."

Mathim closed his eyes, and A'zine felt him centering his magic energy. She restrained her own powers, giving him space to imagine loving Belrina, forging an unbreakable magical bond with her. If he could, she would know Belrina was safe.

He opened his eyes, and A'zine could not filter the density of emotions she saw. She waited for him to speak.

"I am not the one," he said.

When it was apparent he would not say more, A'zine prompted, "I noticed you have a unique understanding of Belrina."

"My experience among the People allows me to understand her," Mathim explained, his eyes displaying his emotions. "Like the humans who raised her, Belrina is generous and forgiving, but I continue to struggle with my decision to bring her here. I will do what I can to be worthy of her forgiveness."

"As our conversation is sealed, I will tell you: your choice to bring her here has preserved the only chance the Empire has to avoid demise. Do not question whether you made the right choice." After Mathim quietly nodded, A'zine added, "Belrina chose to stay, vaxili. She has bravely embraced her fate." She smiled, remembering that conversation.

Finally, he relaxed, returning her smile. "Thank you for sharing this with me, Seer."

A'zine nodded. "As you are close to Belrina, perhaps you will see a suitable sakitha candidate. You are welcome to speak to me at any hour on this matter."

"As you have permitted me to speak, Seer," Mathim said, "I will note that Belrina does not seem. . . prepared for the sakitha rites."

"Thank you for your observation. Contrary to sensationalist reports, all conduct within the sakitha is voluntary."

Mathim bowed formally. "I will leave you to work towards a solution. Good evening, Seer."

"Thank you, Vaxili Mathim," A'zine said in farewell.

As soon as he departed, an apprentice glided into the room, settling into a bow.

"Seeker Kristal, please rise. Is there a message?"

"Seer, the magisthild indicated his matter is urgent."

"I will not keep him waiting any longer. Please escort him to me now." While A'zine waited, she meditated, hoping she could find a kernel of insight from her latest visions.

Every day, the consequences of failure became clearer while the possibility of succeeding against Primth grew more tenuous. At least A'zine now had a concrete task: finding Belrina a sakitha partner. Yet, doing so would likely require exposing her to Kalehala society, and then they would have to protect her from the entire Empire.

When Magisthild Lythk entered, A'zine felt his presence, and she opened her eyes. He knelt in an effortless bow, but his patience was not effortless. "Magisthild Lythk, please rise and tell me about this urgent matter."

"Thank you, Seer. The vaxithild has established Belrina is not a citizen, as the law requires proof of a progenitor who is a citizen. Without the legal protections afforded to Asthildi, she is too vulnerable."

"Please sit, Magisthild. I had not considered the legal issue of citizenship, as Belrina is unquestionably of Asthildi blood. The law was written without considering her unique circumstances."

"And yet, it is the law," he replied, sitting in his chair stiffly.

With a few chants, A'zine arranged for Lythk to have a fresh chalice of water before him, and then she announced, "I have Seen a solution that will grant Belrina citizenship status: the sakitha."

Lythk blinked. "This is unexpected, Seer."

"Yes, we must discuss the arrangements." A'zine paused, studying Lythk. He was a young magisthild, a few years shy of his first semi-centennial adornment.

Lythk waited a moment before inquiring, "I assume this will be a private matter, as you know who her partner will be?" He reached for his chalice, but his penetrating eyes remained on her face.

"Alas, I only know that without a sakitha partner, Belrina will become Primth's slave."

Lythk rose from his chair. "My apologies, Seer, for leaving your table. I think better when in motion." He began pacing, his supple white boots quiet on the marble.

"No need to apologize, Magisthild." A'zine examined Lythk more closely. Working with him over the years, she had observed that he gave freer rein to his emotions than other vaxili.

When Lythk had displayed impatience, anger, or disapproval, A'zine had assumed he did so as an effective method of intimidation. For the first time, she wondered if perhaps his emotions were in fact stronger than most vaxili and thus more difficult to conceal.

"This is problematic, Seer. I continue to believe it is best to conceal Belrina from society. Does the sakitha partner need to be found now? This. . . enterprise will distract from

Belrina's training."

A'zine was glad to see Lythk no longer shied away from using Belrina's name without an honorific. "Unfortunately, the possibility of protecting Belrina from Primth grows smaller every day. If we wait, it may vanish altogether."

"I have difficulty conceiving an option that will allow us to keep this enterprise private," he stated, pacing the length of the chamber. "I believe Belrina would seek a male partner, and the only males Belrina has met are Rakti Za and Vaxili Mathim. The first seeks male partners, and the second is ineligible for such partnerships."

"One correction, Magisthild. Belrina has met three male Asthildi in Kalehala."

Lythk glanced at her. "I omitted myself, Seer, but the omission is irrelevant." He continued pacing. "I dislike suggesting the abdication of a vaxili oath, but the importance of safeguarding Belrina is paramount. The vaxithild could allow Mathim to take part in a sakitha." His clenched jaw prevented additional words.

"I discussed the matter with Vaxili Mathim, and he has eliminated himself as a candidate."

"Then, we truly have no option except an Introduction?" Lythk seemed to be speaking to himself.

"Only you can answer that question, Magisthild."

Lythk stopped pacing. He faced away from her, displaying his peridot cloak. "As you are asking for an express refutation, Seer, I will give it." His voice was quiet. When Lythk turned, his eyes were calm. "I, too, remove myself as a candidate. I am unsuitable."

A'zine folded her hands in her lap. "I suspect love does not always respect our notions of suitability. However," she said, forestalling another objection from Lythk, "as we have exhausted all other possibilities, we should turn to discussing how the Introduction should occur." She suppressed her misgivings—she had to trust the Sight.

"The entire Empire will learn of Belrina's existence within hours of the invitations being sent," Lythk noted, his strides lengthening. "She is not ready, Seer. It takes a decade to train most vaxili. How can she be competent at self-defense in a matter of months?"

"Fortunately, Belrina has excelled in all her lessons with me," A'zine said, smiling. "She may be the greatest magician I have ever instructed. Her intuition is keen and her mind is disciplined." She paused before adding, "I should not like to interfere with your training methods, Magisthild, but perhaps you should advance to magical forms of combat."

Lythk returned to the table, shaking his head. "I thought we had more time, Seer."

"I will teach Belrina how to create protective shields. One afternoon should be sufficient for her to achieve mastery."

"Seer, we need to test Belrina's defenses in real-world conditions. She may render a spell when commanded to do so, but does she have the instinct to fight?"

"I trust you can cultivate her abilities, but please do so quickly. I fear we cannot delay the Introduction longer than five days."

Lythk bowed his head.

"I cannot be at peace until Belrina has a sakitha partner," A'zine said softly, listening to the musical cascade of water. "We must begin planning, Magisthild, so that we do not delay the Introduction on account of logistics."

"I would suggest the Introduction occur in the Reflection Chamber," Lythk promptly replied. "I will procure blocks to ensure guests cannot use spells."

A'zine nodded, adding, "I will create a device that provides a protective shield for Belrina. She can activate it before she enters the Reflection Chamber."

"Seer, a first-year recruit could protect Belrina from a few unsophisticated Kalehala elite," Lythk asserted. "What if Primth transports to Kalehala as soon as he learns of Belrina?

We must be prepared to face him." He gazed at the fountain. "If we fail, Primth will execute all those who aided us in opposing him."

"Magisthild, all in this sanctuary are prepared to die to preserve the light. It is part of our work."

"Some vaxili may share that perspective, Seer, but all act pursuant to my command. I am responsible for their lives."

A'zine was suddenly tired. Lythk was so young. "I was at the last battle of Pymia, Magisthild. So many centuries ago, but I will never forget the senselessness of the lives lost." She looked up. "I will always work to preserve life. All the risks we take will be calculated, but they will be great. Survival is a matter of fortune or fate."

She studied the young commander. "But I understand your point. We must plan to protect Belrina from Primth as soon as we announce the Introduction." A'zine rose. "However, we do not need to do all our planning in one night."

"No, Seer," Lythk agreed, rising as well. "Should I summon a seeker? Do you need an escort?" His hand hovered near her arm.

A'zine smiled, appreciating his concern. "I remind you of my age, Magisthild, and now you believe I am fragile?" She summoned Saolmyn telepathically and then held out her hand to Lythk. "Until tomorrow morning, Magisthild."

Lythk lightly clasped her hand, but she gripped his firmly.

"There is still hope we shall prevail, Magisthild. We will find a partner for Belrina to love, and he will protect her from Primth." Hopefully he was in Kalehala, for A'zine didn't wish to consider the alternatives and their significant risks to Belrina's safety. "Then all will be well."

"It is unfortunate, Seer, that love defies my comprehension," Lythk said solemnly.

"I fear love is a mystery to us all," Seer A'zine replied.

She had never experienced romantic love herself, preferring to focus all her energy on her craft. Now, she had to assist

Belrina find a lifelong partner of the utmost compatibility. She hoped the Sight would soon illuminate the murky reaches of the path it had placed her on.

11

ANOTHER USE FOR MAGIC

WHEN BELRINA WOKE, SHE did not immediately rise from her bed. For once, she did not have a lesson, and she allowed herself to think of home. She wondered if Luna had adjusted to her new home with Aurelio, filled with the bustle of children. Was Aurelio now at peace after reading the note she had transported to her cabin? She recalled the effort she had expended to summon her notebook across the vast distance, writing a brief message to let him know she was safe. She only knew the spell to return a summoned object to its original location, so she prayed Aurelio would find some reason to visit her cabin.

She would love to believe he was now resigned, quietly looking forward to the day she returned home, but if he had not received her message, she feared he wouldn't be. She could too easily imagine Aurelio desperately worried, eager to launch into action, and yet, what could he do? She couldn't conceive of any comforting answers to that question.

Belrina sighed and rose from bed, seeing Amirtha, a slight vaxili whose golden hair was divided into three equal braids starting at her forehead, standing silently in the corner. But there was no sign of Njal.

After cleansing her face with utilth, Belrina retreated to the dressing room, her favorite feature of her bedchamber in the seer's sanctuary. She slid out of her nightdress to fully cleanse. This morning, she would have appreciated a nice leisurely bath, which would cleanse her spirit as well as her body.

Belrina donned a supportive shift before reviewing her choice of gowns. The styles were so diverse. Finally, she chose a rich azure dress cut in a similar fashion to the seer's simple gowns. The unadorned sleeveless sheath skimmed the floor and a cloak in the same fabric covered her neck and shoulders. Coverage was the only aspect of Asthildi fashion Belrina had an opinion about—some of the designs Njal originally proposed had displayed a shocking amount of flesh.

As Belrina emerged from the closet, Njal arrived, and when she uttered an incantation, bolts of fabric appeared on the bed.

"Good morning, Belrina," Njal said cheerfully. "You have not yet done your hair—good! We have a bit of experimenting to do." She examined the fabric. "Seer A'zine tasked me with creating three formal gowns for you." She smiled at Belrina. "We will dazzle them all."

Belrina paid attention to the last statement. The seer had instructed her how to work the telepathic translation spell properly, which was far more convenient than dispensing a translation device to everyone she wished to speak with.

She inquired in Elvish, "Dazzle, who?" A different spell worked in the reverse, allowing her to translate the words she wished to speak. Thus, she could haltingly speak in Elvish, but her tongue needed much more practice with the new language.

"That, I do not know, Belrina. I'm sure the seer will tell you soon. These gowns need to be done by tomorrow, so we have no time to spare."

Njal gave Belrina her breakfast vial, and then she augmented the light in the room with a chant.

"Let's see which of these colors best suit you."

Belrina stood in place for the better part of the morning as her friend fiddled with the fabrics, draping them first one way and then another. Occasionally, Njal inquired as to Belrina's preferences for the cut, fit, or shape of the gown.

In the past, Njal had resorted to magically sketching designs, as there were often no translations for terms describing the construction of Asthildi gowns. Belrina now eyed Njal's movements, hoping she could prevent any disastrous choices—like that one.

"Oh! That would be too low," she protested.

"How about here? Your shape is so lovely. Curves like yours are rarely seen in Kalehala."

Belrina blushed. "They should not be seen!"

"I know your preferences, Belrina, but the seer said at least one gown should be in the latest fashion."

"I know you'll do your best, Njal. Your work is always beautiful." Belrina refrained from expressing further concerns.

When Njal finished with the fabrics, she began brushing, plaiting, and applying unidentified substances to Belrina's hair.

"Amirtha, has Magisthild advised you of any changes to my schedule? Or any additional need for security?" Belrina inquired of her vaxili guard.

"No, Belrina." Of all the vaxili guards, the slim Amirtha was the strictest at complying with social protocols. Belrina suspected she would be good at keeping secrets if instructed to do so.

"Thank you." Belrina watched her face in the mirror to ensure it remained serene. If Njal finished her styling experiments soon, she could speak with the seer before her afternoon training session with the magisthild.

Alas, it was not until shortly before the afternoon changing of the guard that Njal announced she was done. "I must speak with a tailor, for these will be professionally crafted. Have a good afternoon, Belrina."

"Good afternoon to you, too." Belrina mirrored her friend's smile, though she could not match Njal's enthusiasm for Asthildi fashion.

A light chime announced the arrival of the afternoon guard,

and Amirtha opened the door, admitting Balin, a tall, broad, strawberry blonde vaxili beneath the personal attendant disguise.

After adhering to the social protocols for greeting one vaxili and saying goodbye to the other, Belrina quickly changed into her white tunic and leggings, constructing her magic disguise without a device. She had performed these spells so often that they now seemed simple.

The silent journey to the fortress allowed Belrina ample time to speculate about why the seer had commissioned new gowns, and she arrived for self-defense training with an unsettled stomach.

Glancing at Belrina's face, Magisthild ordered her to complete fifteen minutes of breathing exercises. Today, a dark circular mat covered the floor of the training square. Its presence signaled that she was going to fall. Multiple times.

She closed her eyes, sitting cross-legged at the center of the mat. While finishing her last breathing cycle, Belrina felt, rather than heard, Magisthild sit in front of her, as he had a powerful presence.

Belrina opened her eyes, tilting her head up to look at him.

"Today, we will focus on defending against intrusive spells and using magic offensively," the magisthild announced. "Have you learned any of these spells?"

"No, Magisthild."

He held out his hand, palm down. "Slap my hand using magic."

"I don't know how, Magisthild."

"Can you improvise?"

"I-I don't know." Belrina had gained control of her abilities by painstakingly following the seer's examples. "Is it not dangerous to experiment?"

"If you use energy sparingly, it should not be." His green eyes looked at her, unblinking. "Once combat begins, plans can unravel. It is important to adjust quickly. Innovation can win battles."

Swallowing, Belrina said, "I'll try." Looking down at her hand, she recreated every detail in a mental image above the magisthild's hand, and then she pressed the image into his hand, shoving it with a small magic pulse.

With a loud slap, his hand flew down to the mat.

"I apologize, Magisthild! It felt like the tiniest bit of energy."

Lythk slowly flexed his hand in and out of a fist, displaying a red imprint on the back of his hand.

"If you would permit me, Magisthild? I can heal you." Her hands itched to take away the pain she had caused, but using magic or telepathy without someone's permission was taboo.

After a slight nod from the commander, Belrina cradled his hand in both of hers. She orchestrated the complicated spell, washing away the pain and any slight injury to the small ligaments and delicate bones in the hand.

Belrina smiled, marveling at the magic of healing she had learned from Njal. After releasing his hand, she said, "Perhaps I shouldn't improvise with magic?"

"Do not fear hurting others. You must do so to protect yourself." Then the magisthild uttered an incantation, and it felt like her shoulders were being gripped by powerful hands.

Her surprise was audible in a sharp inhale, which reminded her to breathe evenly.

"Counteract the spell," he instructed.

Belrina imagined brushing the unseen hands aside with a tiny pulse of magic. They remained. She tried again, using more energy. One of the phantom hands vanished.

She struck at the other grip on her shoulder with a precise magic blow. It vanished instantly. . . and satisfyingly. She had grown accustomed to studying the pattern of magic energy before attempting to execute a spell. It felt more natural to allow her desire to give magic its purpose.

Magisthild nodded. "Trust your instincts, Belrina." As he stood, he said, "Balin and I will demonstrate magic grappling."

At the sound of her name, Balin deactivated her disguise, revealing her traditional vaxili garb. As the long-legged vaxili strode to meet the waiting magisthild, Belrina hastily retreated.

As he faced the calm-eyed Balin, Magisthild explained, "Magic is used as an extension of our hands and feet. Any other weapon is prohibited, although magic shields are permitted to counteract your opponent's strikes."

He bowed slightly to Balin, and she returned his bow.

Belrina wondered how they would avoid invisible magic strikes.

"Sixty seconds, Balin," Magisthild said.

Balin nodded, and a chime sounded. Immediately, Belrina felt magic energy swirling, although the combatants chanted too softly for her to hear. Magisthild temporarily floated upwards as Balin reeled backwards from a blow to her chest. As soon as his feet touched the ground, they seemed to be caught by a low, sweeping kick. He rolled into the fall as Balin dodged and weaved, eluding his strikes. Of course! A moving target was always hard to hit, even with magic.

Balin launched her own attacks, which had Magisthild using evasive maneuvers as well. Then he lifted Balin in the air, and she did the same. Sweat appeared on Balin's brow as they exchanged strikes in the air. Magisthild landed two to every one of Balin's blows, as his acrobatic defenses were more effective. Balin flinched when a blow landed, giving a quick exhale to release the pain, whereas whenever one of Balin's strikes landed, Magisthild simply nodded in approval.

Finally, a chime sounded and the two grapplers uttered a final chant in unison, landing on the ground. They bowed to each other again.

"Thank you, Balin," Magisthild said. "Belrina, come to the center of the mat. As this is our first lesson, I will allow you to wear a padding bracelet."

He conjured the magic device, and Belrina held out her

arm for him to fasten the amulet on her wrist. Stepping away from him, she activated the device, immediately feeling magic balloon around her head and body, providing a cushion if she were to fall or be struck.

"I will also reduce the force of my blows. Now, let's start with the most common moves."

"Yes, Magisthild." Belrina bowed.

He bowed in turn, chanting. Unseen hands lifted Belrina a few feet into the air while she memorized the magic currents at work.

"Full body lift." He placed her back on the ground. "Now, you try."

Belrina imagined holding Magisthild by the shoulders and she slowly channeled energy to support his substantial weight in the air, duplicating the spell. She lifted him as high as he had lifted her.

"Can you go higher?" he asked calmly.

Belrina slowly lifted him more than his own height, and when he didn't instruct her to stop, she continued directing energy into the lift.

"That is high enough," Magisthild called when his head might be brushing the sun-shielding canopy.

Belrina set him back in his original position.

His green eyes examined her. "You are not fatigued?"

"No, Magisthild."

"Then we will proceed. Most magic grappling begins with the full body lift, which is why I surprised Balin with a strike instead. As you saw, the entire battle can take place midair, as it then requires greater concentration to execute additional strikes. I will execute the full body lift, and then you do the same," he instructed.

Soon, they both were in the air.

"Now I can dispel your magic."

When he uttered a chant, Belrina felt a shield emanate from him, deflecting the magic energy from her lift. With no magic to sustain him in the air, he fell, gracefully landing in a bent-knee fighting stance.

"Now, you try," Magisthild commanded.

Belrina recreated the magic currents by forming a mental image of a shield and thrusting it in front of her. Instantly, she began falling, and she somehow landed in a watchful crouch.

Then Magisthild Lythk showed her various strikes and shields. After a single demonstration, she could duplicate what he did, matching his power. She knew he was holding back, but so was she, and it was empowering to feel equal to the massive vaxili. If she trusted her instincts, as Magisthild had instructed, magic flowed effortlessly.

When they graduated to exchanging coordinated strikes, Belrina asked, "Is it against the rules to set a spell that will endlessly duplicate strikes? Or set the strikes to follow your opponent, no matter where he goes?"

Before answering, Magisthild inquired, "Can you do this?"

"I think so, Magisthild. Shall I try?" Belrina inquired. After he nodded, she closed her eyes, imagining a repeating side-kick launching at the commander. A complicated pattern of energy vibrated into existence.

Magisthild easily side-stepped, but he remained close enough to feel the breeze of the successive strikes. After he nodded, Belrina ended the enchantment. She remembered the magic currents and could replicate the spell again.

"And the second spell, which would be more useful?" Magisthild prompted.

"Protect your face," Belrina warned before closing her eyes to create a mental image of a repeating punch to her instructor's chin that would keep step with him.

He eluded the first strike, but when he attempted to bob out of the way of the second, the phantom punch aligned with his face, landing a blow.

Belrina halted the spell, refraining from asking if Magisthild Lythk needed healing. She reminded herself that he had been unfazed by Balin's superior blows.

"Effective," he said, once on his feet. "We do not have rules against such spells." He finally answered her question. "The shield used to counteract the lifting spell can defend against magic strikes. Create the strongest shield you can."

Belrina considered, enjoying the discovery process. With a series of mental commands, a swirl of magic enveloped her entire body, solidifying into a protective sphere. "I should be protected from any strike, Magisthild," she announced.

"Let's see," he said, unleashing a string of chanting.

Belrina could not sense any magic currents from his spells—they simply did not exist for her. Magisthild continued chanting, testing the strength of the permanent shield. When she felt the protective shield shudder, she instinctively reinforced it, willing it to become stronger.

Magisthild Lythk halted his chanting, striding towards Belrina. "I can sense the magic residue resulting from your spell, but I do not perceive any active currents." He held out his hand in front of him, trying to touch the protective barrier. Belrina raised her hand experimentally as well, and he stopped his hand just short of touching hers. There was no tangible barrier.

"Can you walk and maintain the shield?" he asked.

"I may have to adjust it." Belrina concentrated, commanding the protective dome to travel with her. She walked, and Magisthild began chanting, launching strikes at her. Belrina completed a circle of the training floor, oblivious to the vaxili's blows. She came to stand in front of him, smiling.

"The seer will teach you additional protective shields," he said. "The law has no prohibitions on using shields to protect yourself and others, but you must only use offensive magic grappling techniques if you are facing a threat of significant or sustained harm." Magisthild paused. "Do you have any questions?"

"Significant or sustained harm," Belrina repeated, listening carefully to the translation. She nodded. "I think I understand, Magisthild."

"Good. Let's discuss how to defend against intrusive spells."

He gestured for Belrina to join him at the fortress rampart. He nodded at her amulet. "You will not need that any longer."

Belrina deactivated it with a simple thought.

"Magic can alter your perception of reality. These illusions can be terminated with the force of your mind," he explained, while surveying the rugged Kalehala landscape.

"By the force of my mind?" Belrina queried.

He faced her, fixing his green eyes on her face. "You must deny the existence of the illusion. When you realize it doesn't exist, the spell will be broken." He waited to see if she had further questions before saying, "Let's try one."

"I must release the protective shield, Magisthild? Wouldn't it protect me from these intrusive spells?" she asked.

"It may, but you must learn how to combat these spells. Shields can be infiltrated, Belrina."

After releasing the shield, she felt the loss of its soft hum of energy around her. "I am ready, Magisthild."

"Pretend you are meeting me, an Asthildi elite, for the first time," he instructed.

Belrina bowed deeply to Magisthild, inclining her head, waiting for permission to rise.

"It is my pleasure to meet such a charming young lady," Magisthild Lythk said, enunciating every word and assuming a languid air.

Belrina felt a soft, warm breeze on her neck when he said the word "charming." She had barely perceived the magic energy of the spell.

"Please, rise," Magisthild Lythk said.

Belrina did so, carefully raising her eyes to meet his, according to Asthildi customs.

"Oh, yes, I am utterly charmed."

With the last word, Belrina felt a feathery kiss on her cheek.

Stunned, she clasped her cheek. Then there was a soft kiss on her mouth, and she gasped.

"You are not counteracting it, Belrina. It is only going to increase in intensity."

As she felt a hand pressing the small of her back, Belrina forced every part of her mind to reject the illusions. The hand vanished. Belrina breathed deeply, feeling warmer than she did after sparring, and she struggled to maintain a semblance of serenity.

"Be wary of that word for there are many elites with little imagination who use it."

She did not want to experience more imaginative ploys.

"I apologize for discomfiting you, but it is necessary for you to learn how to counteract these spells."

"Is there not a permanent way to prevent all intrusive spells?" Belrina asked.

"As I said, all defenses can be penetrated." He stared at her unblinkingly. "Now, these spells can also be initiated with a touch or a magic device. You must avoid being touched directly by any Asthildi not on your security team. Let me show you why."

Magisthild Lythk held out his arm, smiling. "Please, let me escort you into the dancing chamber." He had adopted that languid manner of speaking again.

With halting steps, Belrina moved towards the vaxili, placing her hand lightly upon his hand. He smoothly guided her away, walking for a few paces before stopping. "But before we dance, perhaps we can admire the stars together? Do you enjoy stargazing?" He paused, looking up at the sky.

Belrina hesitated. "Magisthild?"

"Please call me Luke," he said warmly. "Is this not the perfect place from which to take in the night's glory?"

Belrina suppressed her amusement at hearing this language from Magisthild. She obligingly looked up at the blue after-noon sky; the sun would be blistering her eyes if not for the protective magical canopy. "I share your enjoyment of a starry night."

"I knew you did!" As he said the last word, he lightly grazed her hand with his free one, a fleeting touch, but there was a small eddy of magic.

Belrina frowned, looking down at her hand. Nothing was happening. "Luke? I think I should like to dance now," she said.

"Oh? Can I persuade you to stay here in the cool night air? Everything is so beautiful in the moonlight." Magisthild did not move, his arm steady beneath her hand. He looked down at her.

Belrina ventured a glance at "Luke," and she stopped breathing. Emerald eyes shone as luminously as moons, and she wanted to explore every golden fleck they contained. And touch his perfect skin.

Belrina had taken a step towards him before she recalled today's lesson. She adopted the psychic position of denial and pushed his arm away from her in disgust.

"Oh! Was that a crime?" Belrina asked, eyes wide.

"It fits the definition of an assault. However, most elites would laugh at your emotional outburst, and your loss of control would be a victory. It is better to have your rejection be swift and decisive, and then externally, you can pretend his or her magic had no effect on you."

Over and over, Belrina was being advised to suppress her emotions. It was unnatural and fatiguing. She soothed herself with deep breathing.

The magisthild walked away from her, apparently giving her space to compose herself. However, Belrina felt a rush of magic energy, and she instinctively raised her protective shield against the strike. She remained unscathed by his blow, but a trickle of energy needled its way through her shield.

Tingles traipsed down her spine, becoming stronger, pinching her skin. She jumped in surprise, and then she ruthlessly denied the illusion. The pinching vanished.

Magisthild Lythk held up a magic device. "A vulnerability in your protective barrier. Magic emitting from a device is substantively different from magic produced by spells." He forestalled her questions by saying, "You will need to ask Seer A'zine for a more detailed explanation."

"Yes, Magisthild."

"We have finished for today. We will resume our training tomorrow afternoon after your lesson with the seer."

Belrina bowed to him. "Good evening to you, Magisthild."

"And to you as well. Mathim will see you to the seer's sanctuary."

Belrina had not noticed when Mathim had replaced Balin. She turned towards the entrance, smiling at her friend. "Good to see you, Mathim."

Mathim smiled in return. "A good evening to you, Belrina." He activated his disguise, and Belrina wordlessly did the same.

"If you are much fatigued, you can take my arm," Mathim offered.

"Today, I am not fatigued," she replied.

Mathim bowed to Magisthild before opening the door to the stairs leading into the fortress. Belrina conjured a string of lights penetrating deep into the darkness, illuminating the stairwell within.

"Impressive, Belrina," Mathim muttered.

Belrina laughed. "Magic is as easy as thought."

"For you, it appears to be," he replied, before proceeding down the stairs.

Before following, Belrina looked back on the training square, noticing that Magisthild Lythk was watching her. He bowed slightly, as she had only seen him do to acknowledge the seer. After recovering from her surprise, Belrina solemnly returned a deeper bow. There were parts of today's unusual lesson she wished to forget, but now Belrina was beginning to believe she could defend herself against Asthildi elite.

12

ENTERING THE WOODS

I N ONE MORE STEP, Aurelio would be in the Old Ones' forest, entering an absolute darkness his eyes could not penetrate.

It was now well past nightfall, as city dwellers had deterred them at every step. Cesario had asked why once, and the elderly gentleman had waved his wooden cane at them fiercely. With Cesario begging for the old man's pardon, they had scuttled away, circling back to their destination well out of the old man's sight.

In this haphazard way, Aurelio and Cesario had made it to the edge of the woods at the city center, convinced an encounter with the Old Ones was now imminent.

"This darkness seems. . . unnatural," Cesario whispered. "Why can't we see the night sky through these first few trees?"

Aurelio lifted his travel lantern higher, but its light failed to illuminate a single tree. "Gods United, be merciful," he whispered.

As he stepped forward, Cesario clutched his arm, holding him back.

"Wait." Cesario rummaged in his pack, producing a hunting line. "I'll tie this to your pack so we don't get separated." When he had finished, he nodded. "Okay, we are as ready as we can be."

Aurelio stepped into the woods. His lantern created a few feet of hazy light, but there was nothing to be seen. He cautiously walked a few steps, encountering no trees. He turned to his friend, who was looking at the ground.

Cesario stamped his foot a few times. "Shine the light on the ground, Aurelio."

Aurelio did so, blinking in disbelief. They were on an overgrown path paved with perfectly square polished black stone. He squatted to finger the stone, which was cold and smooth. At close range, the lantern revealed lighter flecks of blue and gray in the stone.

"Do you know what this stone is, Cesario?"

"I have read about stone that can be polished like this. . . it might be granite." Cesario touched the dense mossy growth on the stone pavers. "What's the source of the moisture?"

"I don't know," Aurelio replied slowly. "The City seemed dry."

"Precisely." Cesario nodded.

"What? But that makes no sense at all!" Aurelio objected.

"It makes little sense if we are in the City. I do not know that we are."

"How could we be somewhere else?" Aurelio asked, lifting the lantern to peer left and right. Its murky light revealed an empty world devoid even of the night sky.

"I do not know," Cesario said quietly. He wiped his hands on his trousers, standing up. "Let's go farther in, but we should keep to the path."

Aurelio walked slowly, using the lantern to ensure they did not stray from the path. They walked for perhaps an hour with no change in their surroundings.

"I think you're right, Cesario," Aurelio concluded. "If we were in the City's small park, we would have walked the entire length by now."

Aurelio walked faster. "Where are they?" he muttered. "Where are you, Old Ones?" Aurelio called experimentally into the apparent emptiness.

Cesario jogged to reach Aurelio. "Careful! Remember, we want to show respect."

"Yes, yes, of course." Aurelio fingered his prayer necklace, seeking calm. He looked ahead into the same darkness. "Where are they hiding?"

Cesario gripped Aurelio's arm. "What if they are already here?"

Aurelio turned to stare at his friend. "What do you mean?"

"Their magic is everywhere. We cannot see them, but who knows if they can see or hear us?" Cesario steadily returned Aurelio's gaze. "It is a logical possibility."

Aurelio swallowed. "Aye, I suppose it is."

Cesario released his grip, and Aurelio turned to face the unexplored path, lifting the lantern high in the preternatural silence. Its light revealed only the next paver, identical to the one he stood on. Aurelio let the lantern fall to his side, and he proceeded cautiously. They walked for several more minutes while he strained his eyes and ears, trying to detect anything new in his environment, but there was nothing—only the next paver in the path. He questioned whether they were even moving forward.

"I will not stop until I find you, Belrina," Aurelio whispered, leading them on. And on.

Finally, he noticed something different: a few wisps of fog at his feet.

"Maybe this is it." Aurelio turned his head to whisper to Cesario.

"I am ready."

Aurelio smiled briefly. "And you say I am the courageous one?"

"You are."

"I have never been so afraid in my life," Aurelio admitted. "I know the Old Ones can help Belrina, but they won't if I say or do the wrong thing."

"Aurelio, you will speak from your heart, as you always do. It will not lead you astray." Cesario smiled in return.

"Thank you, my friend. You always know the right thing

to say." During their conversation, the fog had risen to their shoulders, obscuring their own feet. "Let's continue."

They resumed their slow progress along the path. Soon Aurelio could see nothing but stagnant mist. He took comfort in the lantern's swing, which indicated forward movement.

"Cesario?" he called behind him.

"Yes, I am here."

Although Cesario sounded close, Aurelio could not see a hint of his friend.

"Perhaps you should take my shoulder?" Aurelio suggested.

Aurelio felt Cesario's hand tap his back and eventually grip his shoulder. They walked on, each step measured, as he listened to ensure his boots landed on a paver.

It became a relief to see a tendril of fog move, allowing Aurelio to focus on a definite object. He experimented, focusing his eyes near and then far, but there was no relief from the unchanging fog. Although time was difficult to track, Aurelio judged it had been at least an hour since the fog had become absolute.

Taking another step, Aurelio realized he could no longer feel his friend's hand.

"Cesario?" he called. There was no response. "Cesario!" Aurelio shouted louder. Still no response. Aurelio stopped breathing.

Then he felt a tug on the hunting line tied to his pack.

As relief flooded through him, Aurelio tugged back on the line. His friend was still with him, but they could not see, hear, or touch each other. The Old Ones must be responsible, watching and listening unseen.

"Old Ones? My name is Aurelio. I have come with my friend, Cesario, to seek your help. Please, will you hear my request?" There was nothing to show anyone was listening, but Aurelio continued, "I am prepared to show my gratitude for your help. I may not have valuable objects to give you, but I am young and strong. And I always keep my promises."

There seemed to be a tension, a presence, that was not there before.

"Let me tell you why I am here." Aurelio took a deep breath. "Her name is Belrina. The kindest and most beautiful young woman you will ever see. She was taken from our village by magic."

There was no mistaking it now: something was listening.

"An elf came to our village, and they vanished together."

A dark figure appeared in the mist. It was hard to judge, but it appeared to be the correct size for a man.

"And what do you want of us?" The words were spoken haltingly, the accent musical. Aurelio could not be sure he had heard the voice with his ears, and his throat went dry. He gave the answer he had prepared. "First, knowledge. I want to know if she is safe and happy. I want her to return home more than anything, but her happiness is more important than my wishes."

There was a sound that might have been laughter. "You are an ambitious boy to ask for more than one thing, but your ambition is not selfish, you say. Very well. This may be amusing." The dark figure said an unintelligible word, and the mist vanished.

Aurelio found himself in a round, windowless room with four elaborate wooden chairs raised on individual platforms. Tall, pale, youthful-appearing creatures occupied three of them. Where was Cesario?

He surreptitiously fingered the hunting line on his pack; it had been cut! He had to convince the Old Ones to bring Cesario here.

Aurelio rested his eyes on the polished floor in front of him, not daring to stare at these impressively dressed and adorned beings. "It is an honor to meet you all. My name is Aurelio. I apologize if I do not know the proper way to greet you. I am a simple farmer from the Mountain Region."

Aurelio paused, waiting for any instructions from the Old

Ones. They were silent, but he could feel the weight of their eyes. They did not seem easily impressed. He feared his and Cesario's plan wouldn't work.

"Gods United, please give me strength and wisdom," Aurelio muttered under his breath.

"There are no gods here. Only us," said a feminine voice with the same musical accent as the dark figure.

Aurelio glanced at the speaker, dressed in deep green velvet to match emerald eyes.

"We are the gods!" a male voice said, laughing.

Aurelio's head swiveled to look at the light-haired Old One in a voluminous gray robe, noticing his elongated ears ending in points. Aurelio quickly examined all the Old Ones.

"You are elves! You must know where he took Belrina." Aurelio stepped forward. "Maybe you know him? He said his name was Mathim."

The emerald elf laughed. "I do not know what you are saying, but your excitement is delicious." She smiled, leaning towards Aurelio. "You must be in love."

"Yes, uh, miss. I love Belrina. An elf named Mathim took her from her home. I need to know if she is safe and happy, or if she needs help. . ." Aurelio's voice wavered.

"You seek knowledge, yes?" The gray-garbed Old One smirked.

"Yes, sir. And in return for this knowledge, which I seek immediately in your presence, I offer, as a sign of my gratitude for your help. . ." Aurelio paused.

"Yes?" the three intoned together.

"It is an offering for all of you." Aurelio nodded to the empty chair. "And it is a gift provided by both myself and my friend who accompanied me here. Would you please allow him to join us?"

The elves looked at each other intently for several moments.

The Old One, who had not yet spoken on his own, rose

to his feet. His black tunic cascaded to his toes, rendering his movement graceful. His cheeks were smooth, but his deep-set gray eyes marked his age. "We will allow it," he said in the same halting voice as the dark figure in the mist.

The Old One gestured and intoned a single word in his own language, and the air at which he pointed dissolved into a small oval portal, showing Cesario standing near a figure in a dark cloak on the misty path.

His friend appeared to be a short distance away, speaking, but Aurelio could not hear his voice. He swallowed, trying to work moisture into his throat.

The cloaked figure next to Cesario gazed at the black-clad Old One. There was an intensity to the silence as the elves looked at each other. Then the portal closed, and the eldest elf said in his halting manner, "It will be a moment."

Aurelio fiddled with his satchel. He hoped he had guaranteed Cesario's safety, but he did not like this delay.

"Tell me about your Belrina. What does she look like?" asked the younger male elf. His pale face was framed by even paler hair, and his delicate eyebrows were nearly invisible. As he leaned forward, his light blue eyes seemed to float towards Aurelio.

"I'm not sure I can adequately describe her." Aurelio felt his cheeks warm. "Her molasses hair is wavy and down to here." He pointed to his elbow. "Her eyes are a deep blue, and when she smiles"—Aurelio sighed—"everything in the world is perfect." He shook himself from his memories. "She is beautiful but also sweet and kind. Truly, she is the best person I know."

As Aurelio finished his pitiful description, he heard movement behind him. Swiveling, he saw Cesario and a dark-cloaked elf, who threw back her hood, revealing intricately plaited red-gold hair. There was no sign of how they had entered the doorless chamber.

Aurelio studied his friend, who appeared calm. He wondered what Cesario had been discussing with the Old One now gliding to the empty chair. Her cold blue eyes interrupted Aurelio's thoughts. At an Elvish word, her cloak vanished, displaying a body-skimming red gown, and then she assumed her seat on the raised platform.

"It is an honor to meet you, lady." Her gaze prevented Aurelio from saying more.

"Your friend has promised much," she replied. "I do not see how he can fulfill his promise."

The Old One in the emerald gown stared at the other female elf for a moment. Then she addressed Cesario. "I am intrigued even more now I see you, little one. What is it you and your friend are offering together?"

Cesario had a quick smile for Aurelio before he removed his hat and bowed to the emerald elf. "I know I am not as impressive as my friend," he said, his voice filling the room, "but I do not wish in vain to be other than what I am." He replaced his hat with a slight smile. "What we offer is a little tune to dispel the current gloom." He stretched his arms into an exaggerated question mark. "May we lighten your time with a bit of song and rhyme? And those who care to take a chance may find an even greater joy in Aurelio's dance." Cesario gestured towards Aurelio, who blinked at the addition to the plan.

The elves once again exchanged intense glances.

Aurelio tried to stand as confidently as his friend. He removed his satchel and prepared his limbs for the performance, as if the Old Ones had already agreed. He studied the female Old Ones, wondering if either would accept Cesario's improvised offer and dance with him.

After an inordinate amount of time, the eldest elf spoke. "We all accept your offer. In exchange for your entertainment, we will immediately provide the one named Aur-a-li-e-o with the knowledge he seeks about Belrina." The black-clad Old One nodded to Cesario. "You may begin."

Cesario flourished another bow to the Old Ones, again gesturing to Aurelio, who performed his own bow while backing away to claim unused floor space. As he straightened, Cesario began a quick rhythmic clapping.

Aurelio duplicated the pattern with fast feet, moving in a circle with his arms outstretched. When he completed the circle, Cesario added vocalizations, punctuating his clapping with foot stomps.

In this second circling, Aurelio added a quick leap, raising one knee, to coincide with Cesario's foot stomp. With each circle, Aurelio's leap became more complicated. He tossed off his hat with one of his leaps, whooping. Perspiration gathered on his forehead, but his pace did not slow.

Cesario added a chant to his clapping, "Who wants to dance with this man? Who wants to dance with this man? His feet are fast, his heart is true, and he wants to dance with you!" Aurelio ended that line with a jump that planted him on one knee, his hand outstretched to the green-eyed elf tapping her fingers rhythmically on the arm of her chair.

Cesario's clapping was the only sound for a long moment before the elf clasped Aurelio's hand. Cesario let out an "Ai-yah!" and then he launched into the next verse.

"Welcome to the dancing wheel," Cesario sang out, continuing his rhythmic clapping and foot stomps, "welcome to the dancing wheel."

Aurelio escorted the elf while tapping the rhythm with his feet, circling her around with one hand on her elbow and the other lightly on her back. On the punctuation, he added a simple leap upwards. In the next leap, his partner gracefully joined him.

After the completion of the first circle, Cesario sang, "Your feet will fly, your heart will soar, and you'll want more and more."

In this circling, Aurelio spun his partner in a tight circle on the punctuation. By the end of the circle, the emerald elf was laughing.

"Life is sweet in the dancing wheel." Cesario clapped and stomped. "Life is sweet in the dancing wheel."

Aurelio spun himself and the laughing elf in small momentum-gathering spins in the final circle before escorting her back to her seat. After she sat, adjusting the folds of her skirt with a flourish, Aurelio moved on to the elf in the red gown, clapping his hands and tapping his feet to the beat in a small circle in front of her.

"Who wants to dance with this man? Who wants to dance with this man?" Cesario sang again. "His arms are strong, his heart is too, and he wants to dance with you!"

Aurelio leaped straight up. He lunged to one knee with his hand outstretched, hoping he would have a willing partner.

There was a long pause, allowing Aurelio to catch his breath. He felt a cool hand lightly touch his and with Cesario's "Ai-yah!" he swept his partner away. Surprisingly, she matched him, step for step.

Aurelio grinned, giving himself over to the dance, remembering the last time he and Belrina had performed it together. Aurelio could hardly recall what spins and leaps he executed, but he knew his partner was light on her feet and a quick study.

He heard Cesario sing out, "Life is sweet in the dancing wheel." Aurelio mustered his remaining strength to lift his partner above his head in the last circle. He thought he heard her say an Elvish word, and he immediately felt restored, as if he had not exerted himself at all.

With Cesario's final stomp, he whirled his partner above his head with extended arms.

Aurelio slowly lowered the blue-eyed elf to her feet, discovering she was the same height as him. She was smiling as she held his shoulders. Aurelio thought she must be able to hear his heart beating.

He pulled away as gracefully as he could, escorting her back to her chair. Cesario joined him, and they stood before the

Old Ones together.

The eldest of the Old Ones spoke. "You provided your song and rhyme as promised, and now we shall give the dancer the knowledge he seeks. Immediately and in our presence, as we promised. Step forward, Dancer."

Aurelio strode towards the black-garbed elf, his heart sounding louder in his ears than his boots striking the floor. *Merciful Gods United, please let her be safe.*

"Kneel," the Old One commanded.

Aurelio promptly complied, looking up at the Old One while he placed a hand on the crown of Aurelio's head.

"Think of her," he instructed in his halting way.

Aurelio recalled the moment he proposed marriage to Belrina. He pictured her lovely face in the fading afternoon light, and he heard the Old One chanting quickly in the Elvish language.

The image of Belrina's face slowly faded, replaced by a barren landscape with impressive rocky formations. His disembodied consciousness flew at break-neck speed through rust-colored tents and adobe buildings, finally plunging into a rocky bluff.

The dizzying images stopped in a large room lit with innumerable glowing lights. Belrina, in an elaborate blue gown, knelt alongside a large muscular elf with hair lighter than Mathim's. A silver-haired female elf in purple robes called to Belrina, who gladly joined her.

Suddenly, Belrina looked directed at him. "Aurelio?" she called.

Aurelio wordlessly reached out to her, and Belrina's emotions flooded him: sadness, longing for home, loneliness, and a desire to retreat from impending danger.

Then his mind was wrenched away by the Old Ones, and he found himself in their windowless chamber, nauseated. The black-garbed elf hastily removed his hand from Aurelio's head.

Aurelio sank to his heels, gasping for air. Belrina was yet unharmed. He silently offered a prayer of gratitude as he filled his lungs with oxygen. When he could observe his surroundings again, he watched the elves staring at each other intently. What were they doing? Had the Old One been able to see Belrina, too?

Cesario gripped him under the shoulder, pulling him up, whispering, "Are you alright?"

He allowed Cesario to lead him away from the Old Ones.

"I think they are talking to each other," his friend said. "Tell me, what did you see?"

"Belrina is safe for now, but she is in danger. She is afraid and wants to come home."

Cesario stared into his eyes. "What do you want to do?"

Aurelio grimaced in pain. "I want her home, where she will be safe and happy again, but who knows how the Old Ones would bring her back?" He considered. "I want to go to her. It is the only thing I can do."

"Do you think you can help her?" Cesario asked, the doubt clear in his voice.

"I don't know." He looked at the Old Ones, shaking his head. "I cannot protect her against the magic of the elves. But how can I stay here, knowing she is in danger? I couldn't live with myself if I abandoned her. I must try to help her escape!"

Cesario closed his eyes. "Let me think."

The Old Ones were still engaged in their silent communication, leaving Cesario and Aurelio to plan what their next request should be, and more importantly, what they could offer to obtain it.

Aurelio was certain the godless Old Ones could take him to Belrina, but he feared the price they would extract. He stared at the beautiful creatures who did not respect the gods, knowing he was prepared to pay it.

13

A Pink Pebble

W AKENED AT AN EARLY hour, Belrina barely recalled the journey to the Reflection Chamber, accompanied by the ever-alert Vaxili Amirtha. Unexpectedly, she saw a peridot cloak over wide shoulders and the pattern of braids worn by Magisthild Lythk.

When he turned to face her, Belrina was as quick as her vaxili escort at lunging into a deep bow.

"Good morning to you both," he said. "Please rise."

Immediately upon rising, Amirtha deactivated her magical disguise.

"Good morning, Magisthild," Belrina said. *It's possible his business with Seer A'zine doesn't involve me*, she told herself.

"Vaxili Amirtha, thank you for your service," Magisthild said. "You may take your leisure this morning."

Belrina bowed to the vaxili as she departed, wrestling with her concern at the magisthild substituting himself as her guard. *He wouldn't be here unless the seer's unannounced plan posed a risk to my security.* She regulated her breathing.

"The chamber is secure," he observed in a quiet voice.

"Yes, uh, thank you, Magisthild." Belrina reluctantly removed the magic disguise. "Please forgive my delay."

Njal had directed her to wear one of the new ballgowns, a deep blue garment with a wide oval neckline, showing skin that had never been seen by the sun. Part of her hair was plaited into a crown on her head, giving her a few inches of height, and the rest was silky, straight, reaching past her waist.

Heeled slippers gave her additional height.

As Belrina contemplated summoning a cloak to cover her shoulders, the Seer of Kalehala entered the chamber. Belrina was as swift as the decorated vaxili in dropping into a bow.

"Good morning to you both. Please rise. Let me see you, Belrina." Seer A'zine held out a hand to Belrina, who promptly grasped it. "Splendid! Njal did as I requested, but I am not sure this is the right approach. Magisthild, what are your thoughts?"

Belrina felt something brush her mind, and she focused on it. *'Aurelio?'* she asked telepathically in surprise. At the thought of him, her repressed longing for home and its safety surfaced strongly. Then the presence was gone.

She blinked, wondering if she had imagined the connection, as neither Magisthild nor Seer A'zine had perceived a telepathic intrusion.

"My apologies, Seer. I have no expertise in fashion," Magisthild was saying.

"I do not ask for expertise, Magisthild Lythk, only your opinion." Seer A'zine smiled.

Belrina looked at the polished marble tile, waiting for his response. If he did not approve, perhaps she would never have to wear this indecent gown again.

"It is not optimal for self-defense. Belrina must focus on the guests, not her attire."

"Seer, what guests?" Belrina's words tumbled from her mouth. "Am I going to be introduced to other Asthildi?"

"Yes, Belrina."

Belrina's chest constricted. After more lessons with Rakti Za, she understood how unique her dual ancestry was in the Empire and how intensely curious all Asthildi would be. She didn't want to attract the attention of the Criers Guild, for then Senator Primth would know she was in Kalehala.

"Come to my garden," Seer A'zine said. "There is much there to soothe the soul."

Belrina followed the seer, stopping on the threshold of the circular chamber, observing the silvery, jeweled vines climbing the wall and the constellation of lights and water gracing the ceiling.

"It is spectacular!" Belrina exclaimed in her native language. After a moment, she noticed Magisthild waiting closely behind her. "My apologies," she murmured before entering the seer's garden. As Belrina watched water circling a suspended stone at the center of the fountain, she said in Elvish, "I could not have imagined splendor such as this."

"Come sit where you can see the fountain." Seer A'zine gestured to the remaining seat. "Please serve the water, Belrina."

Magisthild Lythk took a post by the entrance.

After Belrina filled their cups with a simple incantation, the seer appeared content to sip her water while Belrina gazed at the jewel-studded flowers. The artist must have studied real roses, lilies, jasmine, and orchids. She filled her eyes with them the way she would fill her lungs with their fresh scent at home.

"I had a vision, Belrina," Seer A'zine finally said. "I believe there is only one way to ensure your safety."

Belrina set down her chalice and folded her hands in her lap.

"There is an ancient Asthildi custom, the sakitha, that forges a lifelong bond of love between two individuals. We must find you a sakitha partner."

Belrina stared at Seer A'zine. "I must marry?"

"The sakitha bond is not the same as a marriage among the People; it is a connection formed by magic only if the partners are truly compatible."

Sitting back in her chair, Belrina forced herself to speak in Elvish. "Who must I bond with?" she asked quietly.

"I do not know, Belrina, for you will choose your partner. In three days, I will introduce you to Kalehala society so that you can meet candidates for the sakitha."

"So soon?" Belrina clasped her hands tightly.

"Yes, unfortunately, you must find a sakitha partner as soon as possible."

Belrina sat silently, gazing in the direction of her chalice.

"Dear one, please speak. You will soon find the greatest love that life has to offer. Why are you not happy?"

"Please forgive me, Seer." Belrina's throat felt thick. "This is very. . . unexpected." She recalled using the same words when Aurelio proposed. After a moment, she met Seer A'zine's serene eyes. "A lifelong commitment to an Asthildi—is there no other way? Am I truly without a choice?" Belrina's voice was just a whisper.

"We always have choices. We can continue our current measures to keep you safe, but I fear we will fail."

"I will never return to the Forest People, will I?" As Belrina stared at her hands, a teardrop escaped.

Seer A'zine rose, placing her warm hand on Belrina's shoulder. "I have not Seen it, Belrina, but that does not mean it will not come to be." Belrina placed her hand over the seer's, as she struggled for composure.

"Dear one, please do not despair. I will do everything in my power to ensure that you are happy as well as safe. Be at peace."

Seer A'zine's loving energy soaked into Belrina, easing her tears. Belrina held the aged mystic's aquamarine gaze, imbibing serenity until she could breathe normally. The seer placed Belrina's hand on Magisthild's arm, who had silently approached. "Lythk will escort you to your chamber. Rest now."

Belrina did not trust her voice to reply, and she allowed Magisthild to guide her away wordlessly. Before they exited the Reflection Chamber, he activated his magic disguise, prompting Belrina to do the same. Once inside her chambers, Belrina pulled away from Magisthild Lythk, deactivating her disguise.

As she made her way to the bed, she glimpsed herself in a mirror. She barely recognized herself. She transformed her gown into a woolen dress and shawl, and one long braid replaced Njal's plaited crown. Her eyes swept through the chamber, noting the commander's position by the door.

"Do not be alarmed, Magisthild. I am going to use a great deal of magic."

Closing her eyes, Belrina began creating an illusion. When the torrent of magic receded, she had successfully transformed her chamber into a Mountain Region forest, replete with Luna sitting by her side.

Sinking to her knees, Belrina could not resist trying to pet her dog, but her hand encountered empty air. Sighing, she looked at the stationary images.

"This is a forest?" Magisthild Lythk stepped forward carefully.

"Yes, but it doesn't seem real without the sounds and scents," she said, standing.

Magisthild studied the images, a smile touching his lips. It was the first Belrina had seen on his face. "Your homeland is beautiful, Belrina."

Belrina smiled briefly. "Yes." After a pause, she asked, "Do you think an Asthildi could be happy living among the Forest People?"

He fixed his light-green gaze on her before examining the delicate foliage of a fern. "I believe your sakitha partner would happily live wherever you wished."

His words made her think of Aurelio and the peaceful life he had imagined for them. She pulled her shawl closer, trying not to cry again.

"Do you need a lakri remedy?" Magisthild inquired.

She shook her head, avoiding his gaze. "I will be well. Thank you."

As Belrina breathed deeply, she gazed at the forest she had created and opened herself to prayer, asking the Gods United to grant Aurelio peace and happiness. She sat, leaning against the bed. Although she tried to enjoy the memory-augmented illusion, her mind kept turning to future dangers.

In a few days, she would meet the elite members of Kalehala society, and criers would disseminate the news to the entire Empire. She would then face Senator Primth, discovering whether she could deny his unknown demands. What interest could she be to an elite who enjoyed the greatest luxuries offered by the Asthildi Empire?

All too soon, Seer A'zine summoned Belrina for a lesson. She quickly transformed her woolens into a lavender dress with a high neck, but she hesitated to dispel the larger illusion.

"It will fade in a few hours, Belrina," Magisthild said quietly.

"Yes, of course." Belrina smiled at him. "Thank you." With a backwards glance, she left her forest behind.

A FTER HOURS OF LEARNING how to create magic devices, Magisthild escorted Belrina to the Fortress of Knath, and he began their lesson by describing the Introduction.

"We will hold the event in the Reflection Chamber. The seer is inviting more than a dozen young Asthildi, and each may bring a guest or an attendant. A representative from each of the seven guilds will also be there."

He paused, giving Belrina space to ask questions.

Belrina processed the information, asking, "Will I have my security team?"

"You will have only one vaxili attendant, but I will be there as well. Please act as though we met only when I assessed whether your unexpected arrival presented any security threats."

Belrina nodded.

"You will not have any pretense with regard to Seer A'zine. She will openly acknowledge that she has given you lessons for your own safety," Magisthild added. "After the invitations are sent, I will give the following story to the Criers: your mother is of Asthildi descent, and you accidentally traveled here after finding a transportation device among her belongings. Now fully recovered, you are ready to meet Kalehala society."

"Is this story credible, Magisthild?"

He looked at her. "No one will believe any part of the story until they meet you. I believe most will focus on the facts that are true: you have both human and elven blood and were raised by the People."

"I suppose the truth is difficult to believe," Belrina said softly.

After a pause, Magisthild continued. "We will position magic blocks around the chamber, which will prevent the use of spells. This is a block." He produced a small dark object, holding it for Belrina to view.

It appeared to be hollow glass, ranging from gray to black in subtle concentric rings. She recognized it as a device, which could be manufactured from any material.

"*Beydyn*," Magisthild intoned, activating it. "Invoke any spell."

She executed a summoning spell, intending to conjure a wooden fighting pole from its container. Nothing happened, so she tried transporting it through the air. Again, nothing happened.

"The spells aren't working," Belrina reported.

"Try again when holding the block."

Belrina cautiously removed the fragile-looking device from his hand. It was cool and light. When she tried levitating a fighting pole, she felt her magic flowing into the device. She looked at the block more carefully. "Is the magic held within the device?"

"Every block is different. This one transmits the energy back to the sanctuary reservoir. Set the block down by our cloaks and come with me." He walked to the opposite side of the roof, and as he looked upon Kalehala, Belrina joined him.

"Try again here," he instructed Belrina.

Belrina unquestioningly obeyed. This time, the six-foot wooden pole wobbled when she invoked a levitating spell. She tried again, using more magic energy, and it slowly rose an inch. "It feels like I am pushing a boulder uphill." She let the pole drop.

"Each block has a range. Here, we are on the outskirts of the efficacy of this one. At the Introduction, there will be spots in the Reflection Chamber like this, where the blocks only partially work."

"I cannot use magic to defend myself at the Introduction," Belrina said slowly. "If a device is activated prior to entering the Reflection Chamber, will the block prevent that device from operating?"

"It will not."

"Magisthild, there are so many harmful devices, and we will all be powerless to stop them!"

"Not exactly." He deactivated the magic block and then conjured an unassuming black cube to his hand. "Seer A'zine devised this for you."

After he handed it to Belrina, she activated it. Instantly, a protective shield skimmed her body. Closing her eyes, Belrina felt the currents of magic energy, recognizing the patterns from a lesson with the seer.

"Only magic is prevented from touching me. I may interact with all other aspects of the natural world," Belrina observed. "The shield protects against both active and passive forms of magic." She opened her eyes, smiling. "It shall protect me from devices."

"Correct. There is one other threat to be discussed: telepathy. When you defended against intrusive spells, you did so with telepathy. Magic designed to affect the mind can be combated with the mind." Magisthild held a small, pink pebble between his fingers. "Devices like this one are rare and expensive. Your touch will activate it, releasing a spell akin to telepathic manipulation."

"What does it do?" Belrina asked, eyes wide.

He offered it to her. "You shall see. Release the protective shield and then deny the intrusion as soon as you can."

Belrina disabled the shield, losing its comforting, subtle vibration of magic. She studied the delicate device displayed on Magisthild's open palm. As her hand hovered over the pink pebble, she asked, "Why isn't it activated by your touch?"

"It was crafted so that I am immune."

"I wish I could study this sophisticated device, not succumb to it," Belrina muttered. She carefully picked up the pea-sized stone, detecting a small eddy of magic energy.

The device shimmered, and then a tiny pink rose burst into life, initiating the slightest brush against her mind.

"How lovely!" Belrina exclaimed. "If I had not had warning, I wouldn't have suspected. . ." she trailed off in confusion. What was she suspecting? She stared at the pink stone in her hand. What was this device? Looking up, she stared at the muscular elf in front of her, sensing she should know him.

"Forgive me, I seem to have forgotten. . ." She stopped, realizing she could not recall her own name. Alarmed, she grasped for a fact to anchor her reeling mind. In the frantic swirl of thoughts, an idea surfaced, accompanied by a sense of angelic serenity. It would be so lovely to submit, for then she would be carefree.

She squeezed the pebble in her hand, and the pain recalled her to her surroundings and the massive elf staring at her. Submit? That was not her own thought. She may not know her own name, but she knew she valued her autonomy. Whose thought was it?

She ran away from the green-eyed elf towering over her, but she could not go far. Turning to face the massive elf whose eyes matched his cape, Belrina rested her back against the stone rampart. He had not chased her. He appeared to be waiting—what could he be waiting for? Fear threatened to constrict her lungs. Breathing deeply, she tried to remember.

An impulse to surrender came, flooding her entire being. Her knees buckled, and she sank to the stone floor. She felt the falseness of the emotion, and she fought against it. It did not like her resistance. Lashes of power crashed into her skull, forcing her towards submission.

Gripping her head, she silently screamed into the void, willing it to stop. The menacing force receded. She poured more and more power into willing its end. It was still there. She did not know how much more she could give, but she continued to deny the foreign power.

Finally, the struggle ended, and Belrina regained control of her own mind. In the sudden silence, she heard her heavy breathing. She opened her eyes, only to shut them quickly again. Massaging her temples, she tried to moderate the air flowing through her body. That one small device contained so much evil, and Senator Primth would certainly have more powerful devices. She shuddered, instigating waves of nausea.

Belrina sensed Magisthild kneeling beside her. "Belrina? Are you well?"

"I believe so. I have a severe headache."

"I am summoning Lakri Njal to examine you." He used a transmitter to do so, speaking quickly but quietly.

"Do not move, Belrina," Magisthild said, remaining near.

"What would have happened if I hadn't stopped the tele-pathic manipulation?"

"If you had surrendered, you would have relinquished complete control of yourself to me. You would have been a slave."

"What is a slave?" Belrina asked slowly, memorizing the unfamiliar word.

"You would have been unable to do, think, or feel anything unless I commanded it. I could have told you to jump off this roof, and you would have done so. Do you remember how you stopped the telepathic intrusion?"

"Yes. It took everything I had. . . it was so difficult to remember anything once the manipulation started."

"We will work on this more tomorrow."

"Yes, Magisthild."

A swirl of magic currents announced Njal's arrival by transporter, and she quickly eased Belrina's pain before performing an examination.

"She is perfectly healthy, but exhausted. I have restored what I can, but she will need to recover her strength naturally, too," Njal summarized for Magisthild. "Is there somewhere nearby where Belrina can quarter for the night? It is not safe for her to use a transporter, and I doubt she can walk far."

"Most of the chambers in the upper levels are unfurnished." After a pause, he said, "There is one chamber."

Magisthild helped Belrina to her feet, and when she walked unsteadily on limbs that felt too light, he easily lifted her, carrying her across the rooftop.

"This will be more expedient," he said.

Belrina did not try raising her head from his shoulder. "I'm sorry to inconvenience you, Magisthild," she muttered. Raising her voice, she inquired, "Njal?"

"I'm here," her friend replied.

It seemed a long, quiet walk through the dark fortress until they entered a chamber and Belrina was settled into a bed.

The magisthild retreated, allowing Njal to attend Belrina. "A few drops of this restorative, and you will wake, feeling refreshed," she said, handing Belrina a vial.

After she sipped from the vial, Njal gave her a reassuring smile.

"Good night, Belrina. I shall come to you early tomorrow."

"Thank you, sweet Njal." Belrina smiled, gratefully sinking into the pillow, and within moments, she was fast asleep.

W HEN THE FIRST RAYS of the sun touched Belrina's pillow, she woke, sitting up with a small yawn. She immediately noticed Magisthild standing by the doorway, seemingly unaffected by a night without sleep.

"Good morning, Magisthild." Belrina gazed around the masculine room. The white stucco walls, dark wood furnishings, and the unpolished stone floors achieved an unexpected harmony.

He nodded. "Good morning."

Belrina leaned back on the pillow, waiting for Njal to arrive.

"You can still see a bit of sunrise from that window," Magisthild observed, maintaining his position by the door.

Belrina leaped from the bed to see the immense sky striated with a progression of bright colors, ranging from orange to cerulean. From this height, Kalehala seemed only a slight interruption in the vast desert.

After several moments, she spoke her thoughts aloud. "Kalehala seems so peaceful, and yet, there are so many dangers for me."

"I have been training you to protect yourself from the worst of the Asthildi elite," Magisthild said quietly. "At the Introduction, you will meet honorable young Asthildi. You should not be afraid." After a pause, he continued, "There are few in the Empire who can overpower you. You are an equal match for anyone."

Belrina quickly turned to face the commander, staring at him. As usual, she could not read any emotion on his ageless face. His words had always seemed as truthful as the seer's, but he had not taken an Oath of Veracity. Was he sacrificing the truth to be kind?

"I nearly failed last night," she breathed.

"But you did not," he promptly replied, briefly holding her gaze before returning his attention to the sunrise.

"It did not feel like a victory." Belrina could not celebrate her narrow escape from the evil pink pebble.

"It is always such with hard battles."

Belrina studied Magisthild Lythk's smooth face, wondering what battles he had faced. She slowly turned back to the brilliant sky. The magic shield on the window blocked thermal energy, but Belrina imagined feeling the sun's warmth, lifting her face into the light.

She remembered how effortless it had been at home to love all things in the world. It had been a simple feeling in a simple world.

The greatest love that life has to offer. Seer A'zine's words resounded in her memory. How could love take root in a heart filled with fear? She folded her arms over her body, gripping her elbows.

"Are you cold, Belrina? Should I adjust the temperature in my chamber?" Magisthild had taken a few steps towards her, his green eyes studying her.

"No, Magisthild, thank you." She looked away, unfolding her arms. "It was a human gesture."

He drew nearer. "Truly you are well?"

"I am thinking too much. That is all. Thank you for your concern."

Magisthild nodded. "The only remedy I have for excessive thinking is excessive training." He stood next to her now. "But I shall not recommend that for you today."

"I appreciate that, Magisthild," Belrina said. For once, her polite Asthildi response actually reflected her feelings.

"In a few moments, vaxili will train there." He pointed.

"Is there a thermal shield overhead?"

"No. The temperature augments the training."

A long line of white-clad vaxili marched from the fortress, orderly forming innumerable identical rows. When hundreds of vaxili began the first form, their movement was in perfect synchrony. Magisthild observed the whirl of graceful vaxili as closely as she did.

Soon, Belrina was breathing in harmony with the practicing vaxili, and with every exhale, she regained a measure of equilibrium. Her emotions were as difficult to contend with as the pink pebble, but she would combat her fear as she had the evil device. It would be another hard battle.

14

AN INVESTMENT

WITH LIPS CURLED UPWARDS, Senator Primth stood on a balcony in his personal quarters, surveying the work of his landscape artists. Every day, they magically transformed the land and rock of his estate into any shape and color he desired. The results were always superb, for he naturally had the most talented staff, whom he called Primthildi.

Today, white marble pillars, one representing each character of Primth's name, dominated the estate. Emerald roses with white leaves spiraled in complicated patterns between the pillars. In the next hour, the roses would be sapphire. At midday, they would be amethyst, and at the hour of sunset, they would be a shining silver.

Primth returned to his morning meal, sitting at a heavy, round mahogany table. His matching chair towered above his head even when he was standing. Warm bread and cheese were served on gold plates with intricately worked platinum borders. He enjoyed solitude for the first hour of his day in this purple breakfast chamber with its gold-flecked ceiling and massive crystal chandelier twinkling in the early sunlight.

When he finished his meal, Senator Primth summoned a mirror, examining his face. He used incantations to enhance his natural beauty, shaping his eyebrows into sharply pointed arches. Magic energy darkened and lengthened his lashes. Last, Primth matched his lips to the color of his skin. With his light gray eyes, platinum hair, and white skin, he was a luminous creature.

Now Primth was ready for the most important event of his day. With his white silk robe trailing after him, he strode to his wellness chamber to receive his morning massage and body treatment.

Two young female Asthildi gracefully bowed in unison, displaying long, sleek legs through generous slits in their ochre robes, and then they eagerly removed his robe. Naked, the senator walked to the center of the chamber, marked by a small dark square. He raised both arms, uttering a chant. Therapeutic energy gently propelled him into the air, rotating him so he lay face down for his therapists to begin their work.

Chanting softly and rhythmically, Primth's therapists not only relaxed his muscles but toned and shaped them as well. Through their skilled hands, he achieved a lean physique with no physical effort. He could indulge in as much wine as he wanted, and his waist would never see the effects.

This was a luxury few elite could afford, and most who overindulged had flaccid middles and undefined faces. He shuddered at the thought of Senator Nykitha's fleshy jowls. Nykitha probably abolished the use of mirrors in his home.

Thinking of how favorably he compared to the other senator, Primth smiled, his contentment reflected by the polished silver floor. With such pleasant thoughts, the treatments were soon complete.

Once on his feet, Primth examined himself critically, striking multiple poses in a silver-framed mirror extending across the wall. He put his hands on his waist. "I want it smaller."

"Yes, Senator." The two bowed in unison, resuming their ministrations.

A chime outside the door interrupted Primth's pleasant reveries. His stomach clenched in anger and he responded by casting a magic thunderbolt at whichever ill-mannered attendant sought to disturb him.

"Zaritha!" Primth chanted. His face didn't register a grimace, proving he had achieved the heights of serenity. The

greatest seers could not best him for tranquility!

At the end of the session, his therapists replaced his robe and provided him a vitality draught, along with a vial of water. Senator Primth disliked water, but apparently there was no substitute for its healing effects on the body. He quickly downed them both, and as he exited the wellness chamber, he peered at the young technicians' legs again as they bowed.

Primth headed to his ardhendir, stepping on the circular disc worked in silver that levitated him to the adjacent floor housing his wardrobe. His manor was the tallest personal residence in the Capitol at seventy-seven floors, each occupied by personal treasures or staff. As he stepped off the ardhendir, a pair of fashion advisors greeted him; they wore the same ochre silk robes as the massage artists. He had paid for these two to augment their breasts, and he enjoyed seeing the fruits of his generosity.

The senator looked forward to seeing their selections for him today. The first option was a deep blue velvet robe embroidered with gold thread trailing two feet behind him. Its hem tapered to show the fine white leather boots sculpting his legs to the knee, and the neckline dipped to reveal the white silk tunic that would skim his torso. His second choice was a deep emerald velvet robe of similar cut, trimmed with a soft white fur.

He fingered the fur, smiling. "Winter fox. Yes, I shall wear this one."

Primth's young fashion advisors disrobed him and carefully constructed the ensemble on his person, murmuring their admiration when each piece went on. He enjoyed their roving hands as well as their compliments.

He was in high spirits as he moved on to the next chamber to select his hat. These assistants were male, wearing ochre sashes over their navy tunics. Their guild passed knowledge of hat-making only to male heirs—a ridiculous tradition! The best servants were female, and didn't every guild exist to serve the needs of the elite?

The senator quickly made his selection, donning a white wide-brimmed hat with two large feathers crossing at the back. The young ones nodded their approval, and Primth could not fault their judgment. He gracefully acknowledged their bows prior to departing.

While in the ardhendir, Primth heard a small chime audible only to his ear, and he activated the transmitter to speak with his chief intelligence advisor.

"Orlth, what do you have for me?"

"Good morning, Senator. There is an unusual report from Kalehala: an elf-human hybrid raised by Forest People inadvertently used magic to travel there. The Seer of Kalehala will introduce her to the local elite in three days."

Senator Primth blinked. "Do we have visual confirmation of this hybrid?"

"No, Senator. The Seer of Kalehala is guarding her closely."

Primth petted the fur of his cloak to soothe himself. The sanctuary in the remote Drylands may be primitive, but the Kalehala mystic was renown for her magical abilities. Although, as one of the remaining First Asthildi, Seer A'zine's aptitude may be unduly revered. He flung his cloak aside.

"I want to see this hybrid." Primth continued, "Seers reported a magical anomaly generating from Kalehala more than a month ago. Has this. . . forest girl been residing in Kalehala all this time?"

"I cannot be certain, Senator. I dispatched an associate to investigate, and thus far he has reported only that the local magisthild frequently visits the Seer of Kalehala."

"There is a conspiracy afoot. Unravel it to its origins, Orlth."

"Yes, Senator."

"This is now my highest priority. Thank you, Orlth." Primth deactivated the transmitter, reflecting on this unexpected development. A human-elf hybrid would excite the general populace, and, of course, he would use the sensation to further his objectives. Oddly, a stratagem did not immediately occur to him. He needed to know more about the creature—what elven characteristics did she have? Raised among ignorant savages as she was, he should not expect much. The forest girl might be no more than a momentary respite from monotonous crier reports.

Primth composed a missive to the Seer of Kalehala, commanding her to transport the girl to the Capitol immediately. He should have an answer by the end of his committee meeting. While lamenting the fact that the forest girl had transported herself to Kalehala, rather than a more accessible part of the Empire, Primth proceeded to the lowest level of his manor, which was subterranean.

This was where he stored his greatest treasures, and only he knew how to dispel the magic wards protecting them. After dismantling the complex security network, Primth loaded rings on his fingers and concealed several powerful devices within his robe.

Once on the main level, Primth surveyed himself in a generously sized mirror, verifying he was ready to preside over the Executive Senatorial Committee. The members of this committee were his closest allies, but they could be tedious, seeing complications that did not exist. They were fortunate they had him to guide them to see things correctly.

As the senator stepped into the refreshing breeze guaranteed by weather control devices, an ochre-sashed personal attendant standing at the door summoned Primth's transport, a golden cage of a chariot with fine spindles arcing from the base before resting on the encircling rail. It floated gracefully to Primth's feet.

After mounting his transport, he set it into motion with a chant, enjoying the soft breeze riffling the feathers in his hat. Primth's sojourn immediately attracted attention from the public, and he nodded graciously and waved at his voters. The next election wasn't for another twenty-one years, but the senator always acknowledged his loyal followers.

Only the uppermost echelon of the elite had the means to travel by chariot at the center of the promenade, and Primth knew each of their names. Today, Primth merely waved at them, as his mind was on the hybrid. He tried to imagine what the girl might look like, hoping she was young.

The Executive Senatorial Committee met in a smoky gray skyscraper shaped like a crystal shard. The senator maneuvered his chariot into his assigned stall, defined by green hedges generated by a magician. There had not been plant life in this area of the Capitol for at least five centuries. Primth did not miss it.

As he stepped off his chariot, a personal attendant harnessed it, bowing deeply for the senator.

"Thank you," Primth said. Expressing gratitude to those not in his employ earned votes.

Entering the building, he strode to the ardhendir, barely registering the colorful mosaics enlivening the walls and soaring ceilings. Once on the top floor, he strode to the chamber where the committee had assembled, reserving the chair at the head of the table for him.

"Good morning, Senators," Primth said. They rose collectively, bowing with less deference than the non-elected public. He situated himself and his robe in the cushioned chair. "Let us begin. Anything urgent?"

"Perhaps not urgent, but it is a matter of some delicacy," said Leenk, an extremely tall senator from an outer prefecture; his fortune depended upon the consumerism of the Capitol. "There is a proposal to add a senatorial seat in the Blenktara Prefecture, given its population growth in the last six hundred years. A plain reading of our Governing Articles supports their position."

"At least once a century, we see one of these proposals, but the Empire does not need another senator." Primth had worked for eons to achieve the current balance of power.

"Senator Amthik," he called to a scholarly Asthildi.

The named senator blinked his round eyes in response.

"Prepare a proposal to strike the ability to add senatorial seats from the relevant Governing Article," Primth directed. "To do otherwise would not respect the empire we have built. We are at the most successful moment in Asthildi history; we should be preserving, not changing, our political structures. You shall introduce the proposal tomorrow before the Blenktarian senators can present theirs."

The senators nodded, murmuring their assent.

"Anything else?" Primth prompted the committee.

Rona, a slight senator with watery blue eyes, began tremulously. "It is probably an exaggeration, but magicians say the Capitol's reservoir of magic is at dangerously low levels."

"Do they have a proposed solution?" Primth inquired.

"Prohibiting the permanent transmutation of objects in the Capitol," Rona replied.

Senator Primth considered, stroking the fur trim of his robe. "A fine solution for all, except senators, who set examples of what the public should aspire to achieve. You may write the proposal and present it to this committee when it is ready."

"Yes, Senator Primth."

"Also, we should increase the magic allotment for the Capitol. As the most populous city, the Capitol needs the most energy," Primth added.

"The senators from the outer prefectures will not vote to approve such a measure," said a burly senator who had risen from the ranks of the vaxili. Twyn knew little more than military tactics.

"Thank you for that observation, Senator Twyn, but we don't need their votes to pass any proposal, do we?"

"No, Senator Primth."

"And why is that, Twyn?" Primth looked unblinkingly at the brawny senator, who promptly looked away.

"Because there are twenty-five senators in the Capitol and only fifteen representing all the outer prefectures."

Primth inclined in his chair, his lips turning upwards. "Let me also remind you that magical allotments are not subject to a vote of the Senate. Over two hundred years ago, we had the foresight to make them an administrative issue determined by this committee. And we have just determined what to do, have we not?"

Hearty assents hastily sounded.

"Now, I want to discuss a matter that recently came to my attention." Primth shared the intel he had received from Orlth. Reminding the senators he had a superior intelligence network was almost as useful as exploiting their resources.

As expected, the committee dissolved into disorderly conversation. Primth gave the senators an adequate time for unruliness before raising a hand. Silence immediately followed.

"Does anyone have associates in Kalehala who can verify some aspect of this report?" Primth inquired.

Senator Kahlin, the only female on the committee, spoke. "I am allied with a guildmaster in Kalehala. Consider all his staff at our disposal."

"I have contact with a scholar there," Senator Amthik offered.

"Senator Primth, the seer of my prefecture is a member of the Council of the Wise. The Seer of Kalehala would have to respond to that council's requests," Rona proffered.

"Yes, Senator Rona," Primth acknowledged. "I question, however, whether the Council of the Wise would share any coherent information with us."

Several of the senators chuckled, evincing their shared distaste for seers' cryptic proclamations.

With no other suggestions, Primth instructed, "Cultivate associates in Kalehala and immediately report any information you receive."

After a pause, he called on Senator Amthik again. "Please

inquire with our geneticists whether it is possible to trace the hybrid's lineage with a blood sample. I question whether she is an Asthildi citizen."

"The law requires the person requesting the privilege of citizenship to name an Asthildi progenitor, which naturally occurs with the submission of the birth record," Amthik responded. "It is doubtful the hybrid will be able to do so, and therefore, she would not be a citizen."

Primth smiled as broadly as his sculpted face would allow. "That is interesting."

"Senator Primth," Twyn began timidly, "military code identifies any non-citizen as a threat to the Empire."

"We are free to use any means necessary to control a non-citizen. What threat can one girl—who was raised among savages—be to us?" Primth waved his fingers dismissively.

"I agree, Senator Primth, that the hybrid cannot threaten our interests," said Senator Lanka, a slight, pretty youth. "However, she may be a threat to individuals. The last Banished One who reentered the Capitol killed over a hundred citizens before being recaptured."

"Non-elite citizens without protective devices," Primth responded. "None of us are personally at risk." He surveyed his allies, none of whom could equal his ambition-inspired courage. "Any animal, no matter how vicious, can be caged. I will control this forest girl."

After a moment of silence, Primth declared, "Now, if there are no other matters, I suggest we each pursue whatever personal business pleases us most."

With such a pointed dismissal, the senators would not have raised another issue even if there had been one.

"We are adjourned. Alert me at once if any credible information about the hybrid surfaces." Primth rose from his seat, promptly making his way to the ardhendir.

After most meetings, senators would waylay him, suggesting one scheme or another. Sometimes they were profitable proposals, but he had no time for that today.

Once in the ardhendir, he erected a privacy screen and activated a transmitter to communicate with his clerk.

"Beldwin, have I received a response from the Seer of Kalehala?" Primth inquired. "Yes, read it to me." The seer's polite rebuff stoked his anger. "Please repeat the last two sentences."

"'I will expeditiously arrange for a karth to transport my guest, Belrina of the Forest People, to the Capitol. I share bear all expenses as a token of my regret for declining your request,'" Beldwin read.

"Thank you, Beldwin." Primth deactivated the transmitter, clenching his jaw. A karth from Kalehala would take over ten days!

The seer had insisted that transporting the girl directly to the Capitol could injure her, and the Oath of Veracity made the statement unassailable, but the Seer of Kalehala was not fooling him with her niceties. She took pleasure in thwarting his wishes.

The law protecting seers was broad, but that was not what prevented him from immediately extracting retribution—it was the Seer of Kalehala's perceived eminence, for he didn't want to deal with the political ramifications of quenching his anger against a First.

As Primth contemplated a covert method of retaliating against the Seer of Kalehala, the chime for Orlth's transmitter sounded. "Yes, Orlth."

"A half-hour ago, the Seer of Kalehala announced the Introduction is now scheduled for tomorrow."

The seer was determined for that event to occur when he should be the one to introduce the girl to the Empire. "Anything else, Orlth?"

"Unfortunately not, Senator. The seer is undoubtedly using magical means to conceal the hybrid."

"Thank you, Orlth," Primth said, disconnecting before exiting the ardhendir.

Although time was short, he had the means to send a gift to the forest girl before the Introduction. Tomorrow, the public would learn of her existence and criers would descend upon Kalehala, giving Primth and his associates more opportunities to infiltrate the seer's sanctuary. That First's conspiracy involving the elf-human anomaly could not remain secret for long.

By the time the senator was in his chariot, he had decided what his gift to the hybrid would be—it should be well-received by all females, no matter their origin.

There would be considerable expense in sending the gift, and he would personally visit the delivery team to motivate them properly. Promised rewards were never sufficient, as fear more reliably inspired action. When servants understood the consequences of failure as well as success, their obedience was superior to those under a compulsion spell.

Senator Primth had a talent for controlling others, and he would control this forest girl and profit from her inevitable celebrity. Giving a luxurious gift to her now was an investment, a risky one, but Primth had achieved unprecedented power by taking enormous risks.

If the hybrid proved to be a political disappointment, he could still play with her as much as he liked. He imagined a dark girl accustomed to violence and guilt-free pleasures. She inspired wild thoughts he did not wish to control. Senator Primth smiled.

15

The Bargain

C ALMLY, CESARIO STOOD BEFORE the furious Old One towering over him. Aurelio did not know how he could remain so composed.

"We must receive a benefit now." The eldest elf punctuated every word, his hooded gray eyes glowing. "You are offering nothing but words!"

"Please do sit, Balith," the red-gowned elf said mildly. "This is an interesting proposition. It will need a few amendments, of course." She gave the black-garbed elf a long look.

He was slow to nod and regain his seat.

"For my part," the other female elf began, "I see the slightest possibility of returning home as a gift. In over three hundred years, not one human has offered to help us return. As Alinka said, we are not done discussing the details. I have an idea." She fell silent, and the other Old Ones looked at her.

After a few minutes, Balith announced their decision. "This is what we find acceptable: we will provide you, and your friends, with the means to travel with sufficient food and water to Kalehala, where Belrina can be found. You can be there in a fortnight. Then, you will have one month to arrange for our citizenship rights to be reinstated. If you fail, we will forcibly retrieve you, and you will serve the rest of your days as our personal servants."

The last details of Balith's offer obliterated the hope Aurelio had experienced at the beginning of it.

"Honorable Old Ones, I thank you for your proposal, but we

cannot accept," Cesario replied. "There is no transport back unless we fail, and with only a month to work on restoring your citizenship, we *will* fail. What is ten years for you who are blessed with long lives?"

Alinka shook her head. "It is your sense of time that is relevant. If we give you years to accomplish this task, you will forget your promise or wait until the last moment to start." She stared at him with unblinking blue eyes. "We have learned much about humans in our time here."

"I beg your pardon," Aurelio interjected, "we will not forget our promise. Please give us a fair chance."

"We will provide fairness, Dancer, if you successfully bargain for it." Balith smiled, a twist of his lips devoid of merriment.

Cesario tried again. "If we succeed, you will live in your homeland for centuries. If we don't succeed, you will have decades of free labor. It is in your best interests for us to succeed. We have a far better chance of doing so if you give us five years."

"I tire of this. You speak honeyed words like a senator." Balith adjusted a ring on his finger. "But words mean nothing." He sat back in his chair. "Here is my final offer: you have one year from today to restore our citizenship rights. Both of you must give us an approved personal item."

"Something you have with you now should suffice," the emerald-eyed elf added.

Cesario considered. "And you will provide a map to Kalehala," he said the name carefully. "And to clarify, our group will travel together, and our journey starts today? And none but us two have to pay the price?"

Balith's eyes narrowed. "Fine," he growled.

Cesario looked at Aurelio. "You make the final decision," he said, keeping his voice low. "This is the best possible deal, but is it good enough?"

"I can be with Belrina in two weeks." Aurelio tried to calm

his racing heart. "I would accept, but what about you?" He gripped Cesario's shoulder. "You have climbed your mountain." He lowered his voice. "I couldn't have done any of this without you, but you do not have to risk yourself further." He searched his friend's face. "I could take this deal without you. I would be happy to be with Belrina for a year."

Cesario returned his gaze. "I see more mountains to climb, Aurelio. I can't stop with one." He grinned, but quickly sobered. "I do not want you to do this alone." He glanced at the Old Ones, whispering, "I can't stand the thought of you serving them." He met Aurelio's eye. "I want to accept this bargain."

Aurelio threw his arms around his friend. "Thank you. I'm glad you will be with me." After seeing what his intellectual friend had accomplished with the Old Ones, Aurelio had new hope they could rescue Belrina from whatever danger she faced. "Let's accept the bargain together," he said.

Cesario nodded, smiling, and they turned to face the Old Ones. All elven eyes watched them expectantly. "We accept," the young men said together, their voices filling the chamber.

Balith smiled triumphantly, intoning an Elvish word that sent a ray of heat racing through their bodies, shaking them physically.

"Our bargain is sealed," the Old Ones intoned together.

Aurelio wiped the sweat from his brow. He felt as though he had just finished thinning a field of sugar beets on a hot summer day.

"Your personal items, if you please?" The emerald elf descended from her chair and stood before them expectantly.

Cesario handed over a notebook.

Her white smile flashed. "Yes, this will do nicely," she murmured.

Aurelio searched through his satchel, his hands grasping a handkerchief. He held it out to the green-eyed Old One. She waved her hand over it, shaking her head.

"Not personal enough. Give me something else."

"How about this?" Aurelio removed his prayer necklace with its small satchel of written prayers. He had worn it every day since his last birthday. He hesitantly gave it to the unnamed female elf.

"Very nice." She stroked the leather string and then turned away with a flourish.

The gray-clad elf approached them, saying, "Your boots, please? And your satchels?"

Mystified, the young men handed over the requested items. The Old One chanted over each item before giving them back.

"You will never run out of food or water. Every step you take with these boots will cover a mile." He looked over at Balith, muttering to Cesario, "Use them carefully, of course."

"The map?" Cesario nearly squeaked. "We need to know where we are going."

The unnamed male elf gave him an approving look.

Alinka stepped forward with a small, oiled parchment. "This shows the topography of the ten thousand leagues surrounding you." She tapped a red arrow on the top right before turning the map on its side, and the arrow moved, pointing in the original direction. "The arrow will always point toward Kalehala."

Balith finally approached them to give them each a scroll. "Asthildi officials will need our names and personal identifiers. Do not open them!"

"Yes, thank you," Cesario bowed, bending from his waist. Aurelio quickly did the same.

"Go now," the gray elf said, gesturing to a door that had not been there before. "Bring your friends inside the forest before dawn, and I will enchant their boots and satchels."

Cesario looked at Aurelio meaningfully as he picked up his boots. "Thank you, Old Ones. I hope we will be successful. If not, I will see you in one year." He bowed again.

Aurelio had nothing to add, so he simply bowed and carried his boots to the door, which deposited them back in the woods. When the doorway to the Old Ones' chamber disappeared, Aurelio let out a breath he didn't know he had been holding.

"Cesario!" He clapped his friend on the back. "That was amazing. I have been dying to ask, how did you know the Old Ones were elves who had been banished?"

"My deal with the Old One named Alinka." Cesario looked around. "Can you tell which way to the City?"

Aurelio paused to clad his feet in the running sandals in his satchel. Then he slowly circled, searching for a guiding star in the slivers of night sky visible through the treetops. "I'll have to climb a tree. What deal?" he persisted.

"I'll tell you when we are moving in the right direction." Cesario drummed his fingers on his satchel. "Let's check the map." He lit his travel lantern and then unraveled the map. "The detail is incredible. You can almost see the individual rows of houses in the City. Hey, what is this?"

"What?" Aurelio rushed to his side.

"I think. . . yes, there is a pulsating circle. It might be. . ." He began walking in his stocking feet. "I can't be sure yet."

Aurelio picked up their boots. "Mind your step, Cesario. Did you bring running sandals?"

"No," Cesario responded absently.

"We are going to need non-enchanted shoes in case we don't want to travel a hundred miles in the time it takes to cross a room," Aurelio said. He jiggled his satchel, which did not feel lighter without his sandals.

"Yes! Come and look." Cesario held the map out to Aurelio, pointing to a dense square on the map that, upon closer inspection, depicted trees. His friend pointed at a small dark circle. Almost at the pace of one's breath, the dark circle expanded before quickly contracting.

"That pulsating circle is us. When I moved, it moved. It started here." Cesario pointed a thumbnail's width to the left. He gestured to the right with the map. "The City is that way!"

Aurelio looked at the map again. "I'm not sure, but you are, so let's go that way. But first I want to see. . ." He looked into his satchel. "Ay!"

"What?" Cesario asked.

Aurelio handed a pair of running sandals to Cesario. "I think everything in our satchels—not just the food and water—is replenishing."

"Useful!" Cesario adjusted the sandals to his feet.

Aurelio frowned at the appearance of another pair of sandals in his satchel, and then he took the lead, carrying their boots. "Now, tell me, what was your deal with Old One Alinka?"

"For every true thing I said about her, she had to answer a question truthfully. That was the bargain, and the gift I gave for it was a poem. The one about the Lady and the Silver Serpent."

"You are a genius! Tell me everything," Aurelio exclaimed.

"At first it was simple. I told her she was an elf. She was away from her homeland. My first question was: what do you most desire? It surprised me when she said 'to be entertained.' That made me think of the dancing wheel. You did some fine dancing, by the by."

"Oh, thank you. I was nervous about dancing with the Old Ones." Aurelio pointed out a large tree root to Cesario. "Careful there. What was your second question?"

"I asked why she was far from her homeland, and she said she had been banished because she acted against the law."

"That is another surprising answer." Aurelio adjusted the boots he was holding. "I wonder what she did?"

"I'm not sure I want to know!" Cesario paused, checking the map. "We are almost there."

"What was the next thing you said?" Aurelio prompted.

"That she wished to return to her homeland. She agreed. Then I asked how she could return, and she said, 'If I am pardoned by a senator and cleansed by a seer, then I will be a citizen again.' After that, I guessed she had children back home. I was wrong."

"No children? That is odd. Perhaps she committed her crimes prior to marrying." Aurelio considered. "We will need to find a senator and a seer. I wonder what they are?"

"No idea!" Cesario said cheerfully.

Aurelio broke through into a clearing. His eyes had grown accustomed to the dark woods, and the silvery landscape now appeared well-lit by the crescent moon.

Cesario extinguished his lantern. With a tacit understanding, the young men walked quickly and noiselessly to avoid city dwellers, retracing their steps to the Yellow Lodge.

Fortunately, most folk were inside their residences at this late hour, and two young men hurrying back home did not perturb the few people they passed.

As Aurelio approached the front door of the Yellow Lodge, he noticed that the small yard was tidy, and the steps no longer creaked. Had the mistress put his friends to work immediately?

Aurelio knocked quietly, and Victoriano quickly opened the door.

"Gods United be great!" He pulled Aurelio into a hug, and Cesario received the same welcome. "You are unharmed. Did you find them? We have been waiting for a week!"

"A week? But we only left this afternoon!"

"No. You have been gone seven days." Victoriano looked at them, puzzled. "Come inside. Are you hungry? Thirsty? Mistress Helena lets us help ourselves to whatever is in the kitchen."

Cesario smiled weakly. "I could eat."

"Sit, sit. I will fix you plates." Victoriano quickly made good on his word, and they had fruit, cheese, and bread in front of them almost as soon as they seated themselves. "Eat and I will wake the others, and then you can tell us everything."

"Quietly, Victoriano, please. Let's not wake anyone else."

"Yes, yes, Aurelio, of course," Victoriano nodded, a curl

bouncing on his forehead.

As Victoriano vanished, Luna came loping down the stairs. So joyful was her greeting that she would have knocked Aurelio over had he been standing. Aurelio returned her affection, petting and soothing her.

"Oh, Luna, what are we going to do with you?" Aurelio muttered, his face against her neck.

"Someone will volunteer to take her back to Master Jasefo's ranch," Cesario said confidently.

Their friends soon arrived in twos and threes. Although they whispered, the young men filled the lower level of the lodge with a soft buzz of excitement.

Aurelio stood, and the room quieted. "I'm sorry we caused so much worry." He quickly surveyed the group to ensure all his companions were there. "Cesario and I thought we were gone only half a day. I tell you this, so you know how strange everything associated with the Old Ones is. We met them, and we struck a bargain."

He explained the arrangements for the journey to Kalehala, emphasizing the risks. Every time Aurelio tried to say the Old Ones were elves, he found he could not.

"The Old Ones are. . . they are. . ." Aurelio looked at Cesario for help.

"Aurelio is trying to say that the Old Ones are. . . apparently, we cannot say what they are." A thought occurred to Cesario. "Let's try this. Was the person who took Belrina human?"

"No, he was an elf!"

"Yes, and the Old Ones are. . ."

"Elves?" Noelio guessed.

Cesario and Aurelio nodded vigorously.

"We have explained everything we know. Does anyone want to join us? If so, then we must go within the hour."

"I will go," Epifanio quickly volunteered. "That feeling of mine is growing stronger."

Noelio promptly echoed him, adding, "You could use

someone good with a bow, I wager."

One by one, most of his friends agreed to go, but four decided to return to the ranch where the rest of their companions were waiting.

"I'm sorry, Aurelio. But there is too much fear in my heart. This magic... I want nothing to do with it!" Hector said, before muttering prayers to ward off evil spirits.

"No need to apologize. You four have an important task as well." Aurelio called for Luna, and she trotted to his side. "You will take care of Luna, return home with the rest of our friends, and explain everything to our families."

"You can also help us pack now," Cesario suggested. "If everyone brings their satchels down here, we can decide what's best to take."

It took nearly an hour to pack and get eight young men ready for what promised to be an extraordinary expedition, which didn't leave much time to say their farewells.

"Thank you." Aurelio clasped hands with each of the friends he was leaving behind. "Be well until I see you again."

As the young men continuing the journey parted ways with those who would be returning home, the front yard of the Yellow Lodge bustled with whispered blessings and exhortations.

Now shortly before dawn, Aurelio led his companions in a trot to the Old Ones' forest, jogging past the sites of his previous encounters with disgruntled city dwellers, who were now all asleep.

Under a sky that had lightened into a shimmering purple, Aurelio entered the woods at the city center for a second time. Those who needed enchanted boots and satchels immediately vanished, leaving him and Cesario standing among ordinary trees.

"Those Old Ones!" Aurelio removed his hat to run his hand through his hair. "They always leave something unexplained." He looked at Cesario. "Do you suppose they will be gone a week?" His fingertips played on the brim of his hat, twirling it in a circle.

"I don't know," Cesario said slowly. "Let's study the map while we wait," he suggested, unrolling the oiled parchment.

Aurelio held a lantern for his friend, but he did not need to examine the map. He felt that red arrow in his heart, pointing towards Belrina, no matter which direction he faced.

His friends reappeared as a group, looking around in surprise.

"Everyone okay?" Aurelio hastily asked, surveying them.

"None of you tried to bargain with him, right?" Cesario added.

"No!" was the resounding response from all their friends.

"Let's get out of these woods," Noelio said, setting his own feet in motion.

The other young men scurried after him, clutching their newly enchanted boots. Aurelio lingered with Cesario, who was still studying the map.

"These fields go on for miles and miles. They look like a good place to practice with the boots," Cesario said.

"Are they to the south?" Aurelio asked.

"Southeast."

"That will do."

When they rejoined their friends, Aurelio looked due south, ignoring the rosy hues now streaking across the eastern horizon. In two weeks, he would see Belrina in person. If his feet could gallop as fast as his heart, he would see her lovely face before this morning's dawning sun set.

16

THE SEER'S SOLUTION

L EVITATING IN EMPTY AIR, the large silver box was fashioned from a velvety material, and rose petals decorated the lid in a stunning display of color.

Belrina drifted towards the beautiful gift, observing its intricate design.

"It is from Senator Primth," the seeker announced. "I have alerted Seer A'zine."

Belrina froze.

The lavender-robed apprentice looked at Vaxili Balin. "Please let me know where I should place it."

Belrina sat down on the bed, as her knees no longer supported her. She was not yet dressed for the Introduction, and the guests would soon be arriving. She performed vaxili breathing exercises, seeking calm.

After Njal summoned a small pedestal, Balin nodded towards it. "Please set it there."

The seeker intoned an incantation, and Belrina stared at the box as it floated through the air, settling gracefully on the stand.

As soon as the apprentice departed, Njal exclaimed, "This is a most inconvenient time for a distraction!"

"I'll inspect the package." Balin raised her hands over the box, moving them over all the surfaces. "There is a slight magical resonance, which is too small for anything but a message." She straightened, addressing Belrina. "You have activated the protective shield, and thus there can be no harm to you. Do you want me to trigger it?"

There was no socially acceptable way to reject the gift, and Njal was anxious to resume her work. "I suppose so," Belrina said.

"*Beydyn*," Balin intoned.

A small silvery screen appeared over the box, displaying an elf with pointed eyebrows and elaborately plaited hair. Rakti Za had described this communication device—it was an irisean screen. Belrina swiftly hid herself behind Balin, as she was only in her supportive shift.

"Good afternoon to you, Belrina. I am Senator Primth, and I hope we shall meet in person very soon. To welcome you to our society, I am giving you this gift to wear to your Introduction this evening. I look forward to hearing how lovely you looked. Enjoy!" The image winked out.

"Could he see us?" Belrina asked, hoping Asthildi etiquette prohibited the senator from initiating contact in her personal chamber without her consent.

"No," Balin replied. "It is a recording. Watch." She invoked the message again, and it was exactly the same.

"Oh, I see." Belrina stopped cowering behind Balin. Without thinking, she willed the message to stop, as she did not need to hear it again.

"Belrina, this gift may not complement your ensemble. I must see it immediately!" Njal took a moment to calm herself. "Balin, is it safe to open the gift?"

The vaxili checked again. "Yes."

"May I open it, Belrina?" Njal asked.

Belrina hesitated. "Is there any way I can avoid wearing whatever is in the box?"

"No," they said in unison.

Belrina retreated from the gift, wearing her Asthildi mask of tranquility, which she anticipated wearing all evening. "Please open it, Njal."

Her friend unceremoniously ripped the lid off the box,

tossing it aside. A silken covering followed suit. "Oh!" Njal gingerly touched what lay within. "This is zabalith cloth, and the color will suit you well." She lifted yards and yards of the delicate burgundy textile from the box.

"This is to be made into a gown?" Belrina gave voice to her confusion.

Njal draped the zabalith over Belrina's shoulders. "Magic pervades this cloth. It will easily become anything I wish it to be. This is a spectacular gift."

Trusting her friend's judgment, Belrina let Njal work with Senator Primth's gift. When her friend was finished, she guided Belrina to a mirror. The zabalith cloth was now a burgundy gown with a fitted bodice and flowing skirt.

Descending from her shoulders, folds of the fabric cascaded down her back and ended in a wide pool on the floor. Although her arms were bare, she felt sufficiently covered.

Belrina's hair was swept to her left side, falling in waves over her shoulder. Small diamonds glittered in the two small plaits woven into a delicate crown. A pear-shaped diamond pendant rested beneath her collarbone and matching diamond earrings sparkled on her ears. Her black slippers bore diamonds, too.

"Will the others be dressed like this, too?"

"I doubt anyone in Kalehala has ever worn zabalith."

"How will they know?"

Njal laughed. *"Zabalith!"* she intoned, pointing at the gown and sending ripples of magic energy through it. "Watch what happens when you move, Belrina."

Belrina cautiously walked a few steps, and the fabric in contact with the floor shimmered, emitting diamond-like sparkles. "Oh, that is pretty!" she smiled. "But is it not. . . too much? I would much rather look like everyone else. Well, I know I cannot look exactly—"

Njal interrupted her, grazing her arm. "Belrina." She raised both of Belrina's hands in hers, the distinction in the color of their skin obvious. "Yes, you are different." She held Belrina's gaze. "You are the most beautiful person I know. You only need to let them know who you are, and you will earn their approval."

Belrina's eyes glistened. "I'm so glad I met you, Njal," she whispered.

At that moment, the Seer of Kalehala entered the chamber. The three bowed deeply.

Seer A'zine gazed at Belrina. "I see the zabalith cloth, in an inspired color, is the gift from the senator." Her eyes immediately went to the discarded packaging.

With a few spells, the seer assembled the box again, and then she placed her hand on it, closing her eyes. In a few moments, she spoke slowly. "He personally selected the gift, and"—she grimaced slightly—"made efforts to ensure it arrived in time. He spent some time staging and recording his message." She opened her eyes. "The senator embedded an image-capturing spell within his message, which recorded everything directly in front of his image while the message was playing."

Balin hissed. "Clever! I'm sorry I missed it, Belrina."

"He has images of us? I wasn't fully dressed!" Belrina refrained from pressing her hands to her stomach. She clung to her slipping mask of serenity.

"You were hiding behind me, Belrina, for the first playing of the message," Balin reminded her.

"You listened more than once?" Seer A'zine tilted her head.

"I reactivated the message to show Belrina what a recording is," Balin explained.

"But I stopped the message the second time, a few seconds after it started," Belrina informed Seer A'zine. "I'm so glad I did."

"You destroyed the message?" the seer inquired.

Belrina tried to recall what she did. "I am uncertain—I just wanted it to stop."

After trying to activate the message, Seer A'zine announced, "You destroyed it, which may have prevented the images from reaching the senator. This is an invasion of your privacy, Belrina, but no direct harm has been done." She gave Belrina her hand. "I will give you a few minutes to prepare yourself. Then, when you hear the chime, please descend the stairs." She smiled encouragingly. "I will personally introduce you to everyone. All will be well, Belrina."

As Seer A'zine turned to leave, she grasped Njal's shoulder. "You did well." She nodded to Balin. "Keep close to her, Vaxili." Then the ancient Asthildi glided from the room.

Belrina stood where the seer had left her until Njal ushered her to the bed. "Rest for a few moments now, as you will be standing all night."

Belrina sat and started doing breathing exercises again. *Gods United, please give me strength*, she prayed silently. Within the protective shield created by the seer's device, she knew she was safe from any foul magic, but it was no safeguard against social blunders.

A beautiful chime sounded, and Belrina rose, forcing her spine to hold herself erect. Her prayer was not yet answered, but if she didn't let her mask slip, no one would know.

With a smile for Njal, Belrina wordlessly departed, leaving her friend's comforting presence. Vaxili Balin escorted her to the door that would deposit her on an invisible landing near the cavernous apex of the Reflection Chamber.

After one more deep breath, Belrina opened the door, uttering an incantation before stepping forward. A few stories below, she would appear to be standing midair. By navigating the invisible spiraling staircase, Belrina proved her Asthildi heritage.

Pausing before the first step, Belrina surveyed the Reflection Chamber. She could see the glittering of gems, elaborate hair, trailing gowns, and richly colored robes. Most guests were engrossed in their own conversations.

"I am pleased to introduce to Kalehala society, my guest, Belrina of the Forest People," Seer A'zine's voice rang out.

Immediately, all conversation ceased, and Belrina became the focus of every eye in the room. She stiffened her knees, which had begun to quiver. She felt like a prized Red Cliffs horse prancing before a panel of judges, but she had never wanted to be on display. *Prance, I must prance.* Belrina breathed deeply and bowed deeper, bending her knees.

The assembly bowed in turn.

"Come join us, Asthil Belrina," Seer A'zine invited.

In the silence, the collective scrutiny was palpable, a weight that threatened to immobilize Belrina. She tried looking into the Asthildi faces, but the cool gazes were unnerving. After she rested her eyes on the sacred pool, she could move her feet. When her gown skimmed the first step, its sparkles precipitated a murmur of appreciation and whispering.

After a few more steps, Belrina looked at Seer A'zine, who was looking at someone beside her—Magisthild Lythk. He, like everyone else, stared at her.

Belrina almost faltered, but then Seer A'zine locked eyes with her, smiling. She sensed the seer's blessing and smiled back. With the blood rushing in her ears, she vaguely heard a second round of appreciative sounds from the guests.

As she grew closer to the gathered Kalehala elite, it became harder to ignore the individual sets of eyes in smooth, unreadable Asthildi faces. She did not like some gazes. A flush rose to her face, but Belrina did not lose her smile. She concentrated on breathing evenly, and by the last step, she had regained control over her faculties.

In the next moment, Belrina grasped the seer's outstretched hand, and Balin, in her attendant disguise, strode to her side. Now it was easier to ignore all the eyes on her, and Belrina relaxed.

"Please allow me to introduce you to our assembly. I believe you have met Magisthild Lythk?"

Belrina took to one knee for her bow, her gown shimmering with the movement. "Good evening, Magisthild Lythk."

"Good evening." He returned her bow, as if she were an elite, before looking into his cup.

"And we also have the Silvermaster Bykin, and his son, Asthil Elkyth."

"Good evening to you both." Belrina bowed with bent knees again.

"Good evening," they chimed together. The two could not have looked more dissimilar. The father was extremely tall and burly, wearing a plain dark robe, and the son was slight, wearing a scarlet robe and ornate silver rings on each of his fingers. They had the same pale hair and bright blue eyes, however.

"You have an extraordinary story, Asthil Belrina. One that, well, I must admit, I doubted could be true until this moment," said Asthil Elkyth. "I have to know, where did you get the zabalith?"

Belrina spoke her Elvish carefully, using a few lines rehearsed with Rakti Za. "Yes, I had an unexpected journey to an extraordinary place. There are so many wonderful things here." She seized a fold of her skirt, swishing it back and forth, smiling at the sparkles. "A senator surprised me with this spectacular gift."

A honey-haired elf with hazel eyes planted himself at Elkyth's side. His eyes did not stray from Belrina's face.

Seer A'zine maneuvered Belrina to face the newcomer. "Please let me introduce you to Asthil Myrin, son of Jewelmaster Kirtyn and Kaolinmaster Theona."

Belrina and Myrin bowed to each other.

"It is a great pleasure to meet you, Asthil Belrina. It is our good fortune you traveled to Kalehala. I hope you are recovered from the journey?" His eyes roved over every aspect of her form. "You appear to be very well indeed."

Belrina studied the hem of her gown. "Thank you for your

concern, but I am fully recovered." She looked to Silvermaster Bykin, who was the only Asthildi who did not make her nervous. She said, "The lakri healed me—their healing powers are miraculous!"

"Yes, although we do not acknowledge that fact often enough," a female voice replied.

Belrina pivoted again, meeting the owner of the voice.

"This is Rakti Belwyn, daughter of Silvermaster Karyin, and this is Asthil Morwyth, daughter of Lakrimaster Gytherin," the seer said, and they all bowed to each other.

Belwyn was scarcely taller than Belrina, while willowy Morwyth was of a height with most of the male Asthildi.

"It does not appear you have had any refreshment, Asthil Belrina," Morwyth said in a musical voice, offering a cup to Belrina. "Belwyn and I thought you might like some water? The sanctuary's water cannot be bettered for taste."

"Thanks to you both." Belrina accepted the offered silver goblet, pantomiming taking a sip. Magisthild had advised her not to imbibe anything. "What is the subject you teach, Rakti Belwyn?" Belrina inquired.

"I teach elementary magic to our youngest Asthildi," Rakti Belwyn responded.

Belrina smiled. "It must be a joy to instruct children."

"It is often entertaining," Belwyn replied.

"Kalehala has better entertainment to offer, I daresay." A masculine voice said.

"Yes, indeed," said another young Asthildi.

As Seer A'zine guided Belrina to meet these new elites, Belrina felt a telepathic touch on her mind, which she quickly rebuffed. She reached out to Balin telepathically. *'Someone tried a telepathic intrusion.'*

Balin responded, *'I'll inform the magisthild. If you discover who it is, let me know.'*

One newcomer had intricately braided platinum hair, and the other had a large ruby ring on each hand. Seer A'zine performed the introductions yet again, and Belrina did her best to respond to their inquiries, ignoring their appraising stares.

On and on, throughout the evening, Belrina met each of the guests, accepting their compliments and engaging in superficial conversation while Balin quietly shadowed her.

Several more times, Belrina sensed attempted telepathic intrusions, and on one occasion, she identified a crier as the perpetrator. After a brief word with Magisthild, the crier left the Reception Chamber.

The highlight of the evening was when Myrin declared zabalith was intended for dancing, and the seer arranged for lively and richly complex music to play. Belwyn and Morwyth took partners to demonstrate the dance.

Belrina could see no way to refuse dancing with Myrin, who patiently guided her through the steps. She did not appreciate his firm grasp, but she enjoyed the music, and in a few passes, Belrina mastered the complicated dance—a benefit of learning physical combat routines.

Belrina soon found herself laughing and carefree for the first time since hearing Senator Primth's name. She almost forgot her circumstances entirely until she overheard a guildmaster wearing the red robe of a cultivator say he was surprised a human could dance as well as the Asthildi. The reply from an unseen elite was even ruder.

At the end of the evening, a few male elites vied for her attention, presenting their gifts of silver and porcelain jewelry. She politely admired each piece before giving it to Balin. Belrina was grateful that none produced a device.

Eventually, Seer A'zine announced Belrina appeared fatigued by the dancing and insisted she retire. Belrina hastily bowed to the Asthildi surrounding her, gratefully allowing the seer to escort her away.

Once safely within Belrina's chamber, Seer A'zine did not waste any time to inquire, "Is there one Asthildi you met tonight that you would be interested in meeting again?"

Belrina shook her head. "Most of them frightened me. I have not felt so—what is the word I learned tonight—foreign since I have been here. I felt like a cow among horses." When she saw the seer failed to understand the reference, Belrina tried again. "I felt like onyx among diamonds."

"Dear one, you were the brightest diamond of them all." Seer A'zine paused, considering. "You have not felt this way with Vaxili Mathim? Lakri Njal?"

"No, Seer. Njal devotes her life to healing others. Vaxili Mathim has sworn to protect the Empire. I can understand and respect them." Belrina longed to remove her gown and jewels. "The young elites did not wish to speak of anything important. All conversation was about pretty, but unimportant, things." She did not speak of either the impertinent or unwelcoming stares.

"I did not expect Kalehala's elite to be such a disappointment. I apologize for failing to understand what traits you might find desirable in a sakitha partner."

Belrina blinked. "There is no need to apologize, Seer. I could not have named any traits had you asked. Thank you so very much for hosting the Introduction." She breathed deeply. "But what is the next step since I didn't find. . . a candidate?"

"We shall discuss matters in the morning." Seer A'zine grasped Belrina's hand. "For now, rest. You did well this evening, dear one."

Belrina smiled, relaxing, for it was the seer's opinion that was most important. "Good night, Seer. Sleep well."

Seer A'zine returned her smile. "I believe I shall, sweet Belrina."

A short time later, in her simple linen tunic, Belrina was comfortable at last, and she could reflect upon the Introduction. She had learned more about Asthildi elite in those few hours than all her lessons with Rakti Za, and she knew she would always be a foreigner to them. Not only could she never share all their interests, but some also would never see anything but her "crude human characteristics," as she had heard that evening.

In some attitudes, she sensed a menace, a capacity for foul decisions and acts. Belrina shivered, as it was easier to understand the threat Senator Primth imposed, and as yet, all efforts to protect her from him were slated to fail.

A s SEEKERS REMOVED ALL vestiges of the assembly from the Reflection Chamber, Magisthild Lythk retrieved the magic blocks. A device alerted him to Seer A'zine's entrance, identifying her magic power as a potential threat.

"A successful evening, Magisthild." The seer smiled, her silver hair glinting in the light cast by the magic orbs. "There is a matter I would like to discuss with you."

Lythk promptly bowed.

To her apprentices, Seer A'zine said, "Please ensure we aren't disturbed."

"Yes, Seer," they said in unison.

It was a short walk to the seer's private garden, where the flowing water delighted both the ear and the eye.

Seer A'zine sat, intoning the incantation to pour two glasses of water.

"Please sit, Magisthild. I observed something unexpected tonight." She looked at him for several long moments. "About you." She sipped her water without removing her eyes from his face.

"Please speak directly," Lythk invited.

She nodded. "I fear you will deny it." As she set down her chalice, she said quietly, "I observed you are in love with Belrina."

Lythk stared. "I beg your pardon, Seer, but you are mistaken. I respect her, and I admire many of her qualities. That is all. You are fond of her yourself."

"Did you observe how Belrina failed to connect with the young elites tonight?"

"I did not," Lythk said slowly. "She appeared to enjoy dancing with Asthil Myrin, who is entranced with her."

"Belrina enjoyed the dance, not her partner. She felt estranged from the elite, who lacked substance for her. She feels more connection with Asthildi who have dedicated themselves to helping and serving others."

"If she loves music, and probably other forms of art, perhaps we should introduce her to young artists in Kalehala."

Seer A'zine sipped her water. "Is that what you truly wish?" she asked softly, steadily holding his gaze.

Unaccountably, Lythk had to look away. He chose to remain silent, and the seer seemed happy to let him live with his choice. Lythk filled his senses with the artistry in the garden, seeking calm.

Seer A'zine then noted, "I am making arrangements for Belrina's karth to the Capitol, and I can delay her departure for only a fortnight."

"We must move to the next phase of the search," Lythk responded.

"I agree, and thus we should conduct the sakitha ceremony tomorrow." Seer A'zine smiled at him. "Belrina did not find a suitable candidate, but I believe I have."

"Seer, you are not suggesting. . ."

"Yes, Lythk, I am. You and Belrina should take part in a private sakitha, and if unsuccessful, Belrina can tour every artist guild in Kalehala."

"Seer, I cannot participate in a sakitha, unless you wish for me to resign?" Lythk's green eyes flashed. "Rather than chase after impossibilities, Seer, I should continue to safeguard Belrina in my current capacity as magisthild."

"I believe I can convince the vaxithild to postpone the discussion about resignation until after the sakitha. Time is of the essence for Senator Primth's reach has extended to Kalehala." Seer A'zine set down her silver chalice. "Will you let me speak with the vaxithild?"

"It would not be advisable for me to continue instructing Belrina after an unsuccessful sakitha." Lythk slowly explained to the unworldly seer, "Prior to taking my vaxili oaths, a small circle of elites entertained themselves by compelling me to take part in sakithas. Even if candidates do not form a bond, conduct in a sakitha is. . . difficult to control."

A'zine blinked. "Then both of you can consent to a memory-loss spell. If the sakitha is unsuccessful, it will be as if it never happened."

"Seer, it will be unsuccessful because Belrina would never choose me. This is a needless exercise." Lythk realized his irritation was showing, and he took a measured sip of water.

"You do not know what the outcome will be, Lythk, for I certainly do not. If I can make the arrangements with the vaxithild, what logical reason do you have to refuse participating in a sakitha with Belrina?"

Lythk took a longer sip. "For propriety's sake, I should refuse," he said quietly before meeting A'zine's gaze. "However, I will comply if you can make those arrangements *and* if Belrina consents." He gently set the goblet on the table. "Then, when we have completed this improper exercise, we can return to working on actual solutions."

The seer smiled, inclining her silvery head.

"Is there any other business you would like to discuss, Seer?"

"No, Lythk. Rest well. I will summon you tomorrow when all is ready."

"Good night, Seer." Lythk bowed deeply.

After retreating from Seer A'zine's disconcerting gaze, Lythk calmed himself by walking the exterior perimeter of her sanctuary, ensuring that all devices and vaxili were in their designated positions.

Then he walked in the desert night with his cloak open, facing the cold instead of facing himself. He soon found himself in the training square, and he threw himself into practicing forms. Visible currents of magic energy, coursing in spiraling spheres of white, purple, and blue, culminated each of the forms he performed.

Lythk colored the night sky with his practice until the light of the stars faded, and then he watched the sun rise. For the first time in many, many years, he could not predict how his day would unfold.

If Belrina consented to the ill-advised sakitha, anything eventful would be wiped from his memory, and he would never know if he had behaved honorably, which would haunt him. . . among other improper thoughts not worthy of his reflection.

17

A NEW TOOL

F OR A MOMENT, SENATOR Primth admired his reflection in the silver chalice he held, interrupting his survey of the forest girl images gathered by his associates at her Introduction.

Intoxicatingly young, the girl's skin and hair were shockingly rich in color. He could not find those traits beautiful—they were too human. Curiously, despite her savage origins, she appeared to be genteel and docile, although she revealed a bit of passion in her dancing.

Primth returned to the precious few images captured through the subterfuge of his gift. In her private chamber, the girl had been wearing a thin shift, revealing luscious curves that rivaled those of his favorite enhanced lovers, but none of them were as young as Forest Girl. If she had any Asthildi blood, he could draw in her youthful energy during the act of love, achieving a rejuvenation superior to any therapy.

He wanted her now! But the girl first had to be removed from the Seer of Kalehala. Primth guzzled his wine. Maybe he could find his own way to bring the girl to him. . . if he could communicate directly with her.

Primth dispatched a message to A'zine, requesting that she make the girl available to speak with him before he realized he didn't know the time difference. Kalehala was irritatingly at the far end of the Empire. He activated the transmitter for his clerk, learning the girl would likely be asleep for hours. With difficulty, he avoided grimacing, pouring himself more wine.

He would have to occupy himself with less pleasurable business until it was time to meet with Orlth. Primth took his time selecting the best image captures, suspending them in the air above his desk and uttering an incantation to conceal them from all others' eyes.

With more chanting, he unlocked his data library and images of variously hued envelopes appeared on the white surface of his desk. He created a red envelope for Forest Girl's images, adding it to his files.

With a sigh, he opened a brown envelope, and small images of countless petitions appeared on the large white screen above his desk. He randomly selected three to display on his desk.

Every year, he would grant one or two citizen's requests as proof that he listened to the concerns of his voters. The first petition—taxing the elite to pay for medical services for those who could not afford them—was utter rubbish. He destroyed it. Those who were infirm must be so by genetic defect. True Asthildi were graced with health in perpetuity; those who were terminally ill should embrace their fate quickly, preferably before they could breed.

The second petition was a personal plea for employment in a scholarly field. The senator quickly destroyed that one as well. Anyone of importance had little use for academic pursuits. The third petition was so poorly written that he could not understand its import, and he destroyed it rather than try to comprehend it.

Until he could persuade the public that elections were unnecessary in his case, Primth had to pander to the citizenry, even the non-elites. Each year, he grew more weary of doing so.

The senator's eyes grazed the images of Forest Girl. As a non-citizen, she could use magic in ways Primth could not. Could she operate as his proxy, taking the action he wished he could to augment his power? If so, Primth would be limitless.

It was an exciting possibility, but one that might not be realistic, for Forest Girl would have to be intelligent and magically adept—as well as under his complete control.

Primth smoothed his eyebrows with a finger, realizing it was time to meet Orlth in the countryside. He did not enjoy any time outside the Capitol, but remote locations were optimal for clandestine meetings.

As Primth was changing into a silken cloak that would fare better in the warmer weather in the country, a light chime sounded, indicating he had received a message from the Seer of Kalehala. With an incantation, he constructed a screen, projecting the message onto it. A'zine was declining the interview request due to the hour, but she promised to send a recorded message from Forest Girl later. Primth destroyed the message, cursing A'zine's obstructionism.

His anger did not recede until he reached his vault, where he toyed with a few devices that he would love to use on the Seer of Kalehala. If Forest Girl became his proxy, her first act would be to punish A'zine. He smiled as he secreted the devices he needed for his trip to the countryside, and after activating a few, he was ready to meet Orlth.

Closing his eyes to minimize disorientation, the senator activated the transporter. The moment he arrived, he felt the void of magic currents; Primth had spent many of the long centuries of his life in the Capitol, which hummed with the resonance of weather control and energy channeling devices. This quiet felt unnatural.

Cloaked in an illusion of invisibility, Primth stood outside the residence of Asthil Mawyn, a fervent supporter and an enthusiastic partner in bed. She was not in residence, and he regretted not seeing her today. Mawyn's beauty was always impeccable, the result of copious magical enhancements. He approved of her efforts, as it was right that the elite should prioritize the pursuit of physical perfection.

The senator ignored the uninspired art lining the path to

the large copper door gleaming as prettily as the day it was installed several centuries ago. In the stifling air, Primth walked a few paces before the door opened, allowing him to enter the domicile without missing a stride. Orlth's innate impeccable timing was aided by a device alerting him to Primth's arrival.

When the door shut, Orlth appeared. His thin body was engulfed by his voluminous red linen robe, and the lines at his eyes marked him as centuries older than Senator Primth. His thin silver hair had been a different color at birth. Fortunately, his superlative skills outshone his unsightly appearance.

Orlth bowed formally, lunging deeply and stretching his arms wide.

"Senator, I bid you good morning."

A device allowed Primth to see the magic currents of Orlth's security system. He nodded in approval. "Rise, Orlth. Let us get to business quickly so I may return to the Capitol."

"Yes, Senator. This way, if you please." Orlth's spindly legs were still quick as he moved into a secondary chamber where there was a large black synthetic table.

He sat while Orlth served the chilled punch himself, as all servants were either accompanying Mawyn on her holiday or taking a holiday of their own.

"What news?" Primth sniffed the punch, hoping it contained wine.

"The faction led by Senator Amadahl is gaining members. They are one vote shy of moving their proposal to the floor."

Although it could not succeed, voting would generate publicity, and Primth did not need the public to get involved in politics. "Almost a third of all senators have rallied to that populist?" Primth took a drink. It was an enjoyable concoction. Orlth had learned his master's palate in the last few centuries of service. "We have worked hard to sow dissent among the senators of the outer prefectures, and yet almost all of them are uniting behind Amadahl?"

"Amadahl is capitalizing on the fear of less affluent Asthildi, who see diminishing magic reserves as a crisis because magic is essential to their crafts and livelihoods. Amadahl is promising to fix the problem."

"By depriving everyone of the ability to transmute objects permanently!" Primth was compelled to swig his punch. "Asthildi have the right to exercise our inherent magical abilities—it is an issue of freedom and fundamental rights."

"Of course, of course, Senator. We have painted her as a fanatical ascetic whose anti-Asthildi policies will lead to doom. Now, we need some facts to support this story."

"I'm listening," Primth said. After Orlth described his ideas for discrediting Amadahl plausibly, Primth approved the plan with a few minor alterations. "Now, any updates on Forest Girl?"

"She has not left the sanctuary where vaxili keep a constant guard. The Seer of Kalehala is meeting with both the local vaxithild and magisthild frequently. I am trying to uncover more information about the meetings." Orlth shook his head. "A greater percentage of vaxili in Kalehala are loyal to their local leadership."

"Any theories on the girl's magical abilities?"

"The magician I consulted predicted the girl has minimal magic power given she doesn't have much Asthildi blood."

"We need to determine the girl's capacity," Primth said. "Any progress on locating an Asthildi line with missing descendants? There should not be many."

"But there are many with such claims." Orlth shook his head. "Countless fools are forging their genealogical records to claim a relation to the girl."

"Tell me everything you know about how the public views her," the senator demanded.

"In the Capitol, any report mentioning the forest girl, true or false, is selling. Many do not believe she has Asthildi ancestry, but no dominant perspectives have formed yet. As the crier reports mount, the Empire will accept the truth: a hybrid has been formed and is now living among us."

"What are the views in the outer prefectures?" Primth probed.

"I am still gathering intelligence on them as well as major sects. I am particularly interested in the Zealot reaction. They could want her dead because she is an abomination or they could believe she is a reincarnation of their founder, Helene, and worship her." Orlth chuckled. "Their sacred texts guide them in mysterious ways."

"Mystery is the word we use to describe anything defying reason."

Orlth chuckled more vigorously, a rasping sound akin to a cough.

"Anything else, Orlth?"

"The criers will begin daily briefings on the state of the Capitol's magic reservoir."

Primth smoothed his face. "Unacceptable! We must stop them." He took a sip. "Unfortunately, criers can be as unwavering as Zealots," he complained. Criermasters were always droning on about the citizenry's need for information. "I will contemplate this further." He set his chalice down, admiring the multitude of sapphires entwining his finger, their color progressing perfectly from lilac to royal purple. "Any progress in generating more magic energy?"

Orlth shook his head. "Scientists and magicians continue to work on solutions."

"They have been studying the problem for too long. I will devise some inducements for them." Senator Primth rose. "Thank you for your excellent service, Orlth."

Orlth bowed again. "It is my pleasure, Senator."

Eager to return to the Capitol, Primth activated the illusion of invisibility as he turned away from Orlth. Outside the manor, the temperature had risen, and Primth gratefully transported himself back to his cool study, where he could comfortably contemplate how to determine Forest

Girl's magical capacity.

He dismissed the idea of involving seers, for they were too unreliable. He needed eyewitness accounts, and the only Asthildi A'zine permitted near the girl were seekers or vaxili guards.

Primth had one ally among the vaxili in Kalehala, unbeknown to Orlth. Although Primth had never had cause to question Orlth's loyalty, he did not fully trust anyone with autonomy as a matter of principle. The only loyal servant was a magically or telepathically enslaved one.

He activated an encrypted transmitter. "Vaxili Nokilith," the senator said into the device.

After a moment, he heard, "At your service, Senator."

"Tell me what you know about the hybrid's magic abilities."

"I discovered she performs magic without spells or chants."

"Unconventional, but is she powerful?" Primth inquired.

"I do not know, Senator. All those allowed near her keep their secrets well."

"Find out. This channel will remain open for half an hour. Don't keep me waiting long."

"Yes, Senator." Vaxili Nokilith audibly rushed away.

Senator Primth reclined in his chair, considering whether to order a young concubine. His purveyor should be able to find a silver-haired beauty not yet a half-century.

He set the device on his desk where he could see each bright line on the device as it vanished to denote the passage of a minute. When fifteen more minutes remained, Primth turned his thoughts to punishing Nokilith for his failure. As he recalled, Nokilith had a chestnut-haired sister. Perhaps he would not need to order a concubine after all. When only a few minutes remained, Primth anticipated meeting Nokilith's sister.

"Senator," Nokilith called, returning out of breath. "She is powerful. Every day. . . she receives lessons. . . from the seer. She learns. . . everything taught. Her limits. . . have not yet been discovered."

Primth relaxed into his chair, resting his head on the cushioned back. His greatest ambitions were within his grasp! He began imagining the first actions he would take as emperor, and he smiled as he counted the obstructionists he would eradicate.

"Senator?" Nokilith queried.

Blinking, Primth sat erect. "Thank you, Nokilith. Did you commit a crime against another vaxili that can be detected?"

"I concealed the crime for now, but a transfer to a new post would be helpful."

"It will be forthcoming. You did well, Nokilith." Primth deactivated the transmitter with a quick chant. He leaned back again, pondering how to control Forest Girl and her extraordinary magic. What would it be like to exercise magic without uttering spells? If magic would follow your thoughts, you could act swifter than anyone else. With magic and thought intertwined, the girl could be inventive, following her intuition.

But if her mind became undisciplined, her magic could become erratic and dangerous. For the first time, Primth considered the possibility he might not be able to govern her. She was a magical prodigy receiving lessons from the Seer of Kalehala, whose own abilities were acclaimed.

Primth's fingers stroked one of his prized devices, which he always stored on his person. He may not be a magical prodigy, but he had far more resources than any other Asthildi in the Empire. He would not give up his plan to make the girl his tool for achieving unlimited power.

But he would proceed more carefully.

As Primth finished instructing the magisthild in his district to transfer Nokilith, he heard the chime indicating a message from Kalehala had arrived. Primth swiftly activated it, and the recording played on the large screen above his desk.

Forest Girl's deep blue gown had an interesting neckline,

and her hair was coiled in an intricate crown. Sapphire gems with diamond halos graced her throat and ears. This was a refreshing change from the modest styling she had adopted for the Introduction. Haltingly, the girl spoke in Elvish:

"Senator Primth, I am honored you believe I am worthy of your attention. Thank you for the zabalith. It was spectacular." The girl smiled, as if remembering the delightful sparkles of the gown. "Many said Kalehala society had never seen anything so fine. It was kind of you to choose a gift that all attending my Introduction could enjoy. You are very generous, Senator Primth." She smiled, seeming to meet his gaze. Her eyes were the color of a deep, pristine sea. "As you have requested, I am coming to the Capitol to meet you." Her smile faded. "But I must confess that I'm afraid of the long journey, as traveling to Kalehala was unpleasant." She shook her head, as if to dislodge the painful memory. "Until we meet, please be well. Good evening." She inclined her dark head, and the recording ended.

Primth played the recording again. Forest Girl appeared artless, an impressionable young one who understood his power deserved respect. He smiled until he realized the Seer of Kalehala could also influence the girl. He must combat that influence!

The time difference was an annoyance, but he would secretly send the girl a device to permit instantaneous written communications, and then he would prime her before they met, laying the foundation for her complete surrender.

Primth began planning his next steps, assembling the team for his campaign to conquer Forest Girl. More than an hour into his work, Primth realized he no longer required a concubine. Now, his only desire was to possess Forest Girl, mind and body, and the intensity of his hunger was novel, making him feel alive.

He worked tirelessly, carefully designing his campaign, and Primth wouldn't stop until he had her. And her power.

18

THE WHITE TENT

DEEP WITHIN THE SEER'S sanctuary, Belrina descended a narrow staircase, lighting the way with a magic orb. At her side, Seer A'zine was silent, having imparted what information she would about the sakitha rites. The description seemed incomplete.

Belrina didn't understand why sharing an herbal drink with Magisthild would require a memory-loss spell if the sakitha were unsuccessful. An unwillingness to discuss certain matters directly seemed part of Asthildi culture—the matters that most perplexed Belrina.

To calm herself, Belrina practiced vaxili breathing exercises, as taught by Magisthild. Thinking of the stoic vaxili, Belrina relaxed. He would do nothing improper. Perhaps Seer A'zine had selected Magisthild so he could educate her about the rites.

After Seer A'zine had announced Belrina would begin her journey to the Capitol within a fortnight, Belrina's questions had not been about the seer's chosen candidate. She had only inquired about the enchantments involved in the sakitha, and when Seer A'zine confirmed magic did not dictate or influence conduct, Belrina had no objection. Everything that occurred in the sakitha would be her choice, even though participating in the rites was not.

What do I know about choosing love? Her mind drifted towards Aurelio and the answer she had not given him when he proposed. *Please forgive me, my friend. Please be at peace.*

The tranquil life he had promised her now seemed so precious—and utterly unobtainable. Belrina paused, squeezing her eyes shut as she gripped her Asthildi mask like a shawl in a fierce, wintery gale. She resumed her breathing exercises, set her feet in motion again, and began counting her steps to squelch further thoughts.

The further they descended, the more primitive the stairs became, and Belrina assisted the seer as they navigated them. Finally, Seer A'zine stepped away from the light into a narrow passageway.

Belrina quickly sent the light to follow the seer, but she herself was slower. She did not feel ready for "the greatest love that life has to offer." She would enter the sakitha tent only to evade Senator Primth's control. How could anything beautiful and everlasting be forged in these circumstances?

After fifty paces, the corridor expanded into a low, wide cavern, all in darkness except for a white tent, lit from within. It was a moment before Belrina saw Magisthild in the shadows.

When she was several paces from the tent, the seer stopped. Belrina extinguished her orb, and after a moment, she proceeded alone towards Magisthild. He watched her draw near, his pale face unreadable. Stopping a few paces away from him, she bowed as if they were equals. He returned the same bow.

Belrina noticed a white robe suspended in the air behind the vaxili. Seer A'zine had not explained this. Glancing to her left, Belrina saw another robe, and she placed herself in front of it, facing the commander. Then she looked at the seer.

"It is my honor to commence this sakitha through which love may forever bind these two persons. Enter this tent with no adornments or beautifications."

Magisthild removed his gold medallion, giving it to the seer, and then he began unbraiding his hair.

Seer A'zine approached Belrina, waiting for her to remove

the sapphire and diamond jewelry.

As Magisthild had not used magic, neither did Belrina. She handed her earrings and necklace to the seer, and then began undoing the intricate series of plaits sweeping up her hair, her fingers moving quickly. Yet, Magisthild still finished before she did, and her hands felt unsteady as he watched her. Finally, Belrina's hair was loose.

"Enter this tent as equals without distinction of rank," Seer A'zine pronounced.

Magisthild swiveled to face away from Belrina and he untied the sash holding his tunic while walking to the white robe. Belrina quickly turned away, using magic to remove all her garments. If she violated a rule, she did not know, but she was happy to be properly robed in an instant. Grateful for the gloom that concealed her warm cheeks, Belrina organized her hastily discarded attire into a neat pile.

When she stood, it was silent. She cast a quick glance over her shoulder, glimpsing Magisthild standing with his back to her. Thankfully, he was robed. Belrina returned to her original position, and he did the same, more slowly.

The Asthildi across from her no longer looked like the magisthild who had been in charge of her vaxili training. With his pale hair falling alongside his face and his slow steps, he appeared younger. Uncertain. Perhaps he did not know all the rites, either.

Belrina watched the Seer of Kalehala approaching them.

"You must also release all enchantments, Belrina. You both must enter in your natural states," Seer A'zine instructed.

Belrina had relied on the telepathic translation spell for so long, she didn't know if she could communicate without it. "May I use a translation device, Seer?"

She shook her silvery head, summoning a translation device for herself. "It is against custom to use devices within the tent."

Closing her eyes, Belrina discontinued the spell for telepathic translation. Then she cleansed herself of magic residue, which released all the enchantments she was passively maintaining.

From the corner of her eye, Belrina saw her blue gown revert to the dress she had donned that morning.

Seer A'zine smiled at them both. "Enter this tent as individuals and if it is your destiny, you shall leave as partners united by love." The reedy voice of the translation device was jarring in the cavernous space.

The Seer of Kalehala produced a slender gold chain. "Exchange your vows and then enter." She looked expectantly at Magisthild.

He took Belrina's hands, interlacing his fingers with hers, creating a bridge between them. The seer carefully wound the golden chain around their forearms.

Magisthild Lythk spoke his Elvish slowly, and Belrina tried memorizing the words without understanding their full import.

Belrina began repeating the vow in Elvish, but when she faltered, Seer A'zine guided her to say, "I enter with no adornments or beautifications so you might know me as I am."

When Belrina correctly finished the vow, she felt a ripple of magic draw her closer to the magisthild.

He uttered another Elvish vow, the melodious words filling the dark space.

With the seer's help, Belrina said in Elvish, "I enter as your equal, as we would be equals in our partnership." Again, magic compelled Belrina to step closer to Magisthild. Their elbows were now touching.

The last vow, Magisthild said quietly, looking over Belrina's shoulder.

Belrina repeated, "If it is our destiny, I will be your partner and our love will unite us in all things for the rest of our lives."

Then she gasped as the golden chain seared into their skin, leaving glittering tattoos. She stared at the golden lines on her wrists until Magisthild released her hands. She looked for Seer A'zine, but she was already fading into the darkness of the cavern.

Magisthild moved away, and for the first time she felt the damp air of the cavern and the chill of the stone on her bare feet. He opened the tent flap, waiting.

Belrina slowly entered the tent, finding the floor comfortably padded with soft, white textiles. She could stand upright, but Magisthild would not be able to do so. Belrina stepped aside to give him room to enter.

A rectangular wood tray in the center of the tent held three cylindrical objects: a glass carafe filled with a clear liquid and two vessels of light with subtle markings, which she recognized as corresponding to time. The glow within both cylinders reached the highest marks.

Magisthild Lythk entered, blocking the light momentarily before taking a seat on the opposite side of the tent. His voluminous robe allowed him to sit cross-legged, as if to begin meditation.

Belrina considered how she should sit. Her plush robe was a simple garment with two flaps crossing at the top, secured by a knotted sash at the waist. It was intended for more slender female figures. She decided to sit on her heels with her knees almost touching the tray.

"You may begin, Belrina." He gestured to the tray.

"Yes, Magisthild." Belrina carefully raised the white cup, discovering the liquid was odorless. Belrina took a cautious sip. "Oh! It is delicious." She reverted to her native language, eagerly raising the cup again, but the vaxili's quick hand prevented her from drinking. His finger around the cup rested against her lips.

She released the cup. "I apologize, Magisthild," Belrina muttered, but she didn't know what she had done wrong.

"Be careful of drinking too much azuka at once." He watched to see if she understood. He took a small sip, demonstrating. "Drink a very little." He placed the cup back on the tray. "Also, it is best to allow time between sips."

"Why? The seer say," she shook her head, correcting herself, "she said 'azuka is a relaxing herbal liquor.'"

Magisthild Lythk's mouth twitched upwards in a small smile. "Yes, it is relaxing. It also enhances sensations and reduces inhibitions."

"Sensations? Inhibitions?" Belrina repeated the foreign words. "I do not understand all words."

After a moment, Magisthild said, "The seer's explanation is true, but not complete."

Belrina looked at the azuka suspiciously, trying to guess the meaning of the commander's words. He did know more about the sakitha rites than she did. Perhaps he could explain the tattoo. Belrina held her wrist to the light to look at it, her sleeve falling to her elbow. She fingered the glittering marks prominent on her brown skin.

"The seer did not explain." Belrina looked at Lythk, whose eyes were on her arm. "Stay forever?"

Magisthild Lythk raised his green eyes to hers. "Only if we become partners."

Belrina studied her forearm. "It's pretty," she said before drawing her sleeve down.

In the ensuing silence, her gaze kept straying to the wooden tray. "We must drink all?"

"Yes, Belrina."

Belrina took a delicate sip of the azuka, closing her eyes to enjoy the flavor. Smiling, she handed the cup to Lythk.

"It is so delicious." Then, in her own language, Belrina said, "It tastes like pears or maybe peaches."

Belrina watched Magisthild take another sip with no apparent enjoyment.

"Has you taste something more delicious, Magisthild?" Belrina asked, certain her grammar was incorrect.

Setting the cup down on the tray, he considered. "Chocolate. A rich, warm drink."

She smiled. He had understood her question, politely ignoring her blunders. "Chocolate." Belrina tried the word, committing it to memory. She watched the light in the cylinders. There was a flicker akin to candlelight as the light receded with each minute.

Interrupting the uncomfortable length of silence, Belrina asked, "Is there chocolate in Kalehala?"

"No. Only the most exclusive commercial centers in the Capitol have chocolate."

She did not understand the entirety of his reply, but she knew he spoke of the Capitol. "Maybe I can try it there." Belrina tried to keep her voice light.

Magisthild Lythk picked up the azuka cup and guided her hand to take the drink. "Azuka will soothe away your dark thoughts," he said in a low voice. He held his hands over hers until Belrina met his eye. Then he quickly withdrew his hands.

Belrina did not drink immediately. She carefully considered how to conjugate her question in Elvish. "Am I not better at concealing my thoughts?" It was a vulnerability she struggled to eliminate.

His eyes flickered over her face. "Perhaps I know too many of your fears."

I suppose he does. Belrina sought calm, peering into the azuka cup. She tried abolishing all thoughts of Senator Primth, and her likely failure to stand against him. She did not know what the price of failure would be, but that did not lessen her fear.

"Drink, Belrina."

"I am happy to take your advice, Magisthild." Belrina thought that was a proper Asthildi response. She took a larger sip of the azuka and a pleasant warmth spread through her chest.

She watched the magisthild's smooth face as he carefully took the cup from her. He did not look at her, preferring to keep his eyes on the azuka.

Belrina wished he would say something. She looked towards the cylinders of light, wondering if they needed to remain in the tent until all the light was extinguished. How many times would she need to partake in a sakitha? There was so little time remaining until she left Kalehala.

It was very warm now. Belrina moved to sit on one hip, with her legs tucked behind her. As her legs grazed the soft textiles, she enjoyed the sensation. She smoothed her soft robe over her knees and her hand felt every plush fiber.

She lifted her hand to her face, examining it. Her vision seemed clearer, noticing details on her hands that she normally overlooked. Although the light had diminished, she could see everything within the tent as clearly as before.

"Things. . ." Belrina said, struggling to find the right Elvish words, "seem different. This is the azuka?"

"Yes."

"Do you feel different?" Belrina looked into Magisthild's clear eyes.

"Not yet," he said quietly.

"Hmmm." Belrina stroked the soft coverlet upon which she sat, experiencing every silken strand. She smiled. "You were right, Magisthild. I no longer have dark thoughts."

"I am glad, Belrina." His voice was deep and musical. After a pause, he said quietly, "You should call me Lythk."

Belrina looked up at him, seeing a person instead of the commander for the first time. She had made little effort to decipher the emotions beneath his smooth face. Why did he now wish for her to use his first name? As she studied him, he seemed to grow uncomfortable.

She promptly looked down, pondering. Ah, he was supposed to be her equal in here. He was gently correcting her error. Oddly, he had taken his time to do so.

Her gaze found the wooden tray. "Is it my turn to drink, Lythk?" It was a pleasant name to say. Was this why the forgetting spell would be necessary? To forget the familiar manner they were adopting, which would be improper outside this tent?

Asthildi were so preoccupied with rank. She could respect Magisthild as her instructor after calling him by his first name.

"Yes, Belrina," Lythk replied languidly.

Belrina smiled in response, realizing it was more pleasant not to question Asthildi culture at the moment.

Within a few minutes of drinking another sip of azuka, Belrina found she wished to lie down. Since arriving in the Empire, she had had little rest. Her elbow bent of its own accord, and she stretched out on her side.

She rested her head in her hand. Her hair was so soft. She petted the soft textiles with her free hand. She looked at the cylinders, noting the light had diminished to the second marking. Only an hour had passed?

Belrina noticed the azuka cup rested back on the wood tray.

"Is it my turn to drink again?" Belrina asked, finding she was no longer concerned about speaking Elvish properly.

"Yes," came Lythk's soft reply.

Belrina reluctantly sat up on her knees again. She stared into the cup. "There is so much left! I think I have had more than you." Belrina took the smallest of sips. "You should drink more, Lythk." It was easy to say his name now.

Smiling, she lifted the cup to him.

"Perhaps I should." Lythk's hair and skin were luminous in the dim tent.

So fair are elves! Belrina thought, watching Lythk. He indeed took a larger sip, causing her to smile again.

But now it was her turn. Belrina looked at Lythk again, sitting seemingly unchanged. She could think of nothing to say, so she stared at the small cup of azuka.

This drink is as effective as a lakri elixir to induce relaxation, Belrina thought, blinking at Lythk, whose green eyes shone in the soft light.

Finally, Belrina pressed the azuka cup to her lips once again. She closed her eyes as the sweetness filled her mouth. After a few moments, she carefully placed the cup on the tray again.

Belrina happily sank back into the plush textiles. "It is so warm." She untucked her legs, letting them drift to the side. She rested her head on her elbow, lightly sliding a leg over the silken coverings. "Are you not warm?"

Lythk held the azuka cup on his knee, and his eyes traveled the length of her. He did not answer her question, gazing at her face.

Belrina felt even warmer. She dropped her eyes, and then she realized how much of her legs were exposed. She drew her knees behind her, and she adjusted her robe. "I apologize." Belrina did not wish to say his name aloud now.

"There is no need for you to apologize." Lythk was staring into the azuka cup.

Belrina reflected upon his statement. With the azuka flowing through her veins, she heard the emphasis he placed on certain words. Lythk thought he had done something wrong? Belrina sat up to look at him closely.

His skin looked like it would be soft under her fingertips. His robe was open at his chest, hinting at his muscular physique. She gripped her knees. "I don't think I should have any more azuka."

"You must. We both must comply with protocol, Belrina." It was a characteristic statement from the magisthild, but his voice was uncharacteristically intense.

"Does azuka change truth?" Belrina asked.

"I do not understand your question." Lythk sat still, the azuka cup untouched on his knee. He looked into the cup for another moment before taking a sip.

She considered how to phrase her question. "Azuka will not make me see or hear something that is not"—she strained to remember the correct word—"real?"

"It should not."

Lythk was examining her face with his eyes, as she had seen him do many times after she had had a rigorous lesson.

Belrina smiled. "I am well, Magisthild." By habit, she reverted to using the honorific.

Lythk settled back, appearing to be confused by her statements.

"I am confused, too," Belrina admitted.

"And now my thoughts are easy for you to see?" There was a slight curve to Lythk's lips.

Belrina shook her head slightly. She could see Lythk was amused, but she did not know what to say in response. To prevent having to say anything at all, she slowly lifted the azuka to her lips.

As she drank, the memory of his finger on her lips came to her unbidden. She blushed now, although she had not then. With both hands, she returned the cup to its tray. She was so hot. The robe was too thick. She loosened the flaps around her neck but stopped when she saw the skin it showed.

Wondering if Lythk had seen, blood rushed to her face again, increasing her discomfort. She settled on cuffing her sleeves, exposing her forearms. The gold lines on her wrists caught her attention, shimmering in the light.

Belrina blinked. The shimmer wasn't confined to her new tattoos. Her skin itself was glowing. She held out her hands, seeing a silver aura alive with prismatic sparks. For some time, she watched the diamond-like fluorescence.

Could Lythk see this? She looked across the tent to where he sat, eyes closed. Every exposed part of his white skin glowed with a subtle green light flickering with intense blues and purples.

It was mesmerizing. As Belrina studied Lythk's aura, she could discern more complexity in the sparkling colors. She didn't remember traversing the distance between them, but suddenly she was kneeling beside the magisthild and his eyes were opened wide in surprise.

Belrina sat back on her heels. "I did not mean to. . ." She couldn't remember the right word. "I am watching your aura." She smiled as she watched the play of violet sparkles on the crown of his head. *There are patterns as if it has a language of its own,* she thought.

Belrina reached for his hand, feeling his smooth, warm skin. She raised it for him to view. "Can you see it? Your aura?" she asked softly.

Belrina looked at their joined hands. Where their auras overlapped, the fluorescing of colors intensified. "Oh!" Belrina gasped. "It is so beautiful!"

Lythk was silent. Belrina looked into his light eyes. "You do not see?"

"I do not." Lythk slowly withdrew his hand.

Belrina placed her hands on her knees. "Is it because I had more azuka?"

"No, Belrina, it is a manifestation of your magical talent."

Belrina considered. It was against custom to use enchantments within the sakitha tent, but she didn't think a small enchantment would interfere with the ceremony. "I can use magic to show you," she said to Lythk.

He hesitated, not meeting her eyes.

"Let me share this." Belrina touched his hand again.

When Lythk gave a slight nod, Belrina closed her eyes, intuiting the flow of magic energy needed to share her vision with Lythk.

"Look at me, please," Belrina instructed. Lythk turned his head, fixing his eyes on her, and she smiled. "Thank you. Now close your eyes." He again complied, and she grazed his forehead with her finger, sending magic energy into him. With the azuka in her blood, magic vibrated through her body, as exhilarating as sprinting through a flowering meadow. "When you open your eyes, you will see."

Lythk opened his eyes. "I see your aura, Belrina," he

breathed. "It is more beautiful than I had imagined." He reached towards her, and then he stopped, staring at his own hand.

"Your aura is far more interesting, is it not?" She raised her hand to meet his. "And watch now." When their auras overlapped, the frequency of the flashes of violet, blue, and diamond-like sparkles increased, and they watched the dance of colors together.

Belrina sensed that Lythk held himself still, breathing shallowly, and she raised her eyes slowly to his face, absorbing every graceful detail.

He was looking at her, his unguarded green gaze revealing a storm of emotions flowing like endless clouds in a violent wind.

Belrina grasped his hand more tightly. "Lythk, why are you so troubled?"

He did not answer, lowering his eyes.

"Shall I remove the enchantment?" Belrina asked in confusion.

"Yes, please." He looked away from her.

Reluctantly relinquishing his hand, Belrina reached out to touch Lythk's temple, her fingers encountering a few strands of his hair. She smoothed the loose strands behind his ear, smiling at their soft texture. When Lythk turned his head to look at her, Belrina's hand suddenly cradled his cheek.

She slowly lifted her hand away from his cheek to finish her task, but Lythk clasped her hand, preventing her from removing the enchantment.

"A moment, please," he breathed.

Belrina looked into his green eyes, which now only displayed delight.

"I should like to look upon you like this for a moment longer."

Smiling, Belrina was content to hold Lythk's hand and enjoy the extravaganza of light around him. The warmth of his skin radiated into her, and she closed her eyes to relish the sensation.

Then Belrina sensed energy flowing between them, subtle like the first drops of rain. Breathing deeply, she felt the magical exchange grow stronger. When she opened her eyes, there was a visible cord, their auras extending and entwining from his point of power to her point of power.

"Lythk," Belrina breathed.

He stared at the magic cord joining them, and then his eyes leapt to Belrina's face. When he smiled softly, the connection blossomed into a coruscating light illuminating the tent.

It slowly receded, but even when it was gone, the deep bond it had forged remained; Belrina could feel the strength of his heartbeat, the tranquil movement of his breath, and the warmth of the blood coursing through his body.

She stared at him in wonder, and his now tranquil eyes stared deeply into hers. She forgot to breathe as she discerned other emotions in his gaze.

Lythk slowly collected her hands in his, lifting first one hand to his lips and then the other. Belrina closed her eyes to savor his kisses, leaning towards him. When he ran a finger lightly along her face, Belrina opened her eyes. He smiled and her heart danced.

When Lythk kissed her lips, the pleasure of it sent waves of joy throughout her body.

19

Through Grassy Plains

A URELIO SCANNED THE ARID, inhospitable land dwarfed by an immense blue sky. Occasionally, cloud cover provided relief from the intense sun, which stunted trees and desiccated plant life.

It had been days since they had last seen a village, which was just as well, for he did not want to frighten any more Palms People.

Cesario suspected their swift passage through the last two regions would engender a lasting story. Aurelio hoped it wouldn't be one with a tragic ending, and every day, he prayed for his friends' safety as they continued their journey to Kalehala.

When Aurelio stepped back to rejoin his friends, there was a stomach-dropping lurch to the world until he planted his feet, shod in the enchanted boots, side by side again.

Many of his companions would develop headaches by the end of the day, which they would treat with Cesario's never-ending supply of pain medication. At least he could be thankful for that aspect of the Old Ones' gifts.

"We are on a plain," Aurelio reported to his friends, smiling. They could really travel some distance now.

While experimenting with the boots outside the City, they had discovered that one step placed them at exactly the same elevation a mile away. Thus, if someone was standing on a hill when they took a step, they would fall to the lower ground. Everyone had earned scrapes and bruises while using the enchanted boots. Cleofas had severely sprained his wrist a few days ago, and at every step, Aurelio feared worse would happen.

Traveling to higher ground created the greatest risk, which they had queasily observed when Epifanio ended up in the middle of a haystack. Because it was too dangerous to use the enchanted boots in hilly terrain, they had journeyed a quarter of the distance to Kalehala in the last fourteen days.

The Old One had lied when he said they could be in Kalehala in a fortnight. Aurelio should not have expected honesty from the godless elves. Using their faulty gifts would have resulted in catastrophe if not for Cesario's precautions.

It had been Cesario's suggestion to have one person scout ahead whenever they could not see clear terrain stretching out for miles before them. They had had to scout far too often, but fortunately, this grassy plain was flat for as far as he could see.

"Ready?" Aurelio inquired. When his friends assented, he instructed, "Step."

Standing in a line, shoulder to shoulder, the group stepped forward together, finding more knee-high yellow grass, and Aurelio welcomed the monotonous scene.

"Let's take a few steps," he suggested.

Victoriano groaned, clutching his stomach already. "Slowly, please."

Guided by Aurelio, the young men advanced across the plain, pausing a minute between each step.

"What is that?" Noelio pointed at a slender, tall shape in the distance.

Those with bows traveled with them at the ready, for in this unknown terrain, the enchanted boots did not pose the only danger.

Noelio drew an arrow from the quiver on his back with his eyes locked upon the creature grazing on the high, yellow grass. All human eyes studied the unfamiliar beast.

"It is not a carnivore," Rogelio observed.

"Even cows can be dangerous if they are frightened," Noelio mildly replied. "I expect these animals are not familiar with humans."

A few of the young men muttered their agreement.

"We should travel around it." Aurelio pointed slightly to the right.

Accustomed to such maneuvers, the group pivoted a small degree to the right without taking a step. If their boots did not leave the ground, they didn't invoke the Old Ones' magic.

Aurelio checked that all feet were set at the same angle. "Okay, all at once. Go."

There was no sign of the unknown animal in front of them. Noelio slid to one knee, swiveling to the left and drawing his bow smoothly at the same time. But he quickly lowered it. "It is still peacefully eating. It is like a mule with a very long neck."

Eager to see the animal for themselves, the young men found their own ways to shift without lifting their feet, creating an awkward ruckus.

The creature, which was mostly yellow with brown spots, chewed some vegetation with its long face. Its ears were pricked forward, indicating it knew they were there.

"Do you know what it is, Cesario?" asked Emiliano.

"Nope. I don't think anyone has written books about this place and its animals." He smiled. "At least not yet."

Victoriano tapped the dusty ground in front of him. "This animal might not be so friendly." The print was similar to that of a wild cat, but much larger. He squinted into the distance, trying to follow the trail.

"Let me investigate," Noelio suggested, eagerly unlacing and abandoning his enchanted boots. In his running sandals, he set off with light, quick steps.

"Archers, spot him," Aurelio directed, setting an arrow in his own bow, ready to shoot any threatening animal.

The others grabbed the opportunity to wipe their sweat

with handkerchiefs, drink water or splash some on their heads. Some nibbled on flat bread, which helped with the queasiness.

"It took off that way," Noelio called back to them, pointing. "Fast." He grimly trotted back towards them. "I think it is a carnivore. It is too big and fast to survive on grass. We should get out of this region as fast as we can."

Cesario looked at the map while Noelio re-shod his feet in the enchanted boots. "I don't think we can do that today. Or tomorrow."

"Well, let's get moving, then. Three steps, lads," Aurelio directed. "Be at the ready. Remember, if there is anything dangerous, we do not stand and fight. We can move faster than any animal; with one step backwards, we will be safe."

Gods United willing! Aurelio added to himself.

The young men traveled for several hours, none of them wishing to rest, even for a meal. They sustained themselves on quick nibbles of salted meat and other fare from their replenishing satchels.

Aurelio frequently reminded his friends to drink water. The tepid water was not refreshing, but it was necessary.

Just before dusk, they saw three dark, massive shapes lumbering in the distance with odd appendages on the front of their faces. Thankfully, the beasts were traveling away from them.

"Let's not get closer to those!" Epifanio muttered.

Aurelio silently agreed—any animal that large could not be trusted. Each of those dark gray creatures looked like it outweighed four bulls!

"We should find a defensible shelter for the night." Noelio scanned the landscape.

"Cesario, does the map show any potential shelters?" Aurelio inquired.

Cesario lifted the map inches away from his face to study its details. "There are some dark marks here that might be rocky hills."

"Let's proceed carefully," Aurelio replied. "Point the way, Cesario."

Cesario looked at the map again and then pointed slightly eastwards. "There."

The group advanced for twenty more miles before the terrain grew more rugged and varied in elevation, and then Aurelio asked Epifanio to scout ahead.

His friend returned a few seconds later, breathlessly reporting, "I ran into a pack of animals that look meaner than ositos. One charged at me."

"We need to move. Going back will take us towards the big carnivore. If these things are like ositos, they could stalk us all the way back to the Palms People. Can we go forward?" Aurelio asked.

"No." Epifanio shook his head. "I saw a rocky ridge. There could be a steep drop on the other side."

Aurelio looked to either side, noting the elevations. It was growing risky to use the enchanted boots.

"The pack could be here in a few minutes. Can we stand and fight?" Noelio asked.

"Do we stand a chance against them, Epifanio?" Cesario interjected.

"Aye. They can't outrun our bows."

Noelio pointed to a hill a short distance away. "There! We should make our stand up there."

"Aye. Change shoes and then circle up on that hill." Aurelio promptly sat down to change into his running sandals. The rest of his companions did the same. Once on his feet, he took Cesario's blanket roll and satchel, because he was the slowest runner.

Free of the boots, it was a luxury to stretch his legs, but Aurelio restricted himself to Cesario's pace. His bookish friend was soon gasping. They were the last to arrive on the hill, hastily adding their baggage to the pile created by the others.

Before Aurelio took his place in the circle, he gave his sling to Cesario. He hoped his friend's eyesight was good enough to score a hit. Then he notched an arrow in his bow and waited. His mind was clear and his hands were steady—he would shoot as many arrows as necessary to protect his friends.

The silence was as intense as the sun that had sweat gathering on his forehead as he peered into the foreign landscape, anticipating an attack by the aggressive creatures living here.

They heard a peculiar, wild chittering first, and it quickly grew closer. As he listened to the energetic beasts loping towards them, Aurelio's heartbeat quickened.

"I see them!" Noelio roared. "Not yet in range."

A moment later, Aurelio could see them through the grass. About twenty tawny dog-like animals, ridges of hair projecting from their backs, trotted towards them. Their round, bear-like ears and dark eyes reminded him of ositos.

But ositos did not have those gaping jaws and impressive teeth.

Aurelio drew an arrow and unleashed it, hitting the hind leg of a foul-fanged creature, but it merely snarled and kept approaching.

More arrows and projectiles launched at the pack, and two beasts went down, but the rest of the pack surrounded them in a wide, constantly moving and yipping circle.

Cesario loaded his sling and fired. His projectile fell among the black-eyed hecklers, and a few of them lunged for it, fighting each other.

"What was that?" Aurelio yelled.

"Meat," Cesario cried, as he fired more morsels, distracting and dividing the pack.

"Keep it up," Aurelio exhorted. He aimed for any shaggy beast charging up the hill, his arrows finding a chest, a shoulder, and finally, a throat. The struck animal immediately fell.

As their arrows and stones rained on the pack of sharp-fanged animals, the survivors grew skittish. Finally, the pack members that still could, loped away, snarling and yipping their complaints.

Aurelio lowered his bow, panting as if he had run several miles in this heat.

Nine of the beasts remained, injured and bleeding.

Epifanio lifted his bow again.

"Save your arrows," Noelio instructed.

"They are suffering," Cesario countered.

"Aye." Noelio raised a large hunting knife. "I'll take care of it."

"I'll look for arrows we can use again," Epifanio said, and a few others joined him, carefully avoiding Noelio and his gruesome duty.

When his work was done, Noelio noted, "We need to get away from here. These carcasses will attract scavengers and other meat-eaters."

Aurelio looked at the sky, ablaze with a vibrant sunset, seeing only that darkness would soon fall. "We need to find our campsite," he said, loading himself with baggage. "Let's run, lads!"

"Arrows at the ready," Noelio added, and they arranged themselves in a semi-circle as they jogged, with the slower runners in the middle and those most skilled with their weapons on the outer edges.

After several miles, they found a suitable resting place for the night—a sharp rise from the surrounding ground upon which a large boulder, taller than most men, perched. Three of them could sit with their backs to it around a fire.

The group quietly set up camp, having had much practice in doing so.

It had been strange to find that the extreme heat of the day was followed by cold nights requiring fires. Perhaps a half-hour in the evening was comfortable before the chill of the night prevailed. There was no such reprieve in the morning, which dawned hot as soon as the sun appeared in the sky.

After most of his friends had settled in around the fire to eat their dinner, Aurelio ambled around the camp, chewing on flatbread. He peered as deeply into the distance as he could in the failing light.

All seemed to be quiet, but only the Gods United knew what other dangerous beasts these lands contained. Where was the animal who made the prints Noelio had investigated earlier? He hoped they would be able to hear it coming.

Aurelio made another circuit of their small camp.

Cesario joined him, asking, "Are you going to be taking the first shift?"

"I may as well. I cannot sleep."

Cesario said quietly, "I cannot say all will be well, but I can say that we are well-prepared and all of us have useful skills. We are no easy prey."

"True." Aurelio slowed his pace. "If all of us had minds as sharp as yours, Cesario, I could rest easy. Your quick thinking has saved us more times than I can count."

Cesario ducked his head, but Aurelio could see his smile. "Archery skills are much more valuable right now."

"Never doubt that your skills are just as valuable, my friend." Aurelio reconsidered, reaching to grasp the shorter man's shoulder. "In truth, more valuable," he said. "Now that your words have had their intended effect, you should sleep." He resumed walking. "Rest well," he called back, embracing the cooler air on his face.

The camp quickly quieted as the weariest of his friends found sleep in their blankets, and those who stayed awake kept their voices low.

Soon, Aurelio had to keep active to stay warm. As he circled their camp, he kept his ears alert, and his eyes roved the darkness, looking for any shadows moving closer to their camp. For hours, he found none, eventually yielding his post to Victoriano.

Then he fell into a fitful sleep, from which he woke when Noelio gripped his arm.

"Something is out there," his friend whispered. "I can't see it, but I know it is there. Victoriano felt it, too."

Aurelio sat up. "Where?"

"I think it is circling." Noelio looked into the darkness.

"You can't see it at all?" Aurelio quietly gathered his sling and stones.

"No. Maybe it isn't close."

Aurelio listened. It was too quiet. Insects sang when everything was at peace. He rose, crouching alongside Noelio. "Let's wake up all the archers. Quietly."

Aurelio and Noelio quickly woke up a few of their companions. The five of them arranged themselves at approximately equal intervals along the perimeter of their camp.

The night stars provided the only source of light as clouds obscured the moon. Aurelio strained to hear any movement outside their camp.

His friends were still, adept at waiting for hours for forest quarry. They all peered into the night in utter silence, as their ears were more important than their eyes for detecting any nocturnal beasts stalking them.

Without shifting his feet, Aurelio moved his knees slightly. He could feel his fatigue in the griminess of his eyes, but the unseen danger kept him alert. He could sense it watching them, perhaps considering whether it was safe to attack. They were foreign to it as well, as there were no people in these dry, hostile lands. If the beast was capable of using caution, it must be highly intelligent—and therefore more dangerous than that pack of hungry hecklers.

As Aurelio scanned the night, he realized the beast was either as dark as the night itself or it kept itself at a safe distance, watching them with unnervingly good eyesight in this deep darkness. If the creature stalking them now was the same as the one who had created the footprints, it was fast, rendering anything within its sights unsafe.

Aurelio wiggled his knees again, resisting the urge to flex his shoulders as well. The strain of not shivering was burning his upper back. His fingers danced on the woven sling.

He may not be able to kill a large beast with a projectile, but he could stun it. Did that shadow blink? He whirled his sling, staring at a spot of darkness about thirty feet away. There was a shifting of the shadow, and he let his stone loose.

A throaty shriek shattered the silence, allowing Noelio and Emiliano, his two closest companions, to loose arrows towards the sound.

"Harry it!" Noelio cried, launching another arrow into the night.

Aurelio shouted at his friends behind him, "Stay where you are! Keep watch—it may circle round."

After a few shots each, the young men stopped firing as they strained to hear anything in the darkness. Aurelio prayed to all the Gods United that they had frightened the creature away.

After twenty more minutes of tense waiting, insects resumed chirping again.

Aurelio exhaled. "Gods United are merciful," he breathed. "Those who can sleep, please do. It will be morning in a few hours."

Most of the young men dutifully returned to their blankets, as sleep was as necessary as water to keep them alive.

Aurelio and the two best archers—Noelio and Emiliano—stood watch while the night lightened and shimmered into morning. As he watched another powerful sun break the horizon, Aurelio thanked the Gods United for giving them all another day.

Turning his gaze towards Kalehala, Aurelio continued his prayers for a long time. He did not know when, or if, he would see Belrina again.

20

A BROKEN OATH

Lying on her side, Belrina nestled against Lythk as he slept, gazing at his luminous face and wondering at the connection she had forged with him.

Although sudden, it felt natural—as if she had emerged from the dark forest into a clearing, delighting in her first view of the snow-capped Majesties. She wanted to explore every part of this new, bright, exquisite world.

She laid her head on Lythk's shoulder, wrapping her arm around his chest.

In response, Lythk wrapped both arms around Belrina. She smiled, realizing he did not need to be fully conscious to embrace her.

The effects of the azuka had faded, but Belrina could still feel the peaceful beat of his heart when she touched his skin.

A few minutes later, Belrina sensed Lythk was awake. She rolled up, looking into his gold-flecked green eyes. The questions she had planned to ask him seemed less important than enjoying this moment.

The cylinder devices were at their lowest setting, faintly glowing. They had to leave the tent soon.

Lythk caressed her face, smiling softly. "The seer awaits."

Belrina did not move. She invoked the spell to aid her in speaking Elvish now that the sakitha ceremony was done.

"Lythk, did the sakitha bond destroy your vaxili oaths?"

"Not all of them." Lythk's fingers grazed her arm. "I do not regret it, Belrina."

She could feel his love flood into her along the path forged by their intertwining auras. Their lips connected, enhancing their sense of each other.

Several moments later, Belrina asked another question. "May I call you my husband?"

"Yes." Lythk smiled without restraint, a rare occurrence akin to a powerful ray of sun in a dense bower.

Belrina forced herself to leave his side. Sitting up, she clutched the coverlet to her chest. Lythk was still in his robe. She had tried several times to remove it, but he had always distracted her from her objective. His distractions had left her completely unclothed.

Belrina did not recall where she had discarded her robe. She began searching the coverings nearest her.

On his feet with his robe properly done, Lythk said, "Let me find it for you."

In a few moments, he held the robe open for Belrina to step into. She rose, not dropping the coverlet until the last moment. Lythk wrapped her in the robe, tying the sash, and then he kissed her neck before stepping away.

Fixing her tousled hair with a quick enchantment, Belrina joined Lythk at the tent flap, clasping his arm. They exited together, walking several paces in the clammy cavern before the seer suddenly appeared, using a dim globe of light.

Belrina was glad the light did not fully combat the gloom.

After a moment, Seer A'zine smiled incandescently, walking to meet them. "The light may yet be preserved," she breathed, grasping their free hands.

The seer's loving energy was amplified as the blessing flowed through Lythk into their bond. Belrina felt the light, without which magic could not exist, suffusing the entire world.

"Congratulations to you both," A'zine said. "Come, I have arranged a celebratory meal."

"Thank you, Seer," Belrina said softly. To Lythk, she added,

"I shall disguise us." In the next instant, they appeared to be personal attendants, as the elite assumed those at the lowest rung of society had no personal business worthy of attention.

As they emerged from the darkness of the inner sanctuary, the seer extinguished the light. Belrina suppressed a sigh. In the sakitha tent, she and Lythk had been the only beings in the universe. She regretted leaving that illusion behind. She exchanged a glance with her husband, gripping his arm.

As Seer A'zine led them through the Reflection Chamber, Belrina sensed turbulence growing within Lythk. She looked at her husband's serene face.

'Must you resign?' she addressed him telepathically.

'I don't believe the vaxithild will accept anything else,' Lythk replied.

'Perhaps the seer can help?' Belrina focused on controlling her emotions. She did not want to be the reason he surrendered his position.

'Perhaps,' Lythk responded, contributing new feelings to the bond.

Realizing her husband was trying to comfort her, Belrina smiled, allowing her love for him to flow freely. It was the only way she knew to support him.

In the hallway behind the Reflection Chamber, Seer A'zine walked past her personal quarters, stopping in front of arched double wooden doors.

"I hope you will find these quarters comfortable. I will wait for you in my garden." Seer A'zine then left them alone.

Lythk used a chant to open a door, scanning and securing the room before allowing Belrina to enter. Then he followed on her heels.

The main chamber of the suite was round, dominated by a circular bed flanked by brass sconces. Two smaller chambers were attached, one of which housed Belrina's gowns and personal items, and she stepped into it, cleansing herself before donning a deep green gown.

Lythk called, "May I be of assistance?"

Belrina laughed, joining him. She was ready, having used a few enchantments to speed the process. "Do you wish to replace Njal as my stylist?"

In two long strides, Lythk was at her side, looking resplendent in his vaxili garb, offering his arm. "I cannot equal Lakri Njal's talents, but whatever talents I do possess, they are yours to use." He raised her hand to his lips, lightly kissing her fingers. His green eyes caressed her face, and Belrina inclined towards him.

"Must you make it so difficult to leave?" Belrina breathed.

Lythk laughed softly. "I wish we could. . . linger." He returned her hand to his arm. "But we must devise how to approach the vaxithild."

Soon the sakitha partners were in Seer A'zine's garden, bowing their respects to their venerable host and admiring the indulgent breakfast she had prepared.

As they took their seats, Belrina inhaled the scent of the freshly baked loaf of bread filled with nuts and seeds. A small crystal bowl held berry jam, and their goblets contained a cool citrus punch.

"Seer, this is amazing! I haven't had bread since I left home," Belrina exclaimed. With a fresh understanding, she remembered Mathim's enjoyment of the simplest meals she had prepared for him.

"I had to express my delight in your partnership. Please eat while it is warm." The seer followed her own advice, and they enjoyed the luxurious meal for a few minutes.

"There are some matters we should discuss," Seer A'zine began. "Lythk, will you resign as magisthild?"

"I will be expected to resign. However, if I unexpectedly step down as magisthild, it will generate unwanted attention."

Seer A'zine pondered. "I have been considering whether to keep the sakitha partnership secret. I fear angering Primth."

Some of the turbulence in the sakitha bond relaxed. "If we

conceal the bond, it is possible I may remain Magisthild of Kalehala."

"Pardon?" Belrina began hesitantly. "Will we be able to conceal our sakitha tattoos?" She held up her arm, displaying the permanent golden lines. "And if not, won't Asthildi know that Lythk and I are sakitha partners?"

"Let me explore whether I can disguise the marks. If you will allow me?" Seer A'zine inquired, already reaching towards Belrina.

"Of course, Seer." Belrina raised the loose sleeve of her gown, exposing the whole tattoo.

Lythk stood, announcing, "Seer, there was a magical intrusion into Belrina's former quarters. I shall investigate." He summoned a transporter.

"We all should go," A'zine said calmly, standing. "You two should not be separated even for a moment. I do not know what aspect of the sakitha bond will protect Belrina. It could be close physical proximity."

Belrina erected a protective shield over herself and Lythk as she stood.

The seer held out a hand to them both. "I will take us all." She began chanting as soon as they grasped her hands.

As magic energy surged around them, Belrina gripped Lythk's hand.

"Close your eyes, Belrina," he whispered.

Following his advice, Belrina focused on powering her protective shield as the world dissolved for an instant. Once she could breathe again, Belrina opened her eyes.

"Stay with Seer A'zine," Lythk muttered, releasing her hand. He activated a device that darkened the room while lighting a swirling pattern of energy on Belrina's pillow, identifying the magical intrusion. With some additional chanting, an irisean screen appeared. Blurred images raced by until the face of a hazel-eyed Asthildi appeared. Lythk had located the perpetrator.

Her husband chanted ferociously, and a torrent of energy swept through the room. Seer A'zine instructed Belrina to adopt an Asthildi disguise. Confused, Belrina hastily did so. Suddenly, the Asthildi from the irisean screen stood before them, her navy tunic askew.

"You have committed a crime against a seer," Lythk pronounced. "I have authority to impose immediate sanctions."

With wide eyes, the Asthildi dropped to her knees. Looking at the medallion on Lythk's tunic, she lunged into a bow. "Magisthild, I beg for mercy."

Belrina felt a pulse of magic energy sail towards Lythk, disintegrating against her protective shield. '*She tried to strike you,*' Belrina informed Lythk telepathically.

"Do you wish to grapple?" Lythk asked his captive, his voice quiet and intense. "In the presence of Seer A'zine?"

The hazel-eyed elf pressed her hands to the floor, bowing her head. "Seer! I beg for your forgiveness." Then she was suddenly on her feet, throwing a fluorescing magic strike at Lythk as she chanted desperately. Before it reached Belrina's protective shield, Lythk retaliated, striking with his hands in a blur, generating green, blue, and purple corkscrews of power, which lit the dim chamber with their brilliance as he battled with the intruder.

A protective shield deflected Lythk's first two strikes, but the third knocked the navy-clad assailant down, incapacitating her as effectively as Belrina's shield had extinguished the storm of magic she had hurled at them.

Lythk unleashed a string of incantations, lifting his attacker to her feet and confining her within invisible magic walls. His fierce green gaze matched the merciless righteousness in the sakitha bond.

The hazel-eyed Asthildi could not conceal her fear as her entire cache of devices floated to Lythk's hand.

"I am confiscating all your magic devices pursuant to Vaxili Code 7A.224," he announced.

The captured elf squeezed her eyes shut. "He will kill me."

"Would you like to question the detainee, Seer A'zine, or shall I?" Lythk inquired, his eyes not leaving his captive's face. His powerful body was primed for action, and Belrina sensed her husband's primal urge to protect her.

"I shall do it," Seer A'zine stepped forward. "What is your name, Asthildi?"

"Kaya."

"What did you do in this chamber?"

Kaya's forehead glistened with perspiration.

The seer lifted her hand. "Do I need to use a confession spell?"

Kaya tossed her head, exclaiming, "No! I concealed a device." She quickly added, "I do not know what it does."

"On whose orders did you do this?"

Clenching her hands into fists, Kaya said, "Senator Primth."

"Do you know whose chamber this is?"

"No, Seer. The senator only tells me what to do." Kaya lifted her eyes, gazing at the Seer of Kalehala. "Please take me into your custody, Seer. He will kill me."

"Only if he believes you failed," Lythk said.

Kaya's eyes swiveled towards him.

Ignoring her, Lythk addressed the seer. "Please ascertain whether Kaya is telling the complete truth."

"I am! Please believe me." Kaya tried to retreat from Seer A'zine, but escape from Lythk's magical construction was impossible.

"What have you done to fear me so?" Seer A'zine's face was sad, but her grip on Kaya's head was firm. "This is not a cleansing. It is merely a brief examination to aid the magisthild's investigation. Close your eyes, Asthil Kaya."

Seer A'zine began a rhythmic chanting. Soon Kaya was twitching, her eyelids fluttering as the seer accessed her memory.

Belrina drew closer to Lythk. Uncertain if it was safe to

speak aloud, she inquired telepathically, *'How did Senator Primth know this was my bedchamber?'*

'I do not yet know. He could have installed a tracker on the zabalith,' Lythk replied, his thought laced with anger.

Alarmed, Belrina realized their meticulous security measures were not impenetrable.

When Seer A'zine concluded chanting, she drifted away from Kaya. "She concealed nothing from us."

Lythk nodded, invoking a privacy screen, blocking them from Primth's associate. "Before we decide what to do with her, let's see what this device does," he stated.

Belrina reinforced the protective shield around them all.

"Thank you, Belrina," Seer A'zine murmured.

Lythk touched the pillow, triggering the spell. The illuminated magic energy swirled into a line, forming a conduit. Energy coursed along the conduit, brightening the room. When the flow of energy ceased, Lythk lifted the pillow, retrieving a small opal. "I do not detect any magic resonance," he said, mystified.

The seer came to his side, and he handed her the gem. She walked towards Belrina. "It is attuned to Belrina, Magisthild. It is a communication device Belrina must activate."

"He wants to communicate with Belrina privately," Lythk said flatly.

"Should we destroy it?" Belrina asked, raising her hand to direct magic energy toward Primth's device.

"That will not stop Primth, and his next ploy may be more difficult to foil." Lythk paced for a few steps. "Belrina, activate it." His face was taut.

Belrina performed a breathing exercise, hoping her apprehension was not flooding the sakitha bond. She carefully collected the device from the seer. At her touch, a written message sailed through the air. "Did you see that?" Belrina had a limited understanding of the Elvish alphabet, which had seventy-seven unique characters.

"No, Belrina," Seer A'zine responded. "However, I can make a minor adjustment." After she waved her hand over the device, a complex eddy of magic settled into it. "Try it again."

Belrina touched a finger to the opal.

Seer A'zine read the script floating above the device. "Belrina, I am enraptured with you. There are things I wish to say to you that others should not hear. Write me back, please. I shall be desperately waiting for your response. Senator Primth."

Belrina held on to her Asthildi mask of calm. Undoubtedly, her husband could feel the strength of her revulsion through their bond, and it was a relief to share her emotions with him.

"Might I be able to respond, Seer?" Lythk asked.

Belrina gratefully handed him the device.

"I can make it so." With some more chanting, the seer altered the device again.

Lythk put the device away. "I will reply as Belrina, and Primth will believe he has succeeded. If Asthil Kaya's memory of the last few minutes is erased, she will believe she has succeeded as well."

"I will not erase a memory without the subject's permission, Magisthild."

"She will give it, Seer. Then I can perform the memory-loss spell pursuant to Vaxili Code 13.177."

As Lythk predicted, Kaya readily agreed to fool both herself and Senator Primth to avoid the consequence of failure. Belrina hoped Primth would never discover the deception. Even with a sakitha partner, she lived in fear of angering him. How would she ever escape the shadow he cast over her life?

Once Kaya had been dispatched, Belrina gladly held Lythk's arm as they followed Seer A'zine through the arched corridors of the sanctuary.

"The vaxithild is contacting me," Lythk announced.

"Invite her to my sanctuary," See A'zine promptly said. "We can receive her in the Reflection Chamber at her earliest convenience."

Regulating her breathing, Belrina listened to her husband's steady heartbeat, as he made the arrangements with the vaxithild. She attempted to match his outward calm, but they hadn't had time to devise a proposal the vaxithild might find acceptable. They would soon discover if their love would cost her husband his position as Magisthild of Kalehala.

One day, Belrina might face the vicissitudes of Asthildi society with equanimity, but now she felt as clumsy as she had when walking on the shifting Kalehala sand for the first time.

21

A New Freedom

S TANDING SEVERAL PACES BEHIND the Seer of Kalehala, who was at the apex of the pyramid they formed to greet the vaxithild, Lythk permitted himself to look at Belrina. She had transformed her hair into an elaborate plaited crown but remained in a modest dress.

Her dark locks reflected the light of the Reflection Chamber as effectively as jewels, and the rich hues of her face were more alluring than a fashionable gown. Lythk was not her equal in appearance or ability, and yet he was her chosen lifelong partner.

Belrina turned her clear blue eyes towards him. Emotion reverberated through their bond, connecting them along the energy channel forged in the sakitha rites. He smiled, delighting in the shared experience, which he had believed impossible.

'We must convince the vaxithild that our love has not blinded us to duty,' Lythk conveyed to Belrina telepathically.

'Yes, Magisthild.' Belrina gave the honorific without hesitation. She sent a pulse of love along their bond and then faced forward, reminding him to do the same.

Tall, the vaxithild swept into the Reflection Chamber behind a seeker, her peridot cloak swaying. Gold medallions covered both shoulders and her reddish hair, laced with silver, was arranged in several horizontal plaits.

Belrina and Lythk immediately bowed, lunging deeply. They stayed in their bows while the vaxithild paid her respects to the Seer of Kalehala.

"Please rise, Vaxithild Serintha," the seer instructed. "Thank you for joining us at my sanctuary. Please allow me to introduce Asthil Belrina."

"The honor is mine, Seer," Serintha said, smoothly regaining her feet. "You both may rise."

The vaxithild's light blue eyes watched Belrina as she rose. "It is a pleasure to meet you."

"Thank you, Vaxithild Serintha." Belrina inclined her head. "I am honored to meet you." Lythk proudly observed that she had adapted to Asthildi culture, suitably concealing the anxiety racing through the sakitha bond.

Then Serintha's eyes searched Lythk. The seer had disguised the sakitha tattoos with some difficulty, but Lythk feared those who knew him well would detect the fundamental change in him.

"Were your vaxili oaths abolished in the sakitha, Magisthild?"

"I remain loyal to the Empire and the law, Vaxithild," Lythk affirmed. "The sakitha bond has not erased my ability to do my duty."

"You believe so?" Serintha's voice was quiet, her face rigidly expressionless.

"Vaxithild, let us sit while we discuss the latest evolution in Belrina's protection," Seer A'zine interjected, gesturing to the benches around the sacred pool. She sat first, and Vaxithild Serintha sat opposite her.

Lythk sat across from his commander, leaving Belrina to sit next to the decorated vaxili. Before he could begin, Serintha brusquely inquired, "How can you be a vaxili without the foundation of all the oaths?"

"If my assignment is to protect Belrina, there shall be no conflict with performing my vaxili duty."

"Love trumps rationality. Can I trust you to execute this duty in a logical manner?"

Lythk met her gaze, but he did not give an affirmative response—he would not resort to deceit. Lythk knew he would use any means necessary to protect Belrina, even if they went against the Vaxili Code.

"At this significant moment in history, we cannot afford any vulnerability in our company," Serintha continued. "Today, I had a request from a magisthild in the Capitol to transfer one of our vaxili to his command, and I suspect Senator Primth is behind that request." Her steely eyes held his as she unclenched her jaw to speak. "I will investigate all circumstances, but I have reason to be concerned for the integrity of all under my command. I cannot tolerate any who are not truly loyal to *all* vaxili oaths."

All Lythk could focus on in his commander's speech was the fact that Primth may have spies among their ranks. He would investigate all members of Belrina's security team to ensure none had had contact with a compromised vaxili.

"Vaxithild Serintha," Seer A'zine's tranquil voice interceded, "I respect your concerns. I am concerned that the magisthild's resignation will raise questions we do not want to answer, for I am convinced Belrina's sakitha bond should remain confidential." She leaned forward slightly. "We do not want Primth's wrath directed towards Kalehala."

The vaxithild nodded. "I see your point. However, Lythk is no longer a vaxili, for he abdicated our guild when he broke an oath."

The sakitha bond quivered with the emotion both Lythk and Belrina experienced in response to the vaxithild's pronouncement.

Serintha cast her cool blue eyes on Belrina again. "On account of the extraordinary circumstances in which we find ourselves, I will seal his resignation." Her eyes narrowed. "He has my permission to wear his uniform and adornments. I dislike the subterfuge, but I will support it. As long as the sakitha bond is concealed, Lythk may present himself as the

Magisthild of Kalehala."

"I deeply appreciate the concession, Vaxithild Serintha." A'zine inclined her silvery head.

"I shall submit my resignation later today," Lythk said quietly. He held on to the sakitha bond as if it were a protective shield and he were outnumbered by highly skilled opponents. He breathed evenly, focusing on the sentiments flowing from Belrina.

"Vaxithild Serintha," Belrina began, "please, will you tell me who will be in command of security during my journey to the Capitol?"

"I will appoint Vaxili Mathim, who will consult with both myself and Seer A'zine."

"Thank you, Vaxithild." Belrina smiled.

The venerable vaxili nodded. "I will employ all vaxili resources at my disposal to protect you, Asthil Belrina." She held Lythk's gaze. "I was prepared to sacrifice valuable assets, but today, I am reminded all sacrifice requires effort." She returned her attention to Belrina. "This reminder has made me poor company, Asthil Belrina. My apologies."

"None needed, Vaxithild." Belrina said quickly, bowing while seated. The gesture was indistinguishable from an elite's, but her sincerity was all her own.

A brief smile touched Serintha's lips, then she addressed Seer A'zine. "Thank you for granting an audience. I must request permission to depart for I have much to do at present."

"You have my leave. Thank you for your understanding and assistance, Vaxithild Serintha," A'zine said. "Good day to you."

Belrina and Lythk bowed formally to the vaxithild as she departed.

"I know this isn't the outcome sought," A'zine said in her sonorous voice. "However, I see a greater freedom for you, Lythk, which you may use to fully protect Belrina."

After a moment, he nodded. "I cannot, however, display this freedom overtly. I must act as though I am a magisthild.

To do otherwise will invite suspicion."

"And to keep the sakitha partnership secret, we must act as though it doesn't exist? We cannot. . ." Belrina blushed, unable to finish her sentence aloud.

Lythk kept his face smooth with effort. His composure was being tested in new ways for the feelings in the sakitha bond were. . . something he could not consider at the moment. "That is correct, Belrina," he affirmed soberly.

A'zine looked at them both. "I want to know more about the sakitha bond, Belrina. What do you gain from it?"

"We are attuned to each other." Belrina laid a finger on Lythk's hand, and he could feel the blood flowing through her veins. "I can hear his heartbeat." She removed her finger. "We feel each other's emotions."

"If Belrina were frightened, you would know, Lythk?" A'zine clarified.

"Yes, Seer."

Seer A'zine nodded in satisfaction. "But I wonder how far the range is? We would have to test it outside the sanctuary; magic works differently here, as you may recall from our lessons, Belrina."

"Yes, Seer. You explained that there are unique currents and eddies of energy in the sanctuary because of the reservoir beneath drawing in magic."

A'zine smiled. "I wish you could stay here with me, Belrina. You could learn so much."

"I wish I could stay, too," Belrina declared. "However, we will continue my lessons on our journey to the Capitol, won't we?"

Lythk permitted himself to take Belrina's hand. There were so many gaps in her knowledge of Asthildi culture.

"Belrina, I shall not accompany you," Seer A'zine said softly. "There are customs almost as strong as oaths binding me to Kalehala. A seer should not leave her sanctuary unless directed by the Council of the Wise."

Belrina stopped breathing for a moment, and Lythk tried fueling her with confidence through their bond. His lovely sakitha partner did not yet understand the strength of her own powers.

"I shall feel the loss of your company acutely, Seer," Belrina finally said.

"Not as much as I will feel the loss of yours." A'zine's smile was brief. "We will communicate each evening, though." With a chant, a transmitter appeared in her hand. "I created this for us. Please tell me, Belrina, the properties of this device."

With a warm smile for Lythk, Belrina removed her hand from his. In the next instant, the device was in her closed hand. After a moment, she said, "This is an encrypted transmitter, which only the two of us may use to communicate, Seer. Its range is extensive, but I cannot gauge the distance."

"Correct. It will permit fifteen minutes of communication when you are in the Capitol," A'zine confirmed.

Belrina pocketed the transmitter. "I'm glad I will be able to consult with you, Seer."

Although her exquisite face was smooth, Lythk knew her fear was not assuaged. He wondered how to address Belrina's concerns. Their bond gave him a greater understanding of her feelings, but it offered no solutions on how to manage them.

"If you wish, you can continue your lessons with Seeker Saolmyn during the journey to the Capitol," A'zine continued. "She has mastered the turvyst, which would allow me to join you in spirit briefly."

"How does the turvyst work, Seer?" Belrina asked. Lythk felt her mind working on the puzzle.

"The turvyst is a spiritual connection in which one person invites another to share her body; for the duration of the turvyst, the two individuals share thoughts, memories, knowledge. It should be used sparingly, for there is a risk of the confluence of the two minds becoming permanent."

Lythk knew his face reflected his disapproval.

"The turvyst should be used only in urgent circumstances, Magisthild," Seer A'zine added. "If necessary, through Seeker Saolmyn, I can protect Belrina."

"I hope we never have cause to use the turvyst, Seer," Belrina said, "But I will take comfort in having Seeker Saolmyn accompany us to the Capitol." Lythk felt some tension ease in Belrina's body, and his own body relaxed as well.

A'zine nodded and then chanted, displaying her correspondence screen. "You have received numerous requests and invitations, Belrina."

Lythk carefully placed his hands on his knees. The onslaught of attention was inevitable, but it—and the sociopolitical difficulties it presented—would always be unwanted.

A'zine chanted again, opening a yellow envelope with a poetic inscription. "This invitation is from an upper echelon elite who arrived in Kalehala yesterday."

Unexpectedly, A'zine stood, and Lythk promptly joined her. He felt a tingle in the sakitha bond, alerting him to Belrina's use of magic. She likely had created a protective shield.

"Seekers informed me Asthil Myrin will not follow their instructions to leave a message. He insists on waiting until he can speak with Belrina personally."

"He should wait," Lythk promptly replied. "We should not reward his disobedience by granting an immediate audience." He suspected the sakitha bond conveyed a jolt of emotion to his partner.

"Belrina," A'zine asked, "what would you like to do?"

"Is he disturbing the seekers? I don't want them to be inconvenienced on my account."

"He is a nuisance," A'zine acknowledged. "Two apprentices are foregoing their duties to attend to him."

"Then, perhaps, we should make him wait a quarter-hour, and then the three of us can meet with him briefly." Belrina looked at Lythk apologetically.

He nodded, agreeing to the plan. A difference of opinion

needed no forgiveness. "We'll dispatch him quickly," Lythk added.

A'zine regained her seat. "Then, shall we return to the invitations? Most, with your permission, Belrina, I can answer for you, politely sending your regrets that you are too busy preparing for your journey to the Capitol. However, the wealthy elite's request for an audience should be given a personal response."

"My impending meeting with Senator Primth is public knowledge?" Belrina asked, straightening in her seat and clasping her hands together in her lap—mannerisms that displayed her concern to any Asthildi eye.

"Yes, dear one." A'zine held Belrina's gaze. "Primth publicized it himself."

"The Empire is abuzz with news of your existence," Lythk said gently. "Primth gains free media attention by associating himself with you."

"The question is, Belrina, do you embrace the attention?" Seer A'zine queried.

"I wish to run from it," Belrina responded quickly. "However, I do not know if that is the best thing to do. What is your opinion, Magisthild?"

"All public events or interviews create security concerns. Additionally, Primth will be displeased if you spare time for these distractions," Lythk responded.

"Seer, what are your thoughts?" Belrina further inquired.

"There is tremendous benefit to earning the public's affection. If they love you, Primth risks losing their approval if he harms you."

"I wouldn't know how to make the public love me!" Belrina exclaimed.

A'zine laughed melodiously. "You have already made a favorable impression. Let me share the report written by the criermaster who attended the Introduction." The seer displayed it on the screen, reading it aloud for Belrina.

Lythk had read it yesterday morning, but he listened carefully now, searching for any implications he may have missed. Belrina's graceful bearing had impressed the crier, but it was clear he had had low expectations due to her upbringing.

"I also recorded a presentation by our local criers," A'zine continued. With a series of chants, she projected the visual media showcasing two sculpted criers tittering with excitement. The report included interviews with several who had attended the Introduction, including Asthil Myrin, who gushed about dancing with Belrina.

"This is what I should expect whenever I appear at public events?" Belrina asked quietly. The bond conveyed a mix of sentiments. Without waiting for an answer, she continued, "I will not seek more attention from criers, as I wish to maintain my privacy."

"There is more, Belrina," Lythk said softly. "Seer, would you please show us Kalehala's square at this hour?"

"Yes, Magisthild." A'zine chanted a few words, and an irisean screen displayed a busy scene at midday. Many richly attired Asthildi wandered without true purpose under the watchful eyes of vaxili stationed throughout the square. A few chariots were tethered wherever space could be found.

"All these Asthildi left their homes for a chance to see me?" Belrina shook her head.

"Yes, most are extremely wealthy with ample time for leisure," Lythk explained.

"Seer, I will personally decline all requests for an audience. It is the least I can do." After a pause, Belrina added, "I think my departure from Kalehala should be publicized, which should allow Kalehala to return to normal."

Lythk began planning the security measures he would employ for the event before realizing that would be Mathim's responsibility. He held himself still, preventing any movement that would betray his thoughts. Belrina looked at him, compassion in her eyes. Perhaps the sakitha bond was not always convenient.

"Thank you, Belrina. A farewell event will be helpful." A'zine smiled. "Regarding a different matter, the Guilds of Kalehala are selecting a member of the elite to join your entourage. Social protocol requires an elite escort to introduce you at social events."

Alarm spiked in the sakitha bond. "Pardon, Seer. What social events?" Belrina maintained a steady voice.

"Primth has demanded you travel directly to him, stopping only for the essentials of travel," Lythk answered. "He has conveniently provided an excuse to avoid socializing and its potential entanglements."

"It will not be convenient to slight a powerful senator or prestigious guildmaster who will hold a grudge," A'zine countered.

"I don't want to incur ill will from anyone, but it seems inevitable," Belrina said, her dissatisfaction infiltrating their bond. "With powerful Asthildi wanting opposite things, I will have no choice but to displease someone."

"Please do not aim to please the elite," Lythk cautioned, suppressing his frustration at being unable to protect Belrina from the irrational dictates of Asthildi society. "Much of what they desire will be in their best interests, not yours."

Seer A'zine broke the ensuing silence by saying, "We have let Asthil Myrin wait long enough. I have instructed Seeker Menilth to escort him in."

Lythk positioned himself by the door so the young one would see him first.

Wearing an elaborately patterned cloak, Asthil Myrin closely followed the apprentice, sparing Lythk a glance before sweeping into a bow for Seer A'zine.

"Thank you, Seeker Menilth," A'zine said. "Rise, Asthil Myrin. As you can see, Asthil Belrina is not free for an audience today."

"Asthil Belrina." Myrin dipped into a flourishing bow. "I am overjoyed to see you if only for a moment." His eyes absorbed every lovely detail of Belrina's person, and Lythk resorted to breathing exercises to remain calm.

Belrina stiffly returned his bow. "Asthil Myrin." She kept her eyes on the floor. "The seer has kindly allowed this interruption, but it must be brief."

Lythk nodded in approval.

The young one gracefully bowed again. "My apologies to everyone." He stepped forward, as did Lythk. "I could think only of you, Asthil Belrina, and how I wished to see your face when you opened my gift." He conjured a small silver box to his hand. "I promise to leave as soon as you open it."

Belrina opened her hand, and the silver box floated towards her, surprising the young elite. "Thank you, Asthil Myrin. Regretfully, I cannot open it now. The seer has other tasks for me at present."

"Please forgive my thoughtlessness. I shall leave you all now." The young one bowed in reverse order, first to Belrina and then to the seer. When it was clear Myrin would not receive a smile from Belrina, he turned on his heel. Finally, he bowed to Lythk, muttering, "My apologies, Magisthild."

Lythk watched until the young elite, and the seeker trailing him, disappeared from view, climbing the spiraling staircase towards the exit.

"Open it, Belrina," A'zine instructed.

After Lythk strode to Belrina's side, she flipped the lid open. Music floated in the air, and Belrina smiled until she saw a pearl nestled on a cushion within. Then she said flatly, "I destroyed a weak enchantment. You can imagine its purpose."

Lythk held his face smooth as he wrestled with his emotions. The young one attempted to coerce Belrina's affections in front of Seer A'zine! This elite's infatuation bordered on lunacy.

The music died when Belrina closed the lid of the silver device, and she quickly dispatched the gift to the sanctuary's vault.

"Asthil Myrin is neither talented nor resourceful," A'zine opined. "He cannot threaten Belrina."

"Perhaps, Seer," Lythk replied. Determination could make any fool dangerous. He intended to heighten security measures. No, he intended to convince Vaxili Mathim it was necessary to do so. His jaw clenched, and he almost gritted his teeth.

The discussion with Seer A'zine continued until midafternoon. To avoid the swarm of criers accosting everyone departing the seer's sanctuary, Lythk transported Belrina directly to the training square. With no witnesses on the fortress rooftop, he slowly unwrapped his arms, enjoying the embrace longer than he should. More slowly, Belrina removed her arms from his waist, staying near him.

"Physical distancing at all times, Magisthild?" Belrina's voice was low. The emotion filling the bond was as complex as a symphony.

"It is safest, Belrina. Privacy can always be interrupted." He stepped away from his sakitha partner and her unimaginably beautiful, upturned face. An instant later, he returned to her. Belrina deserved the entire truth. "Each time I touch you, it will be more difficult for me to refrain from doing so. I am afraid to test my self-control."

"I understand," Belrina said quietly while her anger flared in their bond. "Primth ruins everything, doesn't he?"

"No," Lythk said emphatically. "He has no power over how we feel." He poured the tenderness with which he wished to touch her into their bond.

Belrina closed her eyes as if relishing his touch. Now only tranquility and love remained in their bond. With a soft smile, she inquired, "What training shall we do today, Magisthild?"

Before he could answer, Lythk received an encrypted communication from Seer A'zine. In response, he closed his eyes briefly.

"Magisthild?" Belrina did not conceal her panic. "What is it?"

"I did not mean to alarm you." Lythk monitored his breathing, belatedly suppressing his emotional reaction. "The Guilds have decided you shall have two elite escorts."

"Who?" Belrina breathed, holding his gaze. The color of her deep blue eyes against the warm hues of her face was as striking as the first time he saw her. He had a wild impulse to abscond with her—they could run until they found an isolated, safe place.

"Silvermaster Bykin." Lythk exhaled evenly, rejecting his foolish notion. No place in the Empire was beyond Primth's reach. "And Asthil Myrin." He needed to practice saying the name with equanimity.

The impertinent young one must have bribed the guildmasters for the appointment. Lythk labored to douse his disgust. Every minute of the journey to the Capitol in the confined space of the karth would now be laborious.

Lythk hoped to use his newly acquired freedom from vaxili strictures judiciously, but he knew he would violate any protocol or principle to prevent Myrin from touching Belrina.

22

SURVIVING THE WASTELAND

C ESARIO HAD EXPECTED TO feel relieved when they left the grassy drylands populated with predatory beasts. But he could find no relief in the desolate wasteland they had been traveling across for the last two days.

The scorching sun sucked their vitality as it had done the earth, which was desiccated, unstable grit instead of soil. Black insects with hard, shiny exteriors were the only living things in this desert—other than themselves.

At least these insects did not bite. Cesario still had red itchy welts from the giant mosquitos they had encountered in the drylands.

Their hats provided the only shelter from the noxious sun which burned any exposed skin, leaving it red and tender. They could evade the searing rays of the sun when they took their magic steps, but there was no escaping the pervading heat.

Cesario's head jerked forward, wakening him from involuntary sleep. Lifting his hat, he dumped water on his head and neck again. They had opted to travel continuously through the night in order to traverse these wastelands as quickly as possible.

"Time for another step, lads," Aurelio said. "Let's keep moving."

"Two more days," Cesario added, hoping the reminder would help.

A commotion arose at the end of his line of friends.

It took Cesario a moment to realize that Emiliano had sunk to his knees.

"Water!" Cesario cried to Victoriano, who was trying to help Emiliano stand. "Give him water."

Victoriano guided Emiliano to the ground, supporting him in a sitting position. Squatting, Epifanio poured water from his canteen over his ailing friend's head. Then he helped Emiliano drink his fill.

Victoriano took off his hat, wet it, and used it to fan Emiliano's face. "Emiliano? Emiliano!"

To avoid enacting the magic of his boots, Cesario shuffled closer to better see Emiliano, who was limp and unconscious. Only Victoriano's arms saved him from collapsing.

Epifanio gently poured more water over Emiliano's head, causing him to open his eyes. Cesario breathed easier.

"I'm sorry, Aurelio." Emiliano's voice was a hoarse whisper.

"You have nothing to be sorry for, my friend." Aurelio's voice was gentle. He shuffled towards Emiliano. "We'll get you safely to Kalehala. Don't you worry!"

Victoriano and Epifanio hoisted Emiliano to his feet, supporting him.

"Does anyone have the strength to carry him?" Aurelio asked.

"Wait." Cesario surveyed their equipment. "Give me two walking sticks and some blankets." His friends kicked up sand as they maneuvered to fulfill his requests.

When he knelt to create the litter, Cesario immediately felt the sand burning his skin through his trousers. He worked as quickly as he could, glad for the walking sticks provided by the stunted trees in the grassy drylands.

After a moment, Noelio joined him, using hunting line to lash the blankets to the wood. When Cesario was confident in the construction, they settled Emiliano on the litter, with Noelio at the helm.

"Let's try it out." Noelio shuffled a few steps forward.

"How's the ride, Emiliano?" Victoriano called.

"Fine," Emiliano said weakly.

"Keep drinking water," Cesario instructed. The benefit of any water they consumed seemed to dissipate through their sweat, making their thirst as constant as the heat.

Emiliano complied with trembling hands.

"Should I try using the magic boots?" Noelio asked.

The young men were silent, their uncertainty hanging in the stifling air.

"I think it should work," Cesario nodded. "Watch." He unhitched his satchel from his shoulder, lowering it to the sand, and while he held the strap, he stepped forward with a magic boot. Encountering open air, he yelped until his foot hit the sand several inches lower than expected.

His satchel thumped his back leg as his heart recovered from the jolt. Then he turned around, stepping upwards to rejoin his friends. He displayed his unharmed satchel to his friends.

"There is a little drop, though." Cesario looked at the litter, considering. "We should secure Emiliano. Can I have a sling?"

Aurelio promptly gave him one, and Cesario looped it around a stick, creating a handgrip. "Will that work, Emiliano?"

His heat-affected friend weakly grasped it. "I think so."

"Hmmm. Let's try something else." Cesario asked for another sling, engineering a chest strap around his thin friend. "Is that comfortable?" He helped Emiliano drink more water, after he nodded.

"Ready to try a step with the boots, Emiliano?" Aurelio asked. "I'll go with you."

Emiliano gave another small nod of his head, and then Cesario watched as Noelio disappeared, followed by Aurelio, who shuffled alongside Emiliano, chatting with him.

On the litter, Emiliano's body did not instantaneously travel. It was a disconcerting visual effect, as if there was a line of invisibility traveling to meet Emiliano.

Several in the group whistled or muttered prayers at the sight.

"Uh, let's line up, lads," Epifanio suggested. "Let's join them."

"Remember the small drop," Cesario called.

In one downwards step—which his companions navigated more gracefully than he had—they were reunited with their friends.

Aurelio was grasping Noelio's shoulder, saying, "You let me know when you need a break."

Then they resumed their trek through the wasteland, toiling on for an indeterminate time, developing a halting rhythm: water, step, wake up, water, step, check if Emiliano is comfortable.

What now seemed a long time ago, they had stopped scouting, finding the desolate landscape changeless. Now, the small peaks and valleys in the land posed no danger; tumbles upon the soft ground earned no bruises, and they easily extracted limbs from yielding sand.

Cesario looked for the sun, trying to judge when nightfall might arrive.

"I think there is something ahead," Epifanio said.

Everyone paused.

"We're too far away to see clearly," Noelio responded.

"Then let's continue."

Step, water, step, check Emiliano.

"What is it?" Aurelio muttered.

Step, water, step. Wake up. Step, check Emiliano, step.

Now Cesario could see a subtle smear on the landscape just above the horizon. It was difficult to see anything through the heat waves rising from the sand and the sweat rolling into his eyes.

"Is it a cloud?" Epifanio asked, puzzled.

They watered themselves again and then stepped forward.

"A cloud? But there is no rain here," Cesario shook his head. He splashed water on his face, hoping to wake up his brain.

"It's very far away," Aurelio noted. "Let's continue."

No one objected, as their desire to be in Kalehala now equaled Aurelio's.

After a few more steps, Cesario could make out a large darkish cloud. There was something odd about it. Water, step, wake up.

"What color would you say that cloud is?" Cesario squinted at it.

Water, step, check Emiliano.

"It is a little yellow," Epifanio said.

Water, step, wake up.

"Yellow?" Cesario muttered to himself.

Water, step, check Emiliano, step. Now he could see a haze stretching along the ground, and it was getting closer quickly.

Water, step, don't sleep, step.

"Stop!" Cesario cried. "It's a storm! It's wind kicking up this grit." He pointed. "It's miles long, and therefore, it must be powerful. Without shelter, we need to run away from it." He fumbled for the map.

"Which way?" Aurelio gazed at Cesario, his body tense.

"Kalehala is dead ahead," Cesario informed them. "The storm is sweeping from left to right. We can go back. Or we can go forward and try angling behind the storm." He pointed to the left.

"We can't go back." No one wanted to argue with Aurelio. The ground they had gained was too hard won. "Let's take a few steps and see if the storm stays its current course."

The young men began their rhythmic routine again. The ballooning storm raced towards them, unlike any meteorological phenomena Cesario had ever seen. Only a small piece of sky above the eastern stretch of desert was untouched.

"It's heading towards us," Noelio said, squinting at the sand cloud. "We need to angle mostly eastwards."

"Let's move forward for as long as we can," Aurelio insisted.

In silence, they stepped forward, facing the rising storm. No one struggled to remain awake now; all eyes were on the mountainous cloud, billowing across their horizon. When they started hearing the roar of the storm, giving them a sense of its power, Aurelio turned southeasterly.

"Time to angle towards the left," Aurelio announced, and everyone lined up with him. "Hold shoulders," he advised.

The young men shuffled closer to grip their neighbor's shoulder. Epifanio now held one side of the litter, allowing Noelio to hold on to his neighbor.

"On my count, let's do ten steps," Aurelio instructed. "Hold on Emiliano! Everyone drink or water down. Okay, here we go. One."

Together, the boys stepped forward, and before Cesario could see his new surroundings, he heard Aurelio count two. The world stretched and whirled in a head-throbbing blur. He could feel Rogelio and Victoriano gripping his shoulders.

Aurelio's voice was distant, but Cesario followed the count through the distorted reality, stopping when he heard Aurelio shout "ten."

Panting, Cesario groped for his canteen and he eyed the storm cloud. Still leagues away, its wind howled loudly, lifting his shirt from his sweat-slicked skin.

"Quickly, get ready for another ten steps," Aurelio instructed.

This time, Cesario held on to each of his neighbor's forearms while they grabbed his shoulders. Another ten miles in less than a minute, and they took a break.

Wind battered his head, trying to steal his hat. Cesario threw it into his satchel, blinked rapidly to protect his eyes from the grit sailing on wild air currents. They weren't out of the storm's path yet. He couldn't see an end to the monstrous dust cloud rushing towards them with a clamor greater than a thousand waterfalls.

"We run twenty steps!" Aurelio hollered. "Hold on tightly. Ready and one. . ."

They hadn't tried over ten steps before. Cesario pushed himself, feeling his leg muscles quiver as the world became less tangible with every step.

He closed his eyes, shutting out the disconcertingly vague reality. About mid-point in the run, he heard the storm surround them.

"Can't stop," Aurelio shouted instead of nineteen. "Twenty, twenty-one. . ."

Cesario concentrated on breathing. His head felt like it was two steps behind the rest of his body.

After the count of thirty, Cesario could scarcely hear Aurelio's voice over the raging storm. Keeping count in his head, Cesario strengthened his grip on his friends' arms.

At the count of forty, Cesario's chest burned, his ragged breath almost as noisy as the constant din of the storm. Straining to hear Aurelio, Cesario paused, but he was swept along with the count of forty-one. Rogelio and Victoriano had him!

Cesario ran through the pain as best he could, dimly aware of his surroundings. After the count of forty-nine, he was pulled to a halt.

In the suddenly solid world, Cesario tried to stand still, concentrating on breathing while waves and waves of pain crashed into his head. Falling to his knees, he vomited, hearing other sounds of nausea around him.

He backed away, still on his knees, clutching his stomach. With the smell of sickness in his nostrils, he might not hold on to its remaining contents. He breathed with the rhythm of the throbbing in his head.

Slowly, Cesario sat back on his heels, and his headache increased with the movement. He gripped his knees until the pain receded, and then he opened his eyes, unable to see clearly through large gray specks flooding his vision.

"Everyone well?" Aurelio called.

Noelio was the first to respond. "Aye. I have Emiliano."

Slowly, each of their friends found their voices, and Cesario managed to add, "I'm here." His hands found his canteen, and he rinsed his mouth before drinking deeply.

He could hear Aurelio and Noelio on their feet, tending to the others.

Aurelio found Cesario. "How do you feel?"

"Severe headache. I cannot see clearly," Cesario reported. "The pain medication in my satchel—give it to any who need it, please."

Aurelio gave Cesario the first pellet. "Rest now," he instructed, helping Cesario to arrange his blankets comfortably.

Cesario realized he couldn't feel the sun's powerful rays. He reached out, grabbing his friend's arm. "Where are we?"

"We are close to a rocky mountain ridge, and it blessedly casts a long shadow."

He refrained from asking how close it was—he didn't need to know how few steps remained before they would have run into the mountain with their enchanted boots.

"Continue drinking water, and I'll be back later," Aurelio suggested.

But Cesario did not let go of his friend's arm. "Tell me about the others."

Aurelio spoke softly. "Emiliano is barely conscious. Noelio and I are well, but everyone else is sick to their stomachs."

"I am the only one having trouble seeing?"

"Yes, my friend, but surely, it is just temporary. Rest now." Aurelio removed Cesario's hand from his arm.

Cesario eased back on his blanket, and when he woke, he wasn't certain if it was morning. The large gray motes obscured everything but basic shapes. He blinked rapidly, and the specks became smaller.

Hearing some friends speaking quietly, he sat up carefully, finding his headache more tolerable. Mildly hungry, Cesario felt around for his satchel.

Aurelio was quickly by his side. "Let me help you. Is your headache better?"

"Thank you. Yes, much better." White and gray spots danced before his eyes, but Aurelio's face was visible between the spots. He accepted the flatbread and dried fruit offered by Aurelio.

"How are the others?" Cesario asked.

"Nearly everyone has recovered. Emiliano is talking and able to eat now."

"Thank the Gods United." Cesario drank some lukewarm water. "How close are we to Kalehala?"

"About five miles away—only five steps! But it is mountainous and rocky for miles. It isn't safe to use the boots."

"No great loss. After yesterday, I would be happy to never use them again." Cesario tried to watch his best friend's face. "You need to go on, Aurelio. You already know it, but you do not want to leave us."

"I need to get you all to Kalehala safely," Aurelio protested.

"No." Cesario shook his head, lowering his voice. "It is not your responsibility to take care of us. You should go on ahead. Take Victoriano and Epifanio—they are level-headed and good with their weapons. The rest of us can stay here until you come back with help."

"I imagined you helping me speak with the elves in Kalehala. Without you. . . Cesario, we can wait another day. If you are better tomorrow, you can come with us."

Cesario chose not to argue. "Is anyone scouting for shelter?"

"Yes, Noelio and Epifanio. Can you walk?"

"Yes. My body is fine. Well. . ." Cesario moved his sore legs and stretched his arms, feeling soreness along his ribs as well. "I feel like I ran several miles instead of seventy steps."

"Would you like to try some dried meat?"

"No, thank you. The dried fruit and nuts taste excellent this morning."

"More so than yesterday or the fifty-seven days before that?" Aurelio asked, chuckling.

"Yes, indeed." Cesario nodded carefully. The two friends laughed.

Overhearing, Cleofas said, "Then I'll try some fruit and nuts from Cesario's pack, because mine taste worse than yesterday!"

The boys passed Cesario's pack around, offering their opinions on the fare and Cesario's sense of taste.

"Well, the water won't taste better than it does right now, lads. Drink up!" Aurelio took a long swig from his own canteen. "Rest your eyes now, Cesario."

Cesario promptly followed Aurelio's advice, lying down. Two full days of sleep might be necessary to recover from their marathon trek across the wastelands.

A DROP OF SWEAT rolling onto Cesario's neck woke him. He automatically reached for his canteen and watered down his face. Someone had arranged a blanket into a makeshift canopy to shield him from the sun.

He wet his hat and fanned himself while sitting up. He gave his eyes a moment to adjust. Still too many spots.

"Hey, Cesario. Any better?" Aurelio asked, immediately at his side.

"The same as this morning."

"We found a small cave about a mile away. It's about four hours until nightfall, so in a few hours, we'll walk there. Until then, we can all rest. Are you hungry?"

Cesario allowed Aurelio to fuss over him. "Have you thought about what I said?" he asked quietly.

"Yes. I still want to wait until the morning. Your eyes could be better by then."

"How high is that mountain range?" Cesario sipped water.

"Not as high as the Majesties."

"But?" Cesario could hear that Aurelio withheld information.

Aurelio chuckled. "I can't hide anything from you!" He drank some water, pouring some over his hat. "The range is nothing but rock, and we don't have ropes. We'll have to be very careful."

"You know, I never climbed Old Cedar." Cesario recalled his many attempts to scale the magnificent tree near their village. "I always got too dizzy." He tried meeting his friend's eyes. "It's the height. I-I'm not a climber."

Aurelio was quiet.

"We'll be fine—we have food, water, shelter. We will be safe." Cesario patted his satchel. "Look through this—see if there is anything you can use."

Sighing, Aurelio opened the satchel and began sorting through the contents.

Cesario felt drowsy in the heat, and after drinking more water, he lay down to rest.

Aurelio's hand on his shoulder woke him.

"It's time. I've packed everything for you. Let me help you up." Aurelio pulled Cesario to his feet, starting a wave of dizziness.

Cesario gripped Aurelio's arm until it passed.

"I wish I didn't have to leave you here," Aurelio whispered, supporting Cesario's elbow. "But I'll be back, I promise."

Smiling, Cesario said, "I believe you."

Then Aurelio helped Cesario with his satchel. "I drew a map to Kalehala in your notebook, and I marked the cave where you'll stay on mine." He gripped Cesario's shoulder tightly. "I'll miss you, my friend."

For once, Cesario did not have words, and in the next moment, Aurelio left his side.

Cesario looked down, discovering that the gray and white spots obscured the ground. He felt around with his boot and discovered a palm-sized stone he would have tripped over. "I'm going to need someone's shoulder," he announced.

"You can use mine," Rogelio volunteered, stepping next to Cesario.

Aurelio lifted his voice to address all the young men. "Take care of each other, my friends, until we're together again." Then he swiftly turned on his heel, vanishing into the haze dominating Cesario's vision.

Epifanio and Victoriano followed Aurelio, disappearing as well, but he heard them calling their own goodbyes.

"May the Gods United protect you," Cleofas cried after them.

"Take care, my friends," Rogelio bellowed in his deep voice.

"May the Gods United protect us all," Cesario said softly.

"Let's go," Noelio instructed. "The cave is this way."

Cesario gripped Rogelio's shoulder, and they walked westerly towards the setting sun. Through the motes dancing across his vision, he saw a dark mass covering the entire horizon.

"Is all of that darkness against the sky the mountain range?" he asked Rogelio.

"Yes, it seems to divide the entire world!"

"How are they ever going to climb it?" Cesario muttered.

"They could use the boots. One step, and they would be over it."

"Aurelio said the terrain is mountainous for miles," Cesario commented.

"Oh. Well, perhaps, there is some path we cannot see from here. There are elves not too far away, right?"

"Interesting thought, Rogelio," Cesario said.

He continued thinking, while walking towards what he hoped would be a comfortable sanctuary for them until Aurelio returned. Or until they somehow found their own way to Kalehala. . .

Occasionally, Cesario looked up at the undefined darkness

looming above him, rising higher and higher in the increasingly fiery sky.

23

INTO THE EMPIRE

S HORTLY BEFORE DAWN, BELRINA lifted her face to a temperate breeze, relishing a quiet moment before the spectacle began. She stood on a platform leading to the karth that would take her to the Capitol, flanked by Lythk and Mathim. A privacy screen temporarily blocked her from the crowd's view.

Safe within the protective shield created by the seer's device, Belrina could hear Asthildi gathering. She breathed deeply. Lythk fueled their bond with a loving confidence, and Belrina imbibed it, achieving a tenuous serenity.

Overhead, delicate orbs of light were arranged in a canopy of silver strings. She admired their beauty to distract her from imagining all the mistakes she could make under the public gaze.

'The privacy screen will vanish on the count of three,' Lythk communicated telepathically. *'One, two, three.'*

Instantly, the excited buzz of hundreds of voices sounded in Belrina's ears, as the crowd responded to the sight of her. She was adorned with jewels, and Njal had spent an inordinate amount of time on her face and hair.

Many Asthildi smiled and waved, trying to catch her attention. Not wishing to offend anyone, Belrina forced a smile and nodded, trying to acknowledge every greeting. As she scanned the crowd, she observed some unsmiling faces. If they disapproved of her, why were they here? Belrina ignored them, genuinely smiling at those in the crowd who embraced her despite her background.

She observed that the most excited Asthildi faces belonged to apprentices, attendants, and those wearing plain robes. All of them, like her, had virtually no status in the Empire, and unlike powerful and affluent Asthildi, they did not cling tightly to reserve. Belrina smiled more broadly at their more natural display of emotion. In response, the crowd surged closer, growing louder. Belrina steeled herself from taking a step backwards.

Then the criermaster spoke, magically projecting his voice, and the crowd quieted. They looked expectantly at the slight Asthildi with a pristine platinum coiffure, wearing a heavily embroidered goldenrod tunic.

"Thank you. Good residents of Kalehala and welcome guests, we have gathered to witness Asthil Belrina, honored guest of the Seer of Kalehala, depart for the Capitol to meet Senator Primth."

Transporting to their designated spots on the platform, Silvermaster Bykin and Asthil Myrin appeared amid a swirl of magic, bowing to each other.

"The honor of escorting Asthil Belrina belongs to Silvermaster Bykin and Asthil Myrin, son of Jewelmaster Kirtyn and Kaolinmaster Theona," the criermaster narrated.

Belrina exchanged bows with her escorts. Asthil Myrin lingered in his bow, gazing at her before turning to the crowd, flourishing his scarlet cloak. He smiled and nodded, as if all present were his personal acquaintances.

In the last several days, Belrina had alternately evaded and rebuffed Asthil Myrin, but he wasn't dissuaded. The situation challenged Lythk's discipline, and Belrina worried someone would break social protocols. And now, they were going to share the confined space of the karth. . .

"At Senator Primth's behest, the company must leave immediately." The criermaster injected reverence into his words. Belrina marveled at his ability to mask his distaste for the ceremony's brevity. Until the last moment, he had tried persuading Seer A'zine to permit an interview with Belrina. "To speed Asthil Belrina on her way, the Seer of Kalehala will bless the company."

A silver nimbus appeared before Belrina, resolving into Seer A'zine on an invisible dais above them. She immediately swept into a deep bow in unison with the vaxili beside her, and then all present followed suit.

"Good morning to you all." Seer A'zine's melodious voice filled the air. "Please rise." Turning to Belrina, she smiled, beginning her blessing. "On this day, you embark on a long journey."

Belrina soaked up the magic energy, enjoying the seer's last loving touch.

"May the miles go swiftly and the days pass pleasantly," Seer A'zine intoned. "May your arrival be welcome wherever you go until you return home."

The criermaster led the applause, and Belrina's escorts began boarding the karth. The crowd resumed its enthusiastic waving, but she gazed at Seer A'zine.

'Be at peace, Belrina.' Seer A'zine spoke to her telepathically.

'I do not wish to leave your protection, Seer,' Belrina replied.

'You no longer need my protection, Belrina. You are more powerful than you know. If you ever need my aid, I will be with you .'

Belrina bowed deeply again, turning to board the karth—a matte metallic tube approximately a hundred feet long. Its seamless exterior concealed interior compartments.

Njal and Seeker Saolmyn were already aboard, along with Vaxili Amirtha, who was posing as a second attendant responsible for Belrina's wardrobe and styling needs. The rest of the security team would remain in Kalehala.

Belrina spared a thought for Vaxili Balin. Lythk had discovered that the vaxili had been telepathically manipulated recently, presumably by a Primth associate. Primth proved yet again that nothing was beyond his power—how could she evade succumbing to his will? Belrina breathed deeply to dislodge the fear in her belly, and she reached towards the sakitha bond, gratefully receiving the support her husband always supplied whenever she was afraid.

Lythk offered his arm, and she kept her hand lightly upon his. The seer had publicly acknowledged that Belrina faced a threat that only the magisthild could thwart, and they hoped the proclamation would help conceal their romantic attachment.

Mathim remained on the platform to watch the crowd as Belrina and Lythk walked towards the door elevated several feet above the glossy road by the karth's tall runners, which were fashioned from the same material as the road. Belrina recalled what now seemed long ago, Rakti Za explaining how roads and modes of transport allowed free travel across the Empire.

They entered the karth, finding themselves in what Belrina supposed to be the dining compartment. Asthil Myrin and Silvermaster Bykin had settled themselves on wide high-backed benches upholstered in a plush cream fabric. Dark faux wood tables separated pairs of these benches, which faced each other.

Large windows that had been invisible from the platform lined both sides of the compartment, promising unobstructed views of the imminent sunrise.

At one window, Vaxili Amirtha looked towards the Fortress of Knath. Nearby, Njal and Seeker Saolmyn were talking, and Belrina joined them.

Saolmyn, whose uncoiled blonde hair skimmed her shoulders, bowed, and Belrina returned her bow, signaling they were equals. Seeker Saolmyn's surprise showed in a slight widening of her gray eyes.

Belrina turned to watch Seer A'zine raise her hand, and as

she lowered it again, the karth moved forward, silently gliding on its runners. In a few moments, the Seer of Kalehala was gone from view.

As the karth gathered speed, Belrina centered herself to its magical flow, grounding herself. The others softly chanted an incantation to do the same.

The blur of the landscape quickly became disorienting, and Belrina turned to her travel companions, most of whom were looking at her.

Asthil Myrin readily broke the silence. "Friends, our journey begins very early. Let us breakfast together." He slid along his bench, patting the additional space beside him. "Asthil Belrina, please join me."

"Thank you, Asthil Myrin, but I shall help prepare our first meal." Following Njal's lead, Belrina attempted to make herself useful, learning how to use the various machines to process marine biological matter into liquid nourishment. Njal presented the first vials to Asthil Myrin and Silvermaster Bykin, both of whom remained seated.

Belrina and Vaxili Amirtha distributed vials to everyone else who came to claim them.

"Belrina, come, you must see the sunrise!" Njal exclaimed, beckoning from a table across from Myrin.

Belrina gratefully sat next to her friend. Lythk and Mathim quickly sat opposite them.

"So beautiful," Belrina said in truth. With her eyes on the blooming scarlet sky, she could ignore the eye-wrenching blur of the landscape.

Once everyone took their seats, Bykin raised his vial, and they all did the same. "From Kalehala to the Capitol, I welcome you to journey with me."

The company repeated the statement in unison before sipping their vials. After copious amounts of flavor additives, the concoction was palatable. Belrina sipped her vial, listening to the polite conversation around her.

All too soon, Seeker Saolmyn and Njal excused themselves to settle into their quarters. After a look from Mathim, Amirtha exited with them, bowing briefly to the group.

The sun was now properly in the sky, heating Kalehala to unbearable temperatures. By midafternoon, they would pass into the next district, traveling nearly a thousand miles. Three districts away, the Senatorial City of Knath, called Halith, was known for its astronomical observatory.

"May I ask, Asthil Belrina, what is causing you to smile?" Asthil Myrin approached her table.

Belrina turned away from the window. "I was thinking of the observatory at Halith. Studying the stars seems a peaceful pursuit."

"May I sit?" Myrin gestured to the seat abdicated by Njal.

"I should rest before my lesson with Seeker Saolmyn," Belrina rose, bowing. Lythk and Mathim were swiftly on their feet.

"Please allow me to escort you," Myrin smoothly offered.

"Asthil Belrina has an escort," Lythk said, offering his arm to Belrina.

Accepting, Belrina observed Silvermaster Bykin watching them.

"Ah." Myrin's face was blank. "Magisthild Lythk, I did not hear your offer." He did not step aside.

Belrina tried to soothe the anger flaring in the sakitha bond. "Please excuse me, Asthil Myrin. I am eager to retire."

Myrin bowed slightly, his hazel eyes flashing as he permitted them to pass.

Belrina retreated to her sleeping compartment, shared with Lythk and Mathim, grateful for a respite from Myrin. All female Asthildi would sleep in the adjacent compartment, providing a buffer from Myrin that Belrina feared would not exist during the day.

AS EXPECTED, AFTER BELRINA completed her lesson with the seeker, Myrin joined her in the leisure compartment, which was mostly empty, permitting room to exercise. She stood near a large window, observing the arid terrain in the distance. Flat-topped rises dotted with yellow scrub had replaced the craggy ridges of Kalehala.

A few feet away, Lythk sat on a bench near the only table in the compartment, drafting another missive to Senator Primth. He did so several times a day.

When Myrin entered, he gazed at Belrina unblinkingly. "Good afternoon, Asthil Belrina."

"Afternoon." Belrina returned to the window.

Chanting, Myrin positioned a bench so he could sit and watch her. Mathim rose to look out a window a few feet from Myrin, adopting the wide-legged vaxili stance.

"How does this compare to the lands of the Forest People, Asthil Belrina?" Myrin asked, ignoring Vaxili Mathim.

Belrina glanced at Myrin. "There is no comparison. There is so little that is green here and so little that is yellow there, besides daisies or squash."

"What are daisies?" Myrin tried the foreign word.

"Wildflowers that like the sun," Belrina explained.

"I have not seen a flower. Can you show me what a daisy looks like?"

"You have never seen a flower?" Belrina turned, facing Myrin. Thinking quickly, she plucked a hair ornament from the coif fashioned by Njal. She held it before her, imagining a single yellow daisy in its place, and it quickly grew into being.

Soon, she twirled the stem in her fingers, the petals whirling in a yellow blur.

"Amazing!" Silvermaster Bykin exclaimed from the doorway.

"May I?" Asthil Myrin asked, standing up.

Belrina cautiously approached Myrin, holding out the daisy. Smiling, Myrin quickly closed the distance between them, folding his hands over hers.

The sakitha bond simmered with Lythk's irritation.

Myrin tilted the daisy towards his face. "Incredible. There is even a slight fragrance."

"Please keep it." Belrina hoped he would take the daisy and his hands away from her.

"What a splendid gift!" Myrin squeezed her hands before delicately grasping the flower's stem. Belrina relinquished the daisy and quickly retreated.

"I came to work, but I can return later." Silvermaster Bykin carried a faux leather case under his arm.

Lythk rose. "The table is yours, Silvermaster," he said.

"Thank you, Magisthild." Bykin merrily set his materials on the table.

"May I observe you, Silvermaster?" Belrina wondered what he would be fashioning.

"Of course! I am delighted by your interest, Asthil Belrina." Bykin smiled. "I am always happy to share what I believe to be the greatest pleasure in life—creating art!"

"Pardon, Silvermaster, but I can think of many pleasures in life greater than art," Myrin said, staring at Belrina. She quickly looked away, feeling Lythk's body tense.

"I assume you refer to transitory things, young Myrin," the silvermaster replied, holding a silver necklace in his hands. "The joy of creation is enduring." He handed the necklace to Belrina.

Belrina stretched the necklace between her hands, admiring the delicate, complex pattern. "This is lovely, Silvermaster!"

"Thank you, Asthil Belrina. Your own artistry was very impressive." He opened a satchel holding unformed silver pieces. "Would you like to learn how to work the silver?"

Belrina returned the snowflake-like necklace to the silvermaster. "I would love to learn." She did not restrain her enthusiasm. "The activity will be very welcome on this journey."

Silvermaster Bykin smiled. "That was my thought as well." With an incantation, he activated a device that displayed a three-dimensional design for a silver ring midair.

"Please excuse me, my friends." Asthil Myrin bowed to Belrina. "I am not in the mood for work of any kind."

"Yes, of course, Asthil Myrin," she said, studying the magical projection.

"Farewell, Myrin," Bykin said, sparing the young Asthildi a glance. Then he chanted a word, and the image began rotating.

Myrin watched them for a few moments from the doorway before exiting.

"I had this device commissioned recently. Before, I used magic parchment for my sketches, but this device will not deplete our magic reservoirs," Bykin said, watching Belrina.

"Magic reservoirs are being depleted?" she asked.

"Yes. Vast amounts of magic are used for luxuries enjoyed in the Capitol, depleting the reservoirs faster than magical dissipations can restore them."

"Thank you for this information." Belrina considered, thinking of the daisy she had impulsively created. "I can be more responsible when using magic. I should release any material transmutation, shouldn't I?"

Silvermaster Bykin smiled. "I think that would be helpful, Belrina. Now, you see this point here?" He gestured to a spot on the projection, happily lecturing for some time.

Later, Njal assisted Belrina with dressing for dinner, choosing a plain dark gown and opting for no jewelry.

"Njal, you always know what suits me. What would I do without you?" Belrina held out her arm to Njal. "Shall we go to dinner together?"

Smiling, Njal, wearing the navy blue of a personal attendant, accepted Belrina's escort. They arrived at the dining compartment, closely trailed by Lythk and Mathim, finding Asthil Myrin alone, standing in wait.

The young Asthildi bowed deeply. "Good evening, Asthil Belrina. Please, would you allow me to join your table?" He wore the daisy on his tunic as if it were a jewel.

Belrina reluctantly released Njal's arm to return his bow. "Asthil Myrin, good evening." She could not think of a polite refusal. "Yes, you may."

She sat on a bench, and Lythk claimed the seat next to her. Mathim quickly sat across from her, leaving Myrin to sit in front of Lythk.

'I am disappointed, Belrina.' Myrin's voice sounded in her mind. He shared his injured feelings. Belrina sensed a foreign, unpleasant mental landscape; she insulated her mind from his influence, adopting the psychic position of denial.

'You violate protocols, Asthil Myrin. I did not give you permission to communicate with me telepathically.' Belrina gave him a healthy dose of her disapproval.

'I will not apologize. From the moment I first saw your face, I have been able to think of nothing else but you. I want you. I need you.'

Belrina felt his attempt at telepathic manipulation, which she swiftly deflected. *'I will never love you. You need to stop.'* She closed the telepathic link before she eradicated his amorous feelings without his consent. It would be so easy to do, but that was not a lawful solution.

Myrin rubbed his temples. "I have a sudden headache. Please excuse me." But he did not stand.

"Asthil Myrin, you do not appear to be well," Belrina said politely. She had avoided harming him telepathically, but he did appear distressed. "Do you need a medicinal draught?"

"Yes, thank you. I think that should do." Myrin stared first at Lythk and then at Mathim. Accepting the vial quickly offered by Njal, Myrin downed its contents in a gulp and then rose. "I shall retire early. Good evening to you all."

After a moment, Njal took his seat. "Belrina, what happened?" she whispered when the four of them were alone.

"He forced a telepathic link with me, and I told him I would never love him." Belrina's voice was quiet.

Njal folded her arms over her chest. "I hope he will stop pestering you now."

"That would be a relief," Mathim agreed.

With Lythk, Belrina communicated, *'He may have sensed that I love someone else. We need to be very careful.'*

'Always,' was her husband's brief reply.

Although Lythk did not seem perturbed by the potential exposure of their relationship, Belrina felt a sliver of unease enter her soul, like a splinter of wood under her skin, and she had no means to remove it.

The next day, they passed the Senatorial City of Halith, traversing the space occupied by five million residents in a few seconds. Leagues away, Belrina could see the domed ceiling of the observatory, crafted from clear glass, topping a dark circular edifice, which approximated the night sky. Its windows were glittering portholes arranged in the shape of constellations. A few of them were familiar, reminding her that the vast sky above her now also encircled her homeland.

Now in territory populated by the uppermost echelon of the elite, correspondence began arriving, filling the air with incessant chimes. Sounding through the night, they caused general consternation until Seeker Saolmyn devised a way to silence them. Bykin spent his days answering the elites' missives, preventing further silversmithing lessons with Belrina.

Lythk and Mathim took turns reading Belrina any letter addressed directly to her, helping her learn the Elvish script. She feared it would take years to develop an accurate spell for instantaneous written translations.

Asthil Myrin, who now behaved courteously, displayed an impressive knowledge of the local politicians and noble families, which Belrina appreciated. Occasionally, his hazel eyes were not as respectful as his conduct, and Belrina knew Lythk observed every instance, drawing that sliver of unease deeper.

On the third evening after departing Kalehala, Belrina activated the seer's transmitter in her sleeping compartment, impatient to speak with Seer A'zine within a privacy screen. Lythk stood in front of the door while Mathim sat on his cot.

"Good evening, Belrina. Though it is closer to morning here." Seer A'zine's voice floated through the air.

"Then good morning to you, Seer. I apologize for disturbing your sleep."

"These are no days for rest, Belrina."

"Seer, the correspondence I receive can be informative. Today, I learned that Senator Primth is implying to criers that he and I are friends. He is seen as an authority on my thoughts and feelings!"

"If you do not tell your story yourself, you risk others telling it for you," the seer responded.

"What are you advising, Seer?" Belrina asked.

"You should attract the criers' attention," Seer A'zine replied, and then she addressed both Lythk and Mathim. "Vaxili, we should let the public see Belrina."

"Seer, it is not safe," Lythk objected. "Kalehala gave us Myrin. In a senatorial city, there could be a thousand Myrins, and one or two would have powerful resources."

"I am confident you all can design a safe event to gain Belrina publicity. Belrina, what are your thoughts?"

"I defer to Magisthild and Mathim on safety." Belrina paused. "But I do not want the senator to speak for me."

"Then I expect to see a public appearance from you soon." It sounded as though Seer A'zine smiled.

A delicate chime sounded at the door.

"Seer, we must terminate our call," Lythk interjected. "We will share the details of any plan later." He looked at Mathim, and Belrina foresaw a long discussion between the two.

"Farewell, Seer," Belrina said, deactivating the transmitter and eliminating the privacy screen.

Lythk answered the door, receiving a bow from Njal.

"My apologies for the interruption, Magisthild. Silvermaster Bykin summons Belrina for an urgent matter. He is in the leisure compartment."

"Thank you, Njal," Belrina said, as she and her vaxili escorts swept by her friend. She soon was bowing to the silvermaster.

"Good evening all." Bykin handed her a magic parchment. "Please read for yourself."

"Thank you, Silvermaster." Belrina gave it to Lythk.

"'Greetings, Asthil Belrina,'" he read aloud. "'I would be deeply honored to provide you hospitality while your karth is serviced at Pylena. Please allow me to provide your entire company with suitable refreshment after your long journey. If you wish, my attendants will complete all services required by your karth. I look forward to meeting you at the station. Mnetha, Senator of Lynthia.'"

"Senator Mnetha has preempted all my usual reasons for denying invitations. We must stop in Pylena for at least five minutes for the karth runners to be refreshed. Thus, she does not propose violating Senator Primth's directive," Bykin explained.

Lythk began pacing the length of the compartment.

Belrina came to peer at the map documenting their journey, which adorned a wall. "How long before we are in Pylena?"

Bykin answered, "Day after tomorrow."

'What is known about Senator Mnetha?' Belrina asked Lythk telepathically.

'She is part of an alliance of outlying prefectures against Senator Primth and his council,' Lythk responded. *'Offering her attendants to service the karth is unusual. We should refuse—I'll confer with Vaxili Mathim.'*

"How large a gathering do you suppose this might be?" Belrina asked aloud, holding on to her Asthildi mask of composure. She could not conceive of a way to reject this senator's offer. Once again, the Asthildi custom of deferring to those in power operated to constrain her.

"I think Senator Mnetha will keep this an exclusive affair," Bykin began. "Perhaps only her and her son—"

"Yalin, who has searched for a partner to continue their genetic line for over a century. No one seems to meet his approval," Asthil Myrin interjected. "Pardon my intrusion. I walked this way for some exercise." He bowed to Belrina. "Are we going to meet Senator Mnetha and Yalin?"

Belrina looked at Lythk and then Mathim, but they had no solutions. "It would appear so, Asthil Myrin. Do you have any instructions, Magisthild?"

"Silvermaster, please refuse Senator Mnetha's offer to lend us her attendants," Lythk said. "The Seer of Kalehala has already made all arrangements."

"Thank you, Silvermaster Bykin, for all your work." Belrina offered him her hand. "I hope you do not regret journeying with me for I am grateful you are here."

"It is my pleasure, Belrina." Bykin beamed.

"If you both would excuse me, I would like to retire now." Belrina bowed first to Bykin and then Myrin. "Good evening." She waited for their corresponding pleasantries before heading to her compartment on Mathim's arm, as it was his turn to escort her.

Lythk trailed close behind them, and Belrina initiated a telepathic link with him. *'What do you suppose this Senator Mnetha wants?'*

'She wants to use you. Like Primth, she wants to leverage the media attention you are receiving to support her own interests.'

'Is it possible to stop them from using me?'

'Yes. Become more powerful than them.'

Belrina's profound bewilderment must have flooded the sakitha bond. Only seers outranked senators. Before she could further inquire into her husband's statement, she was at the door to her compartment.

In private, they had a long discussion with Mathim, identifying the safest event that might generate positive publicity.

When Belrina finally rested her head on a pillow, circulating thoughts kept her awake. So much was out of her control. And so much was unknown about what the senators wanted from her.

'Sleep, Belrina,' Lythk sent telepathically, flooding the sakitha bond with love.

Belrina turned on her side to face him. Tenderness arose in their bond as palpable as if he were caressing her face. In the quiet, they breathed together, and the tranquility of her husband's heartbeat eventually lulled her into the temporary respite of slumber, releasing her mind from its preoccupations. . . until she woke.

24

THE CLIMB

T HE SPINY MOUNTAIN RANGE extended for miles, a solid wall of rock blocking the way to Kalehala. Aurelio and his friends inspected the towering crags for the best place to start their ascent, and after hiking along the base of the mountain for the better part of an hour, it was apparent the rock face consistently offered footholds and ledges. If they had ropes, the climb would be straightforward.

Aurelio stopped in a shady section, watering his face and hands. He removed his hat and placed it in his satchel. Epifanio and Victoriano calmly did the same.

"We may as well begin here." Aurelio pointed up and slightly to the right. "That ledge there is our first goal."

"Let me go first," Epifanio volunteered, and he quickly started climbing. His running sandals gave his feet flexibility, but no protection from the rough rock.

Aurelio watched Epifanio ascend for a dozen feet before following. His hands easily found jagged rocks to grasp.

"Ay!" Epifanio yelped, shaking a hand down at his side.

"What is it?"

"These rocks are hot enough to bake bread on!"

"Can you go on?" Aurelio called to his friend.

"Yes, it was just a surprise, that's all." Epifanio continued to climb, angling towards the ledge. "More shade to the right," he called down.

Aurelio concentrated on getting firm footholds once he emerged from the shade. Soon, it felt like his head was hotter than the rocks under his fingertips. He was going to need a lengthy rest on the ledge that Epifanio was just crawling onto now.

Less than ten feet from the ledge, Aurelio could not find stable footholds. He could go to the left and then try to angle down again, but he opted to rely mostly on the strength of his hands, finding the quickest way to join his friend.

Epifanio offered him a hand, and after scrambling onto the ledge, Aurelio promptly sat down, breathing hard. He watered his head before drinking.

Looking down, Aurelio observed Victoriano's nimble ascent.

"Victoriano is always so graceful, isn't he?" Epifanio said with a laugh.

"You both are better climbers than me," Aurelio replied haltingly, still struggling to catch his breath. He got out his hat, watered it and used it as a fan. "Thank the Gods United, we finally found some shade in this wasteland."

As Victoriano joined them, Aurelio looked back over the desert towards Cesario's camp. He flexed his fingers, ignoring the scraped and sunburnt skin, then he blinked.

Bolting upright on his perch, he pointed to a white spot in the endless blue sky. "A kite!" he exclaimed.

Epifanio looked at him a bit worriedly before turning his gaze to where Aurelio pointed. It was unmistakably a large, tattered kite.

"Cesario?" Epifanio questioned.

"What is he doing?" Victoriano asked.

"He's trying to tell us something." Aurelio considered. "Something he thinks will help us reach Kalehala."

"Well, a kite isn't going to help with climbing the mountain. So how else can it be helpful?" Epifanio queried.

"Because a kite can be seen for miles, it can be used as a signal," Victoriano replied.

"I think he is telling us we can use a kite to attract the elves' attention," Aurelio said slowly. "If they see something unusual, they will probably investigate."

"Will they help us?" Victoriano asked.

Aurelio shook his head. "I don't know. Maybe we can strike another bargain?"

Epifanio looked upwards, shielding his eyes against the sun with his hand. "It is dangerous to climb this mountain, and it may be dangerous to signal the elves."

"Our lives are in the hands of the Gods United," Victoriano murmured.

"Aye." Aurelio started searching through his satchel. "What do we have to create a kite?"

"I have kindling sticks," Victoriano replied.

"I have twine." Aurelio had taken it from Cesario's satchel. *Thank you, Cesario!* he thought.

"I have an extra shirt. It's yellow," Epifanio added.

"This might work! We have the room to work here. Let's make the kite and then climb higher." Aurelio's days as an apprentice to Master Silvio seemed so long ago, but his hands remembered the principles of construction.

"Epifanio, will you carry Victoriano's satchel so he can take the kite?" Aurelio looked at his friend. "You are a stronger climber than me. I wish I could help, but the Old Ones' magic prevents us from splitting the contents of his satchel."

"Don't worry about it. Did I ever tell you about the time our ox was sick? I pulled the plow, and Papa said I did a better job of it."

"You told me," Victoriano responded. "And I didn't believe you the first time."

"What?" Epifanio slapped his beefy chest and thighs. "Look at this muscle. How could you doubt it?"

Aurelio laughed weakly, shaking his head. *Where would I be without my friends?*

When their laughter died down, the three of them scouted the best route upwards from their current perch. After more refueling and watering, Aurelio lashed the kite to Victoriano's back with a bit of rope, and Epifanio again led them up the cliff, aiming for what appeared to be a long, narrow ledge.

Now they were high enough to feel the wind. At first, it was refreshing, but the stronger gusts soon became distracting, bouncing Aurelio's satchel on his back or setting his shirt to sail. He began worrying for Victoriano, muttering prayers.

This was a longer climb, and Aurelio's arms protested their overuse. *Merciful be the Gods United*, he thought once Epifanio had a firm grasp on him. The ledge was wide enough to sit upon, if you didn't mind your legs dangling over the edge. Aurelio kept to his feet, grasping the rock against his back as he watched Victoriano. He shook his arms, easing his muscles.

Victoriano had to hold himself flat against the mountain, waiting for the stronger gusts of wind, which set the kite sailing, to pass.

"I didn't think about the wind." Aurelio shook his head, berating himself. "He's lighter than both of us, so he'll feel the gusts more."

"He'll get it here safely," Epifanio said confidently, but he watched Victoriano's ascent as intently as Aurelio.

After several more minutes of silent prayer, Aurelio was helping Victoriano onto the ledge. "Good work, Victoriano!" He held on to his friend's forearms in gratitude.

"This mountain is as easy to climb as a tree!" Victoriano boasted with a smile.

"Not for me," Aurelio replied. Abrasions smarted on his hands and feet, and his fingertips were sore from gripping rocky handholds. He looked across the mountain range, estimating they had traversed perhaps a tenth of the height. "The wind will only get stronger the higher we go." Aurelio tested his arms. "I'm good for one more climb today—after a bit of a rest."

"Hey! There's something up there. It looks like the elves have carved some symbols into the side of the mountain,"

Epifanio announced. "Maybe there's a path the stone carvers used to get up there?"

Aurelio squinted, seeing a large, flat rock, perhaps one hundred feet above them and five hundred feet to the east. "I can't see any symbols, but it looks like a good place to shelter for the night." He drank water, running an unsteady hand through his hair.

"Why don't I go first? I'll stop at the first shelter I see." Epifanio continued peering at what he said were symbols.

"Take a good rest first," Aurelio insisted.

In a few minutes, Epifanio announced he was ready, and he set off. Aurelio marveled at how easily he climbed, oblivious to the sharp rocks and the certain death awaiting any fall. Aurelio shook the alarming thought out of his head.

Belrina was on the other side of this pile of rocks, and they were going to see her again. Aurelio could not afford to doubt. Not here.

"Can you see any symbols?" he asked Victoriano.

"I can't be sure. But you know how sharp Epifanio's eyes are."

Aurelio ate some dried meat and nuts while silently urging Epifanio forward. His friend passed above the smooth rocks, and then he bucked off the side of the mountain, dropping.

"What!" Aurelio gasped.

In the next instant, Epifanio was on his feet, excitedly waving his hat back and forth.

"It must be an enormous ledge. Are you ready to go? I can lead," Victoriano offered.

Aurelio drank some more water and settled his satchel a bit more comfortably. "Let's go," he said confidently to Victoriano, but he prayed desperately for more strength.

As Victoriano climbed, Aurelio noted the rocks he used, fixing those spots in his mind, willing his tired arms and legs towards those points on the rocky cliff. Periodically, Victoriano paused, waiting for the wind beleaguering them to subside. Aurelio relished those moments, breathing as much air into his tired body as he could. The air had not yet thinned, as it did in the snowy mountains back home.

Aurelio did not track his progress. He just followed Victoriano, rock after rock. After several minutes of climbing without stopping on account of the wind, Aurelio wanted a respite, but he didn't dare lose sight of his nimble friend and the handholds he could so easily find.

He willed himself upwards, clinging to the mountain with his battered hands. *I will see Belrina again!* he told himself, using every fiber of his muscles to get closer to her.

After several more minutes, Aurelio saw a large projection of rocks extending from the side of the mountain. It must be the bottom of the ledge found by Epifanio. Hope fueled his tired muscles as he climbed towards his refuge for the night. He saw Victoriano's hand on the ledge, and Aurelio gathered what remained of his strength, propelling himself upwards with quivering arms and legs.

Soon, he saw Epifanio holding out his hand. Aurelio carefully accepted his friend's help, inelegantly scrambling onto the flat surface, which was polished smooth. Aurelio lay on his stomach for a few minutes, catching his breath.

Epifanio removed the kite from Victoriano's back, and he knelt by Aurelio. "It will be difficult to fly the kite in this wind because the twine isn't strong. It might be impossible further up," he opined.

Aurelio sat up slowly, looking up the mountainside. He thought he could see a piece of the sky on the other side of the range, so far away. "Will it rise over the crest?"

Epifanio examined the spindle, judging the length of twine. "One way to find out," he said.

"Aye, go ahead, Epifanio." Aurelio did not feel like standing just yet. He said a prayer as his friends launched the kite, knowing they would need the help of the Gods United.

Epifanio let the spindle twirl and the yellow kite quickly

shot up into the sky.

"Careful!" Victoriano grabbed the kite's string at the expense of his hands, helping Epifanio regain control over the spindle.

Shuddering violently in the wind, their makeshift kite reached only thirty to forty feet above their heads. As his friends battled with the spindle, the kite rose to fifty feet, then sixty. Wind battered at the fabric of the kite, straining twine and wood, and the crest of the range was hundreds of feet above. Seventy feet. Seventy-five.

"Let it go," Aurelio said calmly.

Victoriano released the kite string.

"Aurelio? Are you certain?" Epifanio asked, clutching the spindle as the wind jerked it in his hands.

"Let it fly, Epifanio. It's the only way the elves might see it on the other side."

Epifanio stopped battling the wind, and the twine quickly freed itself from the spindle.

The three young men watched their unharnessed yellow kite ride the wind upwards. In silence, they watched it soar and zigzag its way across the blue sky.

Aurelio said another prayer and a gust of wind propelled their kite to the mountaintop. The distant yellow speck soon vanished—on the other side!

Epifanio let out a joyful whoop.

"We did it!" Victoriano smiled as Epifanio embraced him. Then Epifanio pulled Aurelio to his feet, clapping him on the back.

"The elves will see it for sure," Epifanio shouted excitedly.

"Aye, if they have eyes as sharp as yours," Aurelio said, laughing. Now that he was on his feet, he explored the elven structure on which they stood. The elves had shaped the rocky ledge into a perfectly symmetrical semi-circle upon which fifty people could easily camp.

Victoriano was studying several arched openings in the

rock's face, which held small cubes or cylinders. Large, but worn, etchings curved overhead. Thank the Gods United Epifanio had seen those symbols.

Aurelio joined Victoriano, who cautiously touched a finger to a pearlescent pyramid.

"*Zylth et malith? Zylth et malith?*" a musical voice demanded.

Spinning, Aurelio saw two elves, wearing long light-green cloaks covering everything but their colored eyes.

Aurelio bowed stiffly, remembering the Old Ones had liked that.

"My name is Aurelio, and these are my friends, Victoriano and Epifanio." He motioned for his friends to join him. They did so haltingly, and the more muscular elf reached Aurelio first, pushing him down and gripping his hair.

"Stop!" Epifanio's shout was louder than Victoriano's.

"Do not resist!" Aurelio instructed his friends. They might not survive a direct confrontation with these militant elves. "We mean no harm," he directed towards the elf above him, wincing as the grip tightened. "We are searching for our friend, Belrina."

The other elf intoned a word, immobilizing Aurelio. Unable to see or speak to his friends, he breathed as evenly as possible, straining to hear either Epifanio or Victoriano. Judging from the silence, they were being held by the magic, too.

Aurelio's mind worked furiously, unable to fathom how to soothe the aggressive elves.

The one holding Aurelio released his grip and stepped away, leaving Aurelio with a tender scalp.

The two elves ignored the Forest People while they had a lengthy discussion. Then the one who had assaulted Aurelio vanished. It was frightening to see magic for the first time, and Aurelio could do nothing to console his friends.

The remaining elf inspected them coolly with crystalline blue eyes. He walked around Epifanio twice, then stood in front of Aurelio, who was still on his knees. He threw his robe back on both sides, freeing his arms before intoning another word.

Aurelio was suddenly free to move again, and he stood slowly, backing away from the elf. His friends immediately came to his side.

"I am fine," Aurelio assured them, grabbing their arms and drawing them away from the hostile elf.

Epifanio watched the Kalehala elf assessing them. "He is expecting us to fight."

"I think it is a 'she'," Victoriano commented.

"What?" Aurelio said in unison with Epifanio.

"The voice sounds feminine." Victoriano looked at the ground, keeping the elf in his peripheral vision.

Aurelio looked at the blue-eyed elf again, realizing Victoriano was right.

The elf said something in a ringing voice.

"Does she *want* to fight?" Epifanio asked, bewildered.

"Mistress Elf." Aurelio bowed again. "We will not break the peace. We only wish to see our friend, Belrina."

"Perhaps we should sit?" Victoriano suggested, keeping his eyes averted from the female elf.

Slowly, Aurelio did so, sitting with crossed legs and placing his hands carefully on his knees. His friends followed his lead.

The elf continued to watch them as if expecting an attack.

"Were the Old Ones like this?" Epifanio asked quietly.

"Not at all. They spoke our language."

Suddenly, the elf hissed, and she marched straight to Aurelio's satchel, yanking it off him and removing the enchanted map. She rattled off a string of questions, which he could not understand, let alone answer.

Aurelio attempted a response. "Mistress Elf, the map was a gift to help us find Belrina. I should like it back, please." He looked down while raising his hand, palm open. He would need it to find Cesario's camp.

In response, the elf unleashed a string of chants, lifting Aurelio into the air by the shoulders. He churned his legs, straining to reach the ground again.

Epifanio rushed the elf while Victoriano ran towards Aurelio. Neither took more than a few strides before invisible blows rained down upon them. Then the angry elf immobilized them again, and she wasn't done. She launched Aurelio over the edge of the semi-circle, suspending him in the empty air. He palpated the pressure he felt on his shoulders, finding nothing to grasp.

"Please! Please, Mistress!" Aurelio screamed. "Don't let go!" His thundering heart flooded his body with blood, and the world became vivid. His friends' eyes, alive with emotion, loomed large.

Swallowing his screams, he focused on them, meeting their expressive gazes. "All the promises. . . I made. . . will you try to. . . honor them?"

The blue-eyed elf studied Aurelio's face as his feet dangled in the open air. She seemed to be expecting a greater commotion. Did she want him to beg for his life again? Defiance rose within him, and Aurelio resolved to oppose her in this small way, even though he couldn't prevent her from taking his life.

"The Gods United will welcome me home, Mistress Elf," he said calmly, although he didn't want to accept that fate. With every particle of his being, he lifted a silent plea to the heavens, asking his merciful gods to spare his life until he could see Belrina—and everyone he cared about—safe from harm. Then he filled himself with prayers for all his loved ones.

Finally, the elf chanted again, drawing Aurelio towards her. He sailed through the air until she seized his head with both hands.

'What are you?' a voice sounded in his head.

Aurelio stared into the elf's blue eyes, answering, "My name is Aurelio. I am a man who loves Belrina and the Gods United."

'What are Gods United?'

She understood him! Aurelio tried to explain who the gods and goddesses were, sending memories and feelings.

The elf pushed him away, rubbing at her temple. When she opened her eyes, Aurelio thought she seemed afraid of him.

Chanting, she pinned the young men against the mountainside with invisible tethers around their chests.

"Thank the Gods United you are safe now!" Epifanio cried, scrubbing the tears from his face.

Victoriano's wide eyes roved over Aurelio. "Are you truly unharmed?"

"The Gods United are merciful, my friends. We're all safe now," Aurelio said, keeping his unsteady voice low. He knew their safety wasn't guaranteed, but even Cesario couldn't engineer an escape without being able to converse with the elves.

For hours, their captor paced in front of them, glaring at any movement or sound. Occasionally, she massaged her temple, staring at Aurelio.

Shortly before sunset, Epifanio whispered, "Look to the right!"

A silvery object floated through the air, approaching from Kalehala. In disbelief, Aurelio watched the disc get larger until it hovered above them, stirring the air before quietly landing.

A section of the aircraft opened, becoming a ramp used by a tall, muscular elf, wearing the same light-green cloak as their guard. Several gold medallions were visible on his white tunic. Their captor took a knee, honoring the newcomer.

A second elf exited the aircraft, a frail, silver-haired female with a powerful aquamarine gaze. Aurelio nearly wept, remembering her from the Old One's vision. She knew Belrina! Their captor lunged more deeply for this venerable elf, touching the ground.

"*Kaminth,*" the silvery elf said in a sonorous voice.

Their guard rose and showed Aurelio's map to the latest arrivals.

The lady-elf addressed Aurelio and his friends, and a reedy voice repeated her words in their language. "Good evening. I am the Seer of Kalehala." She chanted a few untranslated words and a sparkling blue gem appeared on Aurelio's shirt. "Please tell us who you are and where you are from."

"Good evening. My name is Aurelio," he replied. An unnatural voice spoke the Elvish language, apparently translating his words for the elves. "These are my friends, Epifanio and Victoriano." He gestured as well as he could, still pinned to the side of the cliff. "We are from the same village as Belrina."

Aurelio did not know if they wished to hear more, but Cesario said information could be as valuable as bartering beads if used appropriately. "Do not use all your beads at once," his wise friend had cautioned.

"Please tell us how you came by this map?" the Seer of Kalehala inquired.

"There are those such as yourselves who live in our City and grant wishes if they are paid. They provided me with the map." Aurelio answered in as few words as he could.

"Please tell us why you asked for this map," the silvery elf asked next.

"I am in love with Belrina, and I needed it to find her." Aurelio could think of no other answer. "Seer of Kalehala, can you please tell me if Belrina is well? May I see her?"

The lady-elf smiled. "Magisthild Banyk, this appears to be a straightforward matter. I should like to take responsibility for these adventurous friends of Belrina. With your permission, I will safeguard the map. I will, of course, make these young ones available for further questioning should that be required."

The muscular elf bowed, and their blue-eyed captor gave the map to the Seer of Kalehala while bowing. After a few Elvish words, the two green-cloaked elves disappeared.

With a few chants, the silvery elf released the boys from the magical tethers. "Now, let's get you treated by our healers." She turned to board the flying contraption. "Please follow me."

"Great Seer," Aurelio said as he followed, his sandals sliding on the ramp, "we appreciate your kindness. If possible, I would accept your offer of healing, but not for myself. We have friends in the wasteland who need medical care."

She turned to look at Aurelio. "How many in all?"

"Five."

"I will happily provide hospitality for all of Belrina's friends." The silver-haired elf sat on a plush, wide seat that spanned the width of the contraption. A second built-in bench faced it. She patted the space next to her, and Aurelio sat. "On the way to Kalehala, you can tell me about your friends. And the other magical objects you carry."

When his friends took their seats across from him, Aurelio breathed easier.

"We did it, Aurelio," Epifanio whispered, shaking Aurelio's hand. "We're going to Kalehala!" He hugged Victoriano at his side, who grinned, nodding at Aurelio.

Aurelio smiled briefly before turning back to their rescuer. "Kind Seer, would you please first tell me about Belrina?" he inquired.

"Belrina is well. However, you cannot see her now, as she is no longer in Kalehala and no one knows when she will return."

"Where is she, Seer? Can I go to her?" Aurelio cried.

"She went far away. Young one, you must recover from this journey first before starting a new, more dangerous one."

Aurelio distantly heard his friends talking excitedly as the aircraft took to the sky. Small windows offered spectacular views of the mountain range lit by the fiery sunset.

He did not notice the tear rolling down his cheek until the silvery elf touched it. She said something softly in Elvish, translated as, "You truly love her."

Aurelio scrubbed his face. After all these days, all these miles, and he could only pray for Belrina's safety.

He had made a colossal error by requesting the Old Ones provide transportation to Kalehala rather than Belrina. Regardless, he had to honor the bargain or else he—and Cesario—would spend the rest of their lives serving those godless tricksters.

Aurelio gazed out a window, watching the luminous, impossible constructions of Kalehala grow closer, but he could not share his friends' wonderment.

Belrina was not there.

25

A DISPLAY OF ARTISTRY

NJAL SURVEYED THE RESULTS of her work, clapping her hands in delight. "You look so lovely, Belrina. Pylena is known for its warm spring breezes—this is perfect!"

After placing her feet in the delicate slippers, Belrina moved in the cream-colored gown, setting the flounces on the skirt afloat. If necessary, she could run and jump-kick, and her hair provided no distractions as it was swept up in a carefree coif. Her only jewelry was a slim platinum bracelet, a device allowing Lythk to transport her to what he called a "safe place."

Taking Njal's hand, Belrina said, "Thank you."

When she did not immediately release her friend's hand, Njal said, "You will do well, Belrina. You always do."

"Sweet Njal, I have never met a senator before." Belrina looked out the window, catching a glimpse of the bright sky. Senator Mnetha would have her own agenda, unlike the two young Asthildi she had met yesterday in an effort to attract the criers' attention. Mathim had engineered a malfunction in the karth's climate-control, prompting a stop outside a homestead, one of the few growing crops for the most affluent elite.

While the silvermaster attended to the problem, Belrina had announced that she wanted to experience the fresh air without a sun shield. With her three vaxili escorts, Belrina had enjoyed the beauty of the few blooming cherry trees, which two young ones were attempting to capture through magical sketches. Belrina had earnestly admired their work, and one elf began sketching her.

Belrina had then insisted his friend was a better subject, transforming the female Asthildi's simple dress into an elegant gown. Without magic, she had adorned the young one's blonde hair with cherry blossoms. Once the portrait was underway, Belrina had had to bid them farewell to continue her journey to the Capitol. Meeting these young ones had reminded Belrina that Asthildi were not wholly different from humans.

The karth stopped, signaling their arrival in Pylena where Senator Mnetha waited.

Drawing a deep breath, Belrina erected a protective shield—one of her own creation that would allow her to detect magic intrusions. After returning Njal's smile, she stepped into the corridor, continuing her breathing exercises. If she erred in protocol, she hoped Senator Mnetha would forgive her. Belrina shook the thought from her head. Lythk was correct—she should not aim to please Asthildi elite or at least not those who were seeking to manipulate her.

Trailing a single step behind her, Lythk and Mathim were loaded with magic devices, which could not protect her from Senator Mnetha's political influence. Through their sakitha bond, Belrina felt Lythk's persistent wariness.

Silvermaster Bykin and Asthil Myrin were already in the dining compartment, wearing fine tunics. Myrin appeared to be wearing every piece of jewelry he had brought from Kalehala.

"Good morning." Belrina bowed, ignoring Myrin's gaze. He wordlessly returned her bow, allowing his eyes to speak for him.

"Good morning to you," Bykin replied. He held out his arm, and after accepting it, Belrina peeked out the window.

She glimpsed the silken top of a crimson tent against the clear sky, and then the door to the karth opened, metal dissolving into empty air. Bykin escorted her into a sunny morning. Inadvertently, Belrina paused on the platform, staring at the cloud-ringed glistening towers in the distance, rising as high as the Majesties on slender stems.

She could feel Lythk close behind her. His heart beat evenly, reminding her that balance was the foundation for all self-defense. Belrina exhaled.

"Come, Belrina," Bykin urged softly, setting them in motion again.

As they ambled down the platform, Belrina noted that the station was empty of any other Asthildi except navy-wearing attendants. The senator had taken measures to ensure their meeting would be private.

Her eyes searched for Senator Mnetha in the crimson pavilion, finding a stately platinum-haired Asthildi in a flowing apricot gown. At her side was a tall silver-haired elf with violet eyes. He seemed only half-interested in Belrina's procession. In contrast, Senator Mnetha's bright blue eyes gathered in every detail about Belrina.

An enchantment was deflected by Belrina's protective shield, minutely diminishing its strength. Smiling, Belrina intuitively performed a spell that would reinforce her shield automatically whenever it suffered a blow.

At the end of the ramp, Belrina and her entourage bowed deeply.

"Please rise," came Senator Mnetha's rich voice.

Belrina did so, looking towards the senator.

"Senator Mnetha, I am Bykin, Master of the Silver Guild in the Prefecture of Knath. Please allow me to introduce Asthil Belrina, a guest of the Seer of Kalehala."

"Very pleased to meet you," Belrina inclined her head, and she felt another assault on her protective shield. The senator gave no sign she was using magic, so Belrina looked to her son, whose lips may have moved ever so slightly, although he appeared to be watching Bykin.

"And this is Magisthild Lythk of Kalehala, Asthil Myrin, son of Kalehala guildmasters, and Vaxili Mathim." Silvermaster Bykin finished his introductions.

"I am pleased to meet you all." Myrin smiled.

"Please allow me to introduce my son, Asthil Yalin." With a small flourish, Senator Mnetha gestured towards the violet-eyed youth.

"Pleased to meet you all," Yalin said, displaying perfect white teeth. He positioned his generous lips into a smile.

Belrina met Yalin's violet eyes as she bowed. He briefly stared back before finding one of his multiple finger rings more interesting.

"Please, let us enjoy some refreshment together. Come, Belrina." The senator retreated to a settee built for two.

Belrina sat as bidden, and when Lythk assumed a position behind her, she felt more confident knowing she had her impressive husband assiduously protecting her.

An attendant presented Belrina with an iced beverage in a silver goblet.

Before sipping, Belrina applied a cleansing spell she had learned from Seeker Saolmyn to the liquid. "The cucumber-lime punch is delicious," she said politely.

"Are you as fond of the culinary arts as you are of the traditional arts, Asthil Belrina?" Asthil Yalin asked. He remained standing, browsing the offerings of a small table laden with fruit.

Myrin and Bykin had taken separate seats facing the settee while Vaxili Mathim stood in the opposite corner from Yalin.

Puzzled by Yalin's comment, Belrina replied, "I am still discovering all the arts Asthildi have perfected." She realized she was being too formal. Leading with a smile, she added, "I am interested in learning as much as possible."

"It appears you have learned a great deal in a short amount of time, Asthil Belrina," the senator noted.

Belrina looked down at her lap, uncertain how to react to

the compliment. The telepathic translation spell only made it appear that she was fluent in Elvish. "Thank you, Senator Mnetha."

"Tell me, what do you most enjoy learning?" Senator Mnetha asked with a smile.

Belrina sipped her punch. "The magic of healing." She smiled at Mathim. "Lakri accomplish miracles."

"Ah, that is noble of you, Belrina," Senator Mnetha commented.

Thus far, Belrina did not detect any political maneuvers, but perhaps there were elements to their conversation she did not understand.

"Are you excited to meet Senator Primth?" Yalin asked, popping a grape into his mouth.

Belrina's heart leaped in alarm, but she held on to her composure. She watched Yalin's face as she said carefully, "Senator Primth honors me greatly."

Yalin did not seem pleased.

Belrina turned to Senator Mnetha. "Although I am very nervous, as I am not accustomed to meeting senators." She met Mnetha's direct gaze. "Please forgive me if I blunder." She did not wish to anger her, after all.

"Dear one," Senator Mnetha took Belrina's hand, and Belrina felt Lythk tense, "do not concern yourself with protocols. I only want to learn more about you. You have an interesting history."

"My story? It is nothing compared to the wonders accomplished every day in the Empire." Belrina spoke the truth as she saw it.

The attendant offered a silver bowl of chilled strawberries. Belrina helped herself, smiling in delight when their taste was as perfect as their color.

"These are wonderful!" Belrina exclaimed.

Asthil Myrin added his agreement. "The best I have ever eaten, Senator."

Belrina noticed several elves coming out of the karth. They must be done with their inspection. On impulse, Belrina turned to Senator Mnetha. "In return for such wonderful hospitality, what can I tell you about myself?" In truth, she was grateful not for the refreshments but for the senator's lack of a political agenda. It appeared she only had a mild curiosity about Belrina, like most other Asthildi in the Empire.

In the sakitha bond, she felt alarm from Lythk, and Belrina worried she had blundered. She would try to proceed cautiously.

Yalin answered before his mother. "Is it true you have the potential to be one of the greatest magicians of all time?"

Belrina blinked. "That is an extraordinary idea, but I do not know how it could be true. There is much I do not understand about magic."

Senator Mnetha responded, "I suspect you are too humble, Belrina. I should like to know more about your mother. Can you tell us what she looked like?"

Belrina looked down. "My mother, Erynanne, was very beautiful." She paused. "I cannot describe her with words, but perhaps I could illustrate. . ." Thinking of the young artists yesterday, Belrina stood, summoning a white linen napkin. She suspended it in the air, spreading it open in front of her like a canvas. She began drawing, not knowing exactly how, the lines of her mother's face.

Watching the image come together, Belrina lovingly added more and more magic energy, willing an accurate image of her mother to come to life. The napkin molded into a three-dimensional sculpture of her mother's face.

Drawing from the materials at hand—strawberries for her lips, bread for her chestnut hair—Belrina didn't stop the transmutation until a faithful likeness of a smiling Erynanne was visible for all.

In silence, everyone stared at Belrina and the image she had created. Eyes shining with tears, Belrina caressed her mother's cheek. She did not wish to destroy the image, but Belrina slowly let the magic dissipate to replenish the local reservoir.

As her mother's face faded, Belrina felt a tear on her own face.

Turning to Senator Mnetha and Yalin, Belrina bowed, unable to meet their eyes. "Please excuse me. Thank you for this lovely breakfast."

"Yes, of course, Belrina," the senator hastily replied. "Thank you for granting an audience. I hope we shall meet again." She rose from the settee.

Belrina waited for Bykin and Myrin to finish their farewells. Lythk stood a pace behind her, but he could not whisk her away.

Penetrating her discomfort, Belrina felt the weight of someone's gaze—Asthil Yalin. Alert, he no longer looked like an insolent youth. What did he want from her?

Finally, Bykin offered her his arm, and Belrina leaned on it.

"Asthil Belrina, you must be weary from travel," Bykin murmured to her. "We will have you settled back in your compartment in no time."

In response, she gripped his hand tighter for she did not trust her voice. Bykin patted Belrina's hand as they ascended the platform, closely followed by Lythk.

Njal was quickly at Belrina's side when she entered the dining compartment.

"I shall leave you to your attendant, Asthil Belrina." Bykin bowed.

Belrina nodded, and she gratefully departed with Njal, who quickly administered a soothing restorative. As the warm elixir spread throughout her body, easing tension, Belrina concentrated on her breathing. After several minutes, she regained her equilibrium, her sorrow for her mother's death returning to a deep, persistent ache.

The karth was at full speed now, reminding Belrina she was

now over halfway to the Capitol.

"Thank you, Njal. I should like to rest now," Belrina said, sitting on her cot.

"Yes, of course, Belrina." Looking at Lythk, Njal said, "Please allow her to rest." Then she bowed before departing.

Once they were alone, Belrina blurted, "I lost my composure. How badly did I blunder?"

Moving quietly, Lythk sat on the edge of his bed. Their knees were inches away from each other.

"On the contrary, Belrina, you did well. Your display of emotion may have earned their compassion. Overall, you maintained the conversation and proved you aren't an easy target by exhibiting your magical talent. Therefore, many will be dissuaded from attempting to enchant you."

"Do you think Senator Primth will be dissuaded?" Belrina asked hopefully.

After a moment, Lythk said, "I do not wish to alarm you, but the report of your magical prowess has undoubtedly reached Primth. He will be better prepared to ensnare you." Lythk reconsidered. "On second thought, Senator Primth does not accept failure. He likely was already preparing to use the full extent of his resources."

"And what chance do I stand against him?" Belrina whispered.

Lythk slid to his knees, embracing her. "You do not have to face him alone. I will always be with you."

The ferocity in their bond reminded Belrina of how Lythk dealt with Asthil Kaya. "I am so happy you will be by my side."

When Belrina's breathing matched her husband's, she commented, "I observed that Asthil Yalin disliked Senator Primth. Also, Senator Mnetha arranged the meeting, knowing she would incur Primth's ire. Do you think I can count on their support against him?"

He held her more closely. "They do not have the power to oppose him themselves." He stroked her hair. "Let's not entangle ourselves with politicians."

Belrina enjoyed her husband's embrace for a few more moments before asking, "Did you understand Yalin's question about my fondness for the traditional arts?"

"He was referring to your encounter with those two young artists yesterday." Lythk released her, sitting back on his bed. "The criers' glowing reports of that incident drowned out all other reports about you."

"And the culinary arts? That has to do with food, I believe?" Belrina partially recalled a lesson from Rakti Za.

"Yes, culinary artists create meals that are masterful in both taste and appearance," Lythk answered. "Your ability to identify the flavors in the punch impressed Yalin."

"I forget most Asthildi will not have tasted the fruits and vegetables I grew in my garden."

Lythk nodded.

There was a gentle chime at the door, and Lythk immediately answered it. "Silvermaster Bykin?" He stood aside to let the large elf in.

"I apologize for the intrusion, Asthil Belrina, Magisthild Lythk," Bykin began quietly. "Senator Mnetha entrusted me with a missive she wished to be read only by you, Belrina." He attempted to hand it to her, but Lythk interceded.

"Apologies, Silvermaster, but I must first determine whether there is a security threat." Lythk examined the small scroll. "How did you come by this?"

"The senator must have slipped it into my tunic pocket or arranged for one of her attendants to do so. There was a scroll wrapped around this one, asking me to convey it directly to Belrina." Bykin shifted his considerable weight onto his other foot, producing a larger scroll from his pocket. "There is also another matter."

Lythk nodded, closing his hand over Senator Mnetha's scroll.

"This is written by Hamyth, the leader of the Zealot society.

He describes their theory that Belrina is descended from an aristocratic bloodline previously believed extinct. A cartographer from this bloodline did not return from an expedition to the human realm. According to their prophecies, an elf from this bloodline is needed to, uh. . ." He looked down at the scroll to quote, "'Restore the balance between Asthildi and the natural world.'" He rolled up the scroll again. "I can leave this here for you both to read. It is quite lengthy." The silvermaster provided it to Lythk.

"There is no request for an audience? Or a reply?" Lythk inquired.

"No, Magisthild Lythk. As you know, the Zealots are, uh, peculiar. I think they say: 'what must be, will be.' With that belief, why would any meeting need to be requested?" Bykin shrugged his large shoulders. He turned towards Belrina. "I regret having intruded upon your privacy, Asthil Belrina. Please forgive me." He bowed as well as he could in the narrow space.

"No forgiveness is necessary, Silvermaster," Belrina responded, smiling to assure him of her sincerity.

When they were alone again, Belrina said, "I'm glad they chose Bykin to accompany us."

"Yes, he was a fortunate choice," Lythk agreed. "I detected nothing suspicious about Senator Mnetha's scroll." He gave it to her.

Belrina probed for any magic residue herself. "It does not seem magical at all. I think this is truly parchment." She opened it, struggling to read the tiny script. She tried reading aloud: "'Belrina, I am writing to you because you have earned my trust. I believe you will—'" Shaking her head, Belrina handed the scroll to her husband.

Lythk continued to read: "'—combat tyranny and injustice. Together, we can work for a more peaceful, fair world. We can protect you from Primth if you help us protect the world from him.'"

"That's it? She doesn't say how she can protect me? What is she asking me to do?" Belrina asked, perplexed.

"Belrina, there are many senators who oppose Primth, but all of them together haven't been able to thwart his control over our government. I doubt Mnetha can deliver on her promise to protect you." Lythk crossed his arms over his chest. "As I see it, they wish to use you to further their political campaigns. They probably hope you can sway public sentiment to support them."

"I wouldn't know how," she promptly replied. "Do you believe Senator Mnetha is working to achieve a more just and peaceful world?"

"If she opposes Senator Primth, she probably is."

"Then why shouldn't I help her? Even if she cannot help me?" Belrina asked.

Lythk blinked, and then their bond swelled with his love. "Your selflessness is noble," he said. "And rare in Asthildi culture. I would caution you against getting involved in politics. It is a complicated world—politicians are masters of deception and manipulation. If Mnetha wants to support you against Primth, she should do so without making you do her bidding first."

"Can I refuse her? I couldn't even deny her request for a meeting." She shook her head. "Perhaps the seer will have some insights when we speak with her later." Belrina gestured to the Zealots' scroll. "And would you read this? Do you think this theory can be true? If so, I have no family here," she said, smoothing her skirt over her knees.

"In my experience, Zealots rarely have proof to support their theories," Lythk replied before reading the Zealot missive to Belrina. When he finished, he said, "I think you need to be a Zealot to understand all of this."

Belrina smiled slightly. "I am relieved to hear you say that. I understood very little. Perhaps the seer will understand more? I will ask Saolmyn about the Zealots. She knows so much interesting history." Belrina released her hair from its coif. "I think I have time to rest before our lesson." She sighed into her pillow. "It is odd that I should feel the loss of family I never met."

Remaining on his bed, Lythk reached out to stroke Belrina's hair.

"The Zealots may be wrong," he said in a soft voice.

Belrina relaxed, marveling at how gentle her husband's powerful hands could be. She closed her eyes, but she no longer wished to sleep. A moment like this was too rare.

Smiling, she imagined the quiet life she wanted with her husband. After a few moments in the beautiful, insubstantial dream, Belrina had to release it from her mind. It was too painful to cherish what they couldn't experience as long as powerful elites governed their lives.

26

An Old Text

"How could the senator do this without my permission?" Belrina sat with the silvermaster in the dining compartment. "I do not want my mother's face to be part of a media campaign." She carefully folded her hands in her lap, forcing her body to remain relaxed. The love coursing through the sakitha bond helped ease some tension. She looked at her supportive husband. "Surely, this violates social protocols?"

The closer they came to the Capitol, the more correspondence the karth received, including missives for the silvermaster. From a guildmember residing in the Capitol, Bykin learned that Senator Mnetha had recorded Belrina's transmutation and converted it into a campaign, urging Asthildi to use magic responsibly. Belrina had inadvertently provided an ideal example of how to use magic without diminishing reservoirs.

Now the silvermaster gently explained, "Your meeting with the senator occurred in a public place. Anything occurring in public can be recorded. If someone used your image for profit, they would be required to share the profits with you, but this media campaign generates no revenue. I do not believe the senator violated any laws."

"Social protocols offer a different analysis, Silvermaster," Lythk replied. "It is unacceptable to use an Asthildi's image without advance permission."

Sensing the rest of the conversation should be held in private, Belrina rose gracefully. "Thank you, Silvermaster, for sharing this information with me." Bykin studied her closely. "It has given me a sudden desire to exercise."

Bykin stood. "My apologies if I caused any distress."

She held out her hand. "Truly, there is no need for you to apologize, Silvermaster. You are not the cause of my distress."

Silvermaster Bykin gratefully took her hand for a moment. They exchanged bows before Belrina exited, escorted by Mathim.

Once outside the leisure compartment, Mathim stationed himself at the door, permitting Belrina and Lythk to enter.

Erecting a privacy screen, Belrina said, "I do not understand why Senator Mnetha did this. She asked for my help." Belrina looked down, noticing she was in vaxili garb. "Now, I do not trust her. It does not make sense, Lythk." She turned to look at her lovely husband.

"I cannot guess at her motivations, but she would not have acted so if she knew you were a citizen. I wonder how long we can prolong providing proof of your citizenship, Belrina."

"My husband." Belrina felt a flare of love in their bond. "Thank you for the benefit of citizenship. When we can safely announce our partnership to the Empire, I shall be so happy." Swept up in the emotional energy uniting them, she could ignore the dangers of instigating Primth's ire. "Will you do the forms with me?"

Lythk smiled, his green eyes shining, and she had to remind herself to breathe. Side by side, they performed the first three forms, breathing and moving in unison. She could feel his strength and power, balancing and fueling her.

Soon, she was conscious only of the sakitha bond and their joint movement. They breezed through the next three forms together, advancing to the power cycles. Belrina performed the magic shields, blocks, and strikes in lockstep with Lythk.

In the ultimate form, she used magic to perform the aerial flips, easily matching Lythk's spinning magic ellipses, the release of power controlled and satisfying.

Belrina held the final pose, breathing deeply for several moments, as she did not wish to break the silence. Smoothly, she returned to the originating position of the first form. In half a heartbeat, Lythk joined her.

Again, they moved through the forms together, sharing their joy in the synchronized movement. As they began the power strikes for a second time, the karth stopped.

Belrina immediately created a protective shield to protect herself and Lythk.

Mathim ran into the room. "Are you secure?" he inquired of them both. When Belrina nodded, he said, "I'll determine why the karth has stopped."

Before he cleared the compartment, Saolmyn was at the door. She backed into the corridor to allow the large vaxili to depart.

"Pardon my intrusion." Saolmyn made a hasty bow for the magisthild. "I could feel tremendous bursts of power." She studied the room as if surprised to find nothing amiss. "I believe they disrupted the karth's motion. If so, we will need a seer to perform the launching spell again."

"You do not know the spell, Saolmyn?" Belrina asked.

"No, Belrina. My studies focus exclusively on magical antiquities."

"Magisthild and I were practicing vaxili forms," Belrina explained. "Saolmyn, was this an oscillation?" When the seeker nodded, Belrina blinked in surprise. "Only powerful magic can cause an oscillation."

"Yes, Belrina," Saolmyn affirmed.

Belrina stared at the apprentice. The magic had felt natural and effortless. After a moment, she said, "Saolmyn, please explain the situation to the silvermaster. And please convey my apologies."

"Yes, of course." Saolmyn bowed again, leaving Belrina alone with her husband.

Belrina did not remove the protective shield, as she sensed

Lythk remained alert.

'Vaxili Amirtha is investigating the perimeter of the karth,' he informed her.

Belrina nodded, grateful Mathim always kept Lythk informed of all security measures. *'Shall we consult with Seer A'zine?'*

'Yes, Belrina.'

She smiled, basking in the emotions Lythk conveyed when he used her name. When their minds were connected, she felt their sakitha bond more acutely.

Belrina soon had the transmitter in her hand, and after altering her protective shield so it served as a privacy screen, she invoked the device. It was almost a full minute before the seer responded.

"This is an unexpected call, Belrina. Are you well?"

"Yes, Seer. The magisthild and I were performing vaxili power strikes, causing the karth to stop. Saolmyn said the launching spell needs to be administered again."

"I can use the turvuyst with Saolmyn if she consents. It should be a brief merger," Seer A'zine proposed.

"I shall discuss with Saolmyn now." Belrina did so, speaking to her friend telepathically.

"I have been informed that a crier's station is near us. There are also several towns within walking distance. If we linger here, we'll draw a crowd," Lythk announced.

Belrina noticed movement in her peripheral vision. Turning to the window, she observed a gangly male Asthildi adorned completely in black except for a golden belt ending in a tassel. Walking at his side, a lady in a deep purple gown with intricate silver patterns on her bodice wore a silver belt identical to Seer A'zine's.

"Magisthild!" Belrina cried out.

Lythk leaped in front of her.

"Seer, there are two Asthildi approaching the karth," Belrina narrated, a bit breathlessly.

"It is a seer and a scholar," Lythk observed. He grimaced briefly, adding, "And a crier has been sent to investigate our karth. We'll have a crowd in less than twenty minutes."

Saolmyn entered the leisure compartment, and Belrina extended the protective shield to include her.

"It is the Seer of Xorth!" the seeker exclaimed.

"Lazbith is a seer only in name. She has abandoned all the principles of our order, and her conduct is highly erratic," Seer A'zine said. "She is affiliated with the Zealots, and I have not determined what their interests are in you, Belrina. Seeker Saolmyn, with your permission, we can join in the turvyst and I will defend against Lazbith."

"Yes, of course, Seer." Saolmyn nodded.

"I will intervene only if absolutely necessary. Magisthild, I will leave the scholar to you."

"The vaxili stand ready, Seer," Lythk replied.

"Saolmyn, please prepare yourself. I will be with you all shortly."

Belrina felt Saolmyn open a funneling energy inviting a merger, and when the Seer of Kalehala joined, Belrina sensed the magical union and observed a change in Saolmyn's bearing.

Belrina bowed deeply. "I am glad to be in your presence again, Seer."

"None of that, dear one," the seer replied through Saolmyn. "I am Saolmyn, a mere apprentice." She gazed at Belrina with a tranquility Saolmyn never had. "Use all your energy to protect yourself, not others. Now, let's meet the Seer of Xorth." She began leading the way, prompting Belrina and Lythk to exchange glances. Before they could correct her, the seer realized her mistake.

"My apologies, Magisthild," she bowed, allowing Lythk to escort Belrina from the leisure compartment first.

As instructed, Belrina adjusted her shield to protect only herself, reinforcing it with a steady flow of magic energy. She breathed deeply, releasing her spiraling thoughts about the Seer of Xorth's motivations. After a few moments, she found balance.

'Trust your instincts,' Lythk sent.

When they arrived in the dining car, Silvermaster Bykin and the two vaxili were rising from their bows to the Seer of Xorth, whose strength of presence dwarfed her taller companion.

In synchrony with Magisthild Lythk, Belrina swept into a bow. Seer A'zine began hers a microsecond later, bowing the deepest of them all.

"Please rise," the Seer of Xorth surveyed them all, her cool blue eyes lingering on Belrina.

"Seer of Xorth, we are honored to receive you," Silvermaster Bykin began.

Without warning, Belrina felt powerful blows, like those used in magic grappling, raining upon her shield. She easily maintained both her serene expression and the protective barrier, feeding it more magic energy as it waned. She wondered how the Seer of Xorth was using magic without chanting.

"I am Silvermaster Bykin of Kalehala. Please let me introduce our company." He did so while the Seer of Xorth shifted her attack to waves of crashing power punctuated with jolting strikes.

'Let me know if you need help, dear one,' Seer A'zine communicated telepathically.

'I am not yet in danger,' Belrina replied. Without her shield, she would have been knocked senseless. Perhaps permanently.

With each onslaught, the protective shield kept drawing more and more energy. Could she continue to power it? She had expended ample energy with the vaxili power strikes. Instinctively, she altered her shield so it absorbed the energy from the seer's strikes. Now, the Seer of Xorth was fueling Belrina's protective shield.

'I have control now. Thank you, Seer,' Belrina sent.

"You may call me Seer Lazbith. Allow me to introduce Bekani Calyn, an Academy philosopher."

The invisible storm of power continued to pommel her shield, and Belrina wondered how the others could be oblivious to the battle in their midst.

"I do not wish to further delay your journey," Seer Lazbith said.

The magical attack suddenly stopped, but Belrina maintained a firm hold on her shield.

"Bekani Calyn and I have come to join your company."

The sakitha partners shared their joint alarm.

Surprisingly, Bykin was the first to protest. "Seer Lazbith, I'm afraid we cannot offer you the hospitality you deserve. We are traveling with the barest of essentials."

"I have not always lived in luxury." Seer Lazbith waved away the concern. "The accommodations will be adequate."

Lythk spoke next. "Will you affirm that your business will not jeopardize the safety of anyone aboard this karth?" His green eyes bored into the Seer of Xorth.

Seer Lazbith didn't hesitate to lock eyes with him. "I will safeguard Asthil Belrina and all aboard this karth to the best of my abilities."

Seer A'zine bowed deeply in her guise as Seeker Saolmyn. "Pardon, Seer, if I may inquire, what do you wish for the meeting between Belrina and Senator Primth?"

Seer Lazbith's eyes narrowed, and then she looked at Belrina. "It is clear you have inspired many to protect you. It is your permission I seek. Please tell me how I can gain your consent?"

"Seer Lazbith." Belrina bowed slightly. "Please answer Seeker Saolmyn's question."

"Very well. I hope you shall prevail in your encounter with Senator Primth."

"Is there a contest between Belrina and Senator Primth?"

Asthil Myrin inquired as he joined their party. Belrina had not seen him arrive, but Lythk had already positioned his body to block Myrin's access to Belrina.

Myrin bowed deeply to the Seer of Xorth. "I am Asthil Myrin, twice heir of guildmasters in Kalehala."

"Young one, everything is a contest with Senator Primth," Seer Lazbith retorted. "Are there no criers in Kalehala?" she muttered before returning her gaze to Belrina. "He seeks to bend everyone to his will."

"Seer Lazbith, I have two additional questions," Belrina said. "First, how did you know our karth would stop here?"

Smiling, Seer Lazbith said, "Calyn and I deciphered a bit of old text. I can explain further in private if you wish. What is your second question?"

"Why did you attack me?"

Several heads swiveled towards Belrina.

"I had to test your abilities. You were clever to use my energy to reinforce your shield," Seer Lazbith replied forthrightly.

"A crowd is gathering," Lythk informed them. "A crier report was issued five minutes ago identifying this karth as Belrina's."

"I can form a protective barrier around the karth," Seer Lazbith offered.

"That has been done, Seer," Lythk answered.

"Then may I join your company and set this karth in motion?" Seer Lazbith asked.

Everyone waited for Belrina to answer. "You may join us," she decided. "I appreciate your candor, Seer." Belrina hoped the Seer of Xorth would continue her transparency, which was so rare in Asthildi society. Even without an Oath of Veracity, Belrina believed Seer Lazbith wished to support her against Primth, and she wouldn't deny that support, although it might come with entanglements.

"Excellent!" Seer Lazbith chanted and two trunks appeared. Before she uttered the launching spell, Belrina asked for a moment.

Through a window, she saw the faces of scores of Asthildi who had come to see her. "What do they seek?"

Bekani Calyn opined, "Even they do not know. They wish to see or experience something novel."

"It seems impolite to ignore them." Belrina looked at the Saolmyn-hosted Seer A'zine. "I should like to address them." She felt Lythk's alarm, and Belrina considered how to do so safely. "I can project an image of myself atop the karth."

"Would you like my help?" Seer Lazbith offered.

"No, thank you. Saolmyn and I can devise the spells." Belrina conferred telepathically with Seer A'zine before manipulating magic energy, creating a life-sized image of herself on the karth and a small receiver on an irisean screen, which allowed her to see the projection.

It was too dark for the crowd to see her image, so Belrina generated a soft glow of light to surround the projected image.

The crowd erupted into applause and cheering, but she could not see their faces. Belrina created a second receiver to capture the images appearing before her projection's eyes. Then she projected her voice above the din, saying, "Thank you for coming to see me. I must continue my journey to the Capitol. Farewell." She smiled and waved, and her twin-image did the same. "Live well!"

Some in the crowd shouted back, "Live well!"

"Shall I start the karth now?" Seer Lazbith inquired.

Belrina nodded, and as the karth crept forward, she continued to wave. "Farewell and live well, Asthildi!"

She continued to wave until all faces were out of sight. Then she ended the flow of magic energy and turned to her silent companions.

"They were so excited and so happy with so little of my attention," Belrina spoke her thoughts aloud.

"In the beginning, the mere sight of your beloved's smile is enough to satisfy you." Myrin gazed at Belrina.

"As the young one implies, Asthildi can demand more and more of your attention. Their appetite can be insatiable for sakilyn. Do not seek to always please them." Seer Lazbith cautioned.

"Pardon, Seer Lazbith," Belrina inquired, "What is a *sakilyn?*"

"A famous one who will always be followed by criers," she replied.

"Fame is earned by eminence. The exceedingly beautiful and fashionable can be sakilyns," Bekani Calyn added.

Belrina sat down on a bench, closely followed by Seer A'zine, who held her hand. She recalled Lythk saying the first night he guarded her: "You will be highly prized." So little Belrina had known then.

The Seer of Xorth gazed at Belrina a moment. "This has been an exciting evening. I should like to retire. If someone would kindly show me to my compartment?"

Myrin bowed. "I will gladly give up my compartment, Seer Lazbith. Please follow me."

"Bekani Calyn, I can show you to our compartment," Bykin gestured for the tall, gaunt elf to follow him. "We shall share with Asthil Myrin."

When only the vaxili remained, Belrina erected a privacy screen. Seer A'zine said, "Thank you. I did not have the strength to do that. I must go, Belrina. This has been a tremendous enterprise. Saolmyn will need rest." She touched Belrina's temple with an unsteady hand. "Your mind is unsettled. Trust yourself and you will do well." Abruptly, Saolmyn's body slumped against Belrina's shoulder.

"Saolmyn!" Belrina performed a healing spell to relieve her friend's fatigue.

The seeker raised her head. "Thank you."

"Let's get you to bed."

Mathim assisted Saolmyn to her feet, and she could walk when Belrina supported her other arm. They ambled along the corridor, Lythk leading them. His mind was active and alert, demonstrating he did not trust their Zealot guests.

When they arrived at Saolmyn's sleeping compartment, they found Njal sheltering from the Seer of Xorth. With a bit of bustle, they settled Saolmyn into her bed, where Njal examined her, proclaiming the seeker merely needed rest.

While Belrina and Njal sat on a cot together, Lythk huddled with the vaxili within a privacy screen, discussing the additional security measures required by the unusual additions to their company.

Looking at Belrina closely, Njal offered, "Would you like some tea?" Belrina had described how she laced medicine into herbal teas, which had inspired Njal to experiment with warming lakri elixirs. There were a few that Belrina had generously declared as pleasant as tea.

"That would be lovely. It has been another long day." Belrina reflected on the day's events, concluding that choices were either frustratingly limited or perplexingly complex in the Empire. And many would bear the consequences of decisions she made with an incomplete understanding of Asthildi society. Her decision to allow the Seer of Xorth to join them may yet end in disaster.

As Belrina sipped Njal's elixir, she questioned the fate Seer A'zine believed to be hers. She had not eased anyone's suffering in the Empire, nor seen any meaningful opportunity to do so.

Belrina looked at the Asthildi surrounding her, her eyes resting on the fatigued Saolmyn. She had only complicated their lives, drawing them into a struggle against the elite who wished to exploit her. Despite all their efforts, Belrina had not escaped being manipulated by Senator Mnetha or attacked by the Seer of Xorth. With no control over her own life, how could she possibly help others?

27

A Promise Honored

P HYSICALLY, AURELIO FELT HEALTHIER than the day he had left his village. Aching muscles and beleaguered feet had recovered with a few chants from elven healers. Abrasions and sunburnt skin had simply vanished.

Yesterday, the Seer of Kalehala had transported Aurelio and his two friends to a vast structure with bright white walls. In a single room, the three young men were treated by blue-garbed elves who did not constrain or question them.

Aurelio was eager to see all his friends treated by these magical healers, although he didn't know whether to trust the silvery seer when she said no repayment was necessary. How could he know anything when his own heart was so untrustworthy? He had believed so fervently that if he reached Kalehala safely, he would see Belrina.

He walked along the perimeter of the windowless room, unable to open the door to inquire about his friends. Aurelio swiveled on his heel as soon as he heard movement at the door. A matronly healer entered their room, gesturing for Aurelio to follow her, and he promptly strode to her side. Both Epifanio and Victoriano rose to their feet, but the elf shook her head, pointing again at Aurelio.

"I must go alone. Maybe I'll get news about the others," Aurelio said to them.

"Come back soon, Aurelio," Victoriano requested, his wide eyes evincing his concern.

Epifanio nodded his agreement, reluctantly stepping back.

"I will, my friends," Aurelio said, doing his best to smile confidently. Then he followed the elf into the bright, long corridor with white, smooth walls and ceilings that humans would have needed months to perfect.

The healer he followed walked surprisingly swiftly. In the elven tunic, Aurelio's long legs were freer than in trousers, and the slippers were lighter than running sandals. He enjoyed the stroll, but each hallway looked the same as the last, and after several turns, he questioned whether he could find his way back to his friends unaided. It made him uneasy to rely upon these elves, who had all the power of the Old Ones.

Finally, the healer opened a door, and Aurelio saw Cesario sitting in a bed.

Cesario immediately smiled. "Aurelio!"

Aurelio resisted the impulse to run to his friend's side, as he did not wish to startle the elf. "You can see!"

"I can see better than ever—it is amazing!" Cesario bowed over his hands towards the matronly elf. "Thank you, thank you so much." He continued looking around the room. "Everything is so clear."

At Cesario's bedside, Aurelio exclaimed, "What miracles these elves can do!" He gripped his friend's shoulder. "I am so happy you are safe. Where are the others?"

"We came here together, but then they brought me to this room." He leaned forward, whispering, "Did you bargain for the healing?"

Aurelio shook his head. "They did not ask for payment. Maybe the Seer of Kalehala paid them?"

"You met a seer?" Cesario sat up straighter.

"You haven't? Who brought you to Kalehala?" Aurelio asked.

"Some elves dressed in lavender. We couldn't understand them, but when they offered us their hands, we took them. Then they used magic, bringing us here in an instant." He smiled wanly. "It was like taking a hundred steps with the boots in one go."

"The Seer of Kalehala must have sent them. She knows Belrina. Oh, Cesario!" Aurelio fell to his knees, grasping the bedsheets in both of his hands. "Belrina isn't in Kalehala anymore."

The healer rushed to Aurelio, placing her hand on his head. He looked up at her, unshed tears in his eyes. "I am well, Mistress." She muttered a word, and Aurelio suddenly felt calm.

Aurelio sat back on his heels. "I think I would rather be upset."

Cesario touched his hand. "Please tell me everything that happened after we separated."

Aurelio complied, his intellectual friend interjecting with frequent questions, but when he finished his tale, Cesario was quiet.

Finally, Cesario said, "A senator to pardon and a seer to cleanse."

"Aye." Aurelio watched his friend think, experiencing a glimmer of hope. "I am so grateful you are here, Cesario."

"As am I." Cesario smiled. "I cannot wait to see what's beyond these walls with my brand-new eyes."

Aurelio ruffled Cesario's hair affectionately, laughing with his friend. How long had it been since he had laughed like this?

Then the door opened, and the Seer of Kalehala swept in. The matronly healer immediately knelt, and Aurelio fumbled into a similar bow.

The silvery elf spoke in her resonant voice, and then the strange voice translated. "Please rise. I am happy to see you recovered, Aurelio." After she said a few untranslated words, the same blue jewel appeared on Aurelio's tunic. "Please introduce me to your friend."

Aurelio nodded. "Thank you, Seer. This is Cesario de Nieve Fresca." As the magic voice translated his words into Elvish, he noticed the blue pendant flashing.

Cesario bowed as best he could from his bed. "It is a pleasure to meet you, Seer of Kalehala." His sharper eyes connected with the seer's aquamarine gaze. "Thank you for arranging my transport and healing. Please let us know if we can offer recompense?"

When the blue pendant didn't translate Cesario's words, Aurelio interpreted them for the silvery elf.

After understanding Cesario's question, the Seer of Kalehala smiled slightly. None of the elves here had animated facial expressions. "It was my pleasure to help friends of Belrina." She considered. "As recompense, you can satisfy my curiosity. Many Asthildi explorers have perished in the wilderness outside the Empire, and they had the advantage of magic." The Seer of Kalehala peered at them.

Aurelio stood still.

"Tell me, how did you survive?" she asked.

"We had weapons," Aurelio answered, not knowing where to begin.

"Key to our survival were the magic gifts provided by the Old Ones," Cesario explained. Aurelio had shown the Seer of Kalehala the enchanted boots and satchels, as she had sensed their magic, and she had eagerly examined the objects.

Aurelio translated Cesario's words again.

The silvery elf stepped closer. "Banished Ones are dangerous. What did you give them for these magic gifts?"

Cesario allowed Aurelio to answer.

"We—Cesario and I—promised to be their lifelong servants if we cannot restore their citizenship rights within a year." He added, "It was more than a promise—magic sealed our bargain." Aurelio rubbed his arms, remembering the Old Ones' magic.

The Seer of Kalehala was quiet. "Only the most egregious crimes subject an Asthildi to banishment: murder, treason, and violence against the person of a seer, senator, or guildmaster."

Aurelio found himself sitting at the foot of Cesario's bed. "They shouldn't escape punishment for their crimes." He lifted his chin. "I am prepared to serve them."

The silvery elf smiled softly, her aquamarine eyes bright. "You have ample courage, Aurelio." Then her smile vanished. "They may treat servants reprehensibly."

"Are there other punishments for citizens who commit crimes?" Cesario inquired. "Our City has a place for people who are a danger to themselves or others. They cannot leave unless they prove they will be peaceful, and even then a relative must supervise them."

After translating, Aurelio said a quick prayer for those few poor souls in prison, hoping they could embrace nonviolence again.

"Interesting." The Seer of Kalehala pondered, and several moments later, she nodded. "The punishment could be amended. In lieu of banishment, these Old Ones could be placed under a binding spell. They would be citizens again, but they could not use magic without the consent of an overseer."

"Would that satisfy our bargain with the Old Ones?" Aurelio asked.

"As soon as these Old Ones are citizens again, you should be released from the oath," the seer affirmed.

"Great Seer, will you help us?" Aurelio held his breath.

"Have these Old Ones bargained with many other people?" she asked.

"Yes. Many have sought their help, and none have been happy with what they received." Cesario shook his head sadly.

Aurelio nodded in agreement, repeating Cesario's words for the seer.

"I will not permit these Banished Ones to terrorize innocent people," Seer A'zine responded. "I will petition to have them returned to the Empire for better punishment."

"What can we do to aid you in this, Seer?" Cesario asked.

After Aurelio's translation, she replied, "I will send a scribe, and you can tell him about the People who have been harmed by these Old Ones. I will use these cases to support my petition." The silvery elf smiled again, looking at Cesario.

"Seer, can you please tell me how to help Belrina? I know she is in trouble," Aurelio pleaded.

In response, the Seer of Kalehala turned her aquamarine eyes on the Elvish healer. "I apologize, Lakri Helene, but I must erect a privacy screen."

The healer said something untranslated, nodding deferentially.

After the silvery elf chanted a word, she turned to Aurelio. "What do you know about Belrina being in danger?" she asked softly.

"The Old Ones gave me a vision of Belrina. She was with you, Seer, and a muscular elf I thought was Mathim at first. I felt Belrina's emotions—she was afraid. She wanted to return home to escape from danger, and although I cannot name the threat, I know it exists. I came here to help her."

The Seer of Kalehala placed her hand on Aurelio's shoulder. "I can see you love Belrina deeply. There is a way you can speak with her to verify she is safe."

"When? When can I speak with her?" Aurelio implored, staring into their benefactor's tranquil eyes.

"Thank you, Seer," Cesario interjected. "Aurelio is very grateful for your help." He stared at Aurelio, trying to communicate with him wordlessly. "If it were me, I would ask how as well as when."

Ah. Cesario was once again reminding him to fully consider all angles before taking action. Yes, he was still dealing with elves, and this one was more powerful than the Old Ones.

The silvery elf stepped away from Aurelio, briefly gazing at Cesario before chanting a single word.

Aurelio was learning to hear the different way elves spoke

when using magic.

Turning to the healer, the Seer of Kalehala had a brief untranslated conversation before speaking again to Cesario. "When you have fully recovered, I would be happy to receive you and all your friends at my sanctuary." To Aurelio, she said, "Please come with me now."

"Pardon, Seer, my other friends may worry if I do not return. May I say goodbye to them?"

"Lakri Helene can send word," she responded. With another magical chant, a gem appeared in the seer's hand. "This is a translation device that will allow your friends to understand her." She bestowed the device to the healer, who promptly bowed.

Aurelio held out his hand to Cesario. "Be well, my friend."

Cesario gripped his hand. "You, too, Aurelio."

"I shall see you tomorrow," Aurelio said reassuringly before following the Seer of Kalehala, who had not yet said when he could speak with Belrina.

She led him down the corridor, and with a word and wave of her hand, a door appeared in the wall. When it smoothly opened, they stepped into an extremely large room lit with silver lamps. Light refracted from white, smooth walls with subtle gray veining.

Aurelio recognized the chamber from the Old Ones' vision. Belrina had been here with the Seer of Kalehala, and his eyes traveled to where he thought Belrina had stood.

The silvery elf sat down on a long birch bench next to an oval pool of still water. Suspended in air, concentric polished stone basins held more water above the pool.

"Please join me," she said, gesturing to the bench.

Aurelio sat down, allowing ample space between them.

"Please tell me, Aurelio, what is your plan now that you have reached Kalehala?"

"I have not yet formed one. I had to see my friends safely here. Now, I only wish to help Belrina if I can." He stared into the silvery seer's serene face, recalling that Belrina seemed to trust her.

"Our Empire differs greatly from your homeland, Aurelio." The seer paused. "Our laws do not protect you and your friends, making you very vulnerable."

"I do not understand, Seer. Is that why Belrina is in danger?" Aurelio asked.

"No. Belrina is of Asthildi blood."

"Pardon, Seer, but an Asthildi is an elf?" Aurelio struggled to make sense of her statement. "You are saying Belrina has Elvish blood? No, Seer, Belrina is human."

"An Asthildi is an elf who is a citizen of the Asthildi Empire." The Seer of Kalehala paused. "Belrina appears to be fully human, but one of her mother's ancestors was Asthildi. Belrina is now an Asthildi citizen."

Aurelio pitched forward, placing his head in his hands. Erynanne and Mathim had the same golden eyes. Belrina's blue eyes were the only ones of that color he had seen until arriving in Kalehala.

"Are you well, Aurelio?"

"Yes, Seer." He sat up, pushing his hair away from his eyes. As he looked at the silvery seer, her crystalline eyes penetrated his. "Does Belrina have magic?"

"Yes, she is extremely talented and powerful."

Aurelio looked away. "Then there is someone more powerful who is a threat to her?" What could he possibly do to help Belrina now?

"You are very astute, as is your friend Cesario." After a pause, the Seer of Kalehala continued. "I need to tell you more about your position in the Empire. The Asthildi who found you are vaxili—soldiers—tasked with protecting Kalehala. They could have seized and imprisoned you indefinitely because you are not a citizen."

"I'm an honest person, and I've never committed a crime. Why should they want to imprison me or any of my friends?"

The silvery elf looked into the oval pool. "You are foreigners of whom the worst can be assumed. Outside my sanctuary, I fear Asthildi would commit crimes against you, but here you are under my protection."

"You are advising me not to leave Kalehala, Seer?"

"Yes, Aurelio. It would be too dangerous for you and your friends."

"Why would anyone commit crimes against us? We have nothing of value. As for violence, why would anyone wish us harm when we wish none to them?" Aurelio did not feel very astute at the moment.

"You have items of value, Aurelio. What is the unlimited food supply you brought with you?" she asked, wearing a small smile.

"Dried meats, dried fruit, nuts, flatbread."

"What type of nuts?"

"Walnuts, almonds, cashews."

"A single cashew is worth ten pounds of silver." She conjured a large silver goblet. "This is perhaps half a pound." She let it float in front of her, and she conjured nineteen matching goblets. They glittered impressively in the Reflection Chamber. "Ten pounds of silver."

Aurelio felt like he had just taken a step with his enchanted boots.

"How can a cashew be worth so much?"

"They are rare here. We have little water to grow trees or vegetation." She added, "The nutritional value of your replenishing fare will diminish, decreasing its value, but Asthildi will pay a great price to taste it."

Aurelio shook his head, not understanding her comment about the food in their satchels. "This is all so strange to me. I think I have a better idea of how there can be. . . misunderstandings." He rubbed his temple. "When may I speak with Belrina?"

"Soon. Are you well, Aurelio? Perhaps you should return to

the lakri?"

"I am well, Seer. Thank you." Aurelio smiled shakily. "I am realizing how little chance I have of helping Belrina."

"There is perhaps one way for you and your friends to be helpful."

"Yes? What can we do?" Aurelio tried to suppress his excitement so that he could fully consider the Seer of Kalehala's suggestion—like Cesario would.

"Would you permit me?" She reached her magical hand towards him.

Aurelio leaned back. "Pardon, Seer, what will you do?"

"Please know that I have sworn an oath to always speak the truth. You may trust me, Aurelio, when I say I will not harm you. I'd like your permission to explore your capacity for magic."

Aurelio's eyebrows rose into his forehead.

"You used the magic objects created by the Banished Ones. What if I can create devices you can use to help Belrina?"

Aurelio smiled, grasping the silvery seer's cool hands. "You are a true friend to Belrina, Seer. Please, do what you must."

Returning his smile, the Seer of Kalehala withdrew her hands to place them on his head. As she chanted softly, he felt a subtle chill snaking into his body. He welcomed it, praying it would become his contribution in the mission to protect Belrina.

28

A Deception Revealed

R ISING FROM HIS CUSHIONED chair, Senator Primth surveyed the members of the Executive Senatorial Committee.

They all are useless, he thought, not for the first time. Suppressing his annoyance, he gazed into the azure diamond ring dominating his left hand. Unfortunately, he needed these imbeciles' votes.

"I understand your concerns about Forest Girl's growing popularity. However, she is firmly under my control," he said, raising his eyes. "The Conservationist senators used her image without her consent. Now, as none of you offered ideas on how we can use her popularity to further our own ends, there is nothing else to discuss. Our meeting is adjourned."

The senators rose hastily, bowing in silent farewell.

Primth strode to the window, admiring the soaring skyline of the Capitol. Its spectacular heights were unrivaled by any other senatorial city in the Empire thanks to his efforts over the last several centuries. The magnificent view always soothed him.

Realizing he wasn't alone, Primth swiveled.

Senator Leenk stood near the chair he had recently occupied. He inclined forward, trying to disguise his ungainly height. The result was an unattractive hunch.

"Yes, Leenk?" Primth inquired curtly.

"I beg your pardon, Senator, but I have fragmentary information concerning Forest Girl."

"Go on." Primth regained his seat.

"At Pylena, the girl's karth weighed three-hundred forty-three pounds less than it did yesterday evening when it traveled through my prefecture." Leenk's voice grew quieter. "It is possible the karth has gained additional occupants."

"Who?" Primth demanded.

"I have identified a person to investigate: an Academy philosopher with known Zealot affiliations, Bekani Calyn, who disappeared suddenly."

"I knew the Zealots would cause trouble," Primth retorted. He caressed the smooth mahogany arm of his chair. "What are you doing to uncover this Zealot plot?"

Leek sat, leaving several empty chairs between them. "A few decades ago, I planted an associate in the Zealot society, but he hasn't yet risen to importance; he has difficulty accessing the most closely held Zealot secrets."

"When you provide the proper motivation, Senator, I am confident he will provide the information we need." Primth gazed at the taller elf.

"Yes, Senator Primth." Leenk bowed while seated.

"Thank you, Leenk." Primth rose. "Contact me as soon as you have credible information on this matter." He resumed his position at the window, no longer seeing his magnificent city.

"Yes, of course, Senator." Leenk untangled his long legs and hastily bowed. "Have a good afternoon."

Once assured of solitude, Primth walked to the ardhendlr. Setting the disc in motion, he activated his encrypted transmitter.

"Senator Primth, how may I assist you?" Orlth's voice was clear in the small space.

"Can you explain why Forest Girl's karth weighs more now than it did at Pylena?"

"A scholar and a seer joined the party. I discovered this while you were in the meeting, which I thought was still in progress."

"Identity confirmation?" Primth inquired.

"Unfortunately not. Images from the karth's brief stop outside Glynth are imprecise. We are narrowing down the possibilities now."

"Could the scholar be Bekani Calyn, an Academy philosopher?"

"Let me isolate his image from Academy records." Orlth paused. "Yes, Senator, we have a positive match. Bekani Calyn is the scholar who joined the girl's karth."

"What seers have Zealot connections?" Primth inquired.

"The Seer of Xorth is the most notable." After another pause, Orlth continued, "We have the second identity confirmation, Senator."

"Investigate the Seer of Xorth and the Academy philosopher named Calyn. Find out what they want." Primth smoothed his face before it developed wrinkles. "Also, arrange a meeting with the seers tonight." He loathed interacting with those mystic charlatans, but they would have the best information about this Seer of Xorth, who was clearly vying for control over Forest Girl.

"As you wish, Senator Primth."

Disconnecting the call, the senator strode to his chariot, a sleek mirrored machine reflecting the beauty of the Capitol on its exterior. He navigated it to the most prestigious media agency in the Empire, for he needed to combat the Conservationist senators' media campaign immediately.

Primth anchored his chariot in front of his media agents' office, certain they would welcome his unscheduled visit. As he entered the opulently decorated antechamber, an impossibly beautiful youth greeted him.

"Senator Primth, what an honor!" he said. "Please let me show you to a private room. I shall summon Criers Venutha and Alena at once."

Primth almost frowned. The young one acted as though they were acquainted! When Primth was comfortably seated, the youth smiled, displaying brilliant white teeth.

"Shall I fetch you a glass of wine, Senator Primth?"

"Summer wine will do nicely."

The young one's violet eyes widened. "If I cannot procure a summer wine, do you have a second choice?"

"No, I do not." Primth showed his own white teeth.

The beautiful young elf silently bowed, exiting. Primth owned one of the last casks of summer wine in the Capitol, and the value of that cask would likely exceed the lifetime earnings of the unnamed youth.

A delicate chime announced the entrance of two richly attired blondes who bowed deeply in unison. Primth appreciated associates whose beauty equaled their value.

"Arise, sweet ones. I have an urgent need for your services. We must bury the Conservationist campaign using the hybrid's image. Starting tomorrow morning, we must inundate the Capitol with images of Forest Girl supporting *me*—not those retrograde-minded senators."

"You will love the advertisements we create." Venutha inclined her head, adorned by a crown of platinum plaits. "With a voice-matching spell, the hybrid will say anything you wish her to."

"Most words should be her own. I will send copies from my personal collection of recordings, and you will see she praises me often."

"Undoubtedly, Senator Primth." Alena's generous mouth smiled confidently.

A glass of summer wine appeared in front of Primth. He ignored the name of the cultivator gracefully etched into the goblet's slender stem. Smiling, Primth wondered what the young one had promised to pay for this extravagance. He sipped the delicate wine, beginning to enjoy himself.

"Tell me your ideas," Primth commanded.

For the next several minutes, the senator was delightfully entertained as the blonde criers competed for his approval.

"The public will love it when the forest girl acknowledges

the greatness of our most powerful senator," Venutha said.

Senator Primth set down his empty glass. "Be sure the public is inspired to love me, not Forest Girl."

"Yes, of course!" Alena exclaimed, her eyebrows arching prettily in sincerity. "She is an unknown, a novelty that will fade."

"Whereas your power and influence will last forever," Venutha said, finishing the thought.

"You two are priceless." Primth beamed. "Let's use the girl's words 'Live well' to inspire citizens to live as I do. Use that for a longer advertisement, and then prepare at least three shorter segments capturing her best praises." The senator rose reluctantly. "Unfortunately, I have other business. I look forward to seeing your work."

The criers bowed gracefully, and then Primth strode to his chariot, encountering no one else, much to his satisfaction. As he made himself comfortable on the plush bench of his chariot, he sent a message to Orlth, ordering him to investigate the enterprising youth with surprising connections. It was best to monitor any Asthildi with political ambition.

At the highest possible speed, Primth navigated to his estate. Only he could sort and send the appropriate recordings of Forest Girl to his media agents. Once in his private library, the senator did so as efficiently as possible. Yet, he could not help staring at Forest Girl's image. Apparently human, but nonetheless a talented magician. Child-like in demeanor, but womanly in appearance. She did not know how powerful she could be. But before she realized her potential, he would gain control over her, and then her power would be his to use!

Surprised to see how much time had passed, Primth activated a device to read Orlth's encrypted messages. The meeting with the seers would occur at the old oak grove, which few citizens visited as it offered no entertainment value. Yet, the public still supported preserving these useless oak trees, which were the last known surviving specimens in the

Empire. Primth was confident he could change that public sentiment in a century or two. Then the Capitol's skyline would become even more impressive, and more importantly, those competing to build on the land would shower him with gifts and favors. Construction was such a lucrative enterprise.

Of course, if Forest Girl lived up to her potential, Primth wouldn't have to wait to achieve any of his goals. He rose from his chair, flourishing his cloak, imagining the adoring crowds at his coronation.

With a light step, Primth proceeded to his vault to prepare for his meeting with the seers, whose mystical motivations made them inherently untrustworthy. He considered the tactics the seers might employ, collecting counteracting magic devices. He visualized how he would vanquish the seers if they unwisely challenged him. It was a useful exercise that further elevated his mood.

When the time for the meeting drew near, Senator Primth used a magic device to alter his physical appearance. He adopted the image of a person who might be interested in visiting the oak grove: a broad-shouldered youth in a drab tunic with hazel eyes and yellow hair.

He turned away from the image in disgust, striding to the secret tunnel leading from the vault to the edge of his estate, where Primth met his driver for the evening. He jumped into the enclosed chariot.

Nearly an hour later, Primth stood in the grove, surrounded by thick trees and the haphazard tangle of their branches and leaves. He did not see beauty in the chaos of nature, which harbored vermin and pests. Primth suppressed thoughts of wriggling worms and winged insects as he trod through the disgustingly spongy terrain.

Primth quickly found the three seers waiting for him. They had disguised themselves as well, although each had left her hair color the same. He stared at them, beginning his slight bow only after they began theirs.

"If you will allow me, I shall set a privacy screen." Seer Melwyn, silver-haired and the eldest of the three, did not sound as though she asked a question, but she waited for his assent before uttering the spell.

"Senator, this is a pleasant surprise," said Seer Jasemyn. Her dark gown augmented her reddish blonde hair.

"How can we help you, Senator?" Seer Weylan asked, her direct manner recognizable. Generally worn in a severe chignon, her platinum hair now flowed down her back.

"I would appreciate any information you can provide about the Seer of Xorth and her interest in the hybrid," Primth responded.

"Lazbith has been enmeshed with the Zealots for centuries," Seer Melwyn replied. "Zealots believe the hybrid is key to replenishing the Empire's natural resources."

Seer Jasemyn laughed melodiously. "Our greatest scholars and magicians have not managed to engineer an ecological revitalization. What can one girl do?"

Primth ignored the tangent. "What does the Seer of Xorth plan to do with Forest Girl?"

The three were silent for a few moments.

"All visions concerning the hybrid are imprecise," Seer Weylan began.

"I See. . ." Seer Melwyn interrupted, peering into empty space. "She will sow disunity and violence. Monumental change is unavoidable. We must prepare. . ." She sagged and Jasemyn leaped to her aid, keeping her upright.

They did not impress Primth. Melwyn's cryptic words could easily be manipulated. He would continue to be the architect of sociopolitical change in the Asthildi Empire as he had been for the last five hundred years.

"I will guide Forest Girl and her choices," Primth informed them.

The three seers were silent again.

"You are withholding information," he said, stepping forward. "Tell me!"

"We all have Seen that the hybrid fears and loathes you," said Seer Jasemyn as she supported Melwyn.

"Impossible!" Primth objected. "I communicate with her daily. She is reverent."

"The girl is not the author of the messages." Weylan looked surprised she had spoken.

"Who is?"

Weylan shook her head. "I do not know." After a moment, she added, "The Seer of Kalehala altered the device."

"Did the Seer of Kalehala turn Forest Girl against me?" Primth spoke through clenched teeth. To erase her antithetical feelings, he needed to see the girl immediately.

"Yes. Seer A'zine wants the hybrid to defy you," Seer Weylan confirmed.

"There will be consequences for her interference! What can you tell me about the Seer of Kalehala's projects and interests? Who and what does she care about?" Primth struggled to smooth his facial contortions.

"I am not aware of any personal attachments. A'zine's work is her life." Seer Melwyn spoke almost normally now.

"She made an odd request for the Senator of Kalehala to pardon four Banished Ones," Seer Weylan volunteered.

Primth smiled. "If you learn of any other enterprises involving the Seer of Kalehala, please let me know. Now, what can you tell me about the Seer of Xorth's power?"

"Seer Lazbith has brute strength, but she lacks finesse and subtlety. Her focus is on battling lions instead of snakes in the grass," Jasemyn answered.

The senator smiled, bowing slightly. "Seers, your insights have been illuminating. As you support me, I shall continue to sponsor your sanctuaries."

The seers returned his bow in unison.

"Thank you for the audience," he said. "I shall not expend any more of your time. Please allow me to depart first." Primth intoned the chant to remove the privacy wall before swiftly retracing his steps. He kept his ears alert for any chanting from the seers or any movement from unseen creatures.

When he judged he was safe, Primth alerted Orlth of his need for a driver, and as he exited the grove, his ride arrived, demonstrating once again Orlth's impeccable timing.

Seated in the enclosed chariot, Primth erected a privacy screen and contacted an associate in Kalehala. Due to the Senator of Kalehala's primitive security measures, it was only a matter of minutes before Primth had an image capture of Seer A'zine's petition.

It was an odd request to pardon and then bind the Banished Ones' magic abilities. When Primth read where the Banished Ones were currently located, he felt the smile on his face. The anticipation of uncovering the secret and leveraging it to his advantage was exhilarating. He could offer these Banished Ones a better option than the Seer of Kalehala—if they proved to be useful.

With discipline, Primth maintained the unattractive disguise until he was safe within his secret tunnel. Then, with alacrity, he shed the illusion, veering into a seldom used corridor. He stopped at a wide-plank wood door locked by more than a heavy iron bolt.

Primth carefully chanted the complex incantation to unseal the door before sounding the chime to announce his arrival. After a moment, he opened the door, spilling light into the dark chamber.

Huddled in grime and filth, a former seeker struggled to bow while seated.

"How may I serve, Senator Primth?" her voice cracked.

"Clean yourself, Lilith. I cannot bear to look upon your wretched state."

"Yes, Senator Primth." Trained to use only the most rudimentary magic for herself, she conjured the utilth cloth to her hand and scrubbed her face quickly. With a single chant, the hem of her dingy tunic was revealed to be white fabric. Inch by inch, the enchantment eradicated the ingrained dirt until Lilith was attired in wholly white garb.

Primth conjured an orb of light. It had taken him over two centuries to turn Lilith into the pitiful, but obedient, magician he needed to act without question.

"I need to communicate with these elves in the People's City," he said, thrusting the image capture before her face.

She blinked against the light to read the names. "Yes, Senator. Which one do you wish to speak with first?"

Primth pointed randomly. "She will do." Then he realized he had to give additional instructions, which was a disadvantage of eradicating independent thought and initiative. Because Lilith would not deviate from his instructions in the slightest, his directives had to be exact.

"I wish for her to see me in my reception chamber, and the light should be favorable," he said. "Also, I need to see her image, and she must not see or hear you at all. You also must encrypt the communication."

"Yes, Senator." With a few incantations, Lilith set the requested illusion and generated the irisean screen for Primth to see his own reflection. "Shall I begin the communication?"

Primth adjusted the lighting. "Proceed."

Lilith began chanting, and another irisean screen appeared, remaining dim. Her sustained chanting grew louder and faster, and as the minutes passed, Primth wondered if he needed to secure a replacement for Lilith.

Finally, the dim screen flickered, showing shadowy images. A pale face popped onto the screen, blinking in surprise.

"Greetings, Alinka. I am Senator Primth. It is dark there. Please light an orb."

"Senator Primth, I am pleased to meet you. I apologize for not being ready to receive you. I was wakened from sleep. Please give me a moment."

The screen went momentarily black before Alinka reappeared, fully dressed in an old-fashioned velvet gown. A few loose auburn-tinted blonde curls framed her face.

His mouth twitched. He had not seen that hair style in a few centuries. If not for the ludicrous fashion, Primth may have been impressed with her self-possession.

"I called to discuss the possibility of a pardon. I would like to explore a mutually beneficial arrangement. Do you have any suggestions?"

As the Banished One spoke, Primth realized the Zealots were utterly wrong—it would not be Forest Girl who replenished natural resources in the Empire. He would be the one who ushered in a new epoch of plenty, enriching himself and all those he determined worthy.

29

TANGLED YARN

"IT IS IMPOSSIBLE," BELRINA said to the Seer of Xorth, who had wakened her early to begin these experiments. For the last few hours, Belrina had tried creating water to fill a small vial. She rubbed her temple.

Mathim and Lythk were standing in identical positions on either side of the door to the leisure compartment. Both wore stony blank expressions.

"I apologize, Seer, but I cannot alter the basic principles of magic." Belrina shook her head. "I cannot generate matter that has not existed before." She did not understand why the Seer of Xorth had set her an impossible task.

"We postulate there is matter we cannot see," Bekani Calyn spoke, ending his silent observation. "The air is not empty."

"Do you have a specific recommendation, Calyn?" the seer asked as she stood to look out a window.

"Unfortunately not, Seer Lazbith." The tall scholar bowed from his seat. "I wanted Asthil Belrina to know it is possible to transmute invisible material, although one would need to discover which is best for generating water."

Seer Lazbith turned away from the window. "The only thing I see of nature is the sky." She sighed. "Asthil Belrina, how would you increase the water supply in the Empire?"

Belrina closed her eyes, wordlessly creating a spell to locate water. She could sense there were two paltry sources nearby, likely reservoirs for the cities they were passing. Bekani Calyn's statement about invisible matter reminded Belrina that clouds contained water droplets.

After a few minutes of searching in the sky, she located droplets in the highest clouds and she slowly extracted and transported them to the vial in her hand, using a continuous channel of magic energy. It was several minutes before she saw the first drop.

"It is working!" Belrina exclaimed.

Bekani Calyn jumped up, peering at the vial. "How?" he inquired.

"I am transporting water droplets from the clouds," she explained, continuing the magic flow until the vial was full.

"How much energy did you use to fill this vial?" Seer Lazbith asked.

Belrina considered. "I think it is comparable to creating a diamond." She nodded. "Yes, it is comparable."

Calyn sat down suddenly. "So much magic energy for so little water? That is not a solution."

"I can convey a greater supply from my homeland." Belrina could clearly visualize the spring running alongside her cabin at home.

"From the People's lands? You have sufficient energy for this endeavor?" Bekani Calyn studied Belrina.

Belrina nodded. "My training with Seer A'zine was rigorous. I could also enlist Seeker Saolmyn's help." However, her friend should continue recovering from last night's turvyst merge with the Seer of Kalehala.

"Use me," Seer Lazbith directed. "You felt my strength yesterday."

"Yes, I did." Belrina looked at Lythk. She sensed through their bond that he trusted her to decide whether to entangle magically with the Seer of Xorth. In this arena, she did know more of the risks than he did. The seer's centuries of experience with magic could not be underestimated—safeguards needed to be in place.

"Seer Lazbith, are you familiar with the turvyst?" Belrina

asked slowly.

"Yes." The seer eyed Belrina cautiously. "Are you sure you have mastered the turvyst, young one?"

"No," Belrina replied. She hadn't witnessed the spell Seer A'zine used in Kalehala. "However, I do not intend to use it. If you place yourself in the position of the host body, I can channel your power instead of merging with you."

"Have you done this before, Belrina?"

"I have not, Seer Lazbith."

"How do you know it will work?"

"I can clearly see the magic pathway in my mind," Belrina replied, looking at the Seer of Xorth with clear eyes. "I cannot explain better."

"Very well, I will trust you." Seer Lazbith turned her blue eyes on the scholar. "Should I be materially damaged, Calyn, please write a favorable history of me."

Startled, Calyn bowed wordlessly to the Seer of Xorth.

Mathim ventured, "Pardon me, Belrina, but should we be worried that a substantial use of power will interfere with the karth again?"

Seer Lazbith waved away the concern. "I can restart the karth again."

Mathim bowed deeply to the Seer of Xorth.

"Thank you, Mathim. While I'm not concerned about an unplanned stop, there is another who might be." Belrina wished she did not have to consider the feelings of Senator Primth. He had written to express his dismay at their progress. "I shall be careful." She looked at a bench, transmuting it into a large copper tub.

"Seer Lazbith?" Belrina held out her hand and the forthright Zealot calmly grasped it. "Please place yourself in the position of a turvyst host."

In a few moments, she sensed the funnel of magic power striving to connect with her. Belrina guarded against the turvyst merge, and with the modifications she envisioned, she accessed the seer's magic capacity. Now, she could use it for her own purposes, depriving the Seer of Xorth access to her own powers.

Slowly, Belrina fashioned a tendril of magic energy, sending it into the clouds. Then, drawing energy in equal parts from herself and Seer Lazbith, she launched the stream of energy through the clouds and towards the spring near her cabin.

In a shorter time than anticipated, Belrina reached her target, and she lovingly touched the creek with her magic conduit, wicking up the water droplets and transporting them towards the karth.

She drew more and more power from the indefatigable Seer of Xorth, and after several minutes, water droplets began filling the copper tub. Belrina continued the flow of energy until the tub was full, and then she released the remaining water droplets from her magical conduit, freeing them into the sky.

With a few additional manipulations of magic energy, Belrina delicately severed her connection with Seer Lazbith, who stared at the water in the copper tub. She released the seer's hand, though she did not appear to notice.

Belrina walked to the copper tub, running her fingers lightly through the cool, fresh water. "Imagine bathing as often as you wished," she said. Unbidden, memories of home surfaced. Her sadness was swiftly washed away by Lythk's love surging in their sakitha bond.

"What is bathing?" Bekani Calyn asked.

Belrina thought it better not to answer.

The scholar approached the tub. "May I?" He had a clear vessel in his hand, ready to sample the water.

She nodded, moving away. "It should be safe to drink. Seer Lazbith, this water is yours."

Suddenly, a thunderous crash sounded, and the vaxili faced the windows in fighting stances.

Seer Lazbith began chanting, fashioning magic missiles.

"It's not an attack!" Belrina cried. "It's thunder—it's going to rain."

"Rain? Impossible." Bekani Calyn said. "Devices route atmospheric water vapor to reservoirs before it can..." His voice trailed off as raindrops splattered against the windows.

The silvermaster rushed into the compartment, breathlessly dropping into a hasty bow for the seer. He stared at the rain for a moment before presenting himself to Belrina.

"Pardon the intrusion, but I have an urgent missive," Bykin said, waiting for Belrina to give him permission to speak in the presence of the other Asthildi in the room.

Seer Lazbith spoke first. "Asthil Belrina, I should like to offer my counsel on this matter."

Belrina nodded slowly. "You trusted me, Seer Lazbith. I'll listen to your counsel and consider it along with the advice I receive from others." The Seer of Xorth had to understand that providing counsel was not the same as giving directives.

"My apologies, Bekani Calyn, but please excuse us?" Belrina requested.

He promptly exited, bowing to her.

"Senator Primth is coming to meet you," the silvermaster said. "He has arranged a public meeting this evening in the next senatorial city after which there will be a private dinner. He has included detailed instructions regarding your attire." As if eager to be rid of it, Bykin handed Belrina the scrap of parchment.

Belrina accepted it, but she did not read it. "Your thoughts, Silvermaster?"

"Senator Primth has proscribed nearly every detail of your meeting. He did not, however, specify who your chaperone or chaperones could be. I would suggest you choose someone without affiliations the senator would consider... antagonistic. As an artisan, I have no political connections the senator would find objectionable."

Seer Lazbith ignored the implication of Bykin's comment.

"I suggest myself for your chaperone. As a seer, I have special legal protections that the senator must honor."

"Seer Lazbith, why do you wish to protect me?"

The Zealot came close to frowning. "It is unwise to speak of prophecy." She chose her words carefully. "I believe you will lead the Empire into a new era of replenished natural resources. Thus, I will do everything I can to keep you alive and well."

"And if I should not choose you to escort me? Can I still count on your assistance?" Belrina asked.

Seer Lazbith did not hesitate. "Of course." She nodded emphatically. "I believe I can aid you best as your official escort, but I will protect you in whatever capacity I can."

"I am grateful for your support, Seer Lazbith." Belrina bowed formally. "Also, I appreciate your offer to escort me, Silvermaster. While I prepare for the meeting, I will consider how to proceed." She attempted a smile. "I will speak with you both soon."

On Lythk's arm, Belrina left the leisure compartment. Her mind seemed numb. In a few hours, she would finally discover what Primth wanted from her—and whether she could deny him.

Following Mathim, Belrina realized she was leaning against her husband, but she allowed herself the indulgence.

'You are prepared to meet him, Belrina,' Lythk conveyed, his loving confidence suffusing the sakitha bond. "We'll review the location of the meeting and select the best devices to aid you," he said aloud.

Belrina grasped her husband's arm tighter, crumpling the forgotten magic parchment containing Senator Primth's wardrobe requirements.

"Mathim, would you please provide this to Njal?" Belrina gave him the unread directives. "Please tell her she should alter any unsuitable recommendations."

"At once," Mathim bowed, striding away.

Once in her sleeping compartment, Lythk escorted her to the nearest bed. "You must restore your magic energy before the meeting." With a series of chants, he conjured a silver device resembling a seashell.

Accepting the device, Belrina invoked it, and several minutes later it concluded its work. "I didn't realize there was so much power within me," she said softly.

"And that is your magic energy. You also have power in your mind, your spirit, your body. You will fight him with everything you are."

A light chime sounded at the door, and Lythk was quickly on his feet. "Please come in," he said.

The silvermaster appeared in the doorway. His hair looked as though he had run his hands through it several times.

"Dear one," the silvermaster addressed Belrina directly, dispensing with formality in his distress. "I received another urgent message: Senator Mnetha and a few other senators intend to receive you when you stop at Rysdahl."

Magisthild Lythk asked to see the parchment, examining its contents.

Belrina stood. "How much time do we have, Bykin?"

"About an hour."

"And how much time before the meeting with Senator Primth?"

Bykin consulted a device. "One hour and forty-seven minutes." He bowed. "Please let me know if I can be of assistance."

Belrina felt like a ball of yarn being shared by two playful kittens, and she was tired of being batted around by the whims of Asthildi elites. The anger rising within her felt righteous. She would fight for autonomy over her own life and earn their respect. With that last thought, her racing mind drew to a halt.

The only thing the senators respected was power. *'You must become more powerful than them,'* Lythk had said.

Belrina looked at her small, brown hands. She had never wanted power. She had always wanted to heal and support others, but this was the only way she could survive in the Empire.

She connected telepathically to her understanding husband, who had given her space for her thoughts. *'I know what I must do. But I do not know if I have the strength to do it.'*

'You do, lovely one.' His light-green eyes caressed her face. *'I am not eloquent enough to express my thoughts in words.'* Lythk shared his memory of the claryth bursting into a magenta sun in the Reflection Chamber, bathing them in radiance. *'I knew then that your power can transform the Empire itself. You can stand against him, Belrina, and remember, you will not be alone when you do.'*

Belrina wished she could bury herself in his arms, but she did not yet have the luxury of meeting her own needs. She needed to prepare for the senators. With renewed focus, she sketched out plans with Lythk and her allies on the karth.

All too soon, it was time for her to dress in the leisure compartment, where Njal had been laboring over Primth's instructions. Behind a privacy screen permitting sound, Njal helped Belrina don a simple black gown, which adhered to her more tightly than her own skin.

"We have fifteen minutes, Belrina." Njal worked quickly, chanting and chattering nervously. "I did my best, but we have never used this material. I didn't know where to start with the modifications. He wanted the gown above your knee! Cutouts around the waist!"

Njal showed Belrina a silvery sheer material flecked with pinpoint diamonds.

"This is supposed to attach to your hair. How long do you wish it to be?" Njal asked.

Belrina summoned a mirror, staring at her reflection. The armless gown skimmed every curve of her body, and the bodice plunged deeply, exposing too much bosom. High slits on both sides of the gown would reveal her thighs when she walked. With a few quick thoughts, Belrina raised the neckline and eliminated the indecent openings in the skirt.

"Njal, can you fashion a covering for the entire gown from the veil? I still feel naked."

Her friend assessed the possibilities, draping the sheer material around Belrina's shoulders. As she chanted, the silver veil scalloped along both arms and then adhered to the back of the bodice before flowing over the sides of the gown, hinting at a full skirt while leaving the black gown visible underneath. Njal left the simple black gown exposed in the front, fashioning a lacy belt from the sheer diamond-dotted material.

"Thank you, Njal. At least this covers my hips." Belrina summoned a large diamond brooch the Seer of Kalehala had gifted her, securing it to the belt.

While Njal began styling her face and hair, Belrina concealed devices upon her person, making them invisible.

"Five more minutes," Lythk called.

Njal hastily finished her work with Belrina's hair before presenting a pair of black arching slippers balanced on slender spikes. "I had to show them to you!" Njal laughed. As she chanted, the arch of the slippers softened, and the heels became solid and studded with faux pinpoint diamonds. With further chanting, the slippers became comfortable, conforming to Belrina's feet.

"Do you approve?" Njal asked, stepping back.

She had arranged some of Belrina's hair into a crown sparkling with diamonds, and her eyelashes glittered with more flawless gems. Subtle shading on her eyelids enhanced the color of her eyes while her lips shimmered a pink paler than her natural lip color.

"I do not look human," Belrina responded in surprise.

The karth stopped.

"You are my beautiful one," Njal breathed, squeezing her hand. "Please safely return, my friend."

"I intend to, Njal," Belrina said, embracing her friend.

"Thank you for. . . everything."

Njal squeezed her tightly before bowing and rushing from the compartment.

Belrina performed breathing exercises while praying to the Gods United, and then she removed the privacy wall.

Lythk was alone. She held out her hands, and he quickly closed the physical space between them. Clinging to his hands, Belrina imbibed the love in their bond, as if it were her first sip of water after wandering in the Kalehala desert without a sunshield.

"You are ready for this, Belrina," Lythk said softly.

"Please, stay close to me," she said, forcing herself to relinquish her husband's strong hands and exit the karth.

30

THE COLOR OF MAGIC

R ISING FROM HER DEEP bow, Belrina waited for Senator Mnetha to finish introducing Senators Rubinsyth and Luken before saying, "Good afternoon, I regret to inform you I am due to meet Senator Primth shortly."

Senator Mnetha's blue eyes narrowed. "The entire Empire is aware of your meeting. I trust we have time to discuss mutually important business."

Belrina nodded slightly.

"Please follow me," Mnetha instructed. "I have arranged a quiet meeting place." She led the entourage away from the public station where an impressively high protective barrier, created by Seer Lazbith, prevented Asthildi from coming near Belrina's karth.

Senator Rubinsyth was elderly, and Belrina noted that Senator Mnetha escorted him with care. Senator Luken, who wore a simple coral gown, politely accepted Asthil Myrin's arm, but she often looked at Belrina as they strolled along the pearlescent path. None of the senators took notice of the vaxili, who silently shadowed Belrina and Silvermaster Bykin.

A short walk led them to a private outdoor room, undoubtedly designed for meetings such as theirs. Fresh fruit and other refreshments decorated a table. A single attendant, tall with silver hair, was ready to serve them.

As individuals took their seats, Belrina asked for permission to create a privacy wall. "It is in place, Senators," she announced the instant all assented.

She actively held a protective shield, as it offered the greatest security. Seer Lazbith had pointed out that the shield-generating device could be confiscated, leaving Belrina vulnerable.

"We work together to preserve and protect what remains of our natural environment," Senator Mnetha began. "We are called Conservationists."

"We are grateful for the aid you have provided to our cause," Senator Luken said, smiling. "Our media campaign featuring you has been extremely successful."

Belrina did not return the smile. Instead, she looked at Senator Mnetha. "I wish I could celebrate this success with you. However, I did not consent to the use of my image or my mother's."

Senator Mnetha's smooth face momentarily displayed a trace of surprise. "It never occurred to me you would find the media campaign objectionable." She added, "It inspired scores of Asthildi to contact us to learn more about conserving precious resources."

In the sudden silence, the youthful attendant stopped offering refreshments.

"Yes, I believe it did not occur to you," Belrina replied quietly. "Focusing on one's own goals often makes it difficult to consider the needs of others."

Senator Rubinsyth coughed. "Young one, we intended no disrespect. For my part, I will acknowledge that I have grown single-minded in the centuries I have devoted to conservation." Though hooded, his eyes still shone a brilliant blue. "I apologize for neglecting to obtain your consent."

"My sincerest apologies, Asthil Belrina," Senator Luken added.

Senator Mnetha nodded contritely. "I hope this misunderstanding will not prevent future work together?"

"Will you all pledge not to use my image without my consent?" Belrina raised her forearm, unraveling Seer A'zine's enchantment. She smiled as her tattoo glittered prettily in the sunlight. "Or perhaps a pledge is unnecessary as I am a citizen?"

"You were bonded in the sakitha!" Senator Rubinsyth exclaimed. "I have not seen a sakitha mark in some time."

"To whom were you bonded?" Senator Mnetha asked, giving voice to her first thought. Her eyes darted to Asthil Myrin, who was frozen, his hazel eyes fixed on Belrina's tattoo.

"I would ask you to respect my privacy in this matter," Belrina responded.

"Yes, of course, Asthil Belrina," Senator Luken promptly said. "If you should require any pledge of me, I shall happily give it."

Belrina folded her hands in her lap, looking at the three senators for a long moment. "I don't believe that will be necessary. I will support your cause if you allow me to determine what help I can provide." To underscore her point, Belrina added, "I will not be used, Senators."

Recovered, Senator Mnetha bowed slightly to Belrina. "You will be a welcome partner in our conservation efforts, Belrina."

Smiling, Belrina rose, holding out her hand to Senator Mnetha. "I look forward to discussing how I can be of assistance." In the handshake, Belrina provided a transmitter to the senator.

She shook hands with Senators Luken and Rubinsyth, covering the elderly Asthildi's delicate hand with both of hers. "I wish we could discuss these matters now, but unfortunately, I am expected elsewhere." She needed to turn her focus on Primth.

Belrina bowed deeply to the senators, and they returned her bow more deeply than required. She also bowed to Silvermaster Bykin and Asthil Myrin.

"I thank you for your escort," Belrina said, holding the silvermaster's eye. "I hope I shall see you soon."

Before she turned to leave, Senator Mnetha asked, "May I walk with you?"

After Belrina nodded, they retraced their steps, Mathim taking the lead while Lythk walked a half-step behind the senator. She adjusted the privacy screen so it traveled with them.

As expected, Asthildi had gathered outside the protective barrier, which extended to the plaza where the meeting with Primth would occur. They could not hear the animated crowd through the privacy screen, but Belrina waved and smiled at them.

"You manage the public well," Mnetha noted. "I suppose they are easier to manage than senators." She smiled slightly, her blue eyes expressive. "You do that well, too."

"I apologize for my boldness," Belrina said, her cheeks warming. "Circumstances compelled me to act so." She felt a sudden surge of wariness in the sakitha bond, which made her realize she might be ceding some of the advantage she recently gained.

"It is I who should apologize, Asthil Belrina." The senator shook her head. "I was overzealous in pursuing your support. I could not tolerate the thought of. . . others. . . securing your allegiance first so I insisted upon this meeting. My apologies for inconveniencing you." Senator Mnetha cast a glance at Lythk, adding, "And your team."

"I will convey your apology to my good friend, who is also my stylist. She will appreciate it." Belrina smiled, thinking of Njal, and then she waved again to the crowd.

A roofless silver chariot, provided by Senator Primth, was only a short distance away. Belrina's pace slowed.

"Several in this crowd will have reported your sakitha tattoo to Primth by now. You are now bound by the laws of citizenship. There may have been advantages to being a non-citizen," Mnetha said.

"I must face him as I am. Even if I were not a citizen, I

would not embrace lawlessness," Belrina replied. "Besides, citizenship grants me legal protections."

"Citizenship will not protect you from Primth. He does what he wants and then claims his victims are villains. He has a talent for construing plausible tales from half-truths." Senator Mnetha eyed the chariot. "However, his love for spectacle outweighs his self-interest." She looked at Belrina. "I wish I could aid you against him."

Belrina smiled sadly. "Many have said the same. If we united our efforts, wouldn't we increase our chances of prevailing?" Her halting feet had reached the gleaming chariot.

"Your perspective is refreshing, Asthil Belrina." Senator Mnetha offered her hand, and Belrina took it briefly. "If I see an opportunity, I will help."

"Thank you, Senator Mnetha." They exchanged bows. Rising, Belrina saw Mathim waiting in the chariot.

After a deep breath, Belrina accepted his hand.

Lythk leaped in after her.

Belrina looked at the path ahead, lined by innumerable excited Asthildi. "I will stand," she announced, creating a heavily fortified shield around them all.

The sakitha bond vibrated with emotion, prompting her to convey telepathically to Lythk, *'I cannot seem afraid. Use the seer's device to see the strength of my shield.'*

After Lythk did so, he sat, joining Mathim. The device allowed him to see magic energy as color; the deeper hues indicated more powerful energy, which would allow him to see and neutralize the greatest threats.

Seer Lazbith had taught Belrina the spell to provide her with the same benefit, and she closed her eyes as she worked the complicated patterns of magic energy. The Seer of Xorth had hastily explained the enchantment would reveal the source of the magic energy, saying "observe the colors and your intuition will guide you."

When Belrina opened her eyes, pale pink patterns of magic

energy swirled in the air outside the protective barrier. Every-one was using magic! The protective barrier itself was a vi-brant purple with undulating currents of energy constructing the magical wall. She surmised that purple denoted passive energy created by devices, whereas the pink color staining the low-level spells identified active energy.

Wanting the public to hear her voice, Belrina willed a slight alteration in the rhythm of the violet barrier's currents. A rosy rope of energy emerged from her core and touched the protective wall, enacting a subtle difference in frequency that rippled across both sides of the long barrier as far as she could see.

She noted that her shield formed a reassuring burgundy dome over the chariot. She stabilized herself to the chariot, and a pink energy nested around her feet.

"I am ready," Belrina said.

Mathim activated the chariot with a thin pink magical ten-dril, starting its stately advance. They crept forward, slower than a leisurely walk. Belrina now better understood Senator Mnetha's comment, for the chariot was designed to invite a spectacle.

"Thank you for coming to see me." Belrina smiled and waved, and the crowd responded. Asthildi jumped excitedly if her eyes seemed to touch them.

When Belrina saw Asthildi being pushed against the magic barrier, she raised her hand in concern. "Be careful! Please be kind to one another."

The pushing stopped and Asthildi chanted healing spells for those they had jostled. "Thank you—that is beautiful!" Belrina called.

From the corner of her eye, Belrina saw a column of scarlet energy streaking across the sky, arcing over the thirty-foot high violet barrier. She didn't know who was striking at her, but the Asthildi was powerful, generating the spell without a device.

She looked back at Lythk, who activated a device to deflect the powerful strike. A wave of royal purple energy eliminated the angry streak of magic.

Belrina hoped her smile remained intact. She waved to a couple of young Asthildi who had crafted magic signs in green letters; one Asthildi displayed a sign saying *Live* and a friend next to him displayed a sign reading *Well*.

"Yes, live well, my friends! Live lives of kindness and generosity," Belrina cried. The young ones seemed confused, but she was moving on.

The sky darkened with purple tsunami-sized waves cresting over both sides of the violet barrier.

Belrina regulated her breathing. Was this Primth attacking her? She hadn't expected to be tested until she disobeyed him.

Lythk and Mathim launched their own magic waves, obscuring the entire crowd.

Belrina saw a spiraling circle of red cutting through the purple barrier, and she neutralized it easily for they could not afford for the protective barrier to be compromised.

She wondered if the Seer of Xorth and Saolmyn had made it to the plaza. She could not have imagined these densely populated streets—Asthildi filled every space between the sky-reaching buildings that were as tall as mountains and as numerous as trees in a forest.

The purple waves continued to battle, and as long as the chariot kept advancing, Belrina kept smiling and waving, even though she couldn't see the Asthildi who had journeyed to see her.

A crimson torrent streaked through the sky to her right. Belrina considered whether to deviate from the plan and counteract it. She was supposed to conserve her energy, but Lythk and Mathim were still occupied with the never-ending waves of purple power.

As she was deciding, the crimson storm swept towards the opposition's purple wave. It must be the Seer of Xorth joining the fray! Belrina smiled in earnest.

The seer had neutralized one of the purple waves of energy, and Belrina waved to the crowd on that side. Young, old, merchants, scholars, so many distinct faces! This was the Empire—individual Asthildi who deserved to live life as fully as the People.

The second purple wave was now eliminated, as Mathim and Lythk had combined their forces against it. Belrina looked back at them. Mathim's hair clung to his forehead and Lythk's expression was grim.

She performed a healing spell, and a soft turquoise glow enveloped them briefly. What was the origin of this blue-tinged magic? Sensing Lythk's disapproval at what he considered an unnecessary expenditure of energy, Belrina filled the sakitha bond with confidence, for she had not drained her magic power in the slightest.

Rising above the crowd, an enormous irisean screen was alive with images. Belrina concluded this was a crier's field, projecting reports and media campaigns for the entire city. As the chariot inched closer, she realized the field displayed her ride to meet Primth.

Then, from the right, countless deep blue missiles of magic launched over the protective barrier. Those definitely weren't healing spells! What was the source of this blue magic that could be both destructive and restorative?

Adhering to the plan, Belrina ignored the onslaught, waving at the Asthildi, who were oblivious to the magic battle, accustomed as they were to magic energy sweeping through their daily existence.

The vaxili destroyed most of the blue magic missiles, but a few sizzled and sparked as they died on Belrina's shield, which throbbed as the currents collided. When the shield stabilized, it was crimson and noticeably thinner. Belrina reinforced her shield until it resumed its burgundy glow.

Mathim noted, "It will be useful to hear the crier's narration if our vision is obstructed again."

"Should I allow sound through the protective barrier?" Belrina asked.

Lythk nodded slightly.

Belrina concentrated, altering the currents of the barrier. The roaring crowd suddenly assaulted their ears, and the crier's narration soared above the din.

"Continuing her historic journey to meet Senator Primth, the forest girl's smile is as bright and beautiful as the diamond jewel at her waist," said the unknown crier. "We are eager to discover the stylist responsible for giving us this ethereal vision of a girl who grew up among savages."

Tuning out the narration, Belrina found faces in the crowd to greet. As they grew closer to the plaza, the garments worn by those in the crowd became more refined. Belrina moderated her wave, nodding to the cultured Asthildi.

The air erupted into purple bursts of magic as they encountered a horde of elite who could afford sophisticated devices. Maintaining discipline, Belrina did not engage in the melee, reinforcing the protective shield when an enchantment penetrated vaxili defenses. Soon, there were too many to combat. Sensing the nefarious purposes of the enchantments, Belrina shivered. Did any elite respect the law?

"We are seeing the first signs of emotion from the forest girl, as she undoubtedly realizes the importance of meeting Senator Primth, the Empire's most venerable senator," the crier continued. "Waiting to receive the forest girl, Senator Primth is serene and resplendent in a fashion-forward ensemble certain to impress his lowly born guest."

Belrina stared at Primth on the nearest crier's field. He was alone, sitting in a monstrous chair floating several feet above the plaza.

As the barrage of magic from the crowd continued, Belrina fed energy into her shield every minute.

From a distance, a volley of purple corkscrew-shaped projectiles flew over the protective barrier. If this attack was from Senator Primth himself, he had uttered no chants. Nor had the crier's field shown any purple energy emanating from him, although Belrina was uncertain Seer Lazbith's enchantment would work through the irisean screen.

Belrina had to assume Primth could conceal his use of magic from others. The Seer of Xorth had done so, projecting an illusion of a silent self when she chanted. It was a complicated process, but Primth could have engineered devices to allow him to do so with little effort.

None of the immense purple projectiles landed, as a bar of bright red energy swept the sky clear of the coruscating corkscrews. Again, the seer had intervened.

Belrina wondered why Seer Lazbith's assistance was intermittent. No comforting explanation sprang to mind.

"The forest girl is decidedly more somber. It is inevitable she will be subdued by the preeminence of Senator Primth, who can determine her fate in our Empire." The crier's voice evinced excitement.

Belrina schooled her features, yanking on her Asthildi mask. She would not allow Senator Primth to believe he intimidated her.

Lythk conveyed, *Belrina, Seeker Saolmyn wishes to speak with you, but your protective barrier prevents her from reaching you telepathically. Do not compromise the shield. Please.'*

Belrina touched him with her love. *'I will not.'* Carefully controlling her thoughts, she changed her shield, allowing telepathic communications only from Saolmyn. Then she made the protective shield self-reinforcing, allowing it to draw power from her as needed. To her eyes, a scarlet light briefly surrounded her.

'Belrina! Seer Lazbith has been detained by Primth's personal guard.' Saolmyn's voice sounded in Belrina's mind.

'I hope to help her escape,' Belrina responded. The Seer of Xorth had assured them the law protected her from any ill

treatment.

Claret-colored energy flowed from her into the protective shield as enchantments from the crowd continued to penetrate vaxili defenses.

'I am overlooking the plaza. I will aid you when you engage with Senator Primth. Belrina, you must prevail!'

The shield required an almost constant infusion of magic energy now as Lythk and Mathim were overpowered. Without thought, Belrina bathed them in turquoise healing energy before activating the device to replenish her magic reserves.

'Through the turvyst with Seer A'zine yesterday,' Saolmyn continued, *'I accessed her visions. Primth cannot be allowed to win.'* Images flowed with Saolmyn's emotions.

Belrina held the smile on her face while she saw visions of Asthildi growing in power and accomplishing new feats; Asthildi laughing and dining with People; natural resources flowing into Asthildi lands; the People enslaved by Primth, natural resources stolen for the Empire; forests stripped of life, creeks running dry; a wasting disease afflicting Asthildi who profited from the People's subjugation.

The last image was of Aurelio's face under Seer A'zine's hand, the examination revealing his capacity to store and augment magic energy. Belrina blinked at the startling discovery—her humanity contributed to her magical ability instead of diminishing it as Asthildi generally assumed.

Belrina stared ahead, unaware of the crowd for the first time. Her mind turned to Aurelio. Was he in Kalehala now or was this a vision of the future? She suppressed her concern for him for she could not help him now. But could she help the People?

'Fight Senator Primth! It is still possible to prevent the death and destruction he will bring to the People and the Empire.' Saolmyn conveyed hope to Belrina before terminating the telepathic connection.

The protective shield was drawing power at an alarming

rate. She wanted to sit down, but she continued to stand tall. The seer's visions were as yet only possibilities—Belrina had a chance to stop Primth from enacting his vile plans. She assessed the scene in front of her; everywhere purple energy sizzled against the protective barrier created by Seer Lazbith, and some currents drilled through that barrier only to be stopped by her shield.

The sky was lit by vibrant reds, purples, and blues, as magic energy vied for dominance. In the violence, there was no distinction between those who desired to vanquish or those who wished to protect. So this was the brutality of war. Belrina stiffened her knees, smothering tender sentiments for they had no place in this struggle for survival.

The silver chariot rounded a corner, and Belrina could see the Plaza of Rysdahl, empty of all Asthildi except a distant, levitating Senator Primth. A long path led to him, densely lined with lacy glass decorations, forming a fanciful version of a crystal forest arching overhead.

There was space for only one person on the path. Senator Primth intended for Belrina to face him alone.

31

THE CRYSTAL FOREST

B ELRINA BREATHED DEEPLY, SEEKING balance. In the sakitha bond, Lythk's frustration was predominant.

'I can follow you,' he suggested.

'He will punish you for intervening. If you were harmed or captured. . .' Belrina schooled her features.

'We cannot always give him what he wants, Belrina. Therein lies danger, too.'

'Yes, but I need you to be safe! Only then can you protect me.'

The bond roiled with competing emotions. *'Very well,'* Lythk conceded. *'Know that I will always be with you.'*

'And I with you.' It took all Belrina's spiritual strength not to look at her husband. She had to conceal his identity for as long as possible to protect him from Primth.

Somehow, she had to protect all those she loved. Belrina stood as tall as her frame would allow, finding, for the first time, a clear purpose in the Empire.

The chariot stopped, as did the magical bombardment from the upper echelon elite for they didn't dare interfere with Primth now.

Lythk and Mathim sprang from the chariot, each offering a hand to Belrina.

"The forest girl descends from the chariot, showing all aspects of her unique gown," the unseen crier whispered excitedly. "Respecting the past while embracing modern sensibilities, it is sensational!"

Belrina took her first few steps, reducing her shield to protect only herself. Her stomach twisted in response, objecting to leaving her husband and friend unprotected. She fiercely held on to the sakitha bond infused with Lythk's warrior spirit.

"The forest girl possesses a tranquility to rival any noble Asthildi despite her origins," the crier opined.

She had reached the crystal forest, and as she attempted to enter, a diffuse force barred her way. She peered at the glass arching overhead, discerning a blue magic resonance. The structure was a device! Belrina suppressed her alarm, trying to ascertain its purpose. The currents reminded her of magic blocks. Was Primth trying to deprive her of magic? Altering her shield to hug her body, Belrina stepped forward with difficulty. It was as if the crystal repelled her shield with a magnetic force.

She reduced the strength of her shield, its maroon lightening to pink. Her steps became easier, but her safety was severely compromised. Now within the crystal forest, the noise of the outside world vanished.

Experimentally, Belrina invoked the device to create a protective shield. Nothing happened. The crystal structure prevented the use of devices! Belrina sought calm, imbibing strength from the sakitha bond. She kept walking forward in the form-fitting gown, finally realizing she had disobeyed Primth by deviating from his instructions for her attire.

If he had attacked her before, why had he stopped? Primth sat imperiously, mildly interested in her progression. His silver robe had sufficient material to clothe ten people and its white fur lining had taken the life of several animals.

As he looked at the crier's field, his pale lips twisted into a smile. A layer of blue magic residue revealed the enhancements that had sculpted his face into a tight mask.

Her slow steps continued, bringing her closer to the figure who had dominated her life since she had arrived in the Empire.

A deep blue bolt emanated from Primth, striking into Belrina's mind the instant she saw it. Her flimsy shield shattered as she used all her mental energy to dispel the telepathic strike. Stunned by it, Belrina felt the rage fueling his attack. She remembered to step forward, resurrecting a thin protective shield.

Hundreds of purple energy threads snaked from the senator, lashing angrily at Belrina. She unleashed all her power, slowly forming a red frontal shield within the constraints of the crystal forest.

Overhead, a red swath of energy cut through most of the threads. Saolmyn! A few of the purple threads escaped, edging around her shield, and Belrina felt their magic currents soak into her. With her next step, she noticed there was a slit in her gown up to her thigh, and her neckline plunged a few inches lower.

She wrapped herself in a protective shield again, and she strained to step forward. Belrina had to blunt the effects of the crystal structure. She reached out to Saolmyn for guidance, but the telepathic connection was somehow blocked.

Belrina's mind raced furiously. Lythk always said she was too reluctant to become the aggressor. She summoned the senator's device, hoping the low-level spell would work.

She smiled when she felt it in her hand. Primth apparently wasn't concerned about thieves, for who would be bold enough to steal from him? The law allowed her to protect herself from intrusive magic, but would he accuse her of theft? Her smile faded. At least he could no longer alter her gown without her permission.

With a simple spell, Belrina could purloin all Primth's nefarious devices, but that *would* be a crime.

In her peripheral vision, Belrina saw a deep purple flash, presumably from a Primth associate. There was an element of concentration in the sakitha bond—Lythk must be launching a counteracting device, but it was too late, the purple energy was already upon her!

Belrina reinforced her shield with a pulse of red energy, hoping it would be enough.

She found herself blinking in confusion, looking at the elf above her. She did not know who he was, but he wore his preeminence gracefully. He was not as beautiful as. . . she could not remember.

Belrina took a step forward along the path lined with glossy limbs arching overhead. It was too quiet in this structure. She looked down at her gown, trying to remember who she was, but nothing seemed familiar. A pretty shower of purple magic raced towards her, but it was interrupted by a purple wave coming from behind her. She was in the middle of a battle!

Instinctively, Belrina created a protective shield, and her magic worked slowly. When the shield was fully formed, it immediately impeded her steps. She stood still while her mind clawed for a solid fact.

She had to go forward. Yes. She resumed her walk, forcing her muscles to propel her body forward. She would not reduce the strength of her red magic shield.

Purple thunderbolts of energy raced towards her, unleashed by the Asthildi in the floating throne. He smiled warmly at her as if to assure her his enchantments wouldn't be harmful.

The wrongness of his smile stopped her in her tracks. Originating from fear, a bright blue magic pulse sprang from her, eradicating the stranger's enchantment. Why hadn't the blue energy been impeded?

She kept walking forward, struggling internally and physically to combat the resistance against her shield. She quested inwardly, searching for one truth in this unknown reality. Within her, there was a constant source of love fueling her.

She connected her consciousness to that love, basking in its purity. Intuitively, she drew from the deep emotion, fashioning a protective shield with deep blue energy.

She stepped closer and closer to her attacker. Purple

streaks of power lashed at her again, but they died on her shield.

She was now safe, but her memory was impaired. She walked forward, desperately wanting to be healed. In the next instant, a healing blue light suffused her shield, restoring her mind.

Belrina smiled as Primth unleashed another powerful volley of purple energy that died upon her shield. She removed the indecent alterations Primth had made to her dress.

With nearly every step Belrina took forward, Primth and his allies hurled magic enchantments at her. Her husband and friends defused some of them while her indigo shield eliminated the rest, remaining resilient no matter how many strikes it suffered.

She was nearly clear of the crystal structure, but Primth wasn't going to stop. How long could Lythk and her friends hold out?

'You cannot penetrate this shield, Senator. Stop your assaults,' she said to Primth telepathically.

He laughed aloud. *'You have made a catastrophic mistake,'* the senator replied. *'I am a telepathic master!'*

Belrina felt a psychic pull similar to the turvuyst—her mind was being siphoned into his! In another moment, there would be nothing left of herself. Again, she fought. She instituted her psychic defenses, slowing the rate at which Primth pulled her into his mind.

Magically, she lashed out, slashing at the connection, but it wasn't magical in nature. She poured more energy into her psychic defenses, but she could not stop Primth. She could feel his will to dominate, his lust for power, and soon her mind would be indistinguishable from his.

Belrina connected to the sakitha bond, choosing to love Lythk until the moment she was gone. As she poured what remained of herself into their unique love, she was intensely her own person. And insulated from Primth.

With each moment seeming to last an eternity, Belrina focused on the love she experienced in the sakitha bond, reclaiming her mind. Using her entire being, she ousted Primth and painstakingly built walls to protect herself from further telepathic intrusion.

When she was able to breathe normally again, Belrina took another step forward. Primth's twisted mental landscape lingered in the same way as storm clouds darken the day. How many had fallen victim to Primth's telepathic manipulations? Almost without thought, a deep blue wave of energy emanated from Belrina, binding Primth's ability to coerce others telepathically.

She emerged from the crystal forest, dropping into a deep bow for the senator. A wild and thunderous applause erupted from thousands of Asthildi.

Now outside the magic-blocking device, Belrina was free to use traditional sources of magic energy, and she reinforced her blue protective shield, fueling it with red magic energy until it glowed a brilliant magenta.

In the sakitha bond, she shared relief with Lythk, but he quickly transitioned to wariness, for the next battle with Primth was beginning.

The senator stood, supported by empty air, relishing the attention of the crowd. The uproar reminded Belrina that she now had to grapple with Primth's political and social power.

With outstretched arms, Belrina kept her head down as if she had no position in Asthildi society.

"Asthildi," Primth said in a resonant voice amplified by a device. "Thank you for your enthusiasm." The crowd quickly quieted. "It is exciting to meet a creature none of us have seen before: a girl raised as a human who claims to be of Asthildi blood. Arise, Forest Girl."

Belrina had to counter the senator's implication that she did not have Asthildi blood. She rose gracefully, transmuting several of the diamonds on her gown into white-winged butterflies swirling around her head. As she smiled in delight, the crowd reacted noisily.

Frozen, the senator stared at the circling butterflies. Belrina waited for him to speak while the fluttering continued around her. When the crowd began murmuring uneasily in the silence, she inclined her head into another bow.

"Senator Primth," she magically projected her voice, "I am honored beyond words." She paused, smiling. "My friends call me Belrina, and I would be pleased if you, too, would call me so." She could not allow him to continue calling her Forest Girl.

The crowd murmured appreciatively. Primth's colorless face was composed, but his eyes augured into her. When his lips twisted upwards into a smile, fear nestled within Belrina's belly.

"Belrina of the Forest People. What are these winged creatures you have conjured?"

"They are butterflies, Senator Primth." She attempted an Elvish translation, not wishing to underscore the senator's point that she was a foreigner. "I hope you like them as much as I do?" His response earnestly puzzled her.

"They distract me from enjoying your beauty." Primth smiled, pleased at his recovery. He resumed his seat, gazing down at her.

"I shall remove the distraction, Senator." Belrina directed the butterflies to land on her gown, where they reverted to diamonds.

Thousands of exclamations created another din.

Senator Primth's eyes narrowed. He adjusted a large sapphire ring, and red bolts and purple waves descended upon Belrina from all sides. She stood calmly within her protective dome, fueled by both emotional and mental sources of energy.

Counteracting purple waves annihilated a few assaults, reminding her that her husband and friends were fighting with her. Belrina connected with the sakitha bond, feeling Lythk's determination.

"Tell me, Belrina of the Forest People, why did you come to our Empire?"

Belrina ignored the magic attacks eradicated by her shield. "My journey to Kalehala was unplanned, Senator Primth." Belrina hoped the Asthildi crowd would hear the truth of her words. "Before I arrived, I did not know of my Asthildi heritage or this vast empire full of wonders."

"Now that you are here, what are your intentions? What plans have you made?"

Magic strikes continued to pummel her indestructible magenta shield, which she continuously reinforced with traditional magic energy. Primth must be alluding to her meeting with Senator Mnetha. Belrina chose her words carefully. "If given the opportunity, I would like to study with the lakri. I enjoy helping others."

"Politicians provide the greatest public service. Do you have political ambition?" Primth inquired icily.

Wide-eyed, Belrina shook her head. "No, Senator Primth. I assure you, I have none of the skills. . . I am not suited at all for politics." She gathered her thoughts as her shield continuously sucked energy to withstand the assaults from Primth's allies. "Nineteen years of life have not provided me with the required wisdom."

Meeting Primth's eyes, Belrina nearly stepped back from his naked desire. She looked down, confused at his transformation. The magic assaults ceased.

She activated the device to restore her magic power.

Senator Primth stood. "Dear one, I should like to continue our conversation, but first, come," he beckoned, "let me introduce you to Asthildi society."

Observing the pink residue of magic outlining the invisible steps leading to the senator, Belrina ascended, keeping her eyes on Primth's shoulder. He held out his arm, which she hesitantly accepted. He swiftly pulled her close.

Like all Asthildi, he was tall, and her head barely reached his shoulder even with the few inches she gained from her heeled slippers. She reminded herself that physicality was irrelevant in magical combat.

Stepping away from Primth, Belrina bowed deeply to the gathered Asthildi.

"Asthildi, we have here in Belrina of the Forest People an extraordinary gem," Primth proclaimed. "She is welcome to sparkle among us."

The Asthildi host clamored and roared.

Rising, Belrina smiled, acknowledging all who had gathered.

Primth raised his hand in the air and silence immediately followed. "We must depart now." He offered his arm again, and Belrina couldn't refuse. "Good afternoon all." After a moment, he added, "Live well."

With a chant, he erected a privacy screen, and then he whisked Belrina away. The invisible platform continued through an ancient stone archway and over a courtyard of colorful art installations.

When Belrina tried to slow their pace, Primth gripped her arm. They marched above the art, her gown flaring behind her. She despaired over the solitude of the place.

"Senator, where are the attendants? I could provide—"

"We do not need them." Primth tightened his grip on her arm.

Belrina's mind raced faster than her feet. She called for Lythk telepathically, encountering emptiness. Primth had somehow disabled telepathic communication, but Lythk would find her. "Senator, you are hurting me."

"Nonsense." Primth pulled her down invisible stairs, pushing her into the ancient stone building. Belrina kept her feet moving, easily regaining her balance.

Experimentally, she used magic powered from her emotions, which had worked in the crystal forest. When she turned to face Primth, Belrina was in vaxili garb.

The cavernous chamber lined with pillars was a good place to spar. In the center rotunda, there was an elegant table heaped with a variety of food and drink.

"You and I are alone at last," Primth said, conjuring a wine-glass to his hand.

"I should like to come to an understanding, Senator Primth."

He laughed. "You are spirited. Excellent!"

Belrina reinforced her shield, which shone a deep blue. She connected to the sakitha bond, sensing Lythk's frustration. Something—or someone—was effectively blocking him from this chamber. Belrina conveyed serenity to her husband.

"Properly attire yourself, girl. Show me the gown as I designed it."

"Forgive me, Senator, but I wish to remain as I am," she replied politely.

"If you do not obey me, I shall harm your friend." With a word, an irisean screen appeared, displaying Saolmyn in a small dark room. "Shall I tell my guards to punish her? Her interference was most inconvenient."

"Seeker Saolmyn is under the protection of the Seer of Kalehala!"

"Oh, I will claim I didn't know that when I instructed my guards." Primth smiled. "How much punishment can your friend endure before the Seer of Kalehala intervenes?" He sipped his wine. "Some perish after a few minutes of torture. My guards are experts, you see."

Belrina transmuted the vaxili whites into the black gown Njal had styled. She blinked away tears, which she knew would only enhance the senator's satisfaction.

"Still not what I had in mind."

Belrina summoned Primth's device to her hand. "If I activate this? Will that. . .?" She looked away.

"Oh, allow me." The senator came to take the device from her, lingering. "Your youth is delicious."

Belrina quickly stepped away.

Primth's face hardened. "Tell me. Who is your sakitha lover?"

"I shall not tell you."

"I suppose it is of little significance now. He cannot stop me from loving you, can he?" Primth smirked.

Alarm flooded through Belrina as she finally realized his plan.

Primth activated the device, and she gasped when the garment cinched her torso. The spiked slippers provided unreliable stability. She struggled to maintain her balance, as Lythk had taught her. Every breath gave her the clarity of mind she needed to fight.

"Ah," Senator Primth sighed, drawing near.

Belrina wanted to run, but what would he do to Saolmyn?

"You are a work of art." He traced a finger along the neckline of the gown, grazing her flesh. "For my eyes only."

Frozen, Belrina didn't know if she could lawfully attack him for touching her. If this wasn't significant or sustained harm, why would she rather be beaten than endure this? *'Lythk,'* she cried out, *'I need you!'*

The senator seized her, and after a moment, Belrina freed herself, using a vaxili technique. She wanted to save Saolmyn, but. . .

"Senator, I cannot. I will not." Belrina made her refusal clear, evading him.

Primth continued stalking her.

"I will use magic against you, Senator, if you continue to assault me."

The senator laughed, filling the space with joyless humor. "Who will believe you didn't consent to me? Me! That you haven't used magic against me reveals your consent."

Belrina stared at Primth, wondering if he was sane. "I will

escape, and I will tell the remaining crowd out there—"

"Tell them what, dear one?" He interrupted, smirking before lunging at her lazily.

Belrina used evasive maneuvers, forced to run on her toes in the odd slippers. "I saw your mind. You intend to enslave the People and steal their resources."

He paused his pursuit to stare at her. "Why should any Asthildi care? It will bring them wealth."

"Because it will lead to their death!" Belrina ran past the table, placing it between them. "The perversity of enslaving humans will corrupt elves. Asthildi who benefit from the evil enterprise will forfeit their immortality."

"Why would they believe you? I certainly do not." Primth slapped the table. "I tire of this." He activated a device that enveloped Belrina's blue shield in purple energy, exerting pressure sufficient to turn carbon into diamonds.

Belrina fed all her emotional energy into her shield, but she did not know how long she could withstand the crushing weight. "The Seer of Kalehala had this vision," she said, her voice breathy.

"But she hasn't proclaimed it, has she? Thus, no one will believe it is her vision." Senator Primth eyed her, waiting for her to break. "My dear, I do not know why you are fighting. I know you will enjoy our love as much as I will."

Belrina tried to invoke the device to restore her magic power.

Primth laughed. "I can use devices, but you cannot. You should not be able to use magic at all." His face hardened. "There will be consequences for my magicians' failure." Malice lit his eyes.

Belrina repressed her fear, which weakened her ability to conjure magic energy from love. She struggled to find something useful from the merge with Primth's mind. "You have many secrets." As she flagged under the pressure exerted by Primth's device, Belrina gripped the edge of the table to remain standing.

The senator leisurely walked towards her. He gripped her arm, and she mustered the strength to spin away.

"You cheated in your first election!" Belrina shouted. "You used telepathy to influence voters." She fueled her shield with every ounce of her being.

"You cannot prove it." The senator seized her waist, holding her against him.

"Let me go!" Belrina growled. She did not have the strength to move her body away from the grotesque elf. "I can prove it, Senator," Belrina breathed, managing to look him in the eye. She could not hold out much longer—the force exuded by the evil enchantment was too great.

Primth began undoing her garments. "You cannot escape me now."

In a panic, Belrina generated a magic pulse, knocking the senator against a pillar. Using the energy weakened her shield, and it collapsed under the weight of Primth's spell.

Energy seared her skin, awakening strange feelings and sensations. She desired to touch and be touched. Belrina struggled for control over her body. This was not love.

Primth struggled to his feet, producing a transmitter. "I will punish your friend for your disobedience."

"Senator, I am ashamed of myself." Belrina smiled at Primth warmly, and her body drifted towards him of its own accord. "Tell me, how can I make amends?" she kept her voice low. *No!* Belrina screamed internally. He was going to hurt Saolmyn if she didn't stop him. Belrina used her whole being to deny the intrusive spell.

Senator Primth chuckled throatily. "You will atone for your crime against me, but so will your friend."

"No!" Belrina shouted, summoning the transmitter. Half a heartbeat later, she divested the senator of all his devices—a stunning number of them sailed towards the chamber's impressive dome. She invoked another spell and blue magic energy briefly engulfed the collection. "You cannot retrieve them," she said. "I have done what is necessary to defend myself and others."

Senator Primth tried to summon the devices, his chants proving futile.

"I have committed no crimes against you," Belrina concluded.

The senator ran towards his devices, chanting furiously.

"Only if you seek to harm me or the People, will I reveal your secret." The senator did not appear to be listening. "Please, Senator, let me go in peace and abandon your reprehensible plans for the People. Then we can forget all this unpleasantness." She had not wished to beg, but she had to end their conflict.

Primth did not respond, fixating on retrieving his devices.

Belrina erected her protective shield again, comforted by its deep blue glow, and then she turned her back to the senator, walking towards the courtyard where she hoped to find Lythk. They needed to rescue Saolmyn and the Seer of Xorth.

Primth chanted, and she turned, seeing a pink magic strike, which she ignored, resuming her escape, as she knew her shield would protect her. With such a weak magical aptitude, Primth was virtually harmless without his devices.

Belrina heard the senator running towards her. Waiting until the last moment, she stepped aside. Primth launched past her through the doorway, falling on the dusty stone pavers.

She darted around him, hustling through the courtyard as quietly as possible. There was no sign of Lythk or Mathim, and Primth's powerful associates could attack at any moment.

A few feet from the stone arch, an enormous guard stepped in her path. Belrina quickly set a spell so the burly Asthildi could not come closer than six feet. She edged around him, transmuting the spiked heels so she could run. Primth's associate continued trying to reach her, striding in place without gaining an inch.

Belrina sprinted, finally escaping the courtyard and its limits on her powers. Using traditional magic energy, she invoked the restoration device, and then, without losing a stride, she donned a light gray gown covering every inch of skin.

Magic missiles rained upon her, eliminated by her bright magenta shield. She should have known Primth would refuse the truce she had offered. Additional guards, wearing Primth's ochre sash, rushed at her, and she used the same spell to keep them at least six feet away.

As long as Primth had power, he was a danger to all she loved. Belrina saw no other choice—she would inform the public about the senator's election fraud.

32

"ALYN NOLA KYNDA"

"ASTHILDI!" BELRINA AMPLIFIED HER voice, standing in the empty Plaza of Rysdahl. She generated an irisean screen to capture her image, connecting it to the crier's fields. "I need your help."

She scanned the plaza, hoping to see Lythk or Mathim but she only saw Primth's associates, who continued their magical bombardment. "I am under attack."

Instinctively, Belrina created a spell to share what she saw with the crier's fields. Red bolts and purple waves of energy emanating from Asthildi wearing ochre sashes popped onto the screen nearest her.

Belrina noticed Asthildi elite coming to stand on balconies overlooking the plaza.

"Senator Primth also holds a friend of mine, Seeker Saolmyn, hostage. He tried to coerce me. . ." Belrina choked on the words. "I escaped, but my friend is in danger. Please help us!"

Primth's associates ceased their attacks just as Belrina heard the murmurings of Asthildi returning to see a new spectacle. Where was Lythk? Primth would soon return to the plaza.

Belrina focused the irisean screen on her face again. "They have stopped attacking for now, but I am still afraid. Senator Primth is a threat to us all!" she rattled on. "He used telepathy to secure votes in his first election, and I can prove it. Many of you know I am a talented magician. I will create a spell to show every Asthildi here who has been telepathically manipulated by Senator Primth."

She closed her eyes, visualizing the complex currents of energy before carefully creating them. Using more power than ever before, Belrina flung the spell as far as she could, sending ripples of magenta energy through the streets of Rysdahl.

Now she needed to convince them to invoke the spell. "The truth will be revealed when you say these three words: *alyn nola kynda*," she said. "Then if you glow with yellow light, Senator Primth has manipulated you."

"Asthildi!" Senator Primth was back on the invisible platform. "The forest girl has gone mad. Don't listen to her! She is the one who assaulted me."

"Senator Primth." Senator Mnetha's voice soared down from a balcony. "You have been accused of a deplorable crime, and to absolve yourself, shouldn't you encourage us to invoke the spell? If Asthil Belrina is insane, then her spell will not work."

Belrina created another irisean screen to capture Senator Mnetha for the crier's fields. From the corner of her eye, she saw a flash of white. Looking across the courtyard, Belrina saw Lythk and Mathim grappling with Primth's guards. The vaxili's swift, deft strikes were quickly disabling their foes, who were superior only in number.

"Asthildi," Senator Mnetha continued, "I advise you to enact the spell." She had more than a dozen friends with her, including several attendants. "Let's say the chant all together," she urged them. "*Alyn nola kynda*."

When they complied, yellow light instantly surrounded one of her associates and two of her attendants. They looked at themselves in surprise.

Belrina glimpsed another Asthildi enveloped in yellow light on a balcony to her left. She sent the irisean screen there, and as it traveled through the air, the screen captured several Asthildi aglow.

The crowd was invoking the spell!

Belrina felt Lythk near her, protecting her once again. Breathing more fully, she began navigating the screen throughout the streets, capturing the extraordinary number of Asthildi whom Primth had coerced for the crier's fields.

"This is an illusion!" Primth cried. "The forest girl is unwell, and she is sharing her delusion with you all. She should be remanded into my care, and I will ensure she receives treatment."

"This is no illusion," Belrina insisted. "A seer can verify the veracity of my magic. Asthildi, visit your seer and the truth will be confirmed."

"I shall not allow you to take custody of Belrina," Senator Mnetha said, again projecting her voice.

Senator Rubinsyth spoke next, also amplifying his tremulous voice, "Nor I."

From a distant balcony, Senator Luken projected her clear voice, "Nor I."

A chorus of senatorial voices joined them in defying Senator Primth.

The crowd responded noisily, and the crier's fields showed Asthildi shouting at each other, arguing. Violence would soon erupt. A raucous chant arose in the streets: "Electorate challenge! Electorate challenge!"

Belrina didn't know what those words meant, but she observed Primth leaving as hastily as decorum would permit.

"My friends," Primth shouted, "I shall be vindicated. The forest girl spouts slanderous lies. She commits another crime against me! Asthildi, I have always fought for your interests." Then he was out of view.

"Asthildi!" Belrina addressed the crowd again. "I have shared the truth with you so you may live freely. Please choose peace and love. Do not turn against each other tonight. Please return home, be with your loved ones, and go in peace."

Various calls and chants competed for her attention, but

there were no more demands for an "electorate challenge."

She relinquished her control of the crier's fields, turning towards Lythk. As she gazed at him, she allowed the irisean screens she had generated to dissipate. He and Mathim were monitoring the retreat of Primth's associates.

"Magisthild, the senator has the Seer of Xorth and Saolmyn," Belrina called out to her husband. "What if Primth is leaving with them?"

Before Lythk could reply, Senator Mnetha appeared before her amid the swirl of a transporter.

Belrina dropped into an unsteady bow.

"Rise, rise! Belrina, that was incredible. The citizens will demand an electorate challenge." After a look at Belrina's face, she said, "I will explain later. We must leave here at once, as it isn't safe. Please come with me."

"Senator Mnetha, I intend to return to Kalehala."

"If you leave now, Senator Primth may convince the public that you are the criminal. You must go to the Capitol, for Primth is not defeated yet."

"My goal has never been to defeat him, Senator Mnetha. I only wish to be free of him."

"Belrina, we must leave." Lythk bowed slightly to Senator Mnetha. Caution flooded their bond.

"To be free of the senator, you must defeat him. He will seek revenge for what you have done tonight."

Belrina closed her eyes. She could not deny the truth of Mentha's words. "Senator." She bowed. "Please allow me to consider what my next move should be."

Mnetha's blonde hair caught the moonlight as she inclined her head. "Can I not persuade you to take refuge with me tonight, Belrina?"

"I cannot seek refuge yet. I will contact you tomorrow, Senator. Thank you for your help tonight."

"I owe you considerably more gratitude, Belrina." Senator Mnetha bowed. "Please stay safe." When she invoked her transporter, she vanished.

Lythk offered his arm, which she gladly accepted. "Please create a privacy screen, Belrina. We need to protect you from the crowd."

Belrina nodded. "It is done. Now, Saolmyn and Seer Lazbith—"

"Is here," the Seer of Xorth suddenly appeared, looking as formidable as the moment Belrina first saw her. "They left me unattended several minutes ago and I escaped."

Belrina held out her hand, and Lazbith grasped it. "I'm so glad to see you, Seer. Did you see Saolmyn?"

"I saw both Saolmyn and Njal."

For the first time, Belrina faltered. Lythk supported her easily, wrapping his arm around her waist. "Mathim is communicating with Amirtha," Lythk said quietly for Belrina's ears.

"Do not communicate with them telepathically," Seer Lazbith was saying to Belrina. "The senator may have set a trap."

"We should not attempt a rescue tonight," Lythk said. *'You are too weary, Belrina.'* Love swept through their bond.

"I do not wish for them to spend one more moment under his control. He will abuse and torment them," Belrina objected.

"I can go," Seer Lazbith volunteered. "It is not in anyone's interests for Primth to have leverage over you." She paused, looking obliquely at Mathim. "It would aid the campaign if I did not go alone."

Mathim promptly bowed. "You will not be alone. Magisthild, take Belrina to safety, and I will handle the rescue."

"Thank you," Lythk said simply.

"Please let me know when they are safe!" Belrina called after Mathim and the Seer of Xorth as they withdrew from the plaza.

Lythk gently drew her against him, wrapping his arms around her. "Please do not worry about your friends. Let me take care of you."

Belrina gladly settled against his chest in the privacy afforded by the screen she used to conceal them from the crowd.

"How did Primth get to Njal?" Belrina murmured.

"Myrin assaulted Amirtha, absconding with Njal. He will be punished for committing a crime against a vaxili," Lythk answered, flooding their bond with his indignation.

"Was Vaxili Amirtha harmed?" Belrina clutched Lythk's tunic.

"She has suffered worse in magic grappling," Lythk responded, his lips against her hair. "We should leave now, Belrina, but your protective shield will not allow us to travel."

Belrina altered her shield, allowing her husband to activate a transporter and engineer their escape.

When the swirls of magic receded, Belrina opened her eyes. They were in a sleeping chamber with a low bed covered by somber-colored linens. Other furnishings, simple by design, were constructed from natural alder. Two large pieces of wall art in muted tones flanked opposite walls.

"Where are we?" she asked.

"A family estate always vacant in this season." Lythk uttered a few incantations. "I have secured our perimeter." He did not release her from his embrace. "You can release your shield, Belrina," he whispered, stroking her back.

He chanted another incantation, opening heavy dark curtains to reveal a night sky streaked with lightning bolts. The vibrant veins of incandescent power eradicated the darkness.

"Rakti Za spoke of the disruptions caused by weather control devices," Belrina muttered against Lythk's chest. Listening to his steady heartbeat, she said, "It is spectacular."

Slowly, Belrina released the magic energy she controlled with her mind, leaving a blue glow around her and Lythk. Holding him tighter, she breathed evenly, releasing the last of the shield that had protected her from Primth.

"I don't know if I want to know everything," Lythk said, stroking her hair. "It is enough that you are safe with me now."

The sakitha bond quivered with emotion, tranquility victorious in the end.

"It was our love, Lythk, that allowed me to survive. Without our bond, I would have been lost."

Her husband kissed her hair lightly as Belrina clung to him, basking in the everlasting flow of his love.

"I came too close to losing you, didn't I?" Lythk asked softly.

"Too close," Belrina sobbed quietly, and he held her for several minutes before carrying her to bed. Under her husband's protection, she could finally rest.

W HEN BELRINA WOKE IN the morning, Lythk was standing by the window, the transmitter to speak with the Seer of Kalehala in his hand. Except for his soft smile, he fit the image of a dutiful magisthild.

She returned his smile, wondering how much longer they could preserve the pretext. "Good morning, husband. What news of Njal and Saolmyn?" Belrina adjusted her robe, joining him.

"They were rescued and are now safely in Kalehala. Mathim was injured, but he is currently being treated by lakri."

"Gods United be praised," Belrina breathed.

Lythk opened his hand, offering her the transmitter to call Seer A'zine. As his gaze rested on her face, their bond came alive, filling Belrina with enough energy to convey an entire river to Kalehala. He wanted. . .

She stepped closer. "No more physical distancing, Magisthild?"

In response, Lythk caressed her cheek, kissing her.

Remembering their time in the sakitha tent, Belrina felt warm. Reluctantly, she disengaged. "There is something I need to share with you before we communicate with Seer A'zine," she informed him. "It would be best if I do it telepathically."

Lythk nodded, and she brushed her fingers against his temple, feeding him the visions Saolmyn had shared with her.

"The boy?"

"Aurelio. He wanted to marry me," she replied softly. "I don't know how he could be in Kalehala."

"It would be impressive if he endured the journey on foot."

"Yes." After a pause, Belrina said, "I would like to know your thoughts, Lythk. Can we return to Kalehala as originally planned?" As Senator Mnetha had pointed out, Primth would try to erase the truth the *alyn nola kynda* spell had revealed. And if he remained in power, no one was safe.

Lythk's green eyes showed conflicting emotions. "Belrina, our empire is on the brink of civil war. As much as I would like you to be safe in Kalehala, you will be a voice of peace in the Capitol. We have not had a war in nearly two millennia. Millions could die."

She gaped. "Millions?" she repeated numbly.

"Yes. I have been involved in border skirmishes resulting in thousands dead. Before our bond, I would have said we must prevent war at any cost, but I will support whatever decision you make."

"We are aligned in this, dear one," Belrina looked into her husband's clear eyes. "I started this conflict, and we must prevent any violence that could result from it." Her voice grew quiet. "I offered Primth a truce, but he didn't take it."

Lythk clasped her shoulder. "You are blameless. It is Primth who is responsible."

She nodded slowly, and then while watching hot white light dance on an energy-capturing grid, she called the Seer of Kalehala.

"Belrina, my sweet one. Are you well? I wish I could be with you now." The seer's voice made Belrina smile.

"I am well. Lythk is with me," she replied. After a breath, she said, "Seer A'zine, through the turvyst mergers, Saolmyn saw your visions concerning the People and the future of the Asthildi. She shared them with me unintentionally."

"Then she has violated the principles of our order."

Belrina's body tensed. "Will she be expelled? On my account?"

"I cannot say now, Belrina. There is much I need to share," Seer A'zine deftly segued. "An associate of Primth's began questioning your citizenship, and therefore I submitted the record of your sakitha partnership, which prompted the vaxithild to unseal Lythk's resignation."

Belrina grasped her husband's hand.

"Also, Forest People came to Kalehala," the seer continued. "One has been desperately waiting to speak with you. Shall I summon him?"

"Yes!" Belrina exclaimed. In a few moments, she could hear Aurelio's voice.

"Where do I speak to her?"

"Aurelio! I can hear you. How did you come to be in Kalehala?" Belrina reverted to her native language with ease. She could hear Seer A'zine's translation stone at work, which helped Lythk follow the conversation.

"Belrina! Is that really you?"

"Yes, Aurelio." Belrina smiled. "The cube you see is a magic device that allows my voice to be transmitted to you."

"Where are you? Are you well? Can I see you soon?" Aurelio asked in quick succession.

"I am well. I hope to see you soon, too, but I cannot yet return to Kalehala. How did you get there, Aurelio?"

"I had to find you, and I knew the Old Ones could help. My mother didn't want me to go alone, so several friends came with me. We bargained with the Old Ones, and they gave us magic items to help us get to Kalehala. It was a long way, Belrina, but I had to come. I had to. . . know you are safe and well."

"But such dangers you must have faced! I am glad you are safe. And everyone who joined you—are they safe, too?"

"Yes, we are all well!" he replied joyfully. Then he lowered his voice. "But Belrina, are you truly safe?"

"It is complicated, Aurelio. Everything here is more complicated."

"Belrina, let me help you."

She could envision his large brown eyes and earnest face—he was utterly defenseless in the Empire. While she considered, Seer A'zine broke the silence.

"Belrina, the Council of the Wise has convened a summit in the Capitol to discuss recent events. I will go, as I must do what I can to prevent war."

"As will I," Belrina responded in Elvish. "I must also protect the People." She reverted to her native language. "Aurelio, I would be happy to accept your help." He was not defenseless; he had survived untold dangers, proving he was as crafty as he was courageous. He would be a reliable ally in her campaign to protect their people, unlike Asthildi, who may not wish to halt an enterprise providing them profit. "You may travel with Seer A'zine to the Capitol, if she permits," she told her friend.

"May Cesario come with me? He is invaluable. I would not have survived without him."

"You may bring as many friends as Seer A'zine allows."

"I will gladly escort any of Belrina's friends to the Capitol," the seer responded.

"Then I shall see you soon, Belrina." Aurelio's voice conveyed all his emotions.

She had become accustomed to the reserve of elite Asthildi, and the transparency of his affection pierced her. Belrina's eyes misted at the thought of causing him pain.

"Yes, but, Aurelio, there are new dangers here. Learn as much as you can about Asthildi culture and stay close to Seer A'zine." Belrina switched to Elvish to say, "I shall see you both in the Capitol soon. Be well until then."

Disconnecting the transmitter, Belrina turned to Lythk, who stared at the lightning flashing in the bright blue sky. She encircled an arm around his waist, fingering the medallion on his chest.

"Shall I remove it all?" she asked softly.

When he nodded, she transmuted his uniform, replacing his peridot cloak and vaxili whites. Then she gently touched a lock of her husband's blond hair, erasing the years of service reflected in his braids. Finally, she dispelled the enchantment concealing his sakitha tattoos.

Lythk kissed her hands as he had in the sakitha tent. "It is not a sacrifice," he said, his voice soft. "I was chosen." His vibrant eyes caressed her face. "By you." His smile was as luminous as the lightning storm outside the window. "I wanted to be your partner. Belrina, I was in love with you before we entered that tent."

Her surprise was swiftly replaced by joy, and she leaned towards her husband, soaking in every precious emotion flowing through their bond. "I do not wish to remember any time before our love," she whispered, gazing into his golden-flecked eyes. "I choose you, Lythk, today and every tomorrow."

He kissed her, his hands pulling her body closer. Her arms encircled his broad back, and all her senses delighted in experiencing her husband's love. Their kiss grew in urgency until he carried her to the bed.

"Lythk!" she exclaimed when she could draw breath again. "We must go to the Capitol." Her hands lightly held his shoulders for it was so difficult to let go.

Her husband sighed, saying, "Duty has never been more burdensome."

"I wish we could linger." Belrina's senses were still heightened as if she had taken a few sips of azuka. "But what action has Primth taken while I have been recovering?"

Lythk extracted himself slowly, helping Belrina rise from the bed. After she attired herself suitably, she summoned the transporter to her upturned hand, her mind turning to the battles which awaited them in the Capitol.

It was open war between them and Primth now, and the entire Empire might be swept into the fray. Belrina would promote peace, but she would not yield to Primth and his evil schemes. She would use the power she had found last night to stand against him once again. Perhaps the Seer of Kalehala's visions of peace for both the People and Asthildi would then be realized.

"It is time to leave, my warrior-husband," Belrina said, her voice steady. The fear that had governed her since she heard Primth's name was gone, replaced by a greater purpose. "This time we'll fight alongside each other, facing whatever may come together."

A ferocious wave of love surged through the sakitha bond in response to her words.

'Always,' her husband replied telepathically, his green eyes conveying his pledge to endure all to remain by her side.

When she held out her hands, Lythk grasped them and they closed their eyes in unison. As Belrina activated the transporter, she unleashed a torrent of energy. It swirled around them in fierce currents reminiscent of the magic that had brought her to the Asthildi Empire.

Sneak Peek

Book 2: A New Savagery

Lifting her head from Lythk's chest, Belrina stared into his lifeless green eyes, open towards, but not seeing, the starry night sky. She had infused him with healing energy, conjuring every magic ability she possessed, and yet breathing remained his only sign of life.

'*You must come back to me.*' Belrina connected with Lythk telepathically, encountering a numbing void that seeped into her. Pulling away, she disconnected, silent tears streaming down her face. As she looked upon Lythk's body, prone on the grassy ground, she probed the sakitha bond, fueling it with love.

"Your love rescued me from obliteration," Belrina whispered. "Let my love guide you now, Lythk." Pouring all her energy into their bond, she clung to his limp hand. Everything she had left, all her hope, all her strength, she tried to give to him. The sakitha bond absorbed her emotion, but conveyed no response from her unconscious husband.

"Please, please, I need you," she sobbed into his chest again, as the arms, which had once encircled her even while he slept, rested on the hard, cold ground.

When Aurelio placed his hand on her shoulder, she looked up blankly.

"They must be very close now, Belrina." Aurelio watched her carefully, his dark eyes revealing all his emotions. "We should leave."

Belrina avoided those eyes, for she had done enough weeping. Rising from her husband's side, she said, "You should go back to the base with Lythk. Please ask Njal to treat him." She began walking towards the enemy.

"I will not leave you," Aurelio protested.

"You will." Belrina continued her even strides. Her feet did not feel the ground nor her skin the chill of the night.

Aurelio's long legs quickly caught up to her. "No, I cannot leave you alone. Not now."

Belrina looked back at her unconscious husband, his pale skin and hair contrasting with the darkness of the night. "I do not wish for him to be alone." She met Aurelio's eyes now. "Please, stay with him. Please do this for me."

Aurelio froze. "Belrina..." Swallowing, he raised his hand towards her.

She stepped away. "You do not need to protect me. Tonight, I won't be the one who dies."

Closing the distance between them, Aurelio planted himself in front of her. "You are angry." He looked back at Lythk, compassion flooding his face. "You have cause to wish them harm." His hands balled into tight fists. "We all do, but violence only leads to foul deeds."

"Do you think we can win this war harming no one?" she asked quietly, looking at him.

Aurelio flinched, whether at her gaze or her words, Belrina did not know.

"I will do what needs to be done to protect the People," she affirmed. When she sensed the use of magic energy, likely an exploratory probe searching for them, she erected a large protective shield, encompassing them all. More slowly, she created three individual shields, letting the larger magic dome dissipate. Turning her attention back to Aurelio, she said, "I will lose no one else I love."

"And how can I let someone I love fight alone?" Aurelio countered. "Together, we will be stronger."

"They are coming." Belrina looked past him. "I have decided what I must do."

Squeezing his eyes shut, her friend whispered, "Once again, you will face danger and the only thing I can do is pray for your safety."

With effort, Belrina gently touched Aurelio's forearm. "Do not be afraid for me." *I am the one who they should fear.* She did not give voice to her last thought, lest she alarm him again. "You need only believe that the Gods United are just. For if there is any justice in this word, I will not fail."

Aurelio gripped her hand. "I fear I will regret this every day the Gods United grant me life." The unshed tears in his eyes reflected the moonlight. Staring into her eyes, he said fervently, "May they allow me to see you again." He released her hand, sprinting away.

Belrina knew Aurelio would honor her wishes, and Lythk would soon receive the healing he needed. *A skilled lakri like Njal can work miracles*, she told herself. As the memory of Lythk's frozen eyes flooded her vision, her fingernails dug into the palms of her hand. Closing her eyes, Belrina drew a telepathic shield over her emotions—they would only endanger her now.

Stepping forward, Belrina contemplated her next move. She needed power, for she did not know how many she would face. Even the weakest Asthildi in their camp would be dangerous with a single magic device from Senator Primth's personal arsenal. At the thought of the senator, Belrina lengthened her stride. He was the root of all this evil, and while she could not reach him now, she could stop his associates, who were converging on her. They did not yet know who they would meet on this battlefield.

Transmuting her black tunic into a blood-red gown, Belrina created an invisible stairway and began climbing it. She would let them see her for leagues. When Belrina stood above the trees, she altered her protective shield to be fueled by the magic energy launched at it. Then she generated light as bright as day.

A moment later, the barrage started. Magic missiles and unknown spells encountered Belrina's shield, which absorbed the energy. With a smile, Belrina lifted her hand to her protective shield, methodically measuring the ebb and flow of magic energy, crafting it for her purposes. Now, all the magic energy they hurled at her, she would use against them.

"Gods United, if you are still in these lands, please understand. This is the only way." Belrina breathed deeply, creating her first spell, which gave her the location of each Asthildi who hurled magic energy towards her. As she fashioned her second spell, which duplicated the magic used by her enemies, her unbound hair lashed at her face as energy swelled within her shield.

It was time to unleash all that power. Belrina lifted both hands, executing the third spell: all who sought her destruction would be destroyed by the same weapon they launched against her.

As her missiles began speeding towards her enemies, Belrina remembered their ruthless crimes. If she had had any tears left, she would have wept for the women violated, the children injured, the people murdered. How many more tragedies would they have to bear if she did not do this? How many more husbands taken? Belrina unleashed a wail, unheard amid the roar of magic energy deafening all elven ears.

When the sun rose in the People's lands tomorrow, all Primth's associates would be gone, casualties of a war the politicians in the Empire ignored when only humans were dying. No one would ignore what happened here tonight.

Preorder *A New Savagery* now at www.almavasquezbooks.com/ products/songs-of-power-book-2.

<u>**EXCLUSIVE OFFER**</u>

This does not need to be the end! Enter your email address at www.almavasquezbooks.com/pages/bonus-content to *instantly* receive:

- A bonus scene featuring the Old Ones

- *The Lady and the Silver Serpent* (Cesario's poem)

- *Unforged Path*, a prequel novella explaining Belrina's elven ancestry

Then, every month, you'll get a peek into the author's creative process as she shares all the latest news about her work.

<u>**READ THE NEXT BOOK NOW**</u>

Want to read *A New Savagery*, the second book in the *Songs of Power* trilogy, as it is being written? By sharing your thoughts on this early draft with the author, you can influence the story before it is published. If that sounds exciting, please visit www.almavasquezbooks.com/pages/readers-guild.

<u>**ENJOY THIS BOOK?**</u>

Please announce it to the world by rating or reviewing *A New Duality* on the retailer's website where you made your purchase. As an independent author, Alma M. Vasquez relies upon reviews to reach new readers, which allows her to continue writing and publishing her fiction. And, of course, she is utterly thrilled to hear your feedback!

About the Author

Alma M. Vasquez's love of writing began when she was a child who preferred to spend school recess in the library. As an adult, she chose to pursue social justice, becoming an attorney rather than an author, but one day, as she sat in a courtroom waiting for a hearing to begin, she jotted down the opening lines of the story that would become her first published novel.

Now both an author and an attorney, Alma lives in beautiful Washington State, where she was born and raised. In her fiction, she enjoys creating worlds in which justice prevails, and her stories often feature diverse characters who defy expectations.

When she isn't combating injustice, she likes taking long walks and tackling home improvement projects with her family. Learn more at www.almavasquezbooks.com or www.facebook.com/almavasquezbooks.